CHECKERED HEARTS

CHECKERED HEARTS

A. G. STARLING

Podium

Cover design by Sam Palencia

ISBN: 979-8-8953-9457-1

Published in 2025 by Podium Publishing
www.podiumentertainment.com

For my agent, Elaine Spencer,
who has been proven right every step of the way.

CHECKERED HEARTS

PROLOGUE

ROCCO AND NICO

@RacingRocco
Formula 3 is not the same as Formula 1, @NicoRaces. The day you show you can handle the kind of power a Formula 1 engine delivers is the day you can critique my racing.

@NicoRaces
Driving an F3 car is hardly like riding a bicycle. But then you already know that, don't you? I can handle any power you can, @RacingRocco. Come out of the Dark Ages and into the sunlight of the 21st century, you male chauvinist amoeba. I wouldn't dare refer to you as a pig. It's an insult to swine.

@RacingRocco
Saying you lack the power is not a sexist comment @NicoRaces. It's a fact. F3 cars are smaller and less powerful. The speed at which you can grip a corner isn't even close. If you want to corner me, you'll have to do better.

@NicoRaces
Based on your performance of late @RacingRocco, it wouldn't be difficult to corner you. Although why any woman would want to is beyond me.

@RacingRocco
What's beyond you @NicoRaces is what to do with me if you ever did corner me, which would only happen if I let it happen. Maybe if you spent more time on the track and less time obsessing over me on social media, you'd move up to F2.

@NicoRaces
Maybe if you spent more time on the track @RacingRocco and less time reading my posts and making sexist comments, you'd finally find your way back to the podium.

@RacingRocco
It's convenient to cry sexism, isn't it @NicoRaces? Y O Y ask Y? It's not for lack of a chromosome you're not racing Formula 1.

@NicoRaces
I should hope not @RacingRocco. The Y chromosome isn't good for much. Climate change. War. Not to mention the Reliant Robin.

@RacingRocco
That's a lot to place on one little chromosome @NicoRaces. Such bitterness can mean only one thing—you're in the wrong sport. Maybe it's time to consider another.

@NicoRaces
I smell projection @RacingRocco. Hemingway said, "There are only three sports: bullfighting, motor racing, and mountaineering; all the rest are merely games." Here's some advice. Give up this game you're playing with me on social media and find some better use of your time. I would say it would be better spent on motor racing if you had any success at it. That leaves bullfighting and mountaineering. But I wouldn't suggest the former. I fear the two amigos, Itchy and Scratchy, alongside the little toy soldier wouldn't fare too well. Ouch!

DM: Direct Message: From @RacingRocco To @NicoRaces
These posts of yours are ripe with frustration. I'll lend you my Kawasaki Ninja H2R. It might help. It's clear you need to put something exciting between your legs.

CHAPTER ONE

ROCCO

"'Bullfighting, auto racing, and mountain climbing are the only real sports . . .'" Rocco said and then paused, distracted by that heart-shaped ass and feeling a little disappointed she wasn't wearing a dress.

The cue stick slid back and forth between her fingers as she lined up the shot. Then in one fast motion the stick shot back, and Rocco watched the ball drop into the side pocket, leaving only one stripe and the eight ball remaining on the green felt.

She turned around and faced him. "'All the rest are merely games,'" she said, finishing the quote before sauntering to the other end of the table.

Rocco's cousin Dario nudged him. "What's with that quote? Didn't—"

Rocco cut him off. "Yes. She did. I don't know why I said it."

What the hell were Nico Angelini's words doing in his mouth? What were they even doing in his head?

"I think I know why," Dario said. "Trouble is, no one else knows. She hit you where it hurts with that first tweet way back when, and you'd rather hit back and make yourself out to be a sexist pig—no, not a pig . . . What was it?"

"Amoeba."

"Yeah, well, you'd rather the world think that than know the truth. I've said it before and I'll say it again. I don't think she was targeting you with that first tweet that started the feud I don't know how long ago."

"I don't want to talk about it," Rocco muttered.

"Look, there's no way in hell Nico Angelini knows anything about the *special circumstances* surrounding your jump from F3 to F1. So how in the hell could she be tweeting about it?"

Those *special circumstances* were one Carolyn Wickham—the real reason Rocco and Dario had left a swanky New Year's Eve party and come to this shithole. Rocco had told his cousin he'd wanted a change of scene. What he didn't tell him was that he'd wanted it because he'd seen Carolyn at the party.

Rocco shifted his feet, unable to keep his body still as he watched the woman glide around the pool table. She picked up the chalk and stared back at him, rubbing the tip of the stick back and forth.

Back and forth.

Back.

And.

Forth.

There was too much fuel pumping through his veins. He needed to be behind the wheel moving at over two hundred miles per hour. Now more than ever, he thought, trying to swallow that fear that had lodged a lump in his throat. There was a real possibility he might not be racing this upcoming season.

He couldn't accept that. Last season—*his* last? No. Especially not after the disaster it had been.

Who was he kidding, the last few *years* had been a disaster. Ever since he'd left Carolyn's Formula 1 team, or rather her husband's, Blue Jet Lightning, he'd been floundering. And that had provided fertile ground for the doubts and fears that festered in his gut. If he couldn't race and get back to that podium, he'd never be rid of the feeling he was a fraud.

He needed to race. He needed it like he needed oxygen.

What he didn't need was to be standing in a dive bar that smelled of whiskey and sweaty balls on New Year's Eve—correction: New Year's Day, now—about to lose a game of pool he'd thought he would win easily.

He watched the woman as she chalked that stick, waiting for the moment she'd purse those luscious lips and blow.

Something about her was unsettling—but not in a good way. Her cheekbones and jaw were too bold, her lips too lush, her eyebrows set too low, and her hair, blinding—platinum blonde cut short and so sleek it looked like a helmet.

But she was sexy. *Damn sexy*, he thought, feeling the hum of a V6 turbocharged engine vibrating from his loins.

He could feel his body itching to go hurtling down that track. And yet there was something else that kept his foot hovering over the brake.

He stared at those eyes as she chalked the cue. They were cat eyes. When they narrowed, he imagined her pupils tapered like the vertical slivers of a cat. Only he couldn't see her pupils. The bar was too dark and her eyes were too dark—or at least they looked it to him.

Finally, she put down the chalk, blew on the tip of the stick, and leaned over the pool table as she lined up her shot.

Rocco's eyes flashed as he stared at that triangle—the small space of flesh at the base of her neck framed by her collarbone.

Most of the women he saw these days were so thin the space collapsed into a deep valley and the collarbone jutted severely, looking like a dry bone in the desert he could snap between his fingers as easy as a chicken wing. But not this one. This one merely hinted at its presence, like a seductive ripple in a stream left by some elusive creature beneath the water.

He glanced at the guys standing behind her. They were ogling her ass. One of them muttered something to the guy who stood beside him. It was probably something filthy given the lascivious looks on their faces.

Suddenly, the woman's cue stick zoomed back, ramming the guy who'd spoken right between the legs. He groaned. Hunching over and clutching his package, he fell into the guy behind him and that guy went down as well, causing the guy behind him to drop too.

Dario chuckled. "Like bowling pins."

The entire bar was lit up with laughter, but she seemed not to notice. As the last guy fell, so did the last stripe, leaving only the eight ball on the table.

Turn the lights back on. Race over.

She had him beat. There was only one shot left, and an easy one at that.

She had pulled back the stick and was just about to make the shot when Rocco had an impulse to hit the accelerator.

"Aren't you going to call it?" he asked.

Only her eyes shot up. "Hardly necessary."

She shifted her glance to the lone eight ball sitting squarely in line with both the cue ball and the corner pocket.

A rank novice could hit that shot, and Rocco had seen enough to know she wasn't a beginner. Although she had faltered here and there when he stood too close and intentionally brushed up against her—supposedly, by accident.

"And hardly interesting," he said as he sauntered over to her end of the table.

She stood up, and he placed himself directly behind her. What was that scent? It wasn't sugary or flowery, and it wasn't crisp like citrus. He liked it. His groin definitely liked it. It was practically viscous—the kind of scent that belonged in the tropics where the sky hung low, pressing on one's shoulders and against one's chest; the air so thick and heavy, everything it touched turned lush and green as luxuriant foliage pushed up from earth black as mud.

He placed his lips near her ear. "We could make it interesting," he said, low enough so that no one else could hear.

Her lip curled as she glanced over her shoulder. "Ah, but what interests you may not be what interests me."

He grinned. She was a bit of a challenge. And that did interest him.

"All right, then," he said, "you name it."

"How much money do you have on you?"

He reared back. He'd thought the conversation was moving in a different direction.

"I'm not sure. I guess—"

"Don't guess, show me."

He reached in his jacket pocket, took out a wad of bills, and tossed it on the table.

"Is that all?"

He smirked. "You want to search me?"

She placed the cue stick on the table and turned around. He hadn't taken a step back, so she couldn't do so without brushing up against him. As she did, a delicious warm fluidity carrying that pungent scent meandered through his body at its own leisure until it felt as though there wasn't one inch of flesh she hadn't invaded.

She looked him up and down dismissively. "All right."

She reached into his other jacket pocket. Finding nothing, he held out his arms, inviting her to search further.

Not taking her eyes off his, she leaned in and reached around him, slipping both hands into the back pockets of his pants.

"Did you just squeeze my ass?" he muttered in a voice that sounded part whisper and part groan.

"No," she murmured, still searching those pockets. "Would you like me to?"

This is just an act, he thought. Her voice might sound cool, but her body definitely wasn't.

Her heart had sped up, and she was breathing more deeply. He could feel both as her breasts swelled against the immovable force that was his chest. He could even feel her nipples, hard as pistons, just begging to be pinched, he thought as he rubbed his fingertips. And he knew what she could feel down below, pressing into him like she was. That pungent and exotic scent had slithered to the crankshaft between his thighs and was now weaving its way around it like the vines of some lecherous plant.

He glanced at her lips, slightly parted and barely more than an inch away from his own. She was close enough. If they were alone, he would have.

Again, her hands came up empty. She moved on to the front pockets. He noticed she took her time. He didn't mind. He was hard as a rock, especially when he felt her fingers brush up against him *there*.

Is she doing that on purpose?

His heart was pounding so hard it was beating in his ears.

I want to bend you over that pool table. Now.

He fisted his hands, trying to quiet the urge to do just that.

"Your search is very . . . thorough." His voice was guttural because the only part of him that had any say now lay south of the equator.

"Anything worth doing," she said, "is worth doing—"

"Well," he murmured as he felt her fingers slide the entire length of his shaft.

Something sparked in her eyes like a match just before it caught fire.

He grinned. "Are you measuring me?"

Her hands suddenly stopped.

"That is all you've got," she said, her tone flippant as she pulled her hand from his pocket.

That's when he caught sight of Dario, arms folded, shaking his head. Rocco knew what he was thinking. *We should have been back at the hotel in bed—hours ago.*

He turned his attention away from his cousin and back to the woman. "And now for me."

She was wearing an elegant black pantsuit. He couldn't tell if there were any pockets but a methodical search would tell him.

He was about to begin when she stopped him, placing one hand gently on his chest. That simple, delicate gesture, her hand over his heart sent his blood surging like high-octane fuel as he felt his entire body accelerate.

"I thought I just took care of you," she said.

That calm and cool tone of hers sounded practiced.

"I need to see if you can match what I put on the table."

"I can."

"You haven't even counted it."

She shrugged. "Doesn't matter. I think we both know I'm not missing that shot."

"And what if that"—he glanced at the money on the table—"isn't what interests me?"

"All right, then, name it. Although you don't need to. I know what interests you."

He arched his left eyebrow. "You do, do you?"

Her eyes told him—*yes*.

He grinned. "All right, then."

She made a move to turn around, but he stopped her, placing his hands in that niche that was her waist. How perfectly they fit. His fingers snug in that bend in the road. Her hips were ample. The arc from her waist, a dramatic curve like the women in old Hollywood movies.

"Don't you think the wager warrants something a little more difficult?" he asked.

The cue ball and eight ball were perfectly lined up; the eight ball only a couple of inches from the corner pocket.

"What do you suggest?"

He made a swift calculation as to what he thought would be the most difficult shot.

He leaned into her, placing his hand by the corner pocket nearest him on the left. "How about you sink the eight ball into this pocket?"

There was no way she could make the shot.

She'd have to be crazy to say *yes*.

"As you wish," she said.

His brow wrinkled. "What's that?"

"As you wish."

Maybe she was crazy. Either that or she wanted to give him what really interested him because it was what interested her. It had to be the latter. Although he wasn't as certain as he usually was when it came to women.

He fisted his hands, resisting the urge to hoist her over his shoulder and take her back to his hotel room. Even that felt like too much foreplay.

He drew a deep breath.

Just a little longer.

After she missed the shot, she'd come back to his hotel room and they'd have mind-blowing sex. There was something raw, primitive, practically feral about the woman. She might even be into a bit of kink. Some women weren't. Whether she was or wasn't didn't matter. What did matter was what happened after sex. But he was confident that wouldn't be a problem with her.

It was no good to be involved once the season began. Besides all the travel, he needed his mind focused on one thing—and one thing only.

Racing.

He could not believe he was done with it.

Would not believe it.

He needed to race. Had to. That was the end of it. Period.

She didn't wait for him to move away. She turned around, causing him to lose his footing and stumble backward.

She bent over.

"Eight ball in the corner pocket," she said, glancing back at Rocco.

It took him a moment to realize she was looking at him because his attention was on her ass.

She wants my hands on that ass.

I want my hands on that ass.

He waited for her to turn around before he wiped his palms on his pant legs.

"This corner pocket," she added, indicating the one just to the left of her before pulling back the stick and hitting the cue ball.

She skimmed the eight ball with it. He'd thought at least she'd make a reasonable attempt and bank it.

Is she looking to lose?

Sure enough the eight ball was moving the right direction. Problem was, it didn't have enough momentum. It was going to come up short.

And then he blinked, realizing she'd done something he hadn't thought of; bank the cue ball, which came speeding to this end of the table just behind the eight ball and, after impact, sank the eight ball in the designated corner pocket.

She tossed the stick on the table and picked up the money.

"Turn the lights back on, boys. Race over."

Rocco glanced over at Dario. "What did she just say?"

He didn't wait for his cousin to respond. He caught sight of her backside as she walked out of the bar and took off after her.

Once outside, he yelled, "Hey!"

She stopped and turned around.

"I have a question for you," he said.

She walked up to him and got so close, her breath tickled his skin.

Before he realized it, his back was up against the wall.

"Why'd you say what you did just before you left?" he asked.

She must have been a racing fan to say something like that. But she hadn't let on that she knew him.

She leaned in, grazing his lips with hers. Her breath smelled like chocolate-covered strawberries. He felt a humming in his chest and his groin. And for a moment, she just left her mouth resting lightly on his.

"Make every easy shot, Rocco," she said, her words vibrating on his lips.

"Do I know you?" he murmured back.

"And make every shot easy." She pressed her lips on his, opened his mouth with her own, and kissed him.

It was a slow and gentle, languid and luscious kiss. Her tongue, plump, wet, and warm.

He hadn't kissed a woman like this in—how long? Had he ever?

It felt as though she had her mouth on his cock. *She might as well have*, he thought as he felt both heart and breath accelerate and a guttural groan throttle low in his throat in syncopation with the throbbing between his thighs.

But there was something else.

Something almost—tender.

It was the kind of kiss you would give a lover, and a lover you actually loved—deeply loved.

He cupped her cheek with one hand and gripped her waist with the other, pulling her deeper into him.

He wanted to put her back up against the wall. He made a move to swing her around. But just as he tried to, he felt a sudden sharp sting.

She pulled away and brushed his lower lip with her finger.

That's when he saw the blood. That's when he tasted metal.

She bit me.

That's also when he realized her eyes were so dark they could have been mistaken for black. There was no light there, no light at all. But just as he had the thought, he saw something. A spark? A glimmer? Whatever it was, it came and went so fast he must have imagined it.

Her lips curved but so slightly he couldn't call it a smile.

"Game over," she said before turning and walking away.

CHAPTER TWO

NICO

Nico's sluggish eyelids opened and immediately slammed shut. The glaring Vegas sun hit hard. She shielded her eyes with one hand and felt around her bed with the other.

"Is this what you're looking for?"

It took her a moment, but finally her eyes were able to remain open beyond a couple seconds and she could make out Charles, his spiky blonde hair and pale blue eyes looming over her, twirling her eye mask with one hand and a platinum-blonde wig with the other.

"Give it to me," she demanded.

"What?" He held up the mask and then the wig. "This? Or this?"

She tried to snatch the mask, but he pulled away and placed both items on the dresser.

When he turned back around, he held up a wad of cash and narrowed his eyes. "Or perhaps you mean this."

"Charles!" Nico cried, sitting up.

That was a mistake, she thought, feeling queasy.

He handed her a glass of green liquid. "Drink this."

"It looks like a specimen you collected in a swamp. Either that or a toxic waste dump. What's in it?"

Charles said nothing as he crossed his lean, muscular arms, showing off his sculpted shoulders.

Nico sniffed and pulled back. She had only one free hand, and she couldn't decide whether to clutch her head or her stomach.

"Come on, Charlemagne. What's in it?"

"Calling me by my birth name changes nothing," he scoffed. "Just drink it already."

She looked up sulkily at her roommate and best friend.

They'd first met at Drink and Dive when Charles rescued her from an angry guy who suspected Nico had conned him. She had.

That had been a first for Nico. Not the con but the rescue. No one had ever jumped in to help her in the past. But Charles did and he did it brilliantly. He suddenly appeared like that angel Clarence from *It's a Wonderful Life* and put on an Oscar-worthy performance of someone on the brink of vomiting. He looked just about to do so all over the man's shirt. The man and anyone standing within a six-foot radius backed away and were so stunned, it gave Nico and Charles the chance to escape.

It didn't take long before they'd decided to pool their resources—his from dealing cards and hers from low-level racing, poker, and pool—and share an apartment just off the Strip.

Best friend? Charles was her only friend. He knew everything about her past and still loved her.

Nico sighed, staring at the murky liquid. Charles's morning-after remedies always worked. And right now, she couldn't decide whether or not that was a good thing.

She knew she should drink it. Knew she would drink it. But that didn't stop her from not wanting to drink it.

Nico shut her eyes and held her nose. "Ugh," she groaned, after downing half the glass.

"So, tell me what happened? Start with how it is you got this." Charles held up the wad of cash. "As if I don't already know."

"Well, if you already know, then you don't need me to tell you."

"I still want details."

Nico made a move to lie back down, but Charles stopped her.

"Uh-uh. Not a good idea." He propped two big pillows behind her. "Sit up and drink the rest of it. Trust me. You'll feel better. When do you have to be there?"

"What time is it?"

"Eight a.m."

Nico groaned. "In a few hours."

"I can't believe you did this the night before—correction—*the morning of* what could turn out to be one of the most important days of your life."

There was more than that Charles would find it hard to believe once Nico gave him the details. If she did. She didn't want to. Not now. And as for some details, not ever.

"I wonder if this is evidence of some kind of perverted psychology," Charles reflected. "Do you want to fail? Or maybe you want an excuse if you do fail? Maybe you want to be able to blame it on this? Wait a minute!" Charles slapped his palm on his forehead so dramatically it was worthy of a Meryl Streep performance. "Of course! Didn't I tell you?"

Didn't you tell me? thought Nico. *Did I miss something? You haven't told me anything yet.*

"Imposter syndrome! That's it!"' Charles cried.

Nico glanced over at the crumpled, faded photo of a woman sitting in a frame that sat on her bedside table. Even flattening it behind a plate of glass hadn't removed the creases and wrinkles from her having carried that photo in her pocket and fondled it with sweaty palms every day for years. She should be grateful for every crease and wrinkle. Had she not carried it in her pocket every day, she wouldn't have had it with her on *that* day. And then she wouldn't have it at all.

Her eyes shifted to the frame next to it—a photo of her grandfather working on a Porsche at his shop. Originally, the photo had belonged to one of her grandfather's loyal customers and later on one of Nico's Formula 3 sponsors, who'd been kind enough to give the photo to her. The man had displayed the photo because the Porsche had been a sentimental favorite of his. But Nico was drawn to it because her grandfather was in it and she didn't have even one photo of him.

She couldn't even see his face in it.

Nico had been raised by her grandfather after her mother died when she was two years old. She'd never known her biological father. He'd disappeared as soon as her mother had become pregnant.

If only she'd carried a photo of her grandfather in her pocket. But why would she when she saw him every day? She couldn't have known *that* day was the last day she would ever see him.

She looked away and was met with Charles's pensive stare.

She knew Charles was right, of course. She shouldn't have gone to that dive bar last night, shouldn't have played pool, definitely shouldn't have played pool with one Rocco Vittori, and most definitely shouldn't have celebrated taking that arrogant prick down a peg if even only for a second at another bar with a bottle of champagne.

Or was it two?

She kept telling herself the champagne was to celebrate. But truth was, she'd needed it after that kiss. The bubbly was supposed to wash his warm, wet tongue and what it did to her from her memory. But it hadn't worked. Her body still hummed when she thought about it.

Stop!

All she needed was a shower and some coffee. And the rest of that green swamp from hell. She braced herself and finished the ghastly concoction.

Charles folded his arms. "I'm waiting."

"Can I tell you later? I really don't feel up to it."

"All the more reason to tell me now. With your synapses focused on that and away from your head and your gut, you'll feel better more quickly. It has something to do with blood flow."

"How do you know that?"

Charles waved his hand. "I read it somewhere. Can't remember where."

Charles was always full of advice, supposedly based on scientific fact and extensive research. Problem was he could never remember where he'd accessed either the facts or the research.

Suddenly Templeton, Nico's pet rat, popped his head out from Charles's pajama pocket.

"See," Charles said, "Temple wants to hear too. We're all eyes and ears. Go. And no skimping. We want the unabridged, uncensored version."

Charles settled himself on the edge of Nico's bed.

She sighed. Might as well get it over with. Charles would eventually get it out of her anyway. At least his charmed potion was beginning to work. She was starting to feel better already.

"That," she said, pointing at the money, "I got winning at pool."

"I figured as much. It was either that or poker."

"I went to a bar, thinking I would just have a drink."

Hopefully Charles wouldn't ask—

"What bar?"

Damn it.

Nico shut her eyes. "Drink and Dive."

"What?!" Charles glared at her. "You promised you would never again set foot in that dump. There are plenty of other places to get a drink. And definitely better places to have a decent cocktail than that rathole." Charles glanced at Templeton. "No offense, Temple." He turned back to Nico. "Did anyone recognize you?"

Nico shook her head. "I don't think so. I didn't recognize anyone there."

Not entirely true.

"Everyone behind the bar was new," Nico added. "The bouncers too."

That was true.

Charles sighed. "Like I said, some kind of perverted psychology."

They both remained silent until Charles finally spoke.

"You really look like your mom," he said, glancing at the photo. He picked up the one alongside it. "I bet you look like Grandpapa too."

Maybe she did. Maybe she didn't.

Nico worried she was forgetting what her grandfather looked like. That was why every day, she did a literal sketch of him, putting pencil to paper. She was convinced that this imprinted the image of her grandfather in her brain more firmly than had she just done a mental one. Charles had actually told her there was scientific research to confirm that view. He'd read it somewhere. He just couldn't remember where.

Charles sighed as he placed the frame back on the bedside table. "I could tell you weren't having a good time last night. You didn't dance once. Do you think maybe today had something to do with why you went to Drink and Dive? Maybe nerves?"

"Maybe."

"Or maybe that letter that's still sitting on the credenza? The one you have yet to open? The one postmarked from Italy?"

Nico swallowed. Why of all places did it have to come from Italy? That meant that asshole was in Italy. Inside that envelope was her past.

She felt as though she'd be opening Pandora's box minus the hope once she unlocked it.

The Formula 1 schedule had been put out months ago. Two of the races took place in Italy.

A thought suddenly occurred to Nico, and she slivered her eyes, peering at Charles. "How do you know the letter came from Italy?"

Charles tossed his head, his tone huffy. "Just because I read the envelope doesn't mean I read the letter . . . or tried to."

Nico smirked. "No success?"

"No," Charles said grumpily. "That envelope is too thick. I couldn't see anything through it. Why doesn't the motherfucker just email or text? Who writes letters anymore?"

"That would leave a digital trail. Remember, Mickey had to skip the country to escape the authorities."

"Oh, right. He is a criminal. There is that."

"Besides, he doesn't have my email address or phone number."

"Oh, I hadn't thought of that. And you still have that post office box."

Nico nodded.

"Wait a minute," Charles said. "Doesn't physical mail leave a trail too? I mean, there's the handwriting and DNA. There're experts who can figure out all sorts of stuff. Look at Gil Grissom and Abby Sciuto."

"Watching reruns of *CSI* and *NCIS* again? You do know they're fictional characters. And there are things like gloves. Not to mention he probably typed the letter. Although he's developed so many different writing styles, even if he did write it, I don't know if there's anyone who could track it back to him."

Charles opened his mouth, and Nico added, "Including Gil and Abby."

Charles waved his hand. "Okay, forget about the letter."

"Easier said than done."

"I mean, forget about it for now." Charles gazed up at the ceiling, looking deep in thought. "I just realized something. We've gone completely off the rails here." He poked her in the chest. "You still haven't given me any details about your adventure at Drink and Dive."

Nico was hoping he'd forgotten.

Charles examined the wad of cash. "I wonder how much is here. Although I suppose it doesn't really matter, does it? You didn't need the money, so why go *there*, once you were *there*?"

Nico drew a deep breath. "It was him."

Charles rubbed his hands together, a greedy expression in his blue eyes. "Details. Details. Him-who? What did he look like?"

"Like an annoying, arrogant, asshole, prick," Nico said emphatically.

"An asshole and a prick; so, he's got both ends covered." Charles leaned back, a devilish grin on his face. "That handsome?"

"How do you get handsome from annoying, arrogant, asshole, prick?"

"Because annoying, arrogant, asshole, pricks are always handsome."

"That's not true."

"Oh yes, it is. There's a direct link between being annoying, arrogant, assholey, and prickish and being handsome. It must be coded or encoded in the DNA. In fact, I think I read that somewhere. I can't remember where."

"He wasn't handsome," Nico insisted as she turned away from Charles's penetrating stare.

She touched her lips, thinking of his.

She'd expected them to be cold and hard. But they weren't.

No, they weren't.

When he'd stood behind her and she could smell him, she felt an overwhelming urge to taste him up and down. Every inch of him. The way he smelled left her thinking even his sweat would taste sweet.

No, both sweet and savory.

And when he'd placed his hands on her hips, holding her firm, she wanted those hands to roam. She wanted them to go down.

Down.

Down.

All the way.

Down.

Like hers had when she'd searched his pockets and felt *him*.

Damn he was hard. Just how big is the man?

Charles went from playful to serious. "Did he get to you?"

Nico blinked. "Get to me? No! What a thing to say!"

"I say it because your face says it."

"Don't be absurd. You know that's not possible. I can't. I don't even know how. At least not in the normal way—the way normal people do . . . normally. I haven't been with anyone other than . . ."

"Him." Charles sighed. "Mickey."

"Yes, *him*. And that was nowhere near normal."

Shaking his head, Charles crossed his arms. "It wouldn't matter anyway. Neither one of you would ever know. You're a steel vault. You can't even break the code. He wouldn't know. You wouldn't know. I might not even know. Not if you did. Not if he did. He wouldn't know if you were interested because you wouldn't know if you were. Because of that, you wouldn't, couldn't make it known, making it impossible for him to know. You wouldn't know if he was because you wouldn't know if you were, and because you wouldn't know if you were and wouldn't make it known that you were, he couldn't know if you were, so he wouldn't, couldn't make it known if he were and thus, wouldn't know if he were. And I wouldn't know—"

Exasperated, Nico threw her hands in the air. "What are you saying?"

"I'm not sure." Charles paused. "But whatever it is, I think I have to stop. I'm getting dizzy."

Even Templeton seemed disturbed. He ducked his head back down and burrowed himself deep into Charles's pocket.

Nico stood up. Unfortunately, so did Charles.

"I think I feel better now. I'm going to jump in the shower."

She tried to get past him, but he blocked her.

"Hold on, we're not done here," he said, opening the wad and tossing some bills on the bed. "Nico, there are hundred-dollar bills here! In fact, all I see are hundred-dollar bills!" Charles clutched his chest, his eyes wide in a look of horror. "You don't suppose he's a drug dealer or connected?"

"I thought all drug dealers were connected."

Charles grabbed a pillow and threw it at her. "Stop making light of this. I'm serious."

Nico picked up the pillow and threw it back. "You're also a drama queen. Trust me, he was no drug dealer, and he was no mafioso."

"He was Italian?"

"Did I say that?"

"Didn't you?"

"I don't think so. But okay, yes, he happens to be Italian. But not all Italians belong to the mob. And we're not talking about hundreds of thousands of dollars. If I found a sack with that much money in it and kept it, then you could be concerned. He was just a rich, annoying, arrogant asshole who decided to go slumming."

"Prick."

"What?"

"You forgot prick. A rich, annoying, arrogant, asshole, prick who decided to go slumming."

"Right."

Charles narrowed his eyes, a look of suspicion on his face. "What makes you so certain? You sound certain."

Nico made a second move to get past him. "I just am. That's all. Now let me go. I've got to get ready."

Charles held out his hand like a traffic cop. "Stop right there."

Nico saw the wheels turning in Charles's brain.

Damn it.

It was only a matter of time.

He narrowed his eyes. "When you said *it was him*, you made it sound as though you know him—as though I know him. Do you? Do I?"

Just get it over with already.

Nico sighed. "Yes . . . well, by sight and reputation. You've never met him. I'd never met him until last night."

To say she'd been shocked when she'd walked into Drink and Dive to see Rocco Vittori was an understatement. What was he doing in Vegas? He couldn't be here to sign with the same team, could he? The team she was set to sign with? In a matter of hours?

Nico looked up at Charles. "Can I borrow those huge sunglasses of yours? You know, the ones that swallow up half your face."

Charles's brow wrinkled. "Why?"

"Because I have a hangover, and the sun will only make it worse."

"But you have your own sunglasses. The only reason why you'd want to borrow mine is to hide." Charles's eyes flew open wide. "From someone who might recognize you. Like maybe the guy you shagged last night at Drink and Dive."

"Shagged? I didn't shag him."

"Didn't you?"

"No! I think you mean fleece."

Charles waved his hands. "Whatever. The point is, you would only feel the need to hide from this fleece-ee if there was the possibility that he might see you and recognize you. But for him to see you and recognize you, he'd have to run into you. And you're not doing anything today other than going to Maverick Racing headquarters to sign the contract, which means you're thinking he might be there."

"I'm not thinking he might be there! He better not be there. Oh, please don't let him be there."

"So, there is a possibility that he might—"

Nico groaned. "Be there."

Charles fell back on the bed. It was as though what Nico said pushed him off his feet. Then the realization of what she'd said tossed him from the bed, and he sprung back up like a jack-in-the-box after you'd cranked the handle.

He grabbed Nico's shoulders, looking fiercely into her eyes. "He's a driver?!"

Nico nodded.

"An F1 driver?"

Again, she nodded.

Charles stared wide-eyed at all the money on the bed.

"No wonder all those hundreds. Damn, how much did you take him for?"

She had no idea. It wasn't about the money. She'd just wanted to beat him. Take the annoying, arrogant, asshole, prick down a notch.

"So, you're thinking he might be there? Is he going to be on your team?"

Nico shrugged. "I don't know who the second driver is."

She must have had a pitiful look on her face because Charles's tone suddenly changed to a more sympathetic one.

"He won't recognize you, if that's what you're worried about. No one ever does. You've had too much experience doing that sort of thing.

I mean, in the past. You become a whole different person. You're good at it. And you did wear the wig."

Nico hoped Charles was right.

Rocco Vittori was without a contract. No one as of yet had picked him up. That was the last she'd heard. With any luck, things would stay that way, he wouldn't be racing, and he'd retire. *For good,* she thought, gritting her teeth.

And yet he was here. In Vegas. Why?

He couldn't be signing onto the same team. Just couldn't.

"Wait a minute," Charles said. "I don't get it. If you knew he was a driver, why would you—" Charles stared at Nico, a look of horror on his face.

He's got it now.

"Not Rocco Vittori?!"

Nodding, Nico drew in and released a deep breath.

Charles placed his hands on his hips. "See, what did I tell you? Annoying, arrogant, asshole, handsome, prick." He sighed. "Oh my, that is a handsome prick."

"He's not handsome!"

"Perhaps handsome doesn't quite capture it. He's not pretty like that manager of his, Dario."

"Definitely not."

"You're right. He's not pretty at all."

"Damn straight, he's not."

"Yeah." Charles gazed dreamily at some obscure spot suspended over Nico's shoulder. "Too coarse. Not polished. All jagged and unkempt. Always looking like he just tumbled out of bed, even when it's a professional photo and he's in a tux. How do you suppose he's always got that shadow on his cheeks and his jaw? I mean, he must shave, right? Otherwise, he'd have a beard. But I don't think I've ever seen a photo of him where he looks clean-shaven. I don't think I've ever seen a photo of him where he looks clean. He always looks dirty . . . and in the best way possible."

Nico shook her head, making another attempt to get past Charles, but he placed his hands on her shoulders. "I get it, Nico. Under the circumstances, given some of the things he's posted on social media, you might even have been justified."

"Might?" Nico angrily pushed Charles so that his arms fell to his sides.

He grinned. "Just tell me one thing. Is that eye-candy as scorching in person as he is in photos?"

Nico shoved her way past Charles and headed to the bathroom.

She placed her fingers on her lower lip. She could still taste the blood—his blood. But it might just as well have been her own. Damn him for leaving yet another mark. She was supposed to have done that. And she'd probably failed. Even if there was a sizeable sum in that wad, it wouldn't make a dent in his bank account. He could afford to lose that and more. And as for his overblown ego, she might have bruised it, but only temporarily. It had probably healed by the time his head hit the pillow.

Who was she kidding? It had probably healed the minute she'd left him standing outside that bar.

She sighed. No, it was probably worse than that.

He hadn't had to heal at all.

That ego was so massive, it was on par with a John Mayer–sized ego receiving a Dear John letter in a song written by Taylor Swift heard around the world by millions, and his only response, a Miss Piggy routine: *Who, moi?*

How could she ever put a dent in that?

She entered the bathroom and looked at herself in the mirror. Without all that heavy makeup and in the harsh truth of daylight, the face staring back at her looked nothing like the femme fatale who had swindled him. Not to mention she'd lost nearly three inches given those boots she'd worn.

Thank goodness she'd had the impulse to wear that wig and do her makeup as dramatically as she had before she and Charles had gone out for the evening.

But where had that impulse come from? She never did herself up like that anymore.

Maybe it did have something to do with that letter. She wished she had it in her to toss it in the trash or, better yet, burn it without reading it.

She sighed, tilting her head as she had at Drink and Dive. Even a small movement like that changed the way she looked. That woman knew how to entice a man. She knew how to walk, how to sliver her eyes, how to purr, how to kiss.

Why couldn't she do that for real? Kiss—the way normal people did.

She gathered up her hair, but as she did, her finger grazed that horizontal scar that ran along the back of her head. It had healed some time ago, and her hair had grown back so that it was completely covered. No one could see it. But now having touched it, she felt unsteady as though she might faint.

She dropped her hair and gripped the counter, clenching her arms and making her body rigid as she drew a few deep breaths.

Rocco Vittori can't be there. He just. Can't.

She was about to become the only woman driver on the Formula 1 grid. She could count the number of Formula 1 women drivers who'd come before her on one hand—there'd been five of them.

She had to race. She didn't just want to. She had to.

How could she explain it to anyone who hadn't grown up as she had?

She. Had. To. Race.

She wasn't fit for anything else. She certainly wasn't prepared for anything else. She hadn't even finished high school, and she'd never had a real job.

If she couldn't race Formula 1, what then? Make money hustling at pool and poker?

She had to prove she was better than that. She had to show that all that work her grandfather had put into her starting at the age of eight when she'd raced her first kart had not been wasted.

It had to count for something. It just had to.

She had to prove that it wasn't just a drawing of her grandfather that she carried with her. She was his granddaughter. She carried *him* with her because *he was in her*. And that meant everything he'd taught her was in her too—his grit, determination, and integrity. She had to prove that everything that had happened after he was gone didn't change that.

She drew one last cleansing breath and then turned on the water, waiting until it was the right temperature. When it was, she stepped in and held her head under the steaming hot water.

Racing Formula 1 was like her blood, her bone. If they were gone, so was she—not just a persona like that femme fatale at Drink and Dive—but *her*, the *real her*.

CHAPTER THREE

ROCCO

Rocco stood alongside Dario in the parking lot of Maverick Racing headquarters and looked around. Nothing but miles and miles of desert.

Why hadn't he thought to stop for another espresso on the drive out here? He was beat. He felt as though his head had just hit the pillow when Dario woke him up.

The team principal asked if they could move the meeting up and stop by today—New Year's Day. It seemed something had come up.

It pissed him off they would change things on a moment's notice.

Dario placed his hand on Rocco's shoulder. "It's a good sign. They want to sign you before someone else gets the chance."

"It's not like anyone's been knocking down the door. You and I both know that."

Dario grinned. "Yeah, but they don't know that."

Rocco was doubtful. He'd raced for just about every top flight F1 team there was. And over the past couple years, he'd burned bridges with all of them. Given the damage he'd done to cars with nothing much to show for it, he'd become more of a liability than an asset.

Maverick Racing must have some inkling none of those teams wanted him back. People talk. And they didn't seem to think twice about moving up the appointment at the last minute—and on a holiday, no less.

Normally, at this time of year, Rocco would have been at home in Italy with his family. But when this offer from Maverick Racing had come through, he'd convinced Dario to come out a few days prior to the appointment to celebrate the New Year here. It was difficult being around his family right now, given it looked like he might not be racing this upcoming season.

It made it even worse that none of them would broach the subject. Not that he wanted to talk about it. It was obvious his grandfather had forbidden anyone to bring it up. Even his two nieces, not known for being quiet or tactful about anything, had been mute. But it didn't matter. Rocco could hear the questions and the concern in his own head when he looked into their eyes. It was easier to be away from them.

Dario placed his hand on Rocco's shoulder. "They want you, Rocco. You're a proven entity."

In some respects, that was a good thing. In others, not so much—especially if you were going by the past couple of years.

They walked toward the building, but Rocco stopped when he heard the roar of an engine—not just any engine—a Formula 1 engine.

Dario was about to open the door, but Rocco stopped him.

"Hold on a minute. Come on."

He walked around the building. Out back was a makeshift track. He watched as a car zipped past.

It couldn't be the car they planned to race this upcoming season. That was against regulations. It must be an older model they'd bought at auction.

He watched the car hug a turn. It looked as though the driver had yet to hit the brakes. Rocco rubbed his hands, feeling that itch just beneath his skin.

"Did they tell you who the second driver would be?"

Dario shook his head. "Every F1 driver is set. They've all signed contracts with other teams. So, I'm assuming it'll be an F2 driver."

"You're sure no one else from F1 was cut loose?"

"I suppose it's possible." Dario paused. "But it's more likely going to be an F2 driver being promoted to F1. And as for that driver there"—he nodded toward the car that flew past them—"the guy behind the wheel could be the second driver, or he could be a #3—someone to help test the car."

No way is that a #3.

Rocco watched the car make another lap.

He drives like a Formula 1 driver.

Just then the throttle roared even louder.

He's really going for it.

Rocco sniffed as the smell of exhaust and dust kicked up by the spinning tires met his nostrils and the car swept past them. It looked like it was going to skid off the track and hit the embankment before the turn, but the driver made a swift and calculated correction.

He didn't even tap the brakes.

Who the hell is in there?

Whoever it was, there was no way that was a #3. That must be the second driver. And then he had a scary thought. They weren't bringing him on thinking he was #2, were they? If whoever was in that car had already signed up, then they'd gone to him first.

"Not a bad idea to have a third driver," said Dario. "Not only to run tests, but what if one of the drivers gets injured?"

"Maybe a driver getting injured is more likely to happen if there's a third driver."

"Why? Because he would make it happen?"

"Exactly."

"Man, you really don't trust anyone. Well, outside your family, my family, and me, of course." Dario paused. "You don't even trust yourself."

He'd muttered that last part. Rocco figured he hadn't meant him to hear it.

"What was that?" he asked.

"I just said you only trust a small circle of people." Dario turned to him. "You do trust me, don't you?"

This made Rocco smile. "You know I do. I trust you with my life."

Dario made a mock gesture, staggering back and clutching his heart. "That's a relief."

"Except when it comes to my supply of GoGo squeeZ. I know I didn't finish that last case on my own."

Dario sighed. "I think we're going to have to write something about that damn GoGo squeeZ into your contract."

They had a good laugh and then were silent watching the car speed past them again.

"Celeste is right," Dario said. "You have trust issues."

Celeste was Dario's girlfriend.

"For good reason."

"Fair enough."

Rocco hesitated. "I saw Carolyn last night at that party."

"No shit! Why didn't you say something? Did she—see you?"

"I don't know. Maybe. She texted me."

"What did she say?"

"Just that she wanted to talk and she wished me a happy New Year."

"Did you text her back?"

"No."

"Oh, well, I'm sorry I brought her up."

"You didn't. At least not directly. But you did bring up the issue of trust. I'm sure she won't be the last woman I can't trust."

He ran his tongue over his lower lip, thinking of that woman at the bar. He'd never been bitten by a woman before.

He wondered what her reaction would have been had he been the one to do that to her, recalling his attempt to swing her around and put her back up against the wall. That slick move of hers had caught him off guard.

He wished now he hadn't kissed her. If he hadn't, maybe he wouldn't be thinking of her now.

Then again, he hadn't kissed her. She'd kissed him.

"Carolyn always needs to be in the driver's seat," Rocco muttered. "Like that woman last night."

"What woman?"

"What's that?"

"You mentioned a woman last night."

Rocco hadn't realized he'd said that out loud. He hadn't meant to.

He shrugged. "That woman at the bar."

"The one who took all your money?"

Rocco nodded.

He could shake off the loss of the money.

But the woman. She was like a thorn that had gotten under his skin. Thinking about her now was like picking at that thorn—not to remove it but just to drive it in deeper.

He didn't like that things had ended on her terms, both inside and outside the bar.

"Why do you suppose she chose me?" Rocco asked.

"Carolyn?" Dario laughed. "Because you're a pretty boy?"

Rocco's brow wrinkled as he surveyed Dario's perfectly symmetrical features, sparkling blue eyes, and dazzling smile. "That's you, not me. And I didn't mean Carolyn. I mean *that woman* at the bar."

"What do you mean, chose you? She probably played pool with lots of guys. Wasn't she playing when we got there?"

Rocco shook his head. "No, she arrived after us. But you're right, she did play with a couple other guys. Only she didn't play them like she played me."

"You mean she was sharking you."

"Yeah. She was a pool shark, all right. But why me?"

"Maybe because you look like a bonehead?"

"I'm serious."

Dario shrugged. "Probably because she figured you'd have money, which you did. I don't remember seeing anyone else in that bar wearing a Hugo Boss suit."

"You were wearing Armani, so why not you? She knew who I was. She said my name when I met up with her outside the bar."

"Well, there you have it. She knew you were a Formula 1 driver, so she figured, reasonably enough, you'd be loaded."

"But if it was just money, then why not you? Your suit was just as expensive, maybe more."

Dario remained quiet, looking as though he were trying to come up with a reasonable answer. Suddenly he grinned. "You said it yourself. I'm pretty."

Laughing, Rocco shoved him. "All the more reason. You look sweet, like a pushover."

"I do not."

"We'll ask Celeste. Let her settle the question. Trust me." Rocco laughed. "She'll see it my way. No one has ever called me *sweet* besides my grandmother."

"And yet I'm not the one who took in two scraggly, flea-ridden, almost feral strays I located in a dumpster behind a club."

"That makes me a humanitarian, not sweet."

"I thought we were talking about a dog and a cat, not humans."

"You're right, it's an insult to them. They're better than humans."

Dario sighed. "It's not going to be that kind of conversation, is it? If it is, I need some coffee or a shot of whiskey. Maybe both."

Rocco chuckled, shaking his head. "Forget it. I'm just saying I don't know why she would pick me over you." He paused, grinning. "Unless of course, she was choosing which one she'd like to sleep with."

Now it was Dario's turn to grin. "Oh, really? Righteous fail there! If she'd wanted to sleep with you, she would have missed that last shot."

The driver slowed down, and the car finally stopped. Rocco saw a man walking toward it.

"That's the team principal," Dario said. "His name is Casey."

Rocco watched as the driver got out and removed his helmet.

He blinked before turning to Dario. "Do you see what I see?"

"I. Think. So."

Rocco's mouth gaped at the sight of a long, wild, and disheveled mane of raven hair that looked almost blue in the sunlight.

"A woman?" he cried.

"Maybe she's a #3," Dario ventured. "A driver from Formula 2."

"There are no women drivers in Formula 2," Rocco snarled, his teeth clenched.

"Formula 3, then," Dario said matter-of-factly.

Rocco glared at him. "And that would somehow be better?"

"Well," Dario said and then paused. "Oh."

Now he gets it.

"Yeah," Rocco hissed. "Oh. Fucking. Oh."

"It couldn't be. How many women drivers are there in Formula 3?"

"Exactly one," Rocco said, his jaw tight.

"Do you know what she looks like?"

Rocco shook his head. "All our interaction has been on social media. I suppose it's possible we might have crossed paths somewhere at some point. But if we did, I don't remember. I don't have any image of her in my head except something to the effect of an annoying, arrogant, asshat, bitch," he spat.

"Yeah," Dario said, a tone of amusement in his voice.

Rocco watched his cousin's face crimson until that olive complexion of his resembled a hothouse tomato. He was holding his breath. And Rocco knew why. He wanted to laugh.

He wanted to laugh.

Real.

Bad.

CHAPTER FOUR

ROCCO

"She's got plenty of experience," Casey said. "Been racing since she was a kid, like you, Rocco. Go-karts, all the rest of it up to Formula 3."

"That doesn't mean she's any good," Rocco bellowed.

He made a point of speaking loudly. She was somewhere behind him, standing a few feet away and talking to one of the mechanics. He wanted her to hear him.

How the hell was he supposed to race on the same team as Nico Angelini?

"And," Rocco added, "it definitely doesn't mean we need a third driver, let alone *her* as a third driver."

Casey glanced behind him. Probably looking to see if she'd heard. Rocco knew he was making the man uncomfortable.

"Well, we're not— We don't see it— We're not thinking in terms of #1 and #2 drivers. We'd like to think of this as a team. We plan on supporting both drivers—equally."

"What do you mean *both*?" Rocco demanded.

"Well, uh, she's not a third driver."

Rocco gaped. He now knew what people meant when they felt like there was steam coming out of their ears. "Are you telling me she's the second driver? She's going to actually race?"

Casey hesitated. "Again, we're not thinking of either of you as the #1 or #2 driver."

"You're forgetting," Rocco grumbled. "I haven't said *yes* yet."

"Look, I don't know how much you saw when she was driving that retired F1 car, but she knows her way around a track. I can show you footage of some of her races."

Rocco remained silent.

"Look, this isn't just me," Casey said. "I've been talking this over with the owner, the technical director, the director of engineering, some of the mechanics and technicians. They're just as impressed as I am."

Rocco was fuming. He felt himself getting ready to say something only the biggest douchebag would say. There was hardly a moment's hesitation before he threw himself headlong onto the heap of the Ghosts of Douchebag Past.

"Yeah, I can guess what impressed them. It's not exactly difficult to figure out. She's sleeping with one of them."

Inwardly he cringed. If he'd heard anyone else say it, he'd have told them they were an ass.

Damn the woman! She brought out the worst in him!

How in the hell was he going to race alongside her?

Not only was it a douchebag thing to say, it was downright stupid. Sex appeal? This woman? Not even an ounce of it. He'd seen enough of her body when she was talking to Casey. The woman didn't possess even one curve. She was about as captivating as Highway 10 in Saudi Arabia. No going up, no going down, no bends left, no bends right—straight as a rod and nothing but desert for 159 miles. Okay, so she was wearing a racing suit. But what did that matter? If she had any curves, he'd have seen them.

"Maybe we should lower the volume," Casey muttered before sighing. "Think about what you're saying, Rocco. Do you really think I would make this kind of decision based on that? That the owner would? Do you think I would manage for an owner who would? And what about the mechanics, the entire team we've got here? You know a lot of these guys. They've worked for other F1 teams, including teams you've raced for."

"He's right, Rocco," Dario said. "Just because you—" He paused when his eyes met Rocco's, and he stammered, "Uh—"

Gaping at his cousin, Rocco's heart stopped.

Jesus, Dario, have you forgotten Casey's standing right here? Not to mention one Nico Angelini who is a couple feet away and within earshot and would like nothing better than to make my name trend . . . but for all the wrong reasons.

Dario quickly recovered. "Just because you don't like the idea of having a woman on the team doesn't mean she isn't any good."

Rocco cringed. He knew Dario was trying to come up with something—anything other than what he'd nearly divulged about Rocco's past. But couldn't he come up with something better?

It wasn't her being a woman that was the problem. It was her being Nico Angelini that was.

"Let me get her, and I'll introduce you," Casey said, leaving them.

Rocco crossed his arms. "Why did you say that, Dar? You know better than anyone I've never objected to having a woman race Formula 1 as long as she can prove she deserves a spot. And you definitely know that I've never had a problem racing alongside one."

Dario sighed. "I know. I know. I couldn't think. I'm sorry. We both know how hard you tried to get Ceci promoted to F1."

"That's right," Rocco huffed.

Ceci Rivers had raced F3 alongside Rocco years ago. When Rocco had been promoted to F1 and was racing for Blue Jet Lightning, he'd tried to persuade the owner to bring on Ceci as a third driver.

Dario nodded. "Right. So, explain to me why you're trying to convince anyone within hearing distance that you're the biggest sexist douche on the planet?"

"Do you really have to ask? It's because of that woman—Nico Angelini. You know our history."

"I know, but you've both said things on social media. Why don't you just give her a chance?" Dario held up his hand. "Don't answer that, here they come."

Rocco lifted his chin, clenched his jaw, and looked off into the distance.

"Rocco, Dario," he heard Casey saying, "this is Nico."

"Dario Berlusconi. Nice to meet you."

Damn, I'll have to look at her now.

He lowered his gaze. She wasn't wearing the racing suit. She was wearing jeans and a white T-shirt. He glanced at that triangle and the subtle ripple her collarbone made beneath her flesh. It reminded him of the woman at the bar. His eyes ventured south. Okay, so he'd been wrong.

The woman does have curves, he thought as his glance dipped up and over her breasts and descended to the valley of her abs, roaming that tight niche where those bountiful hips blossomed out from her waist.

Really. Really. Curvy. Curves.

He lifted his gaze back to her collarbone. He told his eyes to move on to her face, but he was transfixed by the ridge that ran from shoulder to shoulder just above the neckline of her shirt. He fisted his hands.

Go north, his brain was telling him at the very moment his eyes drifted south, landing on her breasts.

Are those . . . ?

He bit his lip to stop from grinning.

Yes, they are.

He blinked when her arms suddenly blocked his view. She'd crossed them.

Dario elbowed him, and he flinched. He looked at his cousin with a blank stare.

What?

"Rocco," Casey said, "this is Nico."

Oh, that's what.

She'd uncrossed her arms and was holding out her hand. He couldn't get a good look at her face with all that hair. Not to mention the fact she was wearing humongous sunglasses. But there was no mistaking the set jaw. He felt pretty certain she was glaring at him.

"Isn't that a boy's name?" Rocco sneered.

"Doesn't Rocco mean *dick* in Italian?" she responded.

Dario chuckled and nudged Rocco, his voice barely a whisper. "Don't be a tool. Shake her hand."

Reluctant, Rocco took her hand. Damn, it was small. A sudden surge of heat coursed through him when he felt her soft flesh up against his calloused palm. He gave her hand one solid shake and prepared to let go, but when he loosened his grip, she didn't reciprocate. So, he closed his hand around hers and waited for her to loosen her hold. When she did and tried to pull away, he wouldn't let her. He could see she was gritting her teeth. He did likewise.

You're going to be here a long time, sweetheart, if you think you're going to dictate when a handshake with me is done.

There was a moment of silence.

Casey clapped his hands. "Okay, well . . ."

Another moment of silence.

Dario sighed. "I'm going to count to three." He held his fist above their clenched hands and indicated with a finger as he counted off like a countdown at a boxing match after a knockout. "One . . . two . . . three."

Both of them unclasped at the same time.

She shook her hand and wiggled her fingers.

Was I gripping her hand that hard? Why didn't she say something?

Another moment of uncomfortable silence.

Dario was the one to break it.

"You looked good out there . . . on the track."

"Thank you," she said, smiling.

"Didn't she, Rocco?"

Rocco was staring at her hand. She was still moving her fingers.

Dario nudged him.

"Huh?" he said, looking over at his cousin.

"I said she looked good out there."

Rocco glanced at her.

"You've raced Formula 3," Rocco said in a harsh voice.

She nodded. "That's right."

"But not Formula 2?"

She shook her head. "No."

"So, what are you doing here?" he hissed.

Dario and Casey were obviously uncomfortable. Rocco wondered if one of them was going to say something to come to her rescue. It turned out they didn't need to.

"Hmm," she said, placing her finger alongside her cheek and then gazing up. He imagined her eyes opening wide but he couldn't be certain since they were hidden behind those shades.

The shades were fitting, given she was about to throw him some.

"I seem to recall someone else going straight from Formula 3 to Formula 1 without racing Formula 2. Who was that?" She snapped her fingers. "Oh, that's right. It was you. So, you tell me. What are *you* doing here?"

CHAPTER FIVE

NICO

"What did he say after you said that?" Charles asked as he placed the bowl of popcorn between them and handed one kernel to Templeton perched on the back of the sofa.

"Nothing," Nico said. "He told Casey he wanted to try out the car I'd been driving. I should have left. There and then."

"But you didn't."

"No, I didn't," Nico huffed angrily.

"How'd he do?"

She shrugged. "Okay."

Charles grinned. "That good?"

Nico frowned. "So he had a faster time. He had the advantage of going after me, and I wasn't going all out."

She grabbed some popcorn, and the three of them, including Templeton, sat gazing out into space as they munched.

"Do you regret it?" Charles asked.

"Regret what?"

"Scamming all that money off him."

Why should she? Especially after the way he'd acted today. She didn't feel bad about what she'd done, not even a little bit. Although that money was still sitting in the top drawer of her dresser. She didn't feel right about spending it. But she could hardly give it back to him.

"Okay," Charles said. "I see by that *Bowser* look on your face, the answer is *no*."

"What?"

"King Koopa?"

Nico frowned.

"Grand pooh-bah of the Koopa race?"

Nico threw her hands in the air. "Oh, of course, now, I see."

"Mario's archnemesis!"

Nico rolled her eyes. "Video games."

"Okay, so you don't regret it. Too bad you're going to be teammates."

"Yeah, too bad," Nico said glumly, plucking one kernel of popcorn from the bowl and tossing it behind her for Templeton, who caught it between his claws. She then scooped out a handful for herself. "You should have heard some of the foul things he said."

"Like what?"

"Like suggesting I only earned a spot on the team because I was sleeping with someone."

"What a dick!"

Nico grinned. "I told him that's what his name meant in Italian."

Charles roared with laughter.

"Maybe he won't say *yes*," Nico mused. "I hope he doesn't. So, what, if there's no one else without a contract in Formula 1; they're plenty of good drivers in Formula 2 who are just as good as him."

Charles remained silent.

Nico glanced at him. "Did you hear me?"

"Even you have to admit he's good, Nico. He might be one of the best ever."

"Don't be ridiculous, he hasn't won the trophy in years. He hasn't even come in second or third."

"Well, in that case, maybe the best ever without the record to show for it. I wonder why that is."

"Isn't it obvious? It's time for him to retire."

"He's not that old. Is he even thirty?"

"I don't care. I wish he would retire. Or at least not join Maverick Racing. You know how Formula 1 teams work. *Team* is an oxymoron. We'll be racing against each other; driving a car that's been built by the same engineers and mechanics. It's like driving the exact same car. So, how would it look if I did well and he didn't? Whether or not he has a shot at winning or making it to the podium, he'll make damn well certain I don't. He'll set me up to fail. I know it. And I can't fail. There's a lot riding on this—not just for me. There are no women drivers racing in Formula 1 right now."

"I'm well aware."

"There've only been a total of five women who've raced F1 since it began. And only one with enough starts to earn any points. And that was Lella Lombardi way back in 1975."

"I'm well aware of that too," Charles said, rolling both his head and eyes toward Nico's bedroom. The walls were papered with images of them all.

"When I said *yes*, I didn't even think to ask who the other driver would be."

"Would it have mattered?"

Nico shook her head. "No. There's no way I would pass up this opportunity, even if it means having to race alongside that asshole."

"You mean that annoying, arrogant, asshole, prick."

"Yes, even if it means having to race alongside him."

"Well, there you are. Your brain knew what it was doing when it decided not to ask who the other driver was. It was preventing even the slightest possibility of doubt on your part."

"Huh?"

"Not giving you a chance to hesitate or second-guess yourself. The brain can do that. It's actually ahead of you, making decisions, figuring out what you're going to do before you have the thought to do it."

When Nico looked at Charles with a wrinkled brow, he added, "It's true. I read that somewhere. Can't remember where."

Of course not.

"So," Nico said, "it was my brain that decided I should go to Drink and Dive and take the annoying, arrogant, asshole, prick for all he's got. And I had no say in the matter."

"What do you mean you had no say in the matter? What— Your brain belongs to someone else? Or maybe it's not even in there"—Charles poked Nico's forehead—"behind that thick skull of yours. Maybe it's floating in a vat of ginger ale in a scientific lab in Duluth or Brainerd."

"Why Duluth or Brainerd? Why couldn't my brain be in a lab in Paris? Or Monte Carlo?"

"Anybody who's stupid enough to think their brain is floating in a vat of ginger ale doesn't deserve to be in Paris or Monte Carlo." Charles heaved a big sigh. "We are going off track here. My point is, if your brain is making decisions, it's making decisions for you and as a part of you. It's not floating in a vat somewhere where Dr. Wily pokes and prods your gray matter, making you do all sorts of wicked things."

"Is this another video game reference?"

"The Dr. Wily part is."

Nico shook her head, exasperated. "How did we get here? I don't know what in the hell we're talking about."

"You were the one who wanted to talk metaphysics."

Nico found that hard to believe, given she wasn't even certain what metaphysics was.

Charles handed Templeton another kernel of popcorn.

"Does it really matter if you're on the same team? You said it yourself. When it comes to Formula 1, *team* is an oxymoron. The drivers don't compete like a team. Although I suppose it means you'll probably have to see him more—up close and personal-like—and you'll have to stop that social media war with him."

"I will if he does."

Charles laughed. "I bet he's saying the same thing."

Nico got up and walked over to the shelf of DVDs. "So, what do you want to watch?"

Tuesday was movie night.

She pulled out one—*10 Things I Hate About You.*

Maybe.

"His cousin sounds nice," Charles said.

"Dario? He is."

How to Lose a Guy in 10 Days.

Maybe.

Nico smiled. "He told him not to be a tool."

Charles laughed. "He did?"

Never Been Kissed.

Um. Uh-uh.

Nico nodded. "When annoying, arrogant, asshole, prick wouldn't shake my hand."

Isn't It Romantic.

Definitely not.

Charles picked up his phone and began scrolling while Nico continued perusing the DVDs.

The Little Mermaid.

That's Disney, isn't it?

Nico pulled it out. The cover didn't look like Disney.

She read the fine print. It wasn't. This one was a Swedish film based on the original Andersen fairy tale. Where did Charles get this?

Nico turned to him. "What happens at the end of *The Little Mermaid*?"

Charles smiled. "Ariel marries Eric, and the two live happily ever after."

"That's the Disney version. What happens at the end of the original one—you know, the Andersen fairy tale?"

"Oh." Charles's smile disappeared. "In that one, she can't bring herself to kill the prince, so she saves his life by killing herself. She jumps into the sea and turns into sea-foam."

"Sea-foam."

"Uh-huh. Sea-foam."

Nico shoved the DVD back into its slot.

Big. Nope.

Charles sighed. "At least annoying, arrogant, asshole, prick didn't recognize you. I figured he wouldn't."

"Wait until you hear the last thing he said before he left."

Staring at his phone, Charles's blue eyes ballooned. "That he'd be trying out the simulator on Friday early in the morning so he'd put in his order now—a double espresso for him and a cappuccino dusted with cinnamon for Dario. Some jelly doughnuts would be nice too."

Nico frowned. "How did—"

Charles held up his phone. Nico grabbed it.

@RacingRocco

It's official. I'm joining the Maverick Racing team. And what do you know? I'll be racing alongside one Nico Angelini. Let me be the first to welcome Nico to Formula 1. I'll be testing the simulator on Friday at headquarters early in the morning, so I'll put in my order now. I'll have a double espresso, and for Dario, a cappuccino dusted with cinnamon. Some jelly doughnuts would be nice too.

Nico stared at it, speechless, feeling like she'd had the wind knocked out of her.

Charles shook his head. "That boy deserves a spanking. I certainly wouldn't mind doing the job."

Nico made a face.

Charles tried to turn that glimmer in his eye to a glower but failed miserably.

She started pacing. "He hasn't given a thought to stopping the social media snark. I suppose he thinks me—the demure woman—will just remain silent."

"You? Demure?"

"Not to mention he went ahead and made the announcement. Not just about himself, but about me! And the way he did it, as though I were just an afterthought. Like the big news is one Rocco Vittori joining the team rather than a woman racing Formula 1!

"They specifically asked me not to make it known publicly. They wanted to wait until they had everything set up and then have a press conference. And now he just goes ahead and shits all over what should be a historic moment! I have to come up with some kind of response."

"You don't have to."

"Yes, I do. I can't just let that sit there." She shoved the phone in Charles's face. "Look at all those likes and comments."

Charles huffed. "Male chauvinists! We need to put our heads together and come up with something." He grabbed a scoopful of popcorn and shoved it in his mouth.

Nico began to pace. "How do I hate thee?" she hissed. "Let me count the ways."

"Ooh, that's good."

"No, I'm just venting. I have to come up with a response to that!" She pointed at the post on Charles's phone, which kept pinging as the likes and comments flooded in. She handed it to him. "Will you please mute that thing already?"

"Sorry." Charles silenced his phone. "You'll think of something. You always do."

"It's more difficult now. We're on the same team."

"Oh . . . *that.*"

"Yes . . . *that.* Trust me, he's already got a response ready to any reaction on my part. He's going to say something like he was just joking, it's all in good fun, part of the team dynamic. He'll accuse me of overreacting, say I'm too sensitive—or worse—hysterical. I wouldn't be surprised if he suggested I was on my period."

Charles nodded. "As though men don't have periods."

Nico frowned.

"You know what I mean," Charles said. "We get moody too."

"Damn skippy, you do."

"Look, you'll come up with something. What's that saying: Revenge is best served as an ice-cold martini—either that or coffee ice cream."

"You mean revenge is a dish best served cold."

"Exactly. So, let's take a deep breath, sit back, watch a movie, cool our jets, and afterward we'll have that ice-cold martini and coffee ice cream and come up with something."

Charles was right. She was too upset to come up with a good response, let alone a coherent one. Better to calm down and think it through.

"Okay. So, what do you want to watch?"

Charles's eyes were gleaming. "You know what . . ."

"Oh, please," Nico groaned. "Not *The Notebook*. Again."

Charles made a face. "How many times have I sat through *The Princess Bride*?"

Nico sighed. "It is your turn, isn't it? Okay, *The Notebook* it is."

Charles's lip curled like the Grinch's when he'd come up with a plan to ruin Christmas for all the Whos down in Whoville. "I'm not thinking of movies. I'm thinking of the perfect response to that post. Who says your response has to be on social media? Well, actually, it'll probably end up there. Oh yeah, there's no way you do this and it doesn't."

"What happened to the martini and ice cream?"

"We can still have them as we plot the details."

"Okay," Nico said apprehensively, "well, let me hear it, and then I'll decide whether or not I'll do it."

"My dear, no one knows you better than I do. You'll do it."

CHAPTER SIX

ROCCO

Rocco and Dario headed down to the ground floor of Maverick Racing headquarters.

The complex appeared to have everything one would need not only to design, develop, and manufacture a Formula 1 car, but also to assemble and operate it and to handle the business end when it comes to packing up the entire works and traveling across the globe with everything in tow.

There was a reason Formula 1 had been referred to as a traveling circus. That's exactly what it was.

Rocco had to admit the owner seemed serious and willing to put money into the operation. The place was equipped with state-of-the-art technology—the latest in AI and machine learning. There was a driver-in-loop simulator, wind tunnel, and dynos. There was also a gym, sauna, showers, and even a cafeteria.

"So, what do you think?" Dario asked.

"About what?" Rocco replied.

"All this," Dario said, holding his arms out wide.

"Not bad. Actually, pretty damn good. Even if I did get the biggest beatdown of my life for posting that stupid tweet."

"What did you expect?" Dario said. "You said it yourself. It was stupid. We're talking major money here. You pissed all over a major, major, *major* announcement the PR team had set up."

Rocco sulked. "I know."

It was such a boneheaded move.

Both Rocco and Dario glanced at the entrance. Celeste, Dario's girlfriend, was due to arrive any minute.

"Nico Angelini brings out the worst in me," Rocco huffed.

"Don't blame it on her. You're the one who hit send. You're going to have to cool your jets, dude. It's in your own—correction—*our* own best interest."

Rocco sighed. "I need coffee."

"They have coffee."

"That's not coffee."

"I suppose you were thinking there'd be a double espresso waiting for you?"

"Very funny."

The mere mention of espresso had him thinking about the dream he'd had last night. She was wearing that white T-shirt. She walked toward him, carrying an espresso and a jelly doughnut. He was sitting down so she had to bend over to hand it to him. When she did, he pierced the doughnut with his finger and scooped out the jelly. He crooked his finger, beckoning her to come closer. The jelly was dripping onto his thighs, and he remembered it feeling hot. He was just about to reach out and trace her nipples with the jelly and then lick it off when he woke up.

It was a good dream. A real good dream. He just wished he hadn't woken up when he did. And he wished it had been some other girl and not Nico Angelini.

He might have told Dario about the dream if she hadn't been in it. Rocco didn't want his cousin reading anything into it. It didn't mean anything. It made perfect sense she'd be in the dream. He'd seen her earlier that day and was hit with the shitty news she'd be his teammate. As for the espresso—well, that was because of his tweet. As for the rest of it, the jelly and all—well—that was because of the T-shirt.

He shook his head. It did him no good to think about any of it now.

He nudged Dario. "Do you think Celeste would go get me some espresso?"

"They have espresso."

"I tried it. It isn't any good."

"Why don't you go get some?"

"I'm too tired. I didn't sleep well last night."

"You don't suppose it has anything to do with your tweet?"

Rocco sighed but remained silent.

"Well," Dario said, "you can ask Celeste."

"Why don't you ask? She's your girlfriend."

"That's precisely why I won't. Not after that tweet."

Rocco groaned. "Am I going to have to apologize to her? I don't want Celeste mad at me. I don't like it when she's mad. She's a real sweetheart, but when she's mad she can be . . ."

Dario grinned. "A big meanie?" He paused. "You know, you're going to have to find a way to get along with her."

"Celeste? We get along great! I love her! Why? Did she say something?"

Dario laughed. "No, I mean Nico."

"Oh. *Her*."

"Yes. *Her*. I'm surprised there's been no response to the tweet."

"I suppose I should consider myself lucky. If she responds, anything I say is going to make me sound like a—"

"Douche?"

Rocco remained silent.

"Wanker?" Dario suggested. "Prick? Jagoff?"

Sounds about right.

Dario patted him on the back. "Don't worry. That ship has sailed."

Rocco sighed.

Just then Celeste entered, and they both waved at her.

Smiling, she waved back.

"We'll hear from her . . . eventually," Rocco said, not ready to drop the subject. "I can see those conniving black eyes as she crafts her response."

Dario frowned. "I don't think I've ever seen black eyes." He paused. "Hey, how do you know her eyes are black? When we met her, she was wearing sunglasses. Unless . . ." Dario grinned, nudging him. "You've been googling her, haven't you? Looking up images?"

Rocco hadn't. Dario was right. He had no idea what color her eyes were.

I must have been thinking of that woman at the bar.

He shook his head. "I haven't been looking her up. I don't know why I said that."

It took a while for Celeste to reach them, as she stopped multiple times chatting with the people she passed. Once she left them, they were all smiles. Everyone loved Celeste.

She had a slender build, wide-set blue eyes, a heart-shaped face, and dimples when she grinned. She was a looker with a wicked sense of humor. That coupled with a heart of gold made her a real gem and Dario one of the luckiest guys on the planet in Rocco's opinion.

Once she'd made it through the trail of admirers she'd left behind, she and Rocco exchanged pecks on the cheek while she shared a more intimate embrace with Dario.

"Celeste," Rocco pleaded, doing his best to look like an abandoned puppy. "Would you go get me an espresso?"

"No," she huffed. "I can't believe you even asked after that stupid sexist tweet."

"Why was that sexist? Okay, stupid, yes. But sexist? I didn't say it because she's a woman."

"'You're so full of shit, if you ever had an enema you'd evaporate into thin air.'"

Dario laughed.

Celeste lifted her chin. "Valentino said that."

Rocco frowned. "Who the hell is Valentino?"

"A character from a novel by Catherine Doyle, *Mafiosa*."

" *Maf*— Wait a minute. Is this from one of those romance novels you're always reading?"

He flinched when Dario's elbow jolted into his side.

Dario shook his head and then quickly transitioned to a smile when he caught Celeste glaring at him.

He turned back to Rocco. "Dude, you know, she's kind of right."

"I am not *kind of right*," Celeste said. "There is no such thing as *kind of* right. There's only right and wrong. I am right." She poked Rocco's chest. "And you are wrong."

Nodding, Dario wrapped his arm around her. "You are right."

"And . . . ?" Celeste prompted.

"He is wrong," he said, jerking his thumb at Rocco.

Dario was biting his lip, and his cheeks were beginning to crimson.

Asshole. He wants to laugh. Again.

There was a sudden stirring, confused utterances, and some catcall whistles and laughing.

Rocco turned his gaze toward the entrance.

"OMG!" Celeste exclaimed with a huge smile on her face.

A crowd of men were walking this way, wearing short black dresses with frilly white aprons. They were carrying pink boxes, pitchers, and paper bags.

What the—

Dario chuckled. "Celeste, did you do this?"

She shook her head. "I wish! I owe a thank-you to whoever did. I'm enjoying the show."

Rocco could guess what Celeste was enjoying. They were all good-looking and extremely fit, with impressive chests, biceps, and tapered waists.

Probably exotic dancers, he thought. They had the bodies for it.

"What the hell are they wearing?" Rocco demanded.

Celeste rolled her eyes. "Don't you recognize a French maid's outfit when you see one?"

Just then a space opened between a couple of the men, and there was Nico Angelini, carrying a tray with what looked like a double espresso and a cappuccino on it.

She was wearing jeans and a long-sleeved shirt, which while not exactly tight was not exactly loose either.

She handed the espresso and cappuccino to two of the men.

One walked up to Rocco. "Your double espresso, Mr. Vittori."

Rocco smiled. "Thank you. How do you manage those things?" he asked, pointing at the heels he was wearing.

"It ain't easy. I have a lot more sympathy for my mother and sisters."

Chuckling, Rocco nodded.

Dario, cappuccino in hand, joined Celeste and walked over to Nico while some of the team members helped themselves to doughnuts and pastries.

Celeste beamed. "This is just about the best breakfast I have ever had!" She held out her hand. "It's a real pleasure to finally meet you, Nico. I'm Celeste. Dario's girlfriend."

They shook hands.

Celeste's eyes were gleaming. "Oh, you and I are going to be good friends! I've been looking at clips of some of your races. Damn impressive."

Nico smiled. "Thank you. That's nice of you to say."

"Nice has nothing to do with it," Celeste scoffed. "I only speak the truth. Ask Dario. He'll tell you. He's usually the one who catches smoke as a result."

They laughed, and the rest of what was said got drowned out by everyone around them.

Hank, the controls engineer, winked at Nico. "You're okay, kid."

Laura, the engine systems engineer, gave her a thumbs-up.

Rocco folded his arms, his temples throbbing.

Why the hell did you send that tweet?

He watched as the mechanics expressed their approval by slapping her on the shoulder, giving her a bro-hug or a high-five. Some welcomed her to the team and said they were looking forward to working with her.

Leave it alone. Leave. It. Alone.

But that part of him that lurked in the deeper, darker depths of him couldn't.

Wouldn't.

"Oh, miss," Rocco called out. He raised one eyebrow when she turned and met his gaze. "May I have some sugar?"

She pasted a saccharine sweet smile laced with arsenic on her face and picked up a small box of sugar cubes.

He scanned the room. Most of the team had ventured off. Only a few remained and, like Dario and Celeste, were focused on the coffee and pastries.

He quickly hooked his foot around a nearby chair, dragging it up behind him, and sat down.

Her hair was even darker than he remembered. It wasn't groomed like he was used to seeing on women. It wasn't straight, but it wasn't exactly wavy either. It was wild. He wondered if he were to put his hand in it whether he'd be able to get it out. It looked like it might ensnare a man. She had on sunglasses. Again. He couldn't get even a glimpse of her eyes.

Once she was opposite him, she stood still—real still. She had bold bone structure, a strong jaw and cheekbones, like that actress his grandmother loved, Anna Magnani.

She must have some Italian in her. Of course she does with that name.

She offered him the box, but he didn't take it.

She wasn't wearing the white T-shirt. Why wasn't she wearing the white T-shirt?

That got him thinking about jelly doughnuts. Tracing circles. And nipples. Her nipples.

He crooked his finger for her to come closer.

She bent over, and that thick mane of hers fell forward, some strands brushing against his cheek. What was that scent? Was she wearing perfume?

A sudden jolt of electricity shot straight to the south pole.

"What do you think you're doing?" he asked, annoyed at the sound of his husky voice.

She tilted her head. "I should have thought it was obvious."

"It's what you've got those guys wearing that's obvious."

"You've never seen a French maid's uniform?"

"I know what it is."

"Of course you do. I'm sure it's standard issue for all your girlfriends."

Now the south pole was rising.

Damn it.

He bit his lip to keep from smiling. "And if I said it was?"

She tossed her head. "It wouldn't surprise me."

He had the feeling he'd seen her tilt her head like that before. But he didn't remember her doing it.

She attempted to stand up but stopped.

"Ow!" she cried.

Her hair had gotten caught in the zipper of his shirt.

Shit.

He grabbed the collar of his shirt and placed his espresso on a nearby table.

"Come closer," he said.

"Why?"

"So I can get your damn hair out of this zipper."

She hesitated. And there was a moment. Was it her breathing? The flush in her cheeks? He wanted to remove those sunglasses and see her eyes.

And then a sudden thought came to him and he grinned. "Are you afraid of me?"

You should be, once we're out on that track.

She scoffed. "Don't be ridiculous."

She sounded breathy.

His grin widened.

"Well, then," he said, his voice low and husky, "come closer."

She sighed as she leaned forward.

When he tried to release the zipper by pulling the tab, it took the hair with it, forcing her to bend lower. Her hands grabbed the armrests of the chair for support, and she dropped the box of sugar cubes.

She looked down at his lap where they'd landed.

He saw where she was looking and chuckled. "Like what you see?"

Her eyes shot up, meeting his. The sunglasses had slid down the bridge of her nose.

Her eyes were dark. Real dark.

They might be black.

She shoved the glasses back up and then quickly grabbed the arm of the chair again to regain her balance.

"You are so full of yourself," she hissed.

He shrugged. "Well, I guess that's better than being full of something else."

"Your ego, as big and overblown as it is, still leaves plenty of room for bullshit."

She heaved a noticeable sigh. His eyes were drawn to her breasts like they were magnets. He didn't know if she could tell where he was looking, but he knew she couldn't cross her arms. Not in the position she was in now. This amused him. It probably shouldn't. But fuck it. It did.

He looked up. She must have seen where he was looking. She was glaring at him. He didn't need to see her eyes to know that.

"You could stand up, you know," she spat.

I could. But I'm not going to.

"Did you hear me?" she asked.

"I heard you. You're not exactly soft-spoken."

"Don't forget demure and genteel."

"No, not that either."

"Characteristics of the ideal lady," she huffed.

"Who says?" He grinned when he heard her sigh. "You think you already know what I think is an ideal lady, is that it?"

"No," she hissed. "Just forget it." She pulled back, but he didn't let go.

"Do you want to rip out your hair? Just be patient. It's supposed to be a virtue."

"You don't strike me as patient," she huffed.

"No good driver is."

"Not true. The fact that you don't know that might explain your performance the last few years. I know patience is a virtue when it comes to racing. That's part of what makes me a damn good driver."

His heart began to thump.

"We'll see," he said, gritting his teeth as he struggled to pull the hair gently from the zipper.

"What's wrong, Mr. Vittori? Does it make you feel uncomfortable to see men so scantily clad?"

"Not at all."

"Perhaps what's bothering you is not so much what the men are wearing but what they're doing."

"What do you mean, what they're doing?"

"A woman's job."

"Serving coffee?"

"That's right."

"I didn't say that, you did."

Now he'd gotten it; he gently pulled the hair loose and leaned back. "There," he said.

She quickly righted herself and crossed her arms. "Is it true you rescued a cat and a dog from a dumpster?"

He frowned. "Who told you that?" He waved his hand. "Never mind. I know who did."

It was either Dario or Celeste. If Dario had told her, he would have said something like *The guy's not really as bad as he makes himself out to be. That's just a wall he puts up. He's like those mangy mutts he rescued from a dumpster. But don't ever call them mangy in front of him. People are mangy but not animals.* If it was Celeste, it would have been more like *The guy's an asshole, we all know that, but he did rescue that cat and dog. He has that going for him.*

He crossed his own arms and sat glaring up at her while she did likewise, glaring down at him.

She was the first to break the silence. "So?"

"So, what?"

"Is it true? Did you rescue a cat and a dog from a dumpster?"

"Yes, it's true. Why wouldn't it be?"

She shrugged. "No reason."

"Animals don't go around showing you one face and then turn around to show the world another. They don't make you think you can trust them, only for you to find out you can't."

Something changed after he'd said that. He tried to spot what it was. Was it in her face? The way she was standing? He tried to pinpoint what it was, but couldn't.

"And people do that?" she asked, her voice suddenly softer.

His heart picked up pace. He wanted out of this chair. But with her standing there, he hesitated. And that made him feel trapped. For some reason the softer voice bothered him. He felt more comfortable with the other one—the one that matched her black eyes.

"Women do," he said, narrowing his eyes. "But then, you being a woman, you would already know that."

There she was. She was back. He could tell by the way she'd squared her shoulders.

She scowled. "I know what's bothering you."

There it was—the black-eyes voice. Why would he prefer it to the softer one?

"You do, do you?"

"I'm sure you would have preferred a woman serve you."

In that outfit, as a matter of fact, yes.

A surge of heat radiated through his body, and that pole between his thighs began to throb.

She glanced down at his lap. "Your sugar?"

The humming he'd felt in his groin went full throttle.

He hesitated before getting her meaning. He picked up the box and handed it to her.

She indicated with her eyes his espresso sitting on the table.

He took it, but before he could hold it up to her, she threw a sugar cube in the cup with enough force, most of the espresso spilled out onto his thighs. He was glad it was no longer hot.

He stifled a grin but not the stirring he felt below his waist.

"I think one should be enough," she said with that arsenic smile. "We wouldn't want you to be too sweet, now would we?" she added before walking away.

CHAPTER SEVEN

ROCCO

Rocco sat tapping his foot, waiting impatiently for Dario and Celeste to show up so they could go to dinner.

He was agitated. Because of that photo. That damn photo. If Nico Angelini hadn't pulled that stunt, her hair never would have gotten caught in his zipper, and there wouldn't be a photo.

Ping.

He groaned.

Another comment he'd been tagged in.

Who was he kidding? It was his own damn fault. If he hadn't called her over and then sat down, all the rest of it wouldn't have happened.

What the hell had he been thinking?

Ping.

He hadn't been.

Thinking.

It was that stupid dream only without the white T-shirt and the jelly doughnut. Is that what had driven him to do it?

He stood up and began pacing.

This would never do.

The first race was only a few weeks away. He needed to focus, find his way back up on that podium. Even though there was bigger competition for him—drivers like Ian Anker and Leo Clarke—in some ways she was more dangerous. Not to his reaching the podium or earning a championship. But to his pride. At least Anker and Clarke were on different teams, driving different cars. The car might account for a loss.

But she'd be driving a car built by the same engineers and mechanics that built the car he was driving. If she beat him in a race, what would that say about him as a driver?

Ping.

He muted his phone and slammed it on the table.

She was messing with his head. And not just his head, he thought, when he recalled the way she smelled.

Was it perfume? Or her?

If she just hadn't— She could have remained standing, and then he would have been forced to get up out of that chair. But she didn't. Why didn't she?

Dario walked in.

Rocco turned to him. "Who the hell took those photos when Nico Angelini pulled that stunt with the coffee? Does Celeste know? Do you?"

Dario shook his head. "I was too busy ogling the pastries in the pink boxes, and Celeste was too busy ogling the ones in the aprons."

Rocco laughed. Sometimes he really hated Dario for getting him to laugh when he wanted so badly not to.

He sighed. "Have you seen the photo?"

Dario grinned. "Which one? There was quite a selection."

"I'm talking about *the* photo."

"What do you mean, *the* photo?"

"If you have to ask, then you haven't seen it. It's gone viral."

"Okay, so I haven't seen it. Why are you asking me about it?"

"Never mind. It's not important."

"Well, now I'm curious."

"It's just a photo of me sitting down and Nico Angelini standing over me."

"And that went viral? What the— Wait a minute, why?"

"I don't know why it went viral," Rocco lied, knowing full well why it had.

"No. Why were you sitting down, and why was she standing over you?"

"I felt like sitting down, okay?" Rocco cried, exasperated, recalling that's exactly what he'd been doing in that dream.

But he wasn't about to tell Dario that.

His cousin blinked, holding up his hands as if in surrender. "Okay. You felt like sitting down. So, why was she standing over you?"

"I asked for some sugar. She brought it over."

Dario shrugged. "Okay. Why did that go viral?"

Rocco didn't say anything and avoided meeting Dario's gaze.

"Let me see it," Dario said.

Rocco hesitated.

"Come on," Dario said, holding out his hand. "You might as well. I can just look at it on my own phone."

Rocco handed him his phone.

Dario stared at the photo. "Hmm. Interesting."

"What the hell does that mean?"

"It's sexy. "

Rocco groaned. He already knew that.

Dario grinned. "Do you have a magnifying glass?"

Rocco snatched the phone from him. "Give me that."

"I'm just saying . . . you sitting there, and her bending over like that."

One eyebrow hiked up Rocco's brow as the corner of his lips slid up his cheeks. "Bending over? Dude, she's facing the wrong direction."

Dario laughed. "Dude, you are such a dog."

"Dude, that is such a bad choice of words."

Dario waved his hands. "I know. I know. It's an insult to dogs."

Rocco stared at the photo. Now he was trying to imagine her bending over, but the other way.

"Explain something to me," Dario said. "Why is she bending over—wrong direction aside?"

"You wouldn't be talking like this if Celeste was here."

"Duh. I'm not a complete bonehead."

"Just part bonehead."

"You're avoiding my question."

"I didn't want anyone else to hear our conversation, so I just asked her to get close enough so they wouldn't."

"What was the conversation about?"

"I don't remember."

"Like hell you don't."

"Okay, how about this? I don't want to talk about it."

"Okay. But why didn't you just stand up?"

Good question, thought Rocco as he stared at the photo, feeling a warmth flood his body, like that scent.

"Hey!" Dario snapped.

Rocco blinked.

"Are you okay?" Dario asked.

"Yeah, of course I'm okay."

"All right, then answer my question. Why didn't you just stand up?"

"I don't know why."

"Is there something more here? Something I, as your manager, maybe should be worried about?"

"Like what?"

"I'm not sure. All I know is, you don't want me to know what you were talking about when the two of you were like that." He pointed at Rocco's phone.

"It's not what it looks like. Her hair fell forward, and some of it got stuck in the zipper of my shirt. So, I got it—unstuck. It just took me some time."

Dario held out his hand. "Let me see it again."

Reluctantly, Rocco gave him his phone.

Dario stared intently at the photo. The ends of his perfectly arched black brows knitted until they nearly met up with each other. "You can't see that in this photo."

"I know you can't. I've looked. Can we drop it already?"

"Fine with me. I'm not the one who brought it up."

Rocco heard the door open.

"Hello!"

Celeste.

"I almost forgot," Dario said. "I'm just giving you a heads-up. I know you hate doing photoshoots, but Celeste said something about doing one for a magazine. Someone contacted her about it. She'll probably mention it now."

Celeste was a prop stylist.

"Guess what?" she cried excitedly.

"Dario already told me," Rocco said. "I'm not interested."

"What are you talking about?"

"The photoshoot. I'm not interested."

"Well," Celeste said, "that's good because neither are they. They don't want you. They want Nico. And Nico doesn't want you there either. So, it turns out perfect. Everyone's happy."

Celeste's phone buzzed. "This is them. I've got to take this." She pulled open the sliding glass door and stepped out onto the balcony.

Rocco stewed.

They only want Nico? She doesn't want me there? Where does Nico Angelini get off, demanding I not be there?

The balcony door opened, and Celeste stepped inside.

"That was fast," Dario said.

Celeste nodded. "Now they want Rocco to do the photospread too. Maybe because of that photo on social media and all the comments. But don't worry, Rocco, I told them you didn't want to do it."

Rocco frowned. "Why'd you tell them that?"

Celeste and Dario were looking at him like he'd suddenly turned green, had horns coming out of his head and a tail sprouting out his butt.

"Uh," Celeste said as her jaw dropped to the floor and she looked with gaping eyes over at Dario, "maybe because you hate that kind of thing; never want to do that kind of thing; and just seconds before I took the call, told me you didn't want to do *that particular* kind of thing."

"I changed my mind. Call them back and tell them I'll do it."

CHAPTER EIGHT

NICO

Nico sat waiting for them to finish setting up the lighting in the studio.

She sighed. Even though she'd had her usual dose of caffeine this morning, she felt tired. She hadn't slept well.

After that coffee stunt, even sleep wasn't a prick-free zone. She kept dreaming about him. And it was always the same dream. Her hair got stuck in his zipper. But instead of him disengaging it, he pulled her down and rolled her over, pinning her shoulders to the ground. His eyes drifted down to her breasts, and it was as though there were some kind of direct connection like an on-off switch between his eyes, her nipples, and that arrogant grin.

Eyes on breasts—check. Nipples engaged—check. Arrogant grin blast off—check.

Rinse. Repeat. Check.

She sighed.

When her hair had gotten stuck like it had, she'd been close enough to smell him. She remembered that smell when her body was pressed into his while she'd checked his pockets and when she'd kissed him outside Drink and Dive—a woodsy, wildlife kind of scent—part cedar and part animal.

Why did you bend over just because he asked? And now that I think about it, he didn't ask. You could have remained standing. Then he would have been forced to stand up.

Why did you let him put you in that position?

What position? Vulnerable?

No, not exactly. But, something.

She knew what the annoying, arrogant, asshole, prick was doing. He was trying to mess with her head. Undermine her racing before the season even started. Make her lose her confidence.

Just as I expected.

No, that wasn't right. Not exactly.

He was doing what she'd expected. He just wasn't doing it in the way she'd expected.

It was different than when they'd gone after each other on social media.

It feels different.

She stood up and began pacing.

At least the dream always ended where it did. That was a good thing. Any other man, and she might have preferred the dream not stop. But given it was that annoying, arrogant, asshole, prick, better it end before . . .

Before what?

Before he did . . . something.

Her phone buzzed. It was Charles.

"How's it going?" he asked.

"Just waiting. We haven't started yet."

"Nervous?"

"A little. You know I don't feel comfortable in front of a camera."

Ping.

"What's that?" Nico asked.

"My phone. Photos of your coffee run. One of them's gone viral."

Ping.

Viral?

And then Nico thought of the men dressed in those outfits.

I guess that makes sense.

"Why are you bending over Rocco Vittori while he's sitting down?"

Someone took a photo of that?

Nico felt beads of sweat sprout above her upper lip. So what if someone took a photo? There was nothing interesting or special there.

So why did someone take a photo of it?

"Nico, are you there?"

"Yeah, I'm here. Uh. My hair got stuck in his zipper. He was trying to get it out."

Charles laughed. "*Your* hair? Got stuck in *his* zipper?" He paused. "How exactly did that positioning even come about? Him sitting down and you standing over him like that."

"He wanted some sugar."

"Well, well, well," Charles chuckled. "Looks like he got it."

"In his coffee, Charlemagne." Nico huffed.

Ping. Ping. Ping.

"You should read some of these comments."

"That's not the one that's gone viral?"

"It is. It's sexy. You should take a look."

Sexy?

"Damn it, Charles. This is your fault. It was your idea."

"Oh"—he snorted—"so now you're done blaming the brain floating in a vat of ginger ale in Brainerd and on to blaming me."

"I thought it was a toss-up between Duluth and Brainerd."

"No, it's Brainerd. Brain-erd. Get it? Clever, no? In any case, just remember, you were all game to do this, Nico. You know you were. Besides, given some of the comments from those socket slingers, gasket gurus, and suspension sensei you'll be working with, sounds like it was a big success."

Ping.

"Who?"

"You know, the guys who put the car together and make sure everything's humming, those wrench wranglers and spark plug samurai."

"You mean mechanics and engineers?"

"Right." Charles paused. "I wonder."

"Wonder what?"

"Rocco's not doing the photoshoot with you, is he?"

"No! Thank God!"

"What are you wearing for the shoot?"

"My racing suit. Why?"

"I believe those suits have zippers, in which case—"

"Stop right there. If the next word out of your mouth is hair or zipper, Charlemagne, I swear—"

"I wasn't going to say anything about hair and zippers."

"Oh, really? Well, that's good because I forbid you to ever utter the word *hair* in conjunction with the word *zipper* within my earshot. Ever again." She paused. "And if you weren't going to say something about hair and zippers, what were you going to talk about?"

"Nothing."

"No, you were going to say something until I stopped you."

"I wasn't going to say anything. I was going to ask you something."

"Oh really," Nico said, rolling her eyes, knowing full well Charles was lying. "What were you going to ask me?"

There was a moment of silence before Charles spoke.

"I was going to ask you what you think the universe is made up of."

"You were not. There's an easy answer to that."

"Oh, really? What is it?"

"Well, matter—molecules, atoms, that sort of thing."

"Uh-uh."

"What do you mean, uh-uh?"

"Only five percent of the universe is made up of atoms, according to astronomers."

"How do you know?"

"I read it somewhere. I can't remember where."

"Okay, I'll bite. What's the other ninety-five percent made up of?"

"That's the question. Maybe dark matter or energy, they don't really know."

"And you thought I might."

"It was worth a try. You want to know what I want to know?"

Not really, but I'm certain you're going to tell me.

"What exactly are these astronomers doing with their time? It's the twenty-first century, and they've only come up with five percent of the answer?" He paused. "Now that is a real concern. But as for you getting your whatchamacallit stuck in the thingamajig of the annoying, arrogant, asshole, prick . . ."

"What are you talking about?"

"You told me not to say the H-word or the Z-word. HZ-Gate is forbidden."

"HZ-Gate?"

"Do you really want me to spell it out? You told me you didn't want me to say those dirty words. But I will do so, for clarification. Hair-Zipper-Gate. You know, like Watergate. Wiggate. Pantygate. Nutellagate."

"You made that last one up."

"I did not. It was a big scandal at Columbia University—widespread theft of Nutella from the dining halls by students."

"I don't really get Nutella."

"I don't either. It's supposed to be chocolate."

"But it's not."

"Exactly! Now there's the real gate!"

There was a moment of silence.

Nico sighed. "Okay, just forget about HZ-Gate. I'm just glad I'm doing this photoshoot alone. That man is trying to mess with me. I don't even want to think about what it's going to be like once we hit the track . . . He's so freaking competitive."

"Not unlike someone else I know."

"I am *not* that bad."

Nico waited for a response, but Charles was unusually silent.

"Did you hear me?"

"I heard you."

"Well?"

"I refuse to answer on the grounds that it might incriminate me."

"I'm hanging up now. Goodbye, Charlemagne."

Nico sighed as she grabbed her purse. If she had a manager, a Dario of her own, then they might have talked some sense into her before she pulled that stupid stunt.

She opened her purse and tossed her cell phone in.

There it was. That damn letter.

Why did she insist on carrying it around with her?

You know why. You have to read it. But what you really want to do is throw it away or burn it. Act as though there were no letter. But you can't do that. You can't go to Italy without knowing what's in that letter.

She stared at the postmark on the envelope before quickly shutting her purse and tossing it on the chair beside her.

Mickey hadn't contacted her in years. Why now? He must know she finally made it to Formula 1. If he didn't know when he'd written the letter, he certainly knew by now.

Wouldn't it be wonderful if she had a Dario who could manage Mickey for her? Was there such a person? Then again, to do that they'd have to know about Mickey. They'd have to know about her past. They'd have to know about Uncle Jack and Aunt Milly—grifters who'd taken off with her when her grandfather had dropped dead of a heart attack. They'd have to know how she'd helped them con people. They'd have to know about how she'd run off with Mickey and what she'd done with him.

Thinking about it made her feel as though the oxygen surrounding her had suddenly been sucked into a vacuum.

She drew a deep breath. That's why she was better off without a manager. She could manage things. She'd been on her own a long time now and had a lot of practice. Look how far she'd come. She'd done all right.

"You ready?" the photographer's assistant said, standing in the doorway.

Nico nodded and followed her into the studio.

"You're gorgeous!" Celeste said. "Why don't you ever do your hair and makeup like this? You look like an exotic Italian actress."

Nico smiled but felt silly being done up so glamorously given she was wearing her racing suit. At least she'd be doing the photoshoot alone. She wasn't comfortable in front of the camera. If she were standing next to Rocco Vittori, she felt certain once the magazine staff looked at the photos, they would want to cut her out.

Celeste's expression changed from bubbly to serious. "I have to tell you something. Two things actually. First, this photographer doesn't like his subjects to remain silent during the shoot. So, he'll ask you questions. I think he thinks it puts people at ease. Or brings out their true self for the camera to capture. Something like that. The other thing—"

"Okay, Celeste, come on now," the photographer said. "I want to get started."

Celeste glanced from him and back at Nico, hesitating. "I'll tell you when he has to change rolls. It's no big deal."

What's no big deal? wondered Nico. Usually when people said that, the something they were referring to was very much a big deal.

The photographer's assistant positioned Nico in front of the lights and the camera.

"What makes a girl want to race?" the photographer asked.

Nico blinked. The question had caught her off guard.

"And I say girl," he added, "because I figure you raced karts as a kid. So, what makes a woman want to race?"

Do they ever ask men that question?

"I imagine what makes a boy or man want to," Nico said.

He nodded. "Sex, money, and an easy hard-on?"

Nico laughed. "Something like that."

"It doesn't frighten you?"

She hesitated.

"You're fearless," he said, "is that it?"

"No. Of course not. I have fears like anyone else. I'm afraid of death and being injured just as any sane person would be." She cleared her throat. "It's just there are other fears, but they're not there when I'm behind the wheel. Or at least they don't seem present at the moment."

Shit. Now he's going to ask what other fears? Say something. Quick.

"I grew up racing," she said. "My happiest moments were when I was racing."

She swallowed.

When it was taken from me and I thought, along with my grandfather, I'd lost it forever, it wasn't a case of me wanting it back. I needed it back. It was the same thing as needing me back.

Not that. She couldn't. Wouldn't. Say. That.

"I just need it," she quickly added. "I guess you could say, I have a need for—"

"If the next word out of your mouth is *speed,* this photoshoot is over."

She burst out laughing. "No, I wasn't going to say that."

She heard the door open and shut. Celeste must have stepped out. It was so quiet. Only the photographer and her.

And that camera.

She was suddenly so aware of that black lens, she couldn't see anything beyond it. It seemed absent of all light, and yet she felt as though it were a window—and one too large into her past. Any answer she gave would only prompt more questions, pushing that window open wider still, until . . . She shuddered, but only on the inside, steeling her body to remain still.

Like anyone who was practiced in the art of lies, she knew the best ones were those that held an ounce of truth. And an ounce of truth was all she was willing to give.

Don't lie. You're through with lying. Tell enough to tell the truth but not enough to tell the whole truth.

CHAPTER NINE

ROCCO

Rocco stared at her.

She looked. Different. And yet. The same.

It's her eyes. There's something about her eyes.

"I don't mean to make you uncomfortable," the photographer said. "I guess it's just the mindset of a Formula 1 driver baffles me. All the work, the time, the sweat, and the tears you have to put into becoming one of only twenty drivers in the world to get in—what is it—seventeen hundred, eighteen hundred, give or take, pounds of metal and send yourself hurtling around a track at over two hundred miles per hour? I always wonder why they do it. What drives them to do it?"

"It's hard to put into words. There's this quote, I don't know who said it. 'Speed has never killed anyone . . .'"

Rocco knew the quote. He recited the rest of it along with her silently in his mind.

"'Suddenly becoming stationary . . . That's what gets you.'"

The camera flashed. She blinked.

The photographer turned toward the door. "Ah," he said, spotting Rocco. He raised his hand. "Good. You're here. I see you're suited up. Ready to go?"

Rocco nodded before glancing over at Nico. The light was shining in her eyes. She held up her hand in an attempt to shield them.

"Okay, Rocco," the photographer said, "get up there."

"What are you doing here?" Nico demanded when he came out from behind the light.

"The same thing you are."

"Could you stand a little closer?" the photographer asked.

Rocco inched over.

Celeste marched up to them, waving the photographer's assistant off. "This was the other thing I wanted to tell you," she whispered in Nico's ear. "They decided they wanted Rocco too, and he agreed to do it. I should have told you sooner. I would have, but I didn't believe he would actually go through with it. He hates this kind of thing." She drew a deep breath as she took a step back and surveyed them. "Normally this isn't part of my job, but can you two loosen up?"

She took them both by the shoulders and pushed them together.

Rocco felt a spark and flinched.

It's these racing suits.

After taking a series of shots, the photographer threw up his hands. "These are awful. Maybe a change of scenery. Let's go outside."

Rocco leaned against the embankment with his arms crossed alongside Dario, who had joined them. They were on the outskirts of Vegas with the desert as the backdrop. It was mid-February, and they were experiencing a heat wave. It was ninety degrees out.

A slight breeze wafted past them. It should have been a relief. He was sweating pistons in this damn racing suit. But in some ways, the breeze made the heat worse because his skin could hardly welcome it before it was quickly taken away by the sun, which was relentless. It was as though he were looking forward to something that never quite arrived, because the moment it did, he was all too aware of its going.

What's more, it was nothing like a breeze in the places he loved, like the small Italian village where he'd grown up. There was no fragrance of pine or magnolia, jasmine or lavender, olive groves or wildflowers. It didn't carry the scent of anything. It only carried sand, which made his skin feel gritty. Rocco guessed that was because there was nothing for the breeze to grab hold of. As far as he knew, cacti had no scent.

"Why the hell did I agree to this?" he grumbled.

"You tell me," Dario said. "You could have said no. You did say no. Until you didn't. Why is that, by the way?"

"Okay, we're ready!" the photographer's assistant cried.

Rocco walked over to the car where Nico was waiting.

"I don't know why you agreed to do this," she hissed.

"Me? What about you?"

"I said *yes* first, with the understanding that I'd be doing it alone. You knew I'd be doing it, so why didn't you say *no*?"

He hadn't liked it when Dario had asked him the question. He liked it even less when she did.

"Why did you agree to do it at all?" he growled. "Haven't you had enough exposure?"

Her brow wrinkled.

He sighed. "Have you not seen the photos posted of that coffee delivery of yours? Seen all the comments?"

Her eyes flashed. If she could shoot laser beams from them, they would have extinguished him on the spot.

"I didn't post those photos," she spat. "Nor did I make any of those comments. And might I remind you what my doing that coffee delivery was in response to? *Your* tweet. So, if there's anyone here who shouldn't be looking for more exposure"—she lifted her finger and poked his chest—"it's *you*."

Why should that jab send a twitch that developed into a tingle settling in his groin?

"Yeah," he said, doing his best to turn that twitch into a shrug, "but those were just words. It's nothing like an image of—"

"You're in the photos too!"

He stared into those dark eyes glaring back at him, and an image of *the* photo, the one that everyone was talking about, flashed before him. He recollected his discussion with Dario. He drew a deep breath and adopted a cool tone.

"Yeah, but I'm not bending over."

Her eyes gaped, and her mouth followed in quick succession. "I wouldn't have been *bending over* if you would've stood up."

"Okay," the photographer cried, "now I got some good stuff. Give me a moment, I need to put in a new roll."

Rocco frowned, looked around, and then walked over to Dario and Celeste.

"Was he taking photos?"

Celeste looked at him as though he had a cabbage between his ears instead of a brain.

"Duh."

Rocco looked at Dario.

"Dar?"

"Yeah," Dario said. "That's what we're here for."

"Yeah, but why didn't he say something? I didn't know he was taking photos."

Celeste grinned. "All the better. It didn't give you the chance to look like you were getting a rectal exam."

"Okay," said the photographer, coming over. "Let's do this!"

When Rocco didn't move, Celeste waved her hand at him.

"Go on."

Rocco stormed back to the car where Nico was still standing, clearly stewing with her arms crossed.

He crossed his arms as well and leaned back on the car.

"Nico," the photographer said, "lean against the car like Rocco." He paused. "Okay but move closer. Rocco, what are you doing? Don't move away. You're already too far apart."

Rocco inched right.

"Still too far."

He inched again.

Exasperated, the photographer snapped his fingers. His assistant came over and pushed Rocco until he stumbled into Nico.

"Sorry," he muttered.

"Humph."

After taking only three shots, the photographer sighed. "We're back to this again? You're both so stiff."

"I have an idea," Celeste said. "Come on, Dario."

She dragged him over to the car and placed him alongside Nico, pulling Rocco away.

"The magazine doesn't want photos of me," Dario insisted.

"I know. They're not going to use any of them. Just be yourself. Tell Nico a joke or just chat. So Rocco can see what he should be doing and maybe he'll loosen up."

"It's not just me," Rocco muttered to Celeste.

She waved her hand. "Shush."

The photographer began taking shots.

"Oh, man," Celeste cried, "these are going to be great!"

Watching, a reluctant Rocco agreed.

Dario was so damn handsome, and she was—

Not beautiful. No. Not beautiful.

Not even pretty, he told himself stubbornly.

But damn if her face doesn't command attention when you look at it.

"Hey!" Celeste cried, nudging him hard. "What planet are you on?"

Rocco looked over at her with a blank stare.

She looked annoyed, held out her arm, and glanced over at the car where Nico was standing. Alone. What happened to Dario? That's when Rocco realized he was standing behind Celeste.

When Rocco didn't move, Celeste muttered under her breath. "Get your ass over there now, Rocco. You said you wanted to do this. Don't think we're just going to up and quit because you haven't budged after the photographer shouted your name three times."

Three times? Three? Times?

The photographer's assistant grabbed his arm and dragged him over to the car, planting him beside Nico.

Once she'd walked away, Nico spoke quietly, barely moving her lips and without glancing at him. "Look, I don't want to do this any more than you do. So, let's just get it over with. Quick."

"Right. The sooner the better."

"Finally, something we agree on."

But it didn't go quick. Whatever they did—the way they stood, the way they looked at each other, the way they looked even when they didn't look at each other—all of it was wrong.

It was a complete disaster. If the assistant wasn't pushing Rocco to get closer to Nico, she was pushing Nico to get closer to him. You would have thought they were manufacturing epic farts the way they both steered clear of each other.

The only thing mildly pleasant was that occasional breeze, because now there was a hint of something beyond sand—a heady scent that he had to attribute to her, much as he didn't want to.

It had to be her. He only smelled it when she was near.

It reminded him of that woman at the bar. But, he thought, it had to be different.

Has to be.

And yet it had that same heavy way of landing in his body.

He would have thought something heavy would scorch his nose, give him a headache. This didn't. It was like the air itself.

The air itself? What does that even mean? Clearly, the heat is frying my brain.

But it was there. Something. Was there.

The heavy suit he was wearing didn't help matters. He could feel tracks of sweat racing down his flesh and pooling under his arms and in his groin, forming lakes that had begun to make his skin itch.

And yet that scent, whatever the hell it was, was welcome.

The only thing that is.

I just wish it came from some other woman.

This photoshoot was probably even worse for her. There's no way he could be smelling good. Not the way he was sweating.

These photos were bound to be awful. The good thing about that—they wouldn't publish any of them.

The photographer groaned. "Let's move on to the Strip."

"What?" both of them cried in unison.

"We're going to take some shots on the Vegas Strip."

"How many?" Rocco demanded.

The photographer was gritting his teeth. "As many as it takes."

CHAPTER TEN

ROCCO

Rocco stood alongside Dario in front of the car. They were on the Strip with the Bellagio fountains in the background. He slipped his fingers under the collar of his racing suit and plucked it away from his damp skin.

"What the hell are we waiting for?"

Dario shrugged. "Don't know."

Rocco tapped the shoulder of a passing crew member. "Do you know what's going on? Why are we waiting?"

"Nico's changing in the trailer."

He stared at Dario. "Why does she get to change?"

Shaking his head, Dario raised his shoulders. "Maybe after she's done, then you'll change."

Rocco tapped the shoulder of another crew member. "How long's she going to be in there? You don't have another trailer for me to change?"

"I think the photographer wants you to stay in your racing suit. Originally, he'd planned to have you in a tailored suit, but I guess he changed his mind."

Rocco stared at his cousin.

"Or had his mind changed by one Celeste Bellerose."

Dario frowned. "Why Celeste?"

"Because she's trying to get back at me for deciding last minute to do this photoshoot. So, she's more than happy to see me sweat."

As he said the word, it was as if he'd signaled his body to send a river of it down the middle of his back.

"God, I want out of this damn racing suit! If she'd stayed in hers, we could have been finished by now."

Just then he heard the trailer door bang open and shut.

"It's about time," Rocco huffed, lifting himself from the car and turning around.

The photographer was coming this way. He was followed by Celeste. And Celeste was followed by her.

Now she looked. Really. Different.

She was wearing a dress like the one Marilyn Monroe wore in that famous photo where she stood over the subway grate. She turned, and he could see the dress was a halter, which left her entire upper back bare, exposing olive skin that glistened in the sun.

He stared at her collarbone. It was stunning, an elegant line rippling beneath the surface of her flesh, hinting at its presence as it emerged and then quickly disappeared behind the white silk only to resurface as it met up with her delicate shoulders.

They'd piled her hair on top of her head into some kind of messy bun. A few strands fell loose across her cheeks. Her neck was.

Bare.

Naked.

Exposed.

Once she was standing beside him, he shook his head to shake those thoughts from his brain.

"How come you got to change?" he demanded at the very same moment she demanded, "How come you didn't have to change?"

There was a beat of uncomfortable silence.

Dario smiled. "You look great, Nico."

Staring at her feet, she crossed her arms. "Thanks."

Dario nudged him.

Rocco swallowed. "Yeah, you look, uh . . . nice."

All he got in response was an exasperated sigh. She didn't even look up at him.

"Celeste wants me," Dario said as he waved.

But when Rocco looked over, he saw Celeste had her back to them. Dario took off before Rocco could say anything. The guy couldn't get away fast enough.

"Nico, stand beside Rocco in front of the car," the photographer shouted.

"What took you so long?" Rocco hissed.

"You have somewhere else to be?" she hissed back. "Go ahead and leave. And why aren't you in a suit? They said you'd be wearing a suit."

"Yeah, well a suit would hardly be much better," he said, pulling his collar as he felt rivulets of sweat make their way to a pool of hot damp he felt between his thighs.

"Would you rather be wearing this dress?"

"At least it would be cooler."

"Trust me, if it was up to me, I would not be wearing this dress. But it wasn't up to me. And if you're wondering why it took so long, ask the wardrobe lady."

He glared at her. "Do you ever take responsibility for anything?"

Those dark eyes glared back. "Do you?"

There was a moment of silence. The only thing he heard was exasperated breathing. He wasn't sure if it was coming from him or from her.

"I don't want to be wearing *this*," she hissed behind clenched teeth, "while you're wearing *that*."

His heart was pounding. "Well I don't want to be wearing *this* while you're wearing *that*."

His eyes drifted down her neck and stopped at that collarbone.

"Ahem!"

He blinked and looked up.

Her eyes narrowed as though pinpointing the most precise target to do maximum damage with those laser beams.

His heart was racing. He actually felt it pounding in his ears.

He glared back at her, but those dark eyes didn't flinch.

He told his eyes not to move, but they did of their own accord as though they'd been drawn by some kind of magnetic force beyond his control. They wandered and only stopped when they'd reached that collarbone again.

He could tell she was breathing more deeply. And if he'd had to guess, he'd wager her heart was beating fast too. His eyes drifted to her breasts. It was hot enough to fry a tamale on the sidewalk, and yet her nipples—his fingers twitched, and he fisted his palms. She quickly crossed her arms. His glance slipped down to the hem of the dress. It was just past her knees. If there was a strong enough wind, that dress might—

"Ahem!"

He stared a moment longer before looking up and meeting her gaze.

Say something. But his brain was flooded with the image of her leaning over him when she'd brought him the sugar, only now she was wearing that dress.

Say.

Something.

"You could have said *no*," he said.

But not. That.

She blinked. "What are you talking about?

You're stuck with it now.

"When I asked for the sugar. You. Could. Have. Said. *No*. What's more, you could have just handed me the sugar and walked away."

"Why are you talking about that?" She uncrossed her arms, fisting her hands. "You were the one who wanted me to lean in close so you could talk without anyone else hearing."

He shrugged. "Yeah. But like I said, you could have said *no*. If you'd just stood there, I would have been forced to get out of that chair. In which case, your hair never would have gotten caught in my zipper. And then those photos of you with you . . ."

"What?" she spat.

"You know." His eyes drifted down. Damn, he wanted to bite those nipples. Hard. He grinned and then met her glare. "With you leaning over like that."

She was grinding her teeth. It made her jaw even more bold than it already was.

And then in an instant, her jaw softened.

She took a step back, and her lip curled as her eyes drifted down his chest and his torso. She didn't stop until she'd reached the spot right between his thighs.

Heat swarmed like dragonflies as that terrain became muggy, thick, and swampy. That he could have handled, but his crankshaft had begun to rotate.

Up.

And.

Out.

Damn it.

She was smirking.

Finally, she raised her eyes and met his.

Her pupils narrowed like the two sharp blades of a cat's eyes.

Damn her eyes are dark.

Are they black?

They could be black.

His body twitched involuntarily.

It's only because of that damn dress she's wearing.

He stared into that dark abyss and pitied any man who got entangled with this woman enough to really venture in. Even with a desert or a wasteland, you could see what lay before you. But her eyes? A space that was completely devoid of light? You'd never find a way out if you made the mistake of hazarding it.

She looked like the kind of woman who would put a guy's back up against the wall. She probably would bite his lip. Either that or kick the shit out of him.

"Excellent," the photographer cried. "We're getting some really good stuff here. Gotta get another roll."

Fuck. Not again!

Why doesn't he tell us when he's going to take photos? Isn't he supposed to do that?

Rocco noticed that a crowd of onlookers and fans snapping photos with their cell phones had begun to gather.

Some guy from the crowd yelled, "Get up on the hood and flash us some thigh!"

That was followed by a series of laughter, hoots, and catcalls.

"Come on! You're a total snack!" the guy cried. "Let's see some cake up on the hood of that car!"

Nico faced the man and invited him to jump up. "Be my guest."

This received a hearty round of applause.

Rocco grinned, but he could see a blush traveling up her neck and bursting into a deep red on her cheeks.

Why couldn't they have finished the shots out in the desert without any other people around?

"Hey," he said in a low voice, "just ignore them."

"They're not the problem!" she hissed. "You are!"

"Me? What did I do?"

It was too damn hot. He couldn't think. The two hemispheres of his brain were like polar ice caps, and they were melting fast. He could almost swear he heard a crack as the left and right hemispheres broke apart into two separate sheets of ice, making it impossible to communicate with each other. Not to mention the south pole, which was doing its damnedest to point north.

He wiped his brow.

"It isn't me," he said defensively, "it's that dress."

"What the hell is wrong with this dress?"

There was nothing wrong with the dress. Not really.

"I asked you what's wrong with this dress."

He rounded on her. "What's wrong is the way you look in it, okay!"

He cringed. Not only had he said it, which in and of itself was a real blunder, he'd said it loud enough for others to hear. He never would have made such a mistake if it wasn't for this heat. He cursed the sun.

The red in her cheeks deepened, and she turned away.

"We want to see you up on the hood!" someone from the crowd shouted. It sounded like the same guy.

Just then the photographer returned only having heard that last shout from the crowd. "Not a bad idea," he said, "let's give it a try. One of you get up on the hood."

"Okay," Rocco said, crossing his arms.

She crossed her arms likewise. "Okay."

"Well . . ."

"Well, what?"

Rocco could hear clicking.

Is he photographing us now?

He shoved that thought aside, pushing it to the background.

"Go ahead," he said.

"Go ahead and what?"

"Get up on the hood," he muttered between clamped teeth.

"You get up on the hood."

"He said you were to get up on the hood."

"No, he didn't. The photographer said one of us should get up on the hood."

"Well, okay, not him but the asshole in the crowd."

"Well, we agree on one thing: He is an asshole. But even the asshole never mentioned me by name."

"No, but he said—" He stopped himself.

Her eyebrows flew up like green flags.

He could practically hear her thoughts.

Assholes, start your engines.

"What?" she demanded.

He didn't respond.

"Flash us some thigh?" she ventured. "You're a total snack? Let's see some cake up on the hood?"

He sighed. "Will you stop already with the semantics. It's obvious what he meant."

"Why? Because I'm a woman?"

"I notice you pull that card out whenever it suits you."

"I wasn't the one who pulled the card out, you were. And trust me, that card never suits me. But I guess I can't expect you to understand because you don't know what it's like to go through this world as a woman. Not to mention what it's like to go through *this Formula 1 world* as a woman. The fact of the matter is I never would have done that coffee stunt if you hadn't made it clear to everyone how I should be viewed. Not only as a woman but *only* a woman. Certainly *not* as a serious driver. Not as anyone who has just as much hope and dreams and drive as you do. Not as someone who's worked her ass off to get here. No, not any of that. You made it clear that I should only be seen as some twit who's only here to serve a man—and in particular—to serve *you*."

He stared at her throat. It looked as though she were choking out the words and it was difficult to swallow.

Her dark eyes glistened.

Fuck. She's not going to cry, is she?

He felt like shit.

"Come on, Nico," a guy in the crowd yelled, "show us some leg."

"Among other things," another guy cried.

That was followed by laughter and some lascivious gestures.

"I don't care anymore," she muttered in a voice barely above a whisper. "I just want this over."

She stepped forward, but his arm flew out, stopping her.

"No!" Rocco growled, glaring at the man.

His arm accidentally brushed up against her breasts. He heard the flow of her breath suddenly halt and he hastily lowered it.

He clenched his teeth and glowered at the man. "You. Are. Not. Getting. Up. On. That. Hood." He sighed. "I am."

He turned and jumped up on the car.

The crowd went wild hooting and hollering.

"Okay, Rocco," the photographer cried, "lie across the hood on your side, looking this way."

He did so, propping his head up on his elbow.

He felt like a fool and was fairly certain he looked like one.

"Tilt your head more," Dario shouted. "and thrust out your hip."

"Lick your lips," Celeste cried, "and give that come-hither look."

"Shut the fuck up!" Rocco yelled back. "Let's get this over with already," he said testily.

"Nico," the photographer shouted. "Stand in front of him, just don't block his face. Yes, that's perfect. Now just lean against the car."

"Sorry," he said in a low voice. "When I put my arm out like that, I didn't mean to, um—"

"Get handsy?"

She didn't turn around, so he couldn't see her face when she spoke.

"Yeah," he said. "That."

"Well, that's a relief," she said, her voice suddenly sounding a little lighter. "Given you clearly suck at it."

A laugh escaped his lips despite himself.

She glanced over her shoulder.

"Thanks," she murmured.

Why this hit him in the way it did, he couldn't say. But it compelled him to do something he hadn't planned—something that surprised him every bit as much as it probably did her.

When she looked over her shoulder, a lone strand of hair fell in front of her eye, but before she could do anything about it, he took it between his fingers and slipped it behind her ear.

She turned back to face the camera so quickly he couldn't see the look on her face. But even if he had seen it, he probably wouldn't know how to read it. And if he'd been able to see the look on his own face? He probably wouldn't know how to read that either.

CHAPTER ELEVEN

NICO AND ROCCO

It was preseason testing, and Nico stood in the paddock watching the cars whiz by, knowing any second Rocco would be speeding past. She could hear the race engineer on the radio talking to him. She shielded her eyes from the sun. Even with her dark shades, the bright glare made her blink. It was warmer than when she'd been in the car this morning but not that much. It was still cool enough to make for a fast track.

The heat wave that had scorched Vegas during that photoshoot had come and gone. So, it seems, had that spark of good vibes between her and Rocco.

She'd expected things to be different after the photoshoot. She'd expected something to be different.

Not that we would be buddies.

A shiver coursed through her body as she remembered his flesh grazing her nipples when he'd raised his arm just before jumping up on the hood of that car. And then what he'd done with her hair.

She shook her head as though this might shake the memory from her brain.

No, definitely not buddies. But at least less antagonistic.

When she'd arrived at the paddock, she waited for some sign, some indication she'd been right. But he wouldn't even look at her. Not even during the team meeting. And when they'd accidentally bumped into each other once, he'd mumbled a gruff *sorry* while looking the other way.

Maybe it was better. She'd been nervous about seeing him again and not just because of what had happened at the photoshoot but because of her dreams—yes, dreams, plural—because now she was having more than one.

In one, he was up on the hood of that car. That in and of itself wouldn't have been so bad. But she was up there with him. Under him. And he was—doing things. Things she shouldn't be thinking about. Things she didn't want to be thinking about. Things she kept telling her brain to stop thinking about.

Especially standing here in the paddock.

Now that she thought about it, it was better she be invisible to him. She just had to work on making him invisible to her.

If he could do it, then so could she. Okay, so maybe it was a little more difficult because of those dreams. Still, she was every bit as much a driver as he was. He was focused on one thing and one thing only—winning. And so was she.

There he is, she thought as she saw him swiftly approach and fly down the track.

Nico had been thrilled when she was sitting behind the wheel. The car was creating some definite buzz. It was fast. The owner had spared no expense and had poached some of the best engineers, technicians, and mechanics from some of the premier F1 teams, including Blue Jet Lightning and Elegante Racing—the two teams that had finished first and second last year, for the Constructors' and the Drivers' Championships.

In only twelve days, I'll be on that track—the first race of the season. MY FIRST Formula 1 race.

"Nico Angelini?"

She swung around at the sound of a woman's voice. She was stunning—tall and elegant with auburn hair that was sleek, shiny, and straight and still managed to fall in a graceful wave to just past her shoulders. Her skin was translucent, her features delicate.

Nico found herself wishing she could see the woman's eyes, but she was wearing dark sunglasses.

The woman smiled. "I'm Carolyn Wickham."

Wickham, Nico thought. *Right. Wife of the owner of Blue Jet Lightning.*

They shook hands.

"Nico Angelini. You and your husband must be very pleased. Your car and your drivers look very fast."

"They do, don't they? Especially Ian. We're hoping he can win us both trophies again this year. But, of course, Leo Clarke will be in contention as well. Perhaps even Rocco. He doesn't look too bad out there. Maybe he can recapture some of his old glory. I'm just glad to see he's racing this season. For a while there, it looked as though he might—not be."

Nico remained silent. She had her opinions about the man—plenty of them—but she wasn't about to share them with anyone who was connected to another team.

Carolyn sighed. "Hopefully, he can find a way to contain his emotions. I mean, he looks pretty good now. But that's always the case at the beginning of the season. It doesn't take much for his emotions to get the better of him. He's very sensitive."

The conversation was making Nico feel uncomfortable. Something about it felt . . . strange.

There was a moment of silence as they gazed at the cars that passed before them.

"I know it can't be easy for you," Carolyn went on. "It's not easy for any woman in this F1 world, in any capacity. But then, I'm not telling you anything you don't already know. It will only get harder from here."

She paused.

"I'm not sure how well you know your teammate. Maybe I'll fill you in on some details one of these days."

After that, she smiled and left.

Well, that was sus.

Feeling restless, Nico decided to take a walk. She hadn't gone far before she ran into Ceci Rivers, technical director for Blue Jet Lightning.

Ceci had been one of the first people to call and congratulate Nico when word of her racing Formula 1 had gone public. She'd also slammed Rocco on social media for that coffee run tweet.

Ceci wasn't a close friend, but their paths had crossed here and there, and they'd done some events together promoting women in motorsports. Nico had always liked and admired the woman. If anyone knew what it was like to be a lone woman in a man's world, it was Ceci Rivers.

They chatted for a while until Ceci, looking at something over Nico's shoulder, let out a low whistle.

Nico turned around to see handsome Leo Clarke a few feet away and about to pass them.

"Well, well, well," Ceci murmured. "If it isn't Sir Clarke Kent—the *GQ* king."

He was still in his racing suit. Nico had watched him earlier flying around the track rapid fire and earning the fastest time yet today. You would never know it from looking at him. He looked Antarctica cool, not one bead of sweat on him.

Nico's brow wrinkled. "Did you say *sir*?"

"Rumor is, he's going to be knighted by the king."

"Really?"

Ceci ran her black nails through her mass of copper curls and called out in that throaty voice, "Good morrow, Sir Clarke! Looking for a lady who's pulling the princess vibe?"

Nico chuckled as Clarke stopped suddenly and gave them a blank stare. His cheeks crimsoned and his lips parted as though he might respond. But then he quickly shut them, turned his head, and walked off.

Nico shook her head, laughing.

Ceci grinned. "Hey, that man is so bougie. Someone needs to bring him down to earth."

■ ■ ■

Rocco crossed his arms, gazing out at the track.

I thought things would be different after that photoshoot.

He wasn't exactly sure how they'd be different, but something would be different. He thought at least there'd be less friction between them after he'd jumped up on that hood. He just wished he'd stopped there. He wished he hadn't done that thing with her hair.

He didn't want her thinking he was interested in her—like that.

I'm not.

I just wish I could stop having those dreams.

Now he was getting out of that chair and putting those nipples in his mouth. Running his finger along that collarbone while she looked at him with those dark eyes. And even worse . . . he was putting his hand between her thighs and . . .

Fuck, she was wet.

He shook his body like a dog shaking off water.

He knew coming here today, he just needed to keep things cool and professional. But he'd thought cool and professional could still look—what? Friendly? But no. From the moment he'd first seen her in the paddock, she'd had that frozen look like a deer gets when it's caught in a car's headlights. That look that said to him *Don't come anywhere near me and definitely don't even think about doing that again with my hair.* That told him everything he needed to know. Professional and cool meant more emphasis on the cool.

Just go about your business. Remember why you're here.

He felt a hand on his back. Casey and the crew were pleased with his performance. There were bro-hugs and high fives all around.

So far so good, thought Rocco. Of course, this was only preseason testing. Still, the signs were good. Next weekend would be the first round. With a car this fast, during qualifying next weekend, he expected to come in first or second. He'd actually held back a little today, guaranteeing he'd come in behind Clarke's time. There was already enough buzz about the rookie team's car. Better the buzz not be too good.

Barring some unforeseen disaster, next weekend he'd be starting in the first row, at worst, the second. And in that case, it was a virtual lock he'd be up on that podium.

"You looked good out there," Dario said, slapping him on the back. "Third fastest time. Clarke came in second."

"Who came in first?"

"That would be me." Rocco heard a voice behind him.

Up walked Ian Anker, his blonde hair gleaming and those hard, cobalt-blue eyes of his flashing.

"So, a rookie American team," he said. "Not to mention your teammate, who shall remain dick-less."

"Like you," Rocco said.

"Yeah, but unlike you," Dario added, "she has a set of balls."

Anker grinned, displaying his gleaming white teeth. Rocco could almost swear he saw fangs.

He placed his hand on Rocco's shoulder. "Whatever it takes to make you feel better, ladies."

Before Rocco could respond, Anker dropped his hand and walked away.

Dario shook his head. "That guy definitely looks to rattle drivers off the track."

"On it too," Rocco said.

Anker was notorious for not giving way and making dangerous moves to stop a driver from passing him. He intimidated drivers so that even if they had a path to pass him, they hesitated to do so.

Rocco had experienced this firsthand. While he'd never allowed Anker to intimidate him on the track, the outcome between their duels had never gone well for Rocco. At best, they'd kept him from winning or earning even second or third place on the podium. And at worst, they'd resulted in him crashing and unable to finish the race at all.

Dario stiffened looking at something over Rocco's shoulder. When Rocco turned around, he understood why.

Carolyn.

She smiled and placed a manicured hand lightly on his chest. "It's good to see you back in the saddle, Rocco."

He took a measured step back, which left her hand hanging until she dropped it to her side.

She glanced behind him. "Dario," she said in a tone that made it clear she wanted him to leave.

Dario didn't respond. He also didn't move until Rocco gave him a look, telling him it was okay.

"I met your teammate," Carolyn said after Dario had left. "This is new territory for you, having a woman as a teammate."

He shrugged, though his heartbeat quickened. "It's new territory for everyone. There hasn't been talk about the possibility of a woman racing F1 since Ceci." He shot Carolyn a pointed look. "And we both know what happened in that case."

What had happened was that Carolyn had made damn sure it didn't happen when Rocco had suggested it to Blue Jet's team principal.

Carolyn tossed her head. "Ceci seems perfectly happy where she is now."

Ceci was hired by the team a few years later and was now technical director. Rocco had always wondered why Carolyn hadn't put a stop to that too. Maybe she'd tried and failed. Or maybe it no longer mattered to Carolyn, given Rocco no longer drove for the team.

Even Carolyn had to admit it was a good move. Ceci Rivers had proven herself outside the car as well as in it.

It hit Rocco then.

I know what's bugging her.

It's the fact that Nico is a woman.

He narrowed his eyes, and his tone was icy cold. "Be careful, Carolyn. Green has never been a good look on you. We both know what happened with Ceci, and the two of us weren't even involved—in that way."

She blinked, and her eyes flashed. There was a sudden shift in both her body language and the look on her face.

Her tone changed.

"And you and Ms. Angelini are?"

He blinked. He hadn't meant to suggest that. He was about to say *no*, but Carolyn didn't give him the chance.

"Be careful, dear, a poor performance off the track can produce performance anxiety on it."

She turned and was gone.

Dario came up behind him. "You okay?"

He shrugged. "Yeah, sure."

He sounded doubtful because that's how he felt. But then he thought of the upcoming race next weekend.

I'm better than okay.

I'll be up on that podium. I might even come in first, beating Clarke and Anker.

He could. He knew he could.

He would.

Damn it.

CHAPTER TWELVE

NICO AND ROCCO

ROUND 1: RACE 1: LAS VEGAS, NEVADA

Nico's heart was racing. She'd started #16 on the grid out of twenty drivers after qualifying yesterday. She kept reminding herself it could be worse, she could be last.

She'd passed one driver to move up to #15.

She wasn't looking to finish in the top ten and earn any points. That was next to impossible at this point unless someone crashed. Besides, given this was her first race, no one expected her to—not even herself.

There were just two things she was praying for—not to lose her position, and not to be lapped.

Thank goodness she didn't have to worry about the annoying, arrogant, asshole, prick lapping her. Rocco had started from #13. He was just up ahead. Right now, there was only one car between them.

She wondered if he'd ever started a race that far back. In fairness to him, he'd been unlucky during qualifying when two drivers slammed into each other and went spinning off the track. He'd narrowly escaped major impact, but not without doing some damage to the car.

Race Engineer: Nico, just keep doing what you're doing. You picked up pace on this lap. Just be careful on the turn up ahead. Don't look to make any move. Shepperd is coming up behind and might try to pass. Hug the corner as tight as you can and force him to pass on the outside if he makes an attempt.

Nico: Copy.

The turn was just up ahead. She could feel Shepperd's car creeping up on the inside. There was no space for him. Did he think she wouldn't or couldn't hug the turn? Was he thinking she would give way and he would crowd her out? She'd move over and give him an engraved invitation?

Think again, she thought as she took the turn, hugging the inside.

Race Engineer: Good, Nico, good. Okay, you can push on the straight ahead. You've gained a second on the car up ahead. Let's look to pass him on the next lap. Push. Push. Push.
Nico: Copy.

Nico went all out. The car was just up ahead. She was gaining on him. If she could just pass him, that would put her at #14—right behind the annoying, arrogant, asshole, prick.

■ ■ ■

Rocco: Something's not right. It's not handling right.
Race Engineer: Okay, Rocco. We'll look into it after the race. Just hold steady; you're coming up to the last lap.
Rocco: Where are Clarke and Anker? They're not going to lap me, are they?
Radio silence.

Anker had started the race in pole position, first place; Clarke in second.

Rocco: Hey! Did you hear me?
Race Engineer: They're setting a blistering pace, but we don't think so, no. Not if you can just hold steady.

Hold steady at #13. Fucking #13! He'd never started this far back in the grid. At this point, the way the car was handling, he'd given up hope of making a move to pass anyone. The most he could hope for was that he'd hold position and finish the race without being lapped.

He'd never been lapped. Not once. Not even as a kid racing karts.

Never. Never. Never.

Never.

All he wanted now was for this race to be over. And for the engineers to fix whatever the hell was wrong with this car before the next race.

Race Engineer: You're doing brilliant, Rocco.
Rocco: Thirteenth is hardly brilliant.
Race Engineer: Given the bad luck during qualifying and the trouble with the car, a lesser driver would have—
Rocco: Yeah, yeah, yeah.

Maybe there was some significance to the fact he would finish at lucky number thirteen. Maybe this would be rock bottom. He certainly hoped so. It had to be. Things could only get better from here on out. How could they possibly get any worse?

■ ■ ■

She was gaining on him.

Race Engineer: Nico, back off some. Just hold position.
Nico: Why?

She could hear Casey yelling in the background.

Race Engineer: Just hold position. You gained two positions. Remember, it's your first F1 race.
Nico: But I can do it. There's room on the inside. I can see it.
Casey: Tell her to hold position!

Why? So, the annoying, arrogant, asshole, prick isn't beaten by a woman? Driving the same car he is?

I came here to race, and that's what I'm going to do.

She approached from the inside, but as she started to inch forward, he drifted over. *Fine,* she thought, slipping to the outside. She was so intent on passing him that at first she didn't see the car behind her pick up the pace and move to pass. When she did, she jerked left to avoid a collision, and the car went speeding past, which would have been fine if Rocco hadn't moved right, trying to muscle her to the outside.

Nico caught a flash of metal in her peripheral vision just before they crashed and went spinning off the track.

Anker zipped by them, lapping them both, followed closely by Clarke doing the same.

The damage was extensive enough that those two cars weren't the only ones to pass them.

The one good thing the team had to say to them when they entered the paddock after limping across the finish line was that it was impressive that they'd finished the race at all.

At least I didn't come in last, thought Nico.

That honor was reserved for one annoying, arrogant, asshole, prick.

CHAPTER THIRTEEN

NICO AND ROCCO

Nico stood in the paddock of the Barcelona racetrack, waiting for Casey and feeling sick to her stomach. She'd kept telling herself things would get better after Vegas. Let that first race be the first, last, and only disaster. But that hadn't happened. They'd kept up their losing streak putting in terrible results race after race, including this last one in Barcelona. They hadn't had one good race—not even a decent one.

This is it. They're going to let me go. I'm out.

Casey had told her he needed to speak to her *right now*. But there he stood, talking with a couple engineers while she waited. She was too far away to hear what they were saying. But she could tell it was bad. None of them looked happy. Hardly surprising, given they'd put in another lousy performance here in Barcelona.

How much longer could she expect the owner to wait for her and the annoying, arrogant, asshole, prick to get their acts together? Rocco hadn't made it to the podium once. He hadn't finished any race in the top seven, and she'd failed to earn the team any points at all. It was a disaster.

Nico looked around. Rocco was nowhere in sight.

That prick is just as responsible as I am.

She was sweating bullets and wanted out of this racing suit. She wished she could go to her locker on the second floor and get a change of clothes. But Casey had told her to wait *here*, where she was standing right now. He wasn't more than ten feet away, and she didn't want to take the chance that he might turn around and find her gone. She couldn't risk making him any angrier than he already was.

Her cell phone was in that locker too. But she dreaded seeing the missed calls.

Shortly after that first race in Vegas, she'd begun getting random calls. They were from different phone numbers, and whoever was calling never left a voicemail. Charles had tried to convince her they were just spam calls until she told him they were all from Italy.

They had to be from Mickey. But how had he gotten her number?

She kept telling herself to answer when her phone rang. Just get it over with already. But she always copped out.

She glanced over at Casey. If only she could unzip the top part of the racing suit and let it hang from her hips. But the sweat stains on the long-sleeved flame-retardant shirt underneath kept her from doing so.

Yes, they were that bad.

Maybe if I take off the shirt, that'll cool me off some.

There was a restroom only a couple feet behind her.

She watched as Casey moved farther away to look at something on one of the computers. This was her chance. She quickly slipped into the restroom, removed the flame-retardant shirt, and zipped the suit back up. She hid the shirt behind the wastebasket. She'd come back for it later. She dashed back out and breathed a sigh of relief when she saw Casey still at that computer.

She glanced at her watch. She was supposed to meet Charles and Mateo, a guy he'd met here in Barcelona, at a bar in about an hour. Nico suspected that by the end of the evening, Mateo might qualify as Charles's newest boyfriend.

Charles had already begun what could qualify as a soft launch of such a relationship by posting photos of the man's forearms, biceps, sculpted back, and thighs on social media. All body parts placed strategically near enough to Charles's own to draw the inevitable conclusion.

Barcelona was the only race Charles had attended since that first one in Vegas. She'd been hoping they might do better. He planned to go to the race in Monaco, but now she was worried there might not be a race in Monaco—not for her.

Casey turned around and waved for Nico to follow him. They climbed the stairs to the third floor. Was there no chance of a reprieve? Some clemency? It felt as if she were walking the steps to the gallows.

The third floor was where the hospitality suites were located. During the race, they were frequented by sponsors and wealthy fans who could afford paddock passes. But now all those sponsors and fans had gone, leaving the third floor deserted.

Everyone's focus was on the next race.

Nico followed Casey into a room and was about to shut the door behind her.

"Don't bother," he said, his voice firm.

He was right, of course. There was no one around to hear him when he lowered the boom.

She turned around, and that's when she saw him sitting in a chair.

The annoying, arrogant, asshole, prick. He didn't bother to look up.

Casey surveyed them both. "I don't know what's going on between you two, but whatever it is, it's gotta stop. A few more races like we've had so far, and we can kiss this season goodbye. It's one thing to have mechanical problems or bad luck because of some shit move another driver makes. But this! Undermining each other the way you are! It's as though you're more intent on beating each other than winning! And you're making dumb-ass moves to do it! I've got news for you, you're not the only two drivers on the track. And I don't need to tell either of you what we've got to show for your performances thus far—shit! And with that car—a car that can win! Whatever it is that's the problem between the two of you, you need to fix it. And fix it now!"

Glaring at them both, he drew a deep breath.

"I honestly don't know how much longer the owner's going to put up with this. So, I suggest you work your shit out before the next race and put in a decent showing."

He stormed out and slammed the door behind him with so much force Nico felt the room vibrate like it would during an earthquake.

There was an uncomfortable silence.

She glanced over at Rocco. He had his head down and his arms folded.

She was trying to think what to say when he stood up and stomped to the door.

But when he pulled on it, it didn't open.

He tried again.

"What the—" he yelled, looking down at the doorknob and pulling harder.

"What are you doing?" Nico demanded as she stormed over. "Step aside," she said once she was beside him.

He didn't budge, and he didn't take his hand off the doorknob.

"That's rich," he said, glaring at her, "you telling me to step aside. When have you ever stepped aside?"

"I could ask the same of you," she spat. "Now take your hands off and let me try!"

He didn't remove his hands.

"Fine!" she hissed. She placed her hands over his, but a sudden spark shocked her and she quickly let go. He must have felt it too, given he released his grip at the same time.

They stood a moment, staring at each other.

I'll do it.

Grabbing the doorknob, she pulled. And pulled. And pulled.

He stood, arms crossed, wearing not only his racing suit but a smug expression. "Do you really think you can open it if I can't?"

She scowled and placed both hands on the doorknob, putting all her weight into it.

Hearing him chuckle, she let out an exasperated breath. "What is so damn funny?"

"You," he said. "Forget it. The door's jammed. I don't suppose you have your cell phone on you?"

She shook her head. "You?"

He picked up his water bottle, which he had left on the table, and lifted his arms as if to indicate the answer was *no.*

Nico started pounding on the door. "Help! Somebody! Help!"

Rocco went over to a corner and sat down on the floor, leaning his back up against the wall. "No one will hear you. Everyone's gone. The few people who are still on the first floor won't be coming up here."

"Well, how will anyone find us? I mean, if no one's around . . ."

"Someone will notice we're missing . . . eventually."

"What does *eventually* mean?"

"A week or so."

"What?!"

He laughed. "Are you always so gullible? The maintenance crew will be here in a couple of hours."

"How do you know?"

"Because I know some of them. Sometimes I come up to the third floor after the race to think while the crew is still packing up down below. It's quiet. No one's up here."

"Oh," Nico sighed. "Okay, I can do a couple of hours."

Rocco scoffed. "I can do more than a couple of hours."

She glared at him. "Is everything a competition with you?"

"Isn't it with you? How are you any different?"

Nico turned her back to him and began to pace.

"I thought things were going to be different after . . ." he muttered.

She swung around. "What's that?"

"Nothing," he grumbled.

The words came out from behind his gritted teeth with such force, Nico could almost swear they'd achieved solidity and were sitting there on the carpet.

"I heard you," she said. "You said you thought things were going to be different."

"Well, if you heard me, then why did you ask?"

"You said different *after*. After what?"

He didn't respond.

She placed her hands on her hips. "Oh, I know."

"Oh, you do, do you?"

"I do. You thought because you did one nice thing for me by jumping up on the hood of that car, I should be grateful." Nico clasped her hands and held them against her chest. "My hero! Is that it? And then, what? I'm just supposed to make way for you out on the racetrack, is that it?"

He glared at her, shaking his head. "No, that's not it. I didn't do it to be nice. I did it because it was the right thing to do. I would have done the same for any woman. Don't go thinking you're so special."

"I don't think I'm so special."

"'You are so full of shit, if you ever had an enema you'd evaporate into thin air.'"

Nico sputtered and then laughed. She stopped when she saw he wasn't laughing. He didn't even crack a smile. Not even a hint of a grin.

He sighed, lowering his head as though he were speaking to the carpet. "I did it because of what you said."

"What did I say?" she asked.

He looked up, clearly surprised.

She remembered. But she wanted to hear him say it.

He dropped his chin to his chest and stared at the carpet again.

"You said that I was saying you weren't a serious driver with that stupid tweet. And that you had just as much hope and dreams and drive as I do and that you've worked really hard to get here." He paused and drew a deep breath. "And I realized then what an asshole I'd been, and I felt like shit about it." He looked up with a clenched jaw. "Okay?"

She swallowed. "Okay," she said in a softer voice. "But I think my exact words were that I worked my ass off to get here."

His eyes narrowed. "If you remembered what you said, why did you ask me?"

"Because I wanted to hear you say it," she said, trying hard not to smile.

He stared at her a moment. Now not only was his jaw clenched, he'd fisted his hands, and she saw his chest rise and fall as though his breathing were picking up momentum. Looking at him made her wonder what the next words out of his mouth would be.

Suddenly he stood up, unzipped his suit, and slipped his arms out so that the upper part of the suit was left hanging off his hips.

"It's fucking hot in here," he grumbled.

Nico stared.

That undergarment shirt hugged him.

It hugged his chest. It hugged his torso. It hugged his arms.

It was like milk dripping over every ripple, every muscle, every everything.

It is hot, she thought, wiping beads of sweat from above her lip.

She knew the undergarment pants were made of the same material as the shirt.

She noticed how fragile his hips' hold on that suit was.

It could slide down.

It might slide down.

Was it going to slide down?

If he kept walking back and forth like that, it was bound to.

Slide.

Down.

And if it did.

Got milk?

Yes, please.

Sliding down his legs. Sliding over his ass. Maybe even pooling in those dimples above his ass, if he had them. She wondered if he had them. *He must have them*, she thought, looking at his torso. There was probably some direct connection between a torso like that and above-ass dimples.

Thinking of his backside made her suddenly wonder about the frontside.

The milk would be all over *that* too.

The milk would be gripping *that.*

Dripping over *that.*

Gripping and dripping. Gripping and dripping. Gripping and dripping.

She blinked. He was staring back at her, and she'd been looking at just the place where the gripping and dripping would—

Did he see where I was looking?

She turned away, wiping the back of her neck. It was hot in here. Too hot.

When she turned back around, he had his arms over his head.

He was stretching.

Stretching.

Stretch—ing.

That suit, which was dangling off his hips, was perilously close to slipping, even an inch, and she'd see— *Eyes north*, she told herself, wiping her forehead.

But when she lifted her gaze, all she could do was stare at the shirt and wonder why he didn't take it off.

It was hot.

Hot. Hot. Hot.

Why didn't he take that shirt off?

Take it off.

No. Stop thinking that.

And yet she couldn't seem to stop herself from thinking that.

Take. It. Off.

If she told her brain to stop thinking something, it should stop.

But her brain couldn't stop. Wouldn't stop. Didn't want to stop.

Maybe her brain really was floating in a vat, and Dr. Wily was poking and prodding it, producing her lecherous thoughts.

Poke.

Take.

Prod.

It.

Nudge.

Off.

Take.

It.

Off.

"Hey!"

Nico blinked. "What?!" she shouted.

He frowned.

Had she just shouted? She'd just shouted. Why had she just shouted?

"Are you okay?" he asked.

"Of course I'm okay. Why wouldn't I be?"

"It looked like you might faint."

Her heart started pounding. There it is. Return of the annoying, arrogant, asshole, prick.

"Why would you even— Oh, of course, I'm a woman, and that makes me weak."

"I didn't say it because you're a woman and I think you're weak. I said it because you looked unsteady. Your pupils looked as though they might be dilated."

"I've never fainted in my life!"

"Good for you."

"What makes you such an expert?"

"I never claimed to be an expert."

"Well, how do you know what to look for?"

"Because I've fainted."

"Oh."

"There you go. You have me beat. You've never fainted, and I have."

"Don't be ridiculous."

There was a moment of silence.

He grinned. "You want to know how it happened, don't you?"

She shook her head. "No. Uh-uh. I don't. I have absolutely no interest. Zero. Interest."

He chuckled. "Yes, you do. The question is practically tattooed across your forehead."

Another moment of silence.

He sighed. "Let's see. Well, my family was vacationing in the South of France. My sister and I were left to play while my parents had lunch in the hotel restaurant with some friends. I was six years old, and my sister was twelve. They had saunas in the hotel—one for men and one for women. And of course, some people would sit in the sauna naked. My sister dared me to go into the women's sauna and said I was chicken because I didn't want to. She shoved me in and held the door closed. I was relieved no one was in there, but I wanted out. I was about to bang on the door when I heard a woman telling my sister to stop playing around. The door began to open, and I hid under one of the benches. The woman entered, and I quickly turned around so I was staring at the wall. I was too afraid to say anything. I kept waiting for a moment when I could escape, but women kept coming in."

Nico laughed.

He grinned. "That's funny, is it?"

She shook her head and swallowed her laughter. "Sorry. How long were you in there?"

"I don't remember. By the time they found me, I'd fainted."

"Oh."

"Stop looking at me like I'm a starving puppy."

"I'm not looking at you like that."

He chuckled. "You are. Anyway, I got my revenge. My parents were furious. So, of course my sister was punished."

"How?"

"For the remainder of the trip, I got to decide what we would eat for dinner, what dessert would be, and what we would do each and every day."

Nico smiled. "And I'm guessing you made certain to choose things she hated."

He nodded. "I did."

She laughed and then grew silent, staring at him.

I bet they were furious. Especially your mother. I bet you were a beautiful boy. Your mother must love you something awful. How could she not?

She blinked, suddenly realizing she was staring. He was too. He seemed to become aware of it at the same moment she did. They both turned in unison and began pacing in opposite directions.

■ ■ ■

Rocco mopped the sweat on the back of his neck. When he reached one end of the room and turned around, he stared at her, standing in the corner.

"Aren't you hot in that thing?"

"I'm o-kay."

"You know, that's probably why you looked like you were going to faint. You must be sweating gallons. Why don't you take it off? Or at least do what I did and unzip the top part."

"I can't."

"Why not?"

She looked down. He waited.

"Because," she muttered, "I don't have anything on underneath."

His heart began to pump faster, and it had already been pumping plenty fast.

"What do you mean? You took the undershirt off? This?" He indicated, pulling on his shirt.

"Yes."

"Why?"

"I was sweating like crazy. There were huge sweat stains on it. And Casey said I didn't have time to go change. So, I slipped into the first-floor restroom and took it off. I left it there."

"Oh."

He looked at her zipper and swallowed.

"Do you have a—a bra on?"

"Of course I have a bra on."

Now he was trying to imagine it. Was it black? White? Red? Pink? Maybe something entirely different like lilac. Was it lacy? See-through?

He blinked, suddenly realizing he was staring at her chest. He lowered his eyes.

"Oh, well," he said as though speaking to the carpet, "a bra is just like a bikini top. I mean, they cover up the same amount of skin. It's just this idea that one is a bra and the other's a bikini. There's really no difference. Not really." He ventured a glance and met her eyes. "Unless, I mean, I guess sometimes, bras can be, um, lacy." He paused and then added hastily, "I mean, if you're into that sort of thing."

The shirt and pants he wore under the racing suit were supposed to be flame-retardant, but now he felt as though he'd traveled to a world that was the polar opposite of this one—the south pole was pointing north, and anything flame-retardant was now flammable—highly flammable.

Hastily, he removed his shirt and tossed it to her. "Here," he said, "you can wear this. It probably doesn't smell very good."

Shit! Is she going to faint? She had that same look. It really looked as though her pupils were dilated. But then her eyes were so dark.

He took a couple of steps toward her.

"Are you okay?"

"I'm, I'm okay."

He nodded.

She was looking at the shirt in her hands. He was looking at the shirt in her hands. And then it dawned on him. "Oh, right. I'll turn my back."

He did. He was glad to have the racing suit on down below. That crankshaft was really squirrelly now. It wasn't looking just to point north but east, west, and all points in between.

Finally, she said, "You can turn around."

When he did, he blinked.

She'd taken off the racing suit.

The. Entire. Racing suit.

Not just the top part but the bottom as well. It lay in a heap next to her. And not only that. She'd taken off the flame-retardant pants too.

All she was wearing was that shirt. It covered her thighs, but only a portion of them.

She sighed. "Thank you. That feels a lot better. Your shirt's big enough, it's like a dress."

"Yeah," he muttered, staring at her bare legs.

A short dress.

She sighed. "Much better."

He bit his lip. "Yeah. Better."

He sat down on the ground, picked up his bottle, and brought the straw to his lips just to give him something to do—to distract him from those thighs. And then he pulled it away. "Oh, I'm sorry. Are you thirsty? It's not water."

She was standing on the other side of the room. He made a move to get up, but she had already walked over to him.

"What is it, an energy drink?"

"Not exactly. You might not like it. It's kind of sweet."

He handed it to her.

She took a sip. "Mmmmmm." Her eyes ballooned. "Is this a GoGo squeeZ?"

"Uh, yeah."

She sat down beside him and took another sip. "I love GoGo squeeZ."

As she sat down, that shirt hiked up a bit.

Is she wearing underwear?

Stupid question. Of course she's wearing underwear.

Then again, she did have those flame-retardant pants on, and those are kind of like underwear so maybe—no, she wouldn't take them off if she wasn't wearing underwear.

He stared at the hem of that shirt.

She wouldn't leave herself exposed like that.

He tried to calculate how many inches it was from that hem before he would reach her—

He rocked back and forth and suddenly realized she'd jostled his shoulder. He looked over.

"Didn't you hear me? I asked you what flavor this is?"

"Um, I'm not sure."

She gave him the bottle and he tilted his head down so she wouldn't see him staring at her lips

They were on this straw. That I'm sucking now.

"So?" she asked.

He lifted his head. "Huh?"

"What flavor is it?"

"Oh. Um. Zippin' Zingin' Pear."

He handed it back to her, watching her lips suck on that straw. He quickly slung the sleeves of his racing suit over his lap and placed his hands there.

"I've never had it before," she said. "It's good. My favorite is Max Mango."

"Yeah, Max Mango's good. My favorite is Apple Strawberry Rhubarb."

She frowned. "Rhubarb?"

"What's wrong with rhubarb?"

"Nothing, I suppose. But there's no way it can be better than Max Mango."

"Well, it is. Max Mango is good, but Apple Strawberry Rhubarb is better."

She shook her head. "It can't be."

"Yes, it can."

"Uh-uh."

"Was it written somewhere in your contract that you have to disagree with me on everything?"

She laughed. "No. It's just rhubarb doesn't sound like it would taste good."

"So, you've never actually tasted it."

"No."

"Well, then how do you know?"

"I suppose that's true."

"Next race, I'll bring you one, and you can see for yourself."

She smiled. "Okay."

There was a moment of silence.

He turned to her as she turned to him.

"I—" he started to say.

"I—" she said at the same time.

There was another silent pause.

Rocco needed to say what he was going to say. And he needed to say it before she said anything.

"I never objected to a woman driving Formula 1," he said before glancing over at her. "I know I made it sound like I did. I didn't even really object to you driving Formula 1."

She made a face.

He chuckled. "Okay, well, maybe I did. But that was only because of our spat on social media." He swallowed. "You hit a nerve when you talked about men moving up from F3 to F1 while women were being overlooked. You were right, of course. But I took it as an attack against me."

Her brow wrinkled. "Why? I wasn't even thinking of you when I tweeted that."

That's exactly what Dario kept telling me.

He sighed. "I guess I'm overly sensitive because of the way I made it to F1. I had an advantage over other drivers. There were good F2 drivers—every bit as good as me. So, sometimes it feels like what got me to F1 wasn't solely based on merit—as a driver, I mean."

She frowned. "But you've won three world championships."

"It still bothers me, and when you posted that tweet, I took it as an attack, and so I attacked back."

"Were you always following my tweets?"

"No. Someone else brought it to my attention."

Carolyn Wickham. But he wasn't about to tell her that.

"I never would have said the things I did, Nico, otherwise. Not that I'm making excuses, I'm not. But . . . I'm sorry."

He heard her sigh.

"I'm just as much to blame as you are," she said. "I felt like I was being attacked too. So, like you, I attacked back. I'm sorry too. Some of the things I said . . . even Charles, who's always been my biggest cheerleader, has scolded me for some of the things I tweeted."

"Charles, he's your friend who came to the first race in Vegas and this one in Barcelona?"

Nico nodded.

Rocco grinned. "He told me I should tell Casey to consider changing the color of our car and racing suits. Let's see, uh, he suggested yellow, orange, pink, peach, and lilac. He said those are positive colors, which are bound to yield positive results. He said he'd read it somewhere but couldn't remember where."

Nico laughed. "That sounds like Charles."

"Seems like a good friend."

"He is. Like Dario."

"He mentioned someone else—Templeton? He said you wished he could have come too."

He watched a warm smile like a match light up her face, her cheeks bathed in a warm glow.

She loves him.

Rocco cleared his throat. "Is that your—boyfriend?"

She burst out laughing. It took her nearly a minute to stop.

She grinned. "Templeton's a rat."

He blinked. "A rat?"

She nodded. "He's my pet."

He wrinkled his brow. "You have a pet rat?"

"I do."

"I never knew anyone who had a pet rat."

"Well, now you do."

He nodded. "Now I do."

Rocco peered at her. *What kind of girl has a rat for a pet? An interesting one, that's for sure.*

"Did you grow up in Vegas?" he asked. "Is that where your family's from?"

She stiffened, and he could kick himself for having asked.

I guess family is a sore subject with her.

She was quiet. He had only her profile to look at because she wouldn't look at him. Staring at her throat, he could see her swallow before she spoke.

"Um, yeah, some of them." She handed his bottle back to him. "There's not much left. Sorry."

"That's okay."

She sighed, leaning her head against the wall, shutting her eyes. "I'm tired."

He did likewise. "Me too."

Rocco woke with a start. He blinked, wondering where he was. And then he remembered. It was chilly. He stood up and slipped his arms back in his racing suit, zipping it up. He looked over at Nico. Her head was leaning against the wall. Her eyes were shut.

"Nico," he whispered.

Nothing.

She must be cold, he thought, looking at her bare legs. He crossed the room and picked up her racing suit. As he did, something fell out.

Two things, he realized as he bent down to pick them up.

One was a photo of a woman. She could be Nico's mother. The same dark eyes and hair. The same bold bone structure. The other was a piece of paper—on it, a pencil drawing of what looked like an older man.

Rocco searched and found an inner pocket that had been stitched on the inside of her suit.

She must have sewn this in.

He folded the paper and tucked it along with the photo inside the pocket. Then he placed the suit over her legs, doing his best to tuck it around her without waking her. After that, he sat down beside her and shut his eyes.

The next thing Rocco knew, someone was shaking his shoulder. He blinked. It took a minute for his eyes to adjust and for him to realize where he was. He looked up. It was Frank from maintenance.

"You guys get locked in here?" he asked.

Nodding, Rocco held his finger to his lips.

"I'll leave the door ajar," Frank whispered.

Thanks, Rocco mouthed.

He looked down at Nico. He had his arm draped around her, and she was curled up into the crook of his arm, breathing softly with her head pressed against his chest.

When had this happened? How had it happened? She wasn't in his arms when he drifted off. She wasn't even leaning into him.

He almost tucked the hair that had fallen in front of her face behind her ear, but then thought, *Better not; that might wake her.*

Of course, he'd have to wake her . . . eventually.

He knew that. And he would.

He would wake her.

But.

In a minute.

Just a minute more.

CHAPTER FOURTEEN

NICO AND ROCCO

His fingers brushed against her cheek as he took a strand of her hair and gently tucked it behind her ear.

It was tender and sweet.

But he wasn't those things. Was he?

He leaned in, and his words fluttered over her flesh like winged birds.

"I can be tender. I can be sweet." He placed his hand on her cheek, grazing her cheekbone with his thumb as he gazed into her eyes. And then his eyes flashed as he grabbed a fistful of her hair. "And I can be not tender. And not sweet." He pulled her head back, exposing her throat.

Her breath grew unsteady as though she were choking on it.

He grazed her nipples with his thumb.

She shut her eyes.

He pinched—hard—and thrust his groin into her, releasing a sudden flood of hot liquid that threatened to drown her.

He let go of her hair, and she looked up at him. She suddenly realized he had her up against a car.

"Get up on that hood."

The sound of his voice shook her like the throttle of an engine. She hadn't wanted to before, but now she thrilled at the idea, feeling a humming between her legs as though she had a Ducati between them.

As she hoisted herself up onto the hood, she felt the length of his body rub against her own and began to shake so violently, she thought she might fall. But he gripped her hips to steady her. Once she was sitting on the hood, he glanced down at her thighs. He placed a hand gently on each knee. He didn't need to push. She opened them for him.

As she did, she realized she was wearing his shirt.

"It looks nice on you," he said. " Like a dress."

His hands slid up her thighs.

"Gentlemen, start your engines."

Her heart jumped. Was she wearing underwear?

He grinned.

I'll know. Soon enough.

His hands inched up. And with each inch, the heavy throbbing between her thighs extinguished one of those red lights that signaled the start of the race once they were all out: five—four—three—two . . .

He stopped, his thumb brushing back and forth along the edge of the shirt's hem. Not three inches away from . . .

His hands slid under and . . .

All. The. Way.

Up.

And.

In.

She gasped.

"You've been waiting for me."

There was only a brief flicker in his eyes before they disappeared and she felt his hot breath between her thighs followed by his wet tongue, gliding along the lips of her vagina.

The blood in her veins bubbled, and she began to feel as though every bone in her body had dissolved into some sort of languid liquid.

Soon, I'll be a puddle at his feet.

A sudden jolt shot through her as his wet tongue slipped inside and sparks of electricity flickered through her veins, making her entire body quake.

He took her throat in his hands and pushed her back until she was lying on top of the hood.

He loomed over her and thrust himself so deep inside her, she felt as though he'd stolen her breath.

She clutched his shoulders, needing something to hold on to because every quiver, tremble, and quake cut through what was left of her.

Nico jolted upright.

Damn.

She flung the covers aside, half expecting she might see him there. Once her breathing returned to normal, she went into the bathroom and took a quick shower. Afterward, she walked down the hallway of the Barcelona Airbnb she and Charles were staying in and entered the kitchen.

Her heart leapt in anticipation when she saw the French press sitting on the counter.

She picked it up. There was coffee in it, and it was still hot. She poured herself a cup.

"Good morning."

She swung around at the sound of Charles's voice.

His eyes narrowed as he tilted his head. "If I didn't know better, I'd say there was a man in your bedroom."

"Don't be absurd! There's no man in my bedroom!"

"There's no need to shout about it."

Had she been shouting?

Charles peered intently at her.

"Why are you looking at me like that?"

"Because from the look on your face, there's either a man in your room or you had a very delicious dream and took matters into your own hand."

"I already told you there is no man in my room."

What's more, I didn't need my own hand.

"So, by process of elimination . . ."

Nico sighed. Charles wouldn't let up until she told him. She didn't have to give him details—just enough to shut him up.

"Yes and no."

"What do you mean, *yes and no*? It can't be both." Charles paused. "Unless . . . you didn't need to take matters into your own hands. The dream was that good? Lucky girl. Details, please."

"No, I don't feel like it."

"What's the deal? We've always talked about our sexy dreams before." Suddenly Charles's eyes widened and he slapped both cheeks with his palms. "Oh!"

"*Oh* what?"

Nico took a sip of coffee. It gave her an excuse to lower her head so she wouldn't have to meet Charles's scrutinizing gaze.

"Just tell me this," Charles said. "Is this a fictional man or a man we both know and love?"

"Neither."

"Aha! Is he, by chance, a prick?"

Nico could feel her cheeks burning. "Just stop already!"

"Oh my." He clapped his hands, a giddy smile on his face. "So, the prick makes house calls. If he's that good in the dreaming world, makes you wonder what he's like in the waking one when he's made of all that sumptuous flesh and not just the pixie dust of dreams. It might almost be too good. If there is such a thing."

"Stop already, I don't want to talk about him." Nico pushed past Charles and flopped onto the living room sofa. "When's your flight? Is Mateo still driving you?"

"Yes," Charles sighed. "I plan on enacting a romantic airport scene from a film."

Nico grinned. "Which one?"

"*The Mexican.* Once we hear those ominous words, *Boarding flight 101 at gate 101 in terminal 101*"—Charles struck a dramatic pose—"I will turn to him and say, *If two people love each other, but they can't seem to get it together, when do you get to that point that enough is enough?*"

Nico struck a theatrical pose of her own. "And he'll respond, *Never.*"

"He better," Charles said, collapsing on the sofa beside her. "I'm going to take it as a sign. If he says the right thing, then I know it's meant to be."

"And if he doesn't?"

"Then I'll turn on my heels, fart, and walk away so quickly everyone will think it was him."

They both doubled over with laughter.

"Wait a minute," Nico said once the laughter subsided, "I think there are some potential flaws in your plan. Can you fart on command?"

"I'm getting a smoothie on the way to the airport. It will be comprised of whole wheat, bran, prunes, peaches, apples, pears, asparagus, artichokes, cauliflower, cabbage, Brussels sprouts, and broccoli. Not to mention I'm also going to have a latte and ask for regular milk rather than almond, and you know I'm lactose intolerant."

Nico felt sorry for all the poor souls who would be trapped on that airplane with Charles.

"Well," she said, "that should do it, but what if he says the right thing and his last memory of you is one fabulous, formidable, far-reaching, far-flung, farfegnugen fart?"

"If he says the right thing, that means he's in love. And as everyone knows, love not only leaves you deaf, dumb, and blind but olfactorily challenged. I read that somewhere. Can't remember where. He'll be so flooded with oxytocin, he'll think they should bottle and sell my farts."

Nico's brow wrinkled. "You sure about that?"

"I once had a lover who said my farts smelled like hot cocoa with—get this—marshmallows."

Nico laughed as she went into the kitchen and poured herself a second cup.

Charles followed and poured himself another cup as well. "I just realized something. That quote from *The Mexican* is really more fitting for you than me. I wonder if that's why my brain came up with it. Maybe it was actually thinking of you and Rocco."

Nico's mouth dropped. "There is no me and Rocco!"

Charles's lip curled while one eyebrow made a quick jolt up and down like an ascending elevator that had suddenly been forced to stop as a result of someone pushing the red alarm button.

Nico suddenly felt uncomfortably warm.

"What's going on with you?" Charles asked, looking at her as though her head had suddenly begun spinning around atop her neck. "Why are you acting so strange?"

"Me? You're the one who's acting strange!"

Charles wagged his finger. "Something's different. Something has definitely changed. When I asked about your dream, which featured one Rocco Vittori, you said you didn't want to talk about him."

"So? I don't."

"You don't see it."

"See what?"

"You didn't say *annoying, arrogant, asshole, prick*—you said *him*. What happened when the two of you were locked in that room?"

"I already told you. We came to an understanding and agreed to work as a team. That's it."

Charles gazed at the wall in front of him. Nico felt her cheeks sizzle. She felt as though he could literally see the writing on the wall put there by the fairy dust of her dream.

Here lies Nico's salacious thoughts about the sublime shoulders, agile arms, luscious loins, transcendent torso, awe-inspiring ass, and delicious dimples above said ass of one Rocco Vittori and all her vivid imaginings of his dreamy eyes, the cool bristle of his shadowy cheek, and that voice that hits her right between the thighs, making her swoon.

Swoon?

She hadn't swooned. Never had. Never would.

No swoon.

"How exactly did that understanding come about?" Charles asked. "You never said."

Nico threw up her hands in exasperation and almost spilled some coffee as a result. "We hardly had a choice. I told you what Casey said."

Charles threw her a sidelong glance. "Something happened. I can tell. Your dream has betrayed you, Nico Angelini."

She sighed. "We both apologized for the things we said over social media, and we agreed to work together. Shit, we have to. I know I have to or I'll be out."

"Which one of you apologized first?"

"He did. Now, you have to get ready, or you won't have enough time for the methane smoothie before your flight."

■ ■ ■

Celeste sat on the sofa, sipping her glass of red wine as Rocco collapsed into an overstuffed armchair with a GoGo squeeZ.

She shook her head as he twisted the cap that looked like a helicopter rotor.

"How can you drink that stuff?" she asked as she sipped her Brunello.

Rocco threw his head back and squeezed the pouch, taking a big gulp.

"I like it. This one is Apple Pineapple Passion Fruit. How can you go wrong with that?"

"I'm too thirsty for red wine," came Dario's voice from the kitchen. "Do you mind if I have a GoGo squeeZ?"

"Go ahead."

When Dario came out, Rocco nearly leapt out of his chair. "Wait a minute. What flavor is that?"

"Apple Strawberry Rhubarb," Dario said, holding it up and about to twist off the cap.

"No!" Rocco shouted so loudly, Celeste spilled wine on her blouse.

"Damn it," she huffed, going into the kitchen to rinse the stain.

Dario looked stunned. "What's wrong with my having this one?"

"You can't. I only have two left."

"Okay, Dario," Celeste shouted from the kitchen. "You have a choice between Pedal Peach, Boatin' Banana, Happy TummieZ . . . How many of these do you have? . . . Oh, wait a minute, which of these can he have, Rocco?"

"I don't care," Rocco said, waving his arm. "He can have any of them. Just not Apple Strawberry Rhubarb."

Celeste marched up to Dario, grabbed the pouch from him, and shoved another in his hand. "Here, have some Grippin' Grape."

She returned the Apple Strawberry Rhubarb to the refrigerator and then joined Dario on the sofa, picking up a magazine from the coffee table.

"What's that?" Rocco asked.

Celeste flipped through the pages. "It's the current issue with the photospread of you and Nico. They're publishing a digital copy too, but I wanted to be sure Nico got one of these."

"What about me?" Rocco asked. "Don't I get one?"

"Can I have an Apple Strawberry Rhubarb GoGo squeeZ?"

"No."

"Then no," Celeste said as she flipped briskly through the pages. "And don't pout."

"I'm not pouting," Rocco insisted.

"Yes, you are."

"You're not even looking at me."

Celeste sighed as she turned another page. "I was only kidding. I'll get you one. Here it is," she said, swiftly stopping and slamming her hand on the page, a huge smile spreading her cheeks wide.

"Hmm," Dario said, looking over her shoulder.

Rocco frowned. "What?"

Dario lifted his eyes but not his head. "Just hmm," he said, his eyes darting back to the magazine.

"No, Dar, not hmm," Celeste said, "more like mm-hmm."

"What mm-hmm?" Rocco demanded.

Celeste grinned. "You know, mm-hmm, as in yummy. As in, hot!"

Rocco held out his hand. "Give it to me."

"No," Celeste said, holding the magazine to her chest. "It's my magazine, and I'm not finished with it yet."

Gritting his teeth, Rocco moved to the sofa, plunking himself down on the other side of her.

There was an uncomfortable silence while Rocco stared at the photo.

Had he been looking at Nico that way through the entire photoshoot? He knew what he was thinking when he looked at a woman in that way. Would anyone else looking at the photo know? Would she know?

"I didn't think . . ." Dario ventured.

"What?" Rocco asked, looking over at him.

"I guess I didn't think— I just wouldn't have thought one like this . . ."

Celeste rolled her eyes. "What he means is, he didn't think any of the photos would be any good because it looked as though— "

"As though what?" Rocco demanded. "Can't one of you complete a sentence?"

He looked from Celeste to Dario. He couldn't decide whose expression was more annoying—Celeste's or Dario's. She looked like a sly feline while his cousin looked like a laughing hyena.

"As though the two of you didn't enjoy being photographed together," Dario said diplomatically.

Celeste made a face. "'Didn't enjoy being photographed together'? It looked as though the two of them were having side-by-side colonoscopies."

Rocco opened his mouth.

"Without any anesthetic," Celeste added. "At least, when you two knew you were being photographed."

"What about when I got up on the hood of that car?" Rocco demanded.

Celeste shrugged. "The mood between the two of you did improve after that. Look at that one, Dario, with him up on the hood."

Dario pointed at another photo. "Yeah, but this one was taken before he did that."

"You're right. It was. But like I said, they didn't know they were being photographed when that one was taken. It's like the photo on social media."

Dario lifted his gaze. Rocco knew his cousin well enough to know that look he was giving him now was a look of concern.

Celeste sighed. "Just goes to show you."

Rocco frowned. "Show you what?"

"The camera catches what the eye can't see," she said. "Professional photographers will tell you it happens with their best work—revealing the truth people try so hard to hide. Guess people can succeed at hiding it from themselves and other people. But not the camera."

Rocco's shoulders twitched. There it was, that itchy feeling beneath his skin.

There must be too much sugar in this GoGo squeeZ.

CHAPTER FIFTEEN

NICO

Nico stared at the letter in her lap. She had yet to open it, but she couldn't hold off any longer. She'd made a promise to herself she would read it before she set foot on Italian soil. She looked out the window of the plane. Soon they would begin their descent into Milan Malpensa Airport.

That understanding she and Rocco had come to in Barcelona had been real. Something had changed. They were doing much better. Rocco had earned the team points on every race. He had yet to mount the podium, but he'd come close in the last two races, finishing fourth. Nico had yet to earn any points, but with each race, she got one step closer to finishing in the top ten. The last race she'd finished eleventh. She felt full of hope.

She stared back at the letter.

She'd be damned if she'd let Mickey get in the way. Charles was right. She gave him too much power.

That's about to end. Here. And. Now.

With trembling fingers, she ripped open the envelope.

Ciao My Sweet Angelini,

How long has it been? Were you thinking the last letter I sent so many years ago would be my final one? You didn't think I would let you get away that easily, did you? Especially after that dirty turn you did me, which forced me to leave the country.

I've never stopped thinking of my topolina, my little mouse. I have yet to find another woman so willing, so yielding, so compliant.

Are you still the same?

I hear congratulations are in order. My topolina has finally made it. Formula 1! That is quite an accomplishment. One I am quite proud of, given I helped fund you early on.

I expect a return on my investment. I needn't ask if you remember our agreement. Of course you do.

You were quite adept at keeping me at arm's length, avoiding playing the roper and frustrating me in any attempt to fix on a mark while you were working your way up in the racing world. Now, I see you are to be commended for it.

I'm glad we waited. Enough time has passed since I left, and it is now safe to resume our relationship.

I've seen the schedule. I am in Rome as I write this. Soon I will be traveling up the coast to La Spezia. I'm not sure that I will make it as far north as Monza but perhaps the race in Monaco afterward? No matter, in either case we will meet in the very near future.

Don't worry about finding me; I will find you. You can be sure of it. Just as you can be sure that when you are in my arms once more, I will not make the mistake of ever letting you go again.

Yours Always,

Mickey

Nico shoved the letter back in the crumpled envelope and threw it in her purse.

I have more to hold over him than he does me.

He was the one who'd had to leave the country to escape the authorities. It was obvious he was still grifting. How else could he have survived all these years? All it would take is one call to the police to send him packing. If necessary.

But could she do it? She'd like to prove him wrong—show him she was no longer that compliant topolina.

Topolina. I am not his little mouse.

She wanted so badly to believe that Charles was right. That the man had no power over her anymore. But as she ran her finger along that scar on the back of her head, she couldn't believe it—not in her bones.

Exposing him meant exposing her.

She knew it. And he knew it too.

The fasten seat belt sign turned on. She glanced out the window. They'd be arriving soon.

Mickey was right about one thing. When it came to the racing world she had made a concerted effort not to play the roper for him. She had been determined not to lure anyone connected to that world into some con or scam concocted by Mickey. Any time he'd fixed his attention on someone, claiming they'd be the perfect sucker, the perfect mark, she'd found a way to convince him otherwise.

Everything she ever did in the world of racing had been on the square.

She swallowed. A sickening feeling in the pit of her stomach.

Except once.

That night.

That night at Drink and Dive when she'd performed the short con.

And her mark had been none other than Rocco Vittori.

CHAPTER SIXTEEN

NICO

Nico had booked a room at the Hotel de la Ville, a small hotel in the town of Monza. She'd declined Celeste's invitation to stay at Dario's parents' villa on Lake Como. If Dario was staying at the villa, that meant Rocco was too.

Things are improving between us. I don't want to risk messing that up. Not when we're doing so much better on the track.

So why do you feel more uncomfortable around him now than you did before?

You know why.

That dream.

After paying the driver, she stood alongside her suitcase outside the hotel, gazing up at its cream walls adorned with ivy draping from its rooftop like a stunning emerald necklace.

Entering the hotel felt more like entering the home of a count or a marquis. The mahogany walls were decorated with portraits of what Nico could only guess were members of the nobility from days gone by.

When she walked into her suite, the sun was streaming through the French doors that led out onto a balcony. All the furnishings were made of rich dark wood. Scattered about were Chinese vases, a Tibetan chest, and eighteenth-century painted fans. In the bedroom, a king-sized canopy bed with an intricately carved wooden headboard was draped with fine silk fabric. The marble bathroom was equipped with both a spacious walk-in shower and a claw-foot bathtub.

She sighed, staggered over to the bed, and collapsed. Her sluggish eyelids blinked twice before shutting altogether. She told herself she would nap for an hour. Then she would walk around the town, get some dinner, and then head back here for a good night's sleep. No sooner had she completed this thought than she'd drifted off.

When she opened her eyes, it took her a moment to realize where she was. The sky was a deep purple. Soon, it would be black. How long had she been asleep?

She got out of bed and looked at the clock on the bedside table. It was eight o'clock. Dinner was still possible and, beyond that, a necessity, she thought as her stomach grumbled.

She jumped in the shower and once out, towel-dried her hair. She threw on jeans and a sweater, shoved her feet into a pair of her favorite sneakers, and grabbed her purse.

Maybe I'll bring some food back, buy a bottle of wine, and sit out on the balcony. It's so lovely.

Just then Nico blinked as something flew from the sky.

She opened the French doors and saw two stuffed toys.

One appeared to be either Thing One or Thing Two from Dr. Seuss's *The Cat in the Hat*. She couldn't tell which because the circle on its chest that would have told her was missing, leaving a gaping hole. The other was a doll—a girl with short blonde hair, wearing a superhero costume.

After picking them up, she leaned over the railing, glanced up, and spied two smiling faces looking down at her.

Holding up the two items, she cleared her throat and asked in Italian, "Do these belong to you?"

The girls looked at each other, giggling.

Okay, so her Italian sucked.

"Are you American?" the taller one asked in impeccable English.

Nico nodded. "How can you tell?"

They giggled some more.

"So," Nico ventured. "I take it these belong to you?"

They nodded.

"We meant to throw them onto the patio in the garden down below," the shorter of the two said.

The taller girl rolled her eyes. "Lame, huh? They bounced off the edge of your railing, which made them drop onto your balcony. Would have been cool if we'd meant to do it. Like a Tim bank shot."

"Tim?" Nico asked.

"Duncan, dummy."

"You're the dummy," the smaller one said, pushing the taller one. "More like Kareem."

They must be sisters, Nico thought, smiling.

"You're the dummy," the taller one pushed back. "You're also the shorty."

The smaller girl stuck her tongue out at the other girl. "It's not nice to call someone a dummy."

"Sorry, lady," the taller one said, looking down at Nico. "I shouldn't have called you dummy just because you don't know who Tim Duncan is."

"I know who Tim Duncan is," Nico said. "He played for the San Antonio Spurs. One of the greatest power forwards to ever play the game. He had a wicked bank shot and won five NBA championships." She paused. "Although, I'd take Kareem's skyhook bank shot over Duncan's any day. He won six NBA championships."

The smaller girl extended her spine and appeared to grow a couple of inches taller as she lifted her chin, grinning large at Nico.

The taller girl didn't seem to object and appeared to be just as pleased.

"You know a lot about basketball," she said.

"So do you. Look, I was just headed out. I'll leave these at the front desk, and you and your parents can pick them up whenever you want."

"Our parents aren't here," the shorter one said.

Some adult or family member must be up there with them.

"Well, whoever's looking after you, then."

The taller girl scoffed. "I'm seven, and I can look after myself. She's five, and I can look after her."

"Nuh-uh. I can look after myself too."

The taller girl shrugged. "Fine," she spat. "We can look after ourselves."

"Why don't I bring these up to you?"

They both nodded, smiling, eagerly waving their hands for her to come up.

Nico sighed. She was hungry. She needed to eat something. At this point, she'd settle for some cardboard as long as she could smother it in ketchup.

When she got to the room, she'd barely knocked once before the door swung open and the two girls were standing there. She made a move to hand them the toys, but they grabbed her wrists and pulled her inside.

The place was huge—much larger than her suite. To the left she could see what looked like a living or sitting room. To the right was a hallway, which must lead to the bedrooms.

"Um, don't you have an adult staying with you?" Nico asked, looking around but seeing no one.

"Don't need one," the taller one said before clasping her palms to her cheeks *Home Alone* style and screaming.

Nico jumped. Had she seen a mouse?

"Is that *Calvin and Hobbes*?" she shrieked, pointing at Nico's sneakers.

The shorter one jumped up and down, running circles around Nico. "It is. It is. There's Sally!"

Nico smiled. They were her favorite sneakers. They were colorful and had *Calvin and Hobbes* cartoons covering the body of the shoe.

"Pretty cool, huh?" she said, lifting her feet and showing off the shoes from all sides.

"Very cool," the taller one said, nodding.

"Most decidedly cool," the shorter one said, nodding as well.

Nico had to bite her lip to keep from laughing.

The taller one introduced herself. "I'm Sofia. And this," she said, pointing to the other girl, "is my little sister Beatrice."

"I'm her younger sister," Beatrice said. "Not little. I may be shorter now, but that's only because she's seven and I'm only five. I plan on being taller than her in the future."

Nico stood looking from one to the other, nodding and doing her best to muster a serious expression. They were a real kick.

"And who might you be?" Beatrice asked.

"I'm Nico. Nice to meet you."

"Nice to meet you," Sofia said.

"To be sure," Beatrice said.

A chortle burst from Nico's mouth, which she quickly covered up with a cough. "You both speak English fluently."

"We learn it at school, and our parents, grandparents, and great-grandparents speak it, so we get lots of practice."

"Where are you going?" Sofia asked.

"Out to get some dinner."

"Are you hungry?"

Starving, she thought.

They pulled her into an adjoining room with a sofa, some chairs, and a collection of toys and games strewn about the floor. After passing through two more rooms they finally arrived at the dining room, complete with a table that could seat as many as twelve people and a candelabra chandelier hanging above it.

She had thought her suite was spacious, but it looked like a broom closet compared with this palace.

There on the table was a pizza box.

"It just came. We haven't even started yet."

They lifted the cover, and the delicious smell of cheese, tomato, prosciutto, peppers, and caramelized onions on toasty crust wafted toward her nose. It looked and smelled like it had been baked in a stone oven—a mere hint of charcoal on the golden crust around the edge.

Nico clutched her stomach. She kept her mouth shut so that she didn't drool on the carpet beneath her feet. It looked Persian. And expensive.

"What about your mom and dad?"

"They'll be here soon," Sofia said. "They won't mind."

"Come on," Beatrice said.

They dragged her to the table. Not that she put up much resistance.

"There's plenty." Sofia pulled out a chair for Nico and then sat in the one beside her.

Should she do this?

It was a muddle, and one she couldn't think through with her stomach drowning out her brain.

Well, she knew this much. She couldn't leave them.

And she knew something else. That pizza was within reach, not more than an arm's length away, and it was now screaming at her.

The girls were going to eat it anyway. So, why not join in as long as she was here?

The three of them each grabbed a slice and munched away. Damn, it was good.

"So," Nico said in between bites. "Why did you throw your toys over your terrace? Would Thing One or Thing Two not fly kites in the house?"

More giggling.

"It isn't Thing One or Thing Two anymore, it's just Thing." Beatrice climbed off her chair, grabbed the stuffed toy, and brought it back to the table to show Nico. "See. He's lost some of his stuffing. Cat thought he was a chew toy and destroyed the other one completely. So, there's only Thing now."

Cat?

"I see," Nico said as she shoved a second slice into her mouth.

That's when she heard a voice—a man's voice—coming from the other room.

CHAPTER SEVENTEEN

NICO AND ROCCO

Had someone been here the entire time?

"Okay, flying monkeys, if you've started in on that pizza, you better have left me some. I'm coming to check, and then I'm going to throw on—"

Nico's eyes ballooned at the sight of Rocco wearing nothing but a towel around his waist. His chest was glistening, his hair tousled, the ends shedding drops of water that slid from his sculpted shoulders down his muscular chest, descending to his chiseled abs and carving a seductive stream that didn't escape view until slipping under that towel.

He jerked to an abrupt stop when he saw her. If he'd been wearing shoes, he would have skidded.

Nico's mouth was full of pizza. She stared at that towel wrapped around his torso. Was it her imagination, or had it slipped a fraction of an inch? It was now hanging oh-so-precariously on his hips. Another inch and . . .

No sooner had she completed the thought than a wad of pizza dough caught in her throat.

Nico stood up so suddenly her chair crashed to the floor. There was something she needed to do. Hammacher Schlemmer, Schlummer or Schlepper.

What's it called? What does it matter? Just do it. Do what?

"She's choking!" both girls cried in unison as they scrambled off their chairs and jumped to their feet.

Before her brain could manifest another thought, she felt him behind her.

He threw his arms around her. Making a fist with one hand and clasping it tightly with the other, he placed them just below her rib cage. His face was flush with hers, his cheek pressed against hers, the stubble grazing her flesh. His breathing—rapid fire—rose and fell in waves, beating in rhythm with his heart pounding against her back.

"Please don't let me break her ribs," he whispered as he thrust his fist into her, drawing her body into his own.

"Harder, Uncle Rocco! Harder!" Sofia and Beatrice yelled.

Is he wearing anything underneath that towel?

"Her face is red!" Sofia wailed.

"No, it's purple!" Beatrice screamed.

Of course he's not wearing anything, you idiot. He just came out of the shower. Do you know anyone who wears underwear in the shower?

The grim reaper is holding that scythe over your neck. And he's grinning! Think about that! Not the fact that only a thin layer of terry cloth separates . . .

No! These cannot be your last thoughts on earth.

Recite the Lord's Prayer, a Hail Mary, the Pledge of Allegiance, anything but . . .

"Come on, Nico," he murmured.

I must remember one of the three.

She could hear the girls shouting, "Harder, Uncle Rocco, harder!"

"Come on, girl."

Holy Mary! Lord have mercy and deliver us from evil.

"Uncle Rocco, harder. She's turning blue!"

Pray for us sinners. Lead us not into temptation and pledge allegiance now and at the hour of our death, with liberty and justice for all.

"Please, Nico." His plea sounded to her like a prayer. "Don't leave me now. Come on, girl. Please."

For thine is the power and the glory. Forever and ever. Amen.

One more thrust, and out came a wad of wet red dough with one strip of glistening prosciutto hanging from it.

"Ew," Beatrice said, staring down at the putrid object.

"Yuck," Sofia added, peering at it alongside her.

He released his fist and loosened his hold on her but didn't remove his hands altogether. He held her waist, and she could still feel him behind her.

After a moment, he let go and placed the palm of his hand on her back. She sighed, grateful for her breath—even grateful for the presence of his hand, which was surprisingly comforting.

"Just breathe, Nico. Relax. Take a moment. You're okay now."

■ ■ ■

Rocco kept his hand on her back, watching her closely.

She lifted her sweater and brought it up to her mouth, but he pushed her hand down and reached for a napkin. She made a move to take it from him, but he ignored her hand and gently wiped her lips.

When he was done, she hung her head, staring at the floor. She wouldn't look at him. He placed his hand under her chin and lifted it until he could see her face. Her eyes looked like two black pebbles under a running stream.

"Uncle Rocco," Sofia said, "she's still red."

"Yeah, Uncle Rocco," Beatrice said, "maybe you didn't get it all out. Maybe you should do some more."

He shook his head. "No, she's fine. Just give her a moment."

He smiled and brushed one finger lightly under Nico's chin.

The color in her cheeks deepened.

Quickly, he removed his hand.

No one said a word. Even his nieces were quiet, which almost never happened. He racked his brain, trying to think how best to break the awkward silence, which had become deafening. He could hear it ringing in his ears.

He turned his gaze to the wet mound of dough sitting on the carpet.

"Ew and yuck," he echoed.

He cast a sidelong glance at Nico and saw the corners of her lip twitch, curl, and then rise. Finally, she began to chuckle. That got the girls to snicker. Soon they were all laughing until their breath and their stomachs couldn't withstand any more.

When the laughter finally subsided, his nieces ran over and hugged Nico.

"It would have been a shame to lose you after we just became friends," said Sofia.

"Most definitely," agreed Beatrice.

Then they rushed over to Rocco, throwing their arms around him.

"You saved Nico's life, Uncle Rocco," Sofia cried.

"You're a hero," echoed Beatrice.

"Yes, thank you," Nico muttered.

When he met her gaze, she looked away.

"Wait a minute," Sofia said, looking up at him. "You said her name. I heard you."

Beatrice disengaged herself and stared up at him as well. "I heard you too."

"How did you know her name?" Sofia asked.

"Yeah," Beatrice said, "we didn't tell you."

"Yeah, well," he said, "we know each other."

"How?" they both asked in unison.

He hesitated. You couldn't say one thing around these girls and expect it to be kept quiet or forgotten. They had minds like steel traps. And they were never bashful about releasing those traps and spewing things that at best were awkward or uncomfortable and at worst downright damning.

He heard her voice and felt himself cringe at what might come next.

"Your uncle and I are on the same team."

They smiled.

Okay, he thought, *so far, so good.*

"What do you do?" Sofia asked.

"I'm a driver, like him."

The two girls looked at each other.

Shit.

"You're the cockroach?"

"What?" Nico cried, glaring at him.

"I never said cockroach." He looked from her to his nieces. "I never said cockroach. I said encroacher. Actually, I didn't even say that. I said she was encroaching. Not to mention that was a private conversation with your uncle Dario."

The girls stood with their hands on their hips. They were glaring at him too. "What's the difference?" Sofia demanded.

"Yeah," he heard Nico echo. "I'd like to know that too. What is the difference?"

When he looked over at her, he could see she'd recovered. She was shooting daggers at him.

Man, he thought, *how quickly they forget. Didn't I just save her life? Didn't they just call me a hero?*

"An encroacher is not a cockroach," he said. "An encroacher is um, well, it's a—"

"An interloper?" Nico suggested. "An intruder? Someone who's not wanted?"

Beatrice pushed him. "Why wouldn't you want Nico?"

Sofia did likewise. "Is it because she's a girl?"

He suddenly felt exposed and vulnerable. That's when he realized he was still wearing only a towel. What's more, he could feel it slipping. He grabbed it, holding it in place, looking frantically at the three pairs of glaring eyes.

Escape.

It was the only option.

He turned and ran.

CHAPTER EIGHTEEN

ROCCO AND NICO

ROUND 7: RACE 7: MONZA, ITALY

Rocco was wheel-to-wheel with Anker. Clarke was just up ahead. Anker tried to pass him on his right, but Rocco stayed with him. Out of the corner of his eye, he could see Anker inching left, threatening to make contact with him, but Rocco held firm.

Rocco: Anker's trying to squeeze me out. I don't know if we have more power but if we do, let's use it.
Race Engineer: Go for it, Rocco. Push. Push. Push.
Rocco: Copy.

Rocco increased his speed, got out in front of Anker, and was just on Clarke's tail when Anker approached on the right of him. In another second, all three cars were wheel-to-wheel. Anker pulled out in front, but as he did, he veered left and made contact with the front of Rocco's car. Clarke shot out ahead of them both, avoiding contact while Rocco skidded but was able to regain control and keep the car on the track. Anker slid far right into the gravel.

Rocco: Can you check my front? I was sandwiched.
Race Engineer: We're checking. You got past Anker. Well done. He's back on track. Just behind you.

Rocco: Copy. How far back?
Race Engineer: Looks to be at least three seconds.
Rocco: Copy. Where is Nico?
Race Engineer: She moved up one position. Holding steady at ninth.
Rocco: Copy.

Rocco smiled. She could earn some points this race. They both could. She'd moved up to ninth after starting at tenth, and right now he was second after starting at sixth position. Seven laps to go.

■ ■ ■

Race Engineer: Excellent, Nico. You've moved up to eighth.
Nico: Copy. Where's Rocco?
Race Engineer: He's second, just behind Clarke with Anker a couple seconds behind him.
Nico: Copy.

Nico smiled. He would make the podium, maybe even come in first if he could overtake Clarke. And she was about to earn her first Formula 1 points, if she could just hold position. Six laps to go.

■ ■ ■

Race Engineer: Damage is minimal, Rocco. Car handling fine?
Rocco: Seems to be. How is the rear slip and braking?
Race Engineer: All data looks good. You're keeping pace with Clarke, and Anker's slipped back to fifth. Looks like he did some damage to the car. Nico's moved up to seventh.
Rocco: No shit!
Race Engineer: No shit. Just keep your head down, Rocco. Head down. Focus on the pace.
Rocco: Copy.

Five laps to go, he thought. *Come on, Nico. Five laps to go.*

■ ■ ■

Seventh is good. But sixth would be better, Nico thought as she saw Hans Mendelsohn of Blue Jet Lightning just up ahead. She'd set a faster pace in this last lap. With four laps to go, she might overtake him.

Race Engineer: Excellent pace, Nico. After this turn up ahead, you can pass Anker on the straightaway.
Nico: Did you say Anker?
Race Engineer: I did. He and Mendelsohn swapped positions on that last lap.

Nico's heart was racing. It might be racing faster than the car. The turn was just up ahead, and so was Anker. The safe move was to pass on the straightaway. That's what Anker would expect her to do. And he'd do everything within his power to stop her. If she tried to pass him on the turn, he would expect her to do it from the inside, and he would block her out. He would never expect her to make a move on the turn from the outside. But she'd need to make him think that's exactly what she was going to do.

Nico: Can I use some more power here?
Race Engineer: I told you to pass him on the straightaway, Nico. He's not going to budge on that turn.
Nico: I know. I just want to get close behind him.
Silence.
Nico: Did you hear me?
Race Engineer: I heard you. Go ahead and push. But be careful.
Nico: Copy.

Nico was just behind Anker now. It felt as though there was hardly an inch between the front of her car and the rear of his. Of course, just as expected, he was hugging the inside as they came to the turn. She did likewise. But halfway through, she began to drift out to his right as though she were going to make a move to pass. Anker veered right to block her way. She watched the space to his left on the inside of that turn grow inch by inch. And when it was wide enough, she jerked the car left, almost hitting the embankment when she did. As she slid past Anker on the inside, she felt as though she were scraping up against the wall, she was that close.

Race Engineer: Push, Nico! Push!

Nico shot past him. He hadn't anticipated her move and went spinning to his right, lost control, and hit the outside embankment, coming to a full stop.

Race Engineer: Shit, yes! Nico! Head down, now. One more lap, and then the checkered flag is just up ahead.
Nico: Where's Rocco?
Race Engineer: Second. I think he's got it. I don't think he can overtake Clarke at this point. He's holding off Lopez and Stewart who are just behind him. He's kept them both out of DRS range for the last three laps. Just one more lap to go.

Come on, Rocco, she thought. *One more lap. Just one more.*

When Nico crossed the finish line, her first thought was about her grandfather. As she cheered and thanked the team over the radio, she placed her hand on her heart, where she carried that photo of her mother and the sketch of her grandfather in a small inside pocket. But never in a million years would she have imagined that her next thought would be about Rocco.

She was beaming. He'd come in second and would be mounting the podium.

I can't believe I'm this happy for that annoying, arrogant, asshole, prick.

CHAPTER NINETEEN

NICO AND ROCCO

Nico entered Rocco's suite at the hotel with Sofia and Beatrice and placed the key card on the entryway table.

After the podium celebration, Rocco and Dario had had to run off to do a number of interviews. His nieces had practically tackled Nico and begged their mother, Rocco's sister, Isabella, to let them stay with Nico while she went to go meet some friends. Nico told her she'd be happy to do it, and Isabella agreed.

So, Nico and the girls had gone for gelato and walked through the park before returning to the hotel.

Nico glanced at her watch. Isabella would be picking them up in about an hour.

"I'm glad you're still friends with us," Sofia said once the door shut behind them.

"Of course!" Nico said. "Why wouldn't I be?"

"Well," Beatrice said. "Uncle Rocco did call you a cockroach."

"Yeah, but that was a while ago," Sofia insisted.

"Yeah," Beatrice agreed. "He wanted to explain the other night, but you were gone after he got dressed."

Smiling, Nico nodded. After he'd fled, she'd done the same. She didn't want to make things more awkward than they already were. Since then, he'd tried to take her aside a couple times over the weekend, telling her he wanted to explain, but they were always interrupted by Casey or one of the crew.

"What do you want to do?" Nico asked as they pulled her into the living room.

Nico picked up a collection of Grimms' fairy tales from the coffee table and sat on the sofa. Some of the book's pages looked as though they'd been put through a shredder. "What happened to this?"

The girls sat on either side of her.

"Dog," Sofia said.

"Yeah, Uncle Rocco's supposed to get him a scratching post, but he always forgets."

A scratching post for a dog?

"Is he your pet?"

"Uncle Rocco's."

"Maybe he's bored," Nico said. "Maybe he should take him for a walk or to a park so he can run around."

"You mean on a leash?" Beatrice asked.

"Sure," Nico said. "Why not?"

The girls looked at each other, grinning. "Dog on a leash!" they exclaimed. And they both fell backward, roaring with laughter.

Nico furrowed her brow. Must be some kind of inside joke.

"Uncle Rocco was reading it to us last night," Sofia said, indicating the book of fairy tales when they finally stopped laughing.

Beatrice sighed. "He didn't realize there were pages missing. He started to read us one of the stories, but then couldn't finish. He got so mad."

This brought on another fit of laughter.

Nico chuckled. "What story was he reading you?"

"It was about a girl named Snow White," Beatrice said, "and her evil mother, who's a queen."

"Not her mother," Sofia corrected her sister, "stepmother."

Beatrice looked up at Nico. "If her stepmother is a queen, that would make her a princess, right?"

"That's right. Princess Snow White."

The girls made a face and then said in unison, "Lame name."

Nico nodded. "It is, isn't it?"

"Do you know the story?" Sofia asked.

"I do."

"Can you finish it?" Beatrice asked.

"I could. Or I could tell you a different version. One you wouldn't find in this book."

Their eyes opened wide.

"Yes! Do!" they cried, gleefully.

"But wait!" Sofia said as she jumped up from the sofa. "We need chocolate."

"Most definitely," said Beatrice, running after her.

"But we just had gelato," Nico cried.

■ ■ ■

Rocco approached the door to his suite. He was happy—really, truly, happy.

Tonight, when they all met up to celebrate, he'd find a moment to pull Nico aside. He wanted to explain that cockroach business. He really wanted to do more than explain. He wanted to apologize.

But over the last couple of days, he'd never been able to get a moment alone with her. Someone was always around. When they were at the track, there were team meetings, practice sessions, and qualifying. Off the track, there was his family, who lived only a couple hours from Monza.

He entered the code, heard the click, and opened the door. He paused when he heard a voice. It was a woman's voice, but not Isabella's.

"The stepmother wasn't evil," said the voice. "She was just smart, tough, and a woman who wasn't afraid to speak her mind. And like other women of her ilk, she was both misunderstood and maligned."

He shut the door softly behind him, crept down the hallway, and peered around the corner.

"What does *ilk* mean?" Beatrice asked.

"And *maligned*?" Sofia added.

"Ilk means type. So, women who were like her."

"Smart, tough, and not afraid to speak their mind?" Sofia ventured.

"Exactly. And to malign someone means to put them down, make them look bad."

Beatrice nodded. "Like Uncle Rocco calling you a cockroach."

He cringed.

"Well, I don't think he called me that. Not exactly."

"He said you were encroaching," Sofia said. "He didn't want you on the team."

Beatrice nodded. "Yeah."

"Well . . ."

"It was wrong of Uncle Rocco." Sofia said.

"Yeah," Beatrice agreed. "And not nice."

Sofia lifted her chin. "You can drive just as good as him."

Beatrice nodded. "Most definitely."

"Well, I'm good. But not that good."

This brought a smile to Rocco's lips.

She's honest.

"Yet," Nico added.

He sighed.

And cocky.

"Let's see. Now, where were we?"

"The queen, Snow White's stepmother, was misunderstood," said Sofia.

"And maligned," added Beatrice.

"Right. She worried about her stepdaughter and figured it was her responsibility to look after her and most importantly to raise her so that she could take care of herself when she grew up. Especially since she'd been given the name Snow White. The queen would have preferred another name like Diana Prince, Marla Drake, or Harley Quinn."

Bouncing up and down on the sofa, the girls clapped their hands and squealed.

"Or Jessica Jones!" cried Sofia.

"Or Jessica Drew!" chimed in Beatrice.

"Exactly," Nico sighed. "But the king preferred Snow White. And so the queen worried. She knew her stepdaughter would be an easy mark with a name like that."

"What's an easy mark?"

Watching Nico, Rocco had that feeling of familiarity again. There was something about those eyes.

"Someone who can be taken advantage of. Someone who's easy to trick or fool."

The girls looked at each other, shaking their heads. "Not good," they said in unison.

Nico shook her head. "Most decidedly not."

Beatrice beamed.

"The queen knew she needed to teach Snow White some important life lessons," Nico continued, "so that when the girl finally went out into the world as an adult, she would be able to take care of herself and not have to depend on anyone else. So, one day, the queen disguised herself as a witch, in order to teach Snow White a lesson—never take apples from strangers."

"We know that one," Beatrice said. "Our parents taught us never to take anything from strangers."

Nico smiled, nodding. "That's good. You see, neither of you are an easy mark."

Rocco blinked. Beatrice had spotted him. He put his finger to his lips.

"Uncle Rocco!" she shouted.

Both girls leapt from the sofa and came running toward him.

"Nico's been telling us a story," Beatrice said as she hugged his legs.

He cast her a sidelong glance.

"So I hear."

"It's the story you were telling us last night," Sofia said.

He grinned as he peered at Nico. "It sounds a little different than what I remember."

Nico lifted her chin. "Yes, well when you were their age, the princess was always in need of a prince to save her."

He was still grinning. He couldn't seem to stop himself. "And that's no longer the case, is it?"

"No, it isn't."

He looked down at his nieces. "Your mom will be here soon. Go wash your hands, and I'll order something for dinner."

They took off, and there was a moment of silence.

He sighed. "So, princes have gone out of fashion."

"I don't know about that. But the world finally figured out that princesses can do things for themselves. Even things that were once reserved only for princes."

"And those backward princes, who would call such princesses *cockroaches* when they do things once reserved only for princes, need to realize that or be banished from the kingdom."

She grinned. "Something like that."

"Which I never did, by the way. I never called you a cockroach. My nieces heard me use that word *encroach*, and I was angry when I said it."

"Is this your version of an apology?"

He swallowed. "It is."

She nodded. "It sucks, but I accept it."

He laughed but stopped when he realized she was avoiding looking him in the eye. If she wasn't looking at the floor, she was looking somewhere else.

Was it the way he was looking at her? Did it make her uncomfortable?

He began thinking of those photos—the ones on social media and those in the magazine—and thinking of what Dario and Celeste had said.

Is the way I'm looking at her—intense? Too—intense?

"The backward prince should be glad to hear about this change," Nico said. "For Sofia's and Beatrice's sakes. I'm sure he wouldn't want them to have to rely on a prince to save them. And he certainly would never tell them they couldn't do something just because most of the people doing it were men."

She's got me there.

He nodded. "Most definitely."

She blinked, laughed, and finally met his gaze.

The girls came running.

"Pizza!" they shouted. "We want pizza!"

Rocco frowned. "Again? Your mother will be angry with me if I get you pizza again."

"Hey, can Nico have pizza with us?" Sofia asked.

Beatrice jumped up and down, clapping her hands. "Yeah!"

"No, she's going out to dinner with me."

They stared at Nico and then began to push Rocco with huge smiles.

"You're going on a date?" Beatrice asked.

Sofia ran up to Nico. "What are you going to wear?"

"No, no," she said, the color in her cheeks deepening. "It's not—"

Rocco jumped in. "A date. It's not a date," he stammered. "We're all going. Dario, Celeste, everyone."

Unfortunately, this wasn't enough to stop the shenanigans of the two evil pixies who posed as his nieces.

"Will you wear a dress?" Sofia asked, hiking up one shoulder.

"We've never seen you in a dress," Beatrice said. "Why don't you wear dresses?"

"I, I wear dresses. Sometimes."

Rocco could see they'd made her uncomfortable and figured he'd help her out. "You haven't seen her wear a dress because she's a member of the team. Do you see me wearing one?"

The girls giggled.

"Exactly, there you go."

But when he glanced at Nico, he couldn't tell if he'd made matters better or worse.

He looked down at his nieces. "There are some menus in the kitchen. Go take a look. You can have anything *but* pizza."

They ran over to hug Nico. "Thanks for the gelato and the story."

"You're very welcome."

Once they were gone, Rocco frowned. "Gelato?" He glanced at the table, seeing the empty box of chocolate. "And chocolate." He paused. "Before dinner."

"Sorry. I'm not good with children. I don't really know—what—I'm supposed to do."

"No younger siblings or nieces or nephews to babysit?"

"Uh, no."

She looked around the room.

"Looking for something?"

"My purse."

She seemed in a hurry to leave.

Spotting her bag on a chair in the corner, he walked over and picked it up. "Here it is." He extended his hand, the purse dangling from it. "No babysitting gigs as a teenager to make some quick cash?"

She shook her head, reached for the bag, grabbing the strap. She pulled to take it from him, but he didn't let go.

"I would have thought you had. I mean, you're so good with Beatrice and Sofia. They really like you."

"They're sweet girls."

He laughed. "No, they're not. They're Tasmanian devils. They don't like everybody, and when they don't like a person, they're not afraid to show it. But—they like you."

He tried to read the expression on her face. He felt like he'd touched a nerve. Like he was now the one who might be considered a cockroach, venturing into territory where he had no business going.

"My purse?"

"Sorry," he said, letting go. He didn't realize he was still holding on to it.

Just then her phone rang. She looked down at her purse.

"Aren't you—going to get that?'

She swung the purse over her shoulder. "If it's important, they'll leave a message. I should be going."

Whoever it was, she didn't want to talk to them with him around.

When she walked by him, he grabbed her arm. He let go when he saw her bristle.

"You are coming tonight?"

She wouldn't look at him. "Sure. Why wouldn't I be?"

"Right."

He followed her to the door, taking the last couple of steps swiftly to bypass her and open it.

"By the way," he said, "you were really good today. On the track, I mean."

She was halfway through the doorway when he'd said it.

She paused. He had only the side of her face to go by, but he saw the corner of her lip curl. She was smiling. But then he caught the expression in her eye. It almost looked as though she weren't happy. But that didn't make sense. Maybe it had nothing to do with the racing. Maybe those questions about family?

"You were really good too," she said before turning her back to him and hurrying down the hallway.

CHAPTER TWENTY

ROCCO

"Let's play Never Have I Ever!" Celeste cried when Dario and Rocco came back to the table with a round of drinks.

Everybody else had left after dinner.

Celeste glanced around the table. "Everyone knows the rules, right? Do you know the game, Nico?"

"Yes," she said tentatively, "I know it."

Rocco cast her a sidelong glance, wanting to put her at ease.

Come on, look my way.

Finally, she did. He winked. She smiled.

Celeste clapped her hands. "Just think of it as a team-building exercise. I'll start. Let me think." After a moment, her eyes blew up. "Never have I ever stolen somebody's GoGo squeeZ."

Rocco chuckled, looking over at Nico, who was laughing too. Then he shot Dario a glance. His cousin jutted his chin, crossed his arms, and leaned back.

"See," Celeste said. "What did I tell you? Team Building 101."

"Okay, Tony Robbins," Dario said, "I'm next." He turned to Celeste. "Never have I ever returned a dress after I've worn it. And I don't just mean tried it on. I mean worn it going out."

"Very funny," Celeste said, picking up her glass and taking a drink.

Nico also took a drink.

She was wearing a dress now. When she'd entered the restaurant, a couple of the technicians let out low whistles and made comments, but Rocco shushed them as she'd drawn near.

"Your turn, Roc," Dario said.

Rocco hesitated. "You know, Dario, technically that wasn't fair, given you said *dress*. It's supposed to be something that applies to everyone sitting at the table. And given neither one of us likes to cross-dress, you should have said *something* instead of *dress*, and in that case . . ."

Rocco picked up his glass and took a drink.

"Dude!" Dario exclaimed.

"It was the inseam. The tailor got it wrong."

Celeste giggled. "What? You hang to the right, Rocco?"

"No," he replied, his voice gruff. "To the left. You girls should be thanking me for being so damn upright."

"Upright?" Nico asked, a feigned look of surprise on her face. "I thought you said you hang left."

Dario and Celeste burst out laughing.

"Or"—Nico tilted her head, a wry smile on her lips—"perhaps you think we should be grateful for your coming to our rescue."

Rocco leaned toward her, slivering his eyes and grinning.

"You mean, like a good prince would? Maybe," he said, leaning even closer, "it's just a forward-thinking prince recognizing there ought to be a level playing field."

Even though her dark eyes were hard to read, he thought he saw some change in them as though a window had opened.

"Ahem."

It was Dario who'd cleared his throat.

Rocco righted himself and avoided meeting his or Celeste's gaze. "I guess it's my turn now."

He thought a moment, and then it came to him. *Perfect*, he thought.

"Well," he said, looking around the table, "as long as we're venturing down under, never have I ever gone commando."

He and Dario both took a drink. He glanced over at Nico. She and Celeste were eyeing each other, both of them tapping their fingers on the glasses before them.

Finally, Dario nudged Celeste. "Come on, Cellie, play by the rules. You know I know the answer to this one."

Celeste sighed and took a drink.

Nico put her head down, grinning, and took a drink too.

Well. Well. Well.

Dario's cell phone rang. "My mom," he said. "Let me go outside to take this. Be back in a flash."

Once he'd left, Celeste tapped Nico's arm. "So, what's your costume?"

Dario's parents threw a masquerade ball at their Lake Como villa every year. This time it fell in between the Monza and Monaco races.

Nico shook her head. "You'll know when you see me."

"Oh, come on. I'll tell you what I'm wearing. I'm going as Guinevere, and Dario is going as Lancelot. So?"

"So, you'll know when you see me. It'll be a surprise."

They continued chatting, but the rest of what was said went unheard by Rocco.

He was thinking about that dress. He placed his elbow on the table and his chin in his palm.

It was dark green. Set against her olive skin, it made all those hills and valleys of her body even more sumptuous.

The neckline ran straight across from shoulder to shoulder. He could only catch a hint of her collarbone. The cut of the dress was slim enough to reveal her small waist and that deep arc of her hips.

It was one thing to wear a dress, another altogether to go commando while doing it.

She wouldn't. Would she?

His blood was pumping so heavy, he felt the weight of it in his legs and especially in that area that lay between them.

"Okay, back to it!" Dario cried, clapping his hands.

Startled, Rocco's elbow along with his head slid off the edge of the table. He almost fell out of his chair altogether but quickly righted himself.

When he was back to sitting upright, they were all staring at him.

"You all right, dude?" Dario asked.

"Yeah, sure."

"I guess it's my turn now," Nico said. "Let's see," she said, drumming her fingers on the table. "Okay, I've got one. Never have I ever fake-cried to get something."

Nico and Celeste each took a drink. But Rocco and Dario didn't move.

Celeste prodded Dario. "Dario, do you want me to tell them about the time when you—"

"Okay, okay," he said, taking a sip of scotch.

Rocco laughed.

Nico eyed him and his bourbon. "Never?" she asked.

He shook his head. "Never."

Now she placed her elbows on the table and leaned toward him, smiling. "Not even as a child."

He bit his lip and heaved a big sigh before lifting his glass.

"I thought so." She laughed.

"Oh, you did, did you?"

"I did. You pout sometimes."

"She's right," Celeste said. "You do."

"I don't," Rocco insisted.

Nico grinned. "You're doing it now."

Dario pointed at Rocco. "Dude, she's right!"

Rocco shook his head while the three of them laughed.

They went around, keeping the never-have-I-evers fairly tame until Dario grinned and looked directly at Rocco. "Never have I ever been handcuffed."

"Okay, okay, very funny," Rocco said as he took a drink.

"Oh my," Celeste said, clapping her hands.

"Really?" Dario chimed in.

They were looking at Nico.

Rocco did likewise. Damn if she didn't have a poker face.

Turning to Dario, he pointed his thumb at Nico. "Did she take a drink?"

If they were ever to put an image of what it meant to grin from ear to ear in the dictionary, Dario's face right now would be it.

"She did," he said.

Rocco's heart began to beat in a funny way as though it were uncertain which way it wanted to go. Did it want to slow down and make everything around him, including himself, absolutely still? Or did it want to push the gas to the floor and hurl headlong full throttle?

He leaned toward her, grinning. "Care to share any details?"

She mirrored him. "Do you?"

He shrugged. "It was a misunderstanding. A couple of guys got into a fight at a bar. I was an innocent bystander. But when the police arrived, they handcuffed me too until the bartender told them I wasn't involved."

He waited for her to say something, but she didn't. She just nodded.

It was his turn.

He could smell that scent. He felt a jolt between his thighs, which told him his heart wanted to race.

Looking at her, and only at her, he said, "Never have I ever been handcuffed while in bed."

What was that look in her dark eyes telling him? He felt as though they'd ventured somewhere that might be painful to her, somewhere she didn't want to go. And then just like that, she blinked, her eyes glittering as she grinned playfully, lifted her glass, and took a drink.

"Interesting," Celeste said.

"Very," Dario added.

Anyone else looking at the table would have said they were enjoying themselves and the mood was joyful. But he couldn't forget the painful look in those dark eyes just before she'd turned on that sparkling smile like a spigot.

"It's getting late," Rocco said. "Maybe—"

"It's not late," Celeste cried.

Rocco's eyes shifted left, but Nico's eyes quickly darted away.

They went around again, and everything seemed fine. They were all having a good time, including her.

I must have misread that look.

Celeste dealt Dario a blow when she said *Never have I ever cried watching the film* Titanic, forcing him to reluctantly take a drink.

But Dario paid her back.

"Never have I ever blamed a fart on a pet."

Rocco sighed and drank while Nico laughed. But then Rocco and Dario stared at Celeste.

"What?" she asked.

"Celeste," Rocco said. "Drink up."

"I will not!"

Dario groaned. "We know it was you and not Rocco's dog."

"How could you know that?"

"Because I know what he looks like when he farts," Rocco said. "Not to mention the fact you scared him away. We all saw how he ran out of the room. I found him hiding under the bed."

"That's absurd," she said. "He did not."

Rocco grinned and glanced over at Nico. She couldn't contain her laughter.

Dario was having a difficult time too. But he did his best to squelch it when Celeste gave him a dirty look.

"Cellie," Dario said, placing his hand on her arm gently. "Come on."

Celeste jutted her jaw and had yet to lift her glass.

"There is no way for you to know it was me. You should accept that it wasn't, given I told you it wasn't."

Rocco and Dario looked at each other.

There was a pause.

And then in unison, they said, "Uh, no."

"Fine," Celeste spat, taking a drink. Once she'd slammed her glass on the table, she added, "I did that under protest. I admit to nothing. I just did it so that the two of you would shut up about it and we can move on."

The game continued.

Most of the things they revealed were lighthearted and funny. They'd all used a fake ID to get into a bar, and while at a bar, they'd all given a fake phone number to someone who'd asked for it. Everyone but Celeste had worn something from their dirty laundry. Nico and Celeste had laughed so hard they'd peed themselves. Dario and Rocco had forgotten where they'd parked their cars, and Celeste and Nico had faked orgasms. Although Celeste made a point of reassuring Dario she'd never done it with him.

And then there were the times when only he and Nico took a drink. Dario was the one to make those never-have-I-ever statements, knowing full well Rocco would have to drink. But Rocco would bet he hadn't expected Nico to drink as well. He knew he hadn't. Like when Dario had said *Never have I ever slept with someone whose name I didn't know* and *Never have I ever called a sexual partner by the wrong name when in bed with them.*

When this started happening, Rocco began to think that as much as he was enjoying himself and as much as he didn't want to end the evening, they probably should—and soon.

"My turn." Celeste shot an evil grin across the table at Rocco. Clearly, she had something in mind that would require him, and him alone, to drink.

"Never have I ever had a black eye."

He rolled his eyes as he lifted his glass and took a drink. But as he set the glass down, he saw a look of shock on Celeste's and Dario's faces. They were staring at Nico.

"Nico!" Celeste exclaimed. "I'm sorry."

She laughed, but it sounded false. "Don't be."

"But if I'd known, I never would have— I only did it to tease Rocco, because, well, he and Dario can tell you the funny story when he got a black eye."

Nico looked around the table at each of them. She looked okay, but damn if those eyes of hers weren't dark. Too dark for him to really tell.

"It was an accident—something stupid," she said. "My fault, actually. Something so dumb, I'm too embarrassed to tell you."

She placed both hands flat on the table. "My turn to buy the next round." She stood up and walked over to the bar.

Celeste looked from Dario to Rocco. "Do you believe her?"

"What, that she got a black eye?" Dario asked.

"No, you idiot, that it was no big deal."

"Okay, but don't call me an idiot."

Celeste reached over and placed her hand on Dario's cheek. "I'm sorry, honey. I didn't mean it."

All Rocco could think watching them was that it was probably well past the time they should be going home. He glanced over in the direction of the bar.

"She must be telling the truth, right?" Celeste asked. "About it being nothing, just a silly accident. That kind of thing can happen, right?"

When Dario didn't respond, Celeste looked over at him.

"Rocco? What do you think?"

He didn't know what to think. "She sounded convincing. I mean, it didn't seem to bother her. She didn't have to drink. And if it was something bad, she wouldn't have. No one expected her to. So, given she did, that must mean it was no big deal."

Lowering her shoulders, Celeste drew in a deep breath and let it out as one long sigh. "You're right."

He was glad he'd put Celeste at ease. He just wished he'd been able to do the same for himself.

He glanced back at the bar. He also wished he'd stopped Nico from buying another round. They should call it a night. He had an uncomfortable feeling in his gut that as much as he'd enjoyed the evening, it was about to turn sour.

He was definitely feeling the effects of the alcohol, and he could see Dario was too. Not to mention Celeste. She'd begun to slur her words and giggle uncontrollably every time she hiccupped. Nico had to be feeling the effects too. She was hardly much bigger than Celeste. But if she was, she did a damn good job of not letting it show.

"I think we should call it a night," he said when Nico returned with the drinks.

"But I just bought another round," she said.

She sounded angry.

He looked at her. "Don't you think you've had enough?"

"Me? What about you?"

He shrugged. "I'm fine."

"Well, then why do you want to leave?" She stared hard at him and spoke before he had a chance to answer. "Oh, I know why."

He frowned. "What?"

She shrugged. "Never mind."

"No. Why?"

"You want to stop because you don't like what you heard—I mean, said."

What in the hell was she getting at?

"You know," she said, making another attempt, "maybe you didn't like some of the things that were revealed—about you."

"Why would that be the case? If anything might put me off, it would be—"

"What?" she asked. "It would be what?"

Even as black as her eyes were, he could tell by looking at them, she was seeing red.

"Um," Celeste ventured, "maybe—"

"Go ahead," Rocco said, cutting her off. "But this'll be the last round."

There was a moment of silence.

"It's your turn," Rocco said, staring at Nico.

It wasn't in fact her turn, but he felt compelled to hear what she would say.

Someone's phone rang. He only realized it was Nico's when she pulled it out of her purse and silenced it without even looking at it.

After she tossed it back in her purse, she stared back at him, and once again he was struck by something familiar about her eyes.

"Never have I ever said I love you to someone and didn't mean it."

Not taking his eyes off hers, Rocco picked up his glass and drank.

She blinked, looked away, and took a drink as well.

Why would she say that, knowing she would drink? Did she want him to know that about her?

"Okay," he heard Celeste say in a bright tone that sounded forced and false. "I've got one." She leaned toward Dario, grinning. "Never have I ever had a spicy dream about someone sitting at this table."

Celeste lifted her glass and took a drink. When Dario didn't, she glared at him. "You better . . ."

Raising his glass, Dario laughed. "You already knew the answer to that one."

Rocco's heart was pounding. His fingers were on his glass. Nico's were on her glass too, he noticed as he glanced over at her. Whatever she was thinking, he knew it couldn't be the same thing he was.

He was thinking of that dream he'd had of her—more than once. But he wasn't about to admit to it by taking a drink.

No, for this one, he was going to have to lie.

He flinched as he felt a hand on his shoulder.

He knew who it was. He recognized that overly sweet perfume. It was followed by a voice as smooth as single malt, and just like single malt, burned as it went down. Only difference—it didn't send that warmth flooding through his veins. Not anymore.

"Bottoms up, darling," Carolyn Wickham said, pulling up a chair and sitting beside him.

CHAPTER TWENTY-ONE

NICO

Nico gazed out the window as the taxi drove them back to the hotel. She tried to listen for any sign of life beside her, but there was none. *Too drunk*, she thought, glancing over at Rocco.

He really went to town after Carolyn Wickham showed up.

The woman had made a point of taking a drink as she pulled up a chair next to Rocco. She'd drummed her dark red nails on the table, clearly waiting for him to do the same. But he didn't.

How about this one? she'd said. *Never have I ever lied to anyone sitting at this table.*

Rocco took a drink and grinned at her. *You ought to drink too.*

Fair enough, she'd said, lifting the glass to her lips.

Actually, you should probably drink an entire bottle for that one, he'd said.

After that, she'd stood up abruptly, said good night, and left.

If they'd left then, Rocco probably wouldn't have needed help back to the hotel. But once Carolyn was gone, he went to the bar and came back with a bottle.

Nico wished she could put the day on rewind. It had been such a happy day up until that stupid drinking game. Maybe it wouldn't have been so bad if she hadn't admitted to some of the things she had by drinking.

Why did I do that?

Before Carolyn Wickham's arrival, he'd wanted to end the evening. And she knew why. He wanted to get away from her after learning the things he did about her. The only reason he was sitting next to her now was because they were staying in the same hotel and he was too drunk to make it back without some help. Celeste had insisted they take the cab together.

Admitting to some of the things she had made her—what?—definitely less than appealing. Possibly even repugnant.

Yes, repugnant.

Sleeping with someone whose name I didn't know? Calling someone by the wrong name when I was in bed with them? Saying "I love you" to someone when I didn't mean it?

All things she'd done years ago when she was with Mickey.

Repugnant.

There were other adjectives that came to mind, but for some reason this was the one that stuck—like there was something green lodged in between her teeth, compelling people to turn away at the sight of her.

But he'd raised his glass too. He'd done the same things. Why wasn't she turning away from him? Why was he allowed to turn up his nose in disgust when he'd done the very same thing?

Allowed?

It sounded strange. But that didn't seem to matter. It's the way the world turned. And kept turning. Still, even today.

It wasn't fair. Why must a woman pay for her past when it seemed a man never had to?

But you already knew that. So why admit to those things?

She couldn't blame it on the alcohol. She was the only one sitting at that table who wasn't drunk. She knew how to appear that she was imbibing without in fact doing so. She was as sober as a priest in the confessional.

There's a part of you that wanted to admit to those things, wanted to admit them to him.

She glanced over at Rocco. He hadn't moved since he'd tumbled into the cab.

Who had he said *I love you* to when he didn't mean it? That Wickham woman? Something had happened between them. That was obvious.

Still, the man must have loved at some point. Really loved. He had plenty of good examples in his life to look to. She'd met his family only briefly in the paddock—his parents, grandparents, and sister. They all seemed lovely, and it was clear they adored him.

And then there was Sofia and Beatrice. Nico sighed, getting a warm and fuzzy feeling; one she'd learned never to allow after her grandfather had died; a feeling she'd reserved only for Charles and Templeton.

Charles is right. There is some kind of perverted psychology at work in my brain. Why admit to those things? Now he knows things about me.

He knows things.

Thinking about those things, she cringed.

She'd been handcuffed. In bed. He must be thinking she's a sexual deviant. Better that than the truth.

Maybe if she'd just stopped there, she might not feel like the earth was shifting beneath her feet, and at any moment it might split and she would fall into a dark hole that had no end.

At this rate, she wouldn't have to wait for Mickey to expose her past.

She glanced over. His lips were slightly parted, strands of his hair brushing his shadowed cheek. It was true, he pouted. She could see the child in him now. She could see it when he'd told her that story about when he fainted. When they'd talked about GoGo squeeZ.

And she could see something else.

She could see herself falling for him.

What a cruel twist of fate that the annoying, arrogant, asshole, prick should turn out to be . . .

So. Damn. Lovable.

Who was she kidding? She knew why she'd admitted to those things. It was the safe move, the smart move. She'd done it to stop the falling before it was too late, before she got in too deep.

There was no chance after tonight. If there'd ever been one to begin with.

She gazed out at the passing landscape. The trees looked black, as though they'd been carved out of the dark sky.

"It's cold," he muttered.

"Sorry." She hastily rolled up the window.

"How much farther do we have to go?"

"I don't know. I can ask the driver."

He shook his head. "Never mind. Doesn't matter."

His head lolled to the side, stopping when it hit her shoulder. He made no attempt to lift it, and they rode the rest of the way in silence.

Nico struggled getting him out of the cab and guiding him up the steps and into the lobby. Once there, she managed to steer him to the elevator, although it took some time given they didn't travel as the crow flies. The same was true as they stumbled out of the elevator and headed to his door.

"Do you have your key card?" she asked.

His only response was to stagger backward and use the wall to prop himself up.

"You have it, right?"

He leaned toward her. "Have what, sweetheart? Just tell me what you want, and I'll give it to you. I'm good at that."

She chuckled. "You need to be wearing a fedora to talk like that."

He grinned. "Like what?"

"Like you're a character in a dime-store novel."

"You could have at least said Sam Spade or Philip Marlowe."

"I'm surprised you didn't include Bogie."

"Him too. Why not?"

"Well, then you'd need a Bacall."

"You'll do."

His eyes slipped like silky fingers, tracing every inch of her all the way down to her toes. "I'll give you the key card if you tell me one thing."

Her heart was pounding. "What?"

He stared into her eyes, and she felt as though his eyes, like hands, held her there. Maybe because she couldn't read them.

"Are you going commando now?"

Those words had the force of a hot wind, sweeping over every inch of her.

She swallowed. "No," she managed to say.

"Too bad."

Again, his eyes roamed her body. Only now when he did it, it didn't feel like silk. It felt more like a snake, a snake that could not only slither up and down but could enter her. If it wanted. Now that hot wind had become heavy, wet, and muggy.

"Why do women do that?" he asked.

"Do . . . what . . . ?" she ventured.

"You know."

She hesitated.

A kind of madman grin slithered up his cheek. "Why do women go commando?"

She felt air go in and out of her lungs. Okay, so she was still breathing.

"I—don't—know."

"Yes, you do. You do it. So, you must know why you do it."

She lowered her shoulders, confirming the fact that she could move and his eyes couldn't hold her to this spot like a pair of hands.

"Do you know why you do everything you do?" she asked.

"That's a slick move, answering my question with a question."

"You mean a slick move like changing the subject? Which is what you just did."

He laughed. "Yeah, like that."

She held out her hand. "Your key card?"

He stared at her palm. "You have small hands." He looked up. His eyes met hers. "You're small too, almost tiny." And then that snake slithered south. "Well, some of you."

She could feel Thelma and Louise hit the gas.

"I mean, you're not tall, and you have little hands and feet, and your waist is tiny, but other parts . . ." His eyes darted from her breasts to her hips. "Other parts. Aren't. Tiny."

She'd given up trying to squelch the inferno that was raging through her. A fire she feared made her cheeks look like two hot burners. Either that or like the cheeks of a scary clown.

"You're doing it again," she huffed.

"Am I? Guess I can't help myself."

He opened his arms, making it clear if she wanted that card, she was going to have to find it herself.

That night at Drink and Dive flashed before her.

She avoided his gaze as she reached into his jacket and dipped her fingers in his left pocket. Nothing. His breath rained down, smelling like warm caramel. She'd smelled bourbon on men before, but it had never smelled like this.

She slipped her hand into the right pocket and felt something stiff, plastic—a card. She was about to pull it out, but then her fingers touched a row of raised shapes.

He grinned. "Credit card."

Just then her hand brushed against something that wasn't rigid, paper—money.

"Do you want to make a wager? There's a sizeable sum there."

She quickly pulled her hand out and took a step back.

Grinning, he thrust his hips forward. "Would you like to start with the front or the back?"

Gritting her teeth, she exhaled.

Just get it over with already.

She thrust her hand down his left front pocket and froze.

There was nothing there. Well, no. Not exactly.

There was something there. But it wasn't his key card.

He groaned. "You remembered."

She blinked. "Wha-what?"

He put his lips to her ear. "That I hang left."

Had she remembered? She wasn't thinking about that when she'd— Was she?

She made a move to pull out her hand, but he placed his on top of hers.

"You haven't finished with this one yet. The pocket's deeper than that. You'll have to go farther," he said, his voice raspy.

Her hand slid down.

"That's nice," he murmured. "Anything worth doing, is worth doing—" He paused, staring at her.

She held her breath. It felt as though all available oxygen had been sucked into a vortex.

His brow wrinkled. "Something about this is familiar."

She quickly tugged to pull her hand out but only got about halfway. Her bracelet was stuck.

Not again.

She pulled. She pulled harder. And with each tug, she felt the space in that pocket get tighter.

"Hey," he said, "stop, you're going to rip—"

"Sorry."

He blinked, looking bemused. "What are you sorry for? Why did you stop?"

"You just told me to."

"Well that was stupid of me. Why the hell would I do that?"

She wanted to laugh. But she wanted to get her hand out of his pocket more. She would laugh. Later. When she told Charles, who would definitely laugh.

"Because I was going to rip your pants."

"That's okay. I don't mind."

Yeah, I know what it is you don't mind.

He dipped his own hand in the pocket and began stroking hers. "Let me see if I can help."

"How is this supposed to help?"

"I'm not sure yet. Maybe I can pull the bracelet from the material or thread its stuck on. But come closer so you're not tugging against the pocket so much."

She drew closer but kept her head down, doing her best to concentrate on the intricate pattern of the carpet.

Her heart was pumping in all the places it shouldn't—in her ears, she could hear it pounding; in her wrists, which made her hands tremble; even between her legs, where she could feel it throb.

Don't look up.

Don't.

Look.

Up.

But she did.

Her eyes met his. Her lips parted.

Could she do it? The way normal people did. Not as part of a con or pretending to be someone she wasn't.

Just her and him. Because she wanted to. Hopefully because he wanted to too.

Maybe he will.

I will. If he will.

And then suddenly her bracelet broke free. She blinked and hastily pulled out her hand, forcing him to do the same.

Once her hand was free, she took a step back.

Right about now, she was hoping for a 9.5 magnitude earthquake on the Richter scale. With any luck, a hole would open up under her feet and swallow her so she wouldn't have to face those eyes and that arrogant grin, not to mention that snake.

She remembered Charles telling her about a snake in Chile with both a slow- and fast-twitch tongue.

That's the one. That's the snake. The one with the slow- and fast-twitch tongue.

"I don't have a key card," he said matter-of-factly.

Nico's eye's ballooned. "What?"

Damn her voice. Even that trembled.

"I forgot it. But that's okay. I don't need it."

He stepped around her and punched some keys on a panel to the right of the door. She hadn't noticed the panel. She didn't have one for her room.

The door clicked, and he pushed it open. She turned on her heels and made a move to go, but he grabbed her wrist.

"Aren't you going to come in?"

"No."

Why did he want her to come in? Stupid question. After everything she'd revealed, why wouldn't he? She was here. She was available. And given what he'd learned about her, she was up for anything. Or just about anything. He was too drunk to think about the mess he might wake up to. Too drunk to realize she was a member of his team and all the possible things that could go wrong were they to hook up for one night.

She tried to yank free, but he held on. She might not have minded if the pounding in her wrists wasn't so insistent. There was no way he couldn't feel it beneath his fingers. And she didn't like what it might be telling him. What she knew it was telling her.

"Not even to make sure I make it to my bed safe and sound?"

"I don't think we have to worry about that."

He pouted. "You won't worry?"

A laugh that sounded more like a snort escaped her lips. "Of course not."

"Not even just a little?"

She stared into his eyes. He had to be joking. But he didn't look it—or sound it.

"It's nice to have someone worry about you," he said.

She felt her eyes prick. *No*, she told them.

You will not play misty now. Not when there's no mark and nothing to gain from it.

"Not that you want people you care about to worry," he said. "You don't. But still, it's nice that they do. Don't you think?"

She did.

But he had so many people to do that.

"You have plenty of people who worry about you," she said. "Your nieces, your sister, your parents and grandparents, Dario and Celeste. You don't need me."

"I guess." He looked down at the carpet and muttered. "But it'll be quiet with my nieces gone. Not a bad thing. But sometimes not a good thing." He looked up, trying to peer at her with glazed eyes. "You don't know what I'm talking about, do you?" He swayed right, and the door began to swing. He stuck his foot out just in time to catch it before it shut. "Quiet makes thoughts louder. Specially thoughts you don't want to be having. Specially not before you go to sleep."

"I understand."

He brightened. "You do?"

For some reason, looking at him now, she wanted to laugh. But then she thought he might think she was laughing at him. And she didn't want him to think that.

So, she nodded. "I do."

All too well.

He smiled just before his head fell forward, and he was back to staring at the carpet. Suddenly he looked up, and his eyes brightened. "There's leftover pizza."

When she hesitated, he added, "Oh right. Maybe not pizza."

He bit his lip.

She wished he wouldn't do that. His lips had mastered the Goldilocks principle. They weren't too thick. They weren't too thin. They were just right—perfect. And the upper lip, which he now had between his teeth, dipped in a dramatic way like a curve in the road that showed you something wholly unexpected once you got around it. Something that could make your palms sweat, your heart stop, and maybe even make you gasp for breath.

Suddenly, he snapped his fingers with his other hand. "Chocolate. There's chocolate. Chocolate. And more chocolate. There's so much chocolate, you can put chocolate on chocolate. And more than one kind of chocolate."

She didn't want to, but damn it, she couldn't stop herself. She smiled.

She stopped pulling against him.

"We didn't eat all the chocolate?"

He shook his head. "Uh-uh. I have some stashed away—in three different hiding places. I have to when those two Tasmanian devils are around."

Her smile broadened. She couldn't stop it if she tried. And she wasn't trying. But she still couldn't seem to move one foot in front of the other.

"Where are the hiding places?"

"Uh-uh. I'm not going to give all my secrets away. Not without getting something in return."

She felt herself take a step forward as though gravity itself had pushed her.

"What kinds?" she asked as she took another step.

"Huh?"

"You said there were different kinds of chocolate."

He tugged her arm, gently pulling her closer. "You'll have to come in to find out."

"White chocolate?" she asked as she took yet another step.

He'd pushed the door wide open and was standing in the doorway.

"No. Do you like white chocolate?"

She shook her head. "No. Okay, I'll come in. But just for a minute. You can let go now."

He frowned. "Huh?"

She glanced down at his hand around her wrist.

"Oh."

He let go, and she entered.

"White chocolate's not really chocolate," he said as the door shut behind her. "Why do they even call it chocolate?"

He's. So. Sweet.

Is he really?

This sweet?

He grinned with hooded eyes as he brushed past her. "Don't worry, I don't have any handcuffs in the bedroom."

Apparently not.

CHAPTER TWENTY-TWO

ROCCO AND NICO

Rocco stuffed another piece of chocolate in his mouth and watched Nico as she examined the box. He had more than one question he wanted to ask her. He'd start with the one she was most likely to answer—*or at least answer truthfully*, he thought.

"How do you do that?" he asked after licking his fingers free of chocolate.

"Do what?" she asked.

She was still surveying the box.

"Do you like dulce de leche?" he asked.

"Yes," she exclaimed, nodding with energy.

"This one," Rocco said, taking a piece of dark chocolate out of its black paper cup and handing it to her. "How do you drink like that and look like you do? I mean, not be shitfaced like me."

She bit into the chocolate. "I've had a lot of practice."

What did she mean?

"Where'd you grow up?" he asked.

"Who says I grew up?"

He grinned. "Good answer, but you didn't answer my question."

She hesitated, but then shrugged.

"No one place really. We moved around a lot."

"So, you grew up a nomad. A gypsy."

"Something like that."

"Okay, so how about this one: Why?"

That got her to look up.

She frowned. "What?"

"Why race? When you were talking with the photographer during the photoshoot. You never said."

■ ■ ■

So, he'd been in the room.

She remained silent.

"You don't want to tell me."

That's right. I don't.

"Okay," he said, "well if you won't tell me, then at least you can tell me the truth about the drinking—the whole truth."

"Okay," she said. "I'll let you in on a little secret."

"Come closer," he whispered, "so I can hear."

"You don't have to whisper," she said.

He continued to whisper. "You said it was a secret. Come closer."

She was already close enough. She could smell the bourbon, caramel, and chocolate on his breath. She shivered when she felt his breath tickle her flesh.

"Are you cold?" he whispered.

She shook her head.

"Come closer."

She inched forward but quickly stopped.

His lips were only a few inches away from hers.

"That's close enough," she said. "Any closer, and I'll be behind you."

"Not possible. 'What's behind you doesn't matter.' You know who said that?"

She knew. What she didn't know was why he'd said it. What did he mean by it?

Just remember, he's drunk. He doesn't know what he's saying.

"Enzo Ferrari," she responded.

He grinned. "You're right, but that's too loud."

She blinked. "Does your head hurt?" she whispered.

"No. Does yours?"

She shook her head. Even for a conversation with a drunk, this was loopy. "You should rest," she whispered.

She made a move to go, but he grabbed her wrist.

That hand must have made a pact with that snake. She felt that reptile slithering over the entire square footage of her skin.

Slithering over everything.

Every. Thing.

"You can't go yet," he muttered. "You haven't told me the secret."

He took his other hand and opened hers, grazing her palm with his finger.

Slow-twitch-fast-twitch-slow-twitch-fast-twitch-slow-twitch-fast-twitch.

What is the name of that snake in Chile?

He looked up at her. "Are you okay? You look like you did in Barcelona when you looked like you might faint."

She stiffened. "I told you I don't faint."

He grinned. "That's right. That's me. I'm the one who faints."

She dropped her chin to hide her smile.

He stared back at her palm, running his finger back and forth, her flesh shivering in its wake.

"Your hands are small." He looked up at her. "Did you know that?"

You just told me that.

If he can't even remember that, he won't remember any of this.

"So I've been told. Now please give me back my hand."

"Not until you tell me the secret."

She sighed. "I didn't drink as much as you."

"Yes, you did. You had the same number of rounds as the rest of us. And you drank to a lot of the never-have-I-evers I did. That surprised me."

She felt her heart start to pound but not in a good way. "Why? Because I'm a woman?"

"Maybe."

At least he was honest.

She sighed. "It may have looked to you like I was drinking as much as you were, but I wasn't. Whenever I went to buy a round, I got Coke for myself."

"But Coke is darker than scotch, and it has bubbles."

"Not if you water it down, which is what I asked the bartender to do."

He grinned. "That's cheating."

She smiled. "It is."

"But what about when you weren't buying the round?"

"I didn't always drink it or drink as much."

"If you didn't drink it, where'd it go?"

"I spilled some on the table, which I quickly mopped up with a napkin."

"I never saw you do that."

She smiled. "I also put some in Dario's and Celeste's glasses when they weren't looking, when they got up to use the restroom."

"But not mine?"

"No, not yours."

He smiled. "That was nice of you."

"Niceness had nothing to do with it. They were drinking scotch like me. You were drinking bourbon. Also, you were more—observant."

"Oh."

"Please don't tell them."

"It's a secret. I can't."

"I even managed to spill some in Carolyn Wickham's purse."

His jaw dropped. "You did?!"

She nodded.

His eyes sparkled as he laughed, and then he gazed into her eyes.

It felt as though— *But no,* she thought. She wouldn't allow herself to think it, let alone act upon it.

Better to throw some cold water on the situation and retain her sanity.

"You can let go of my hand now."

"Okay, but you gotta do one more thing."

She narrowed her eyes, suspicious. "What?"

"Come on," he said, dragging her behind him as he headed down the hallway.

She dug in her heels.

He stopped and turned around but still had yet to let go of her hand. She was surprised his hold could be so firm and not hurt.

"Don't worry," he said, that wicked grin on his face, "I'm not going to jump you, if that's what you're thinking."

His response surprised her. Did it also disappoint her? *No,* she thought emphatically. He was drunk. Really drunk. If they slept together, the best she could hope for was that he wouldn't remember it. Because if he did, he was sure to regret it.

He resumed walking down the hallway, pulling her after him, clearly thinking his response adequate.

"Then why . . . ?" she asked but stopped.

She was going to ask why were they going to his bedroom?

But when she looked around, she saw they were already there.

CHAPTER TWENTY-THREE

NICO

"Tell me a story," he said.

Of all the things Nico had been imagining . . .

This.

Was not one of them.

"My grandmother always told me a story when I wasn't feeling well."

She frowned. "You were feeling well enough to eat half a box of chocolates."

"Probably why I'm not feeling good now." He grinned. "But even if I was feeling okay, she would tell me a story before I went to sleep. And if she wasn't around to do it, my mother or one of my aunts would."

Nico chuckled. "It sounds like you grew up in a Fellini film."

He grinned. "Like in *Eight and a Half*."

Exactly, thought Nico. *A beautiful boy with a harem of women fawning over him.*

"And did they call you emir?" she asked, her tone sardonic.

His eyes flashed as he shook his head. "The little prince."

That explains a lot.

"I can't think of a story," she said, trying to pull her hand away.

He placed his other hand over hers, holding on with both hands. "Make one up. I know you can. I heard you do it with my nieces."

Her brow furrowed.

How is it possible to look pleading and arrogant at the same time?

Sighing, she gazed out the window opposite them. The trees were black set against a deep and dark purple sky. Her eyes drifted out beyond the walls of the garden below, beyond the racetrack, even beyond the cities of Monza, Milan, and Lake Como, flying north until she reached the Italian Alps. It was there her story would take place.

Still gazing out the window, she began.

"Once upon a time . . ."

She paused, glancing down at his hands clasped over hers.

He let go, jumped onto the bed, and shut his eyes.

Charles is never going to believe this. I'm seeing it with my own eyes, and I don't believe it.

"Once upon a time, at the foot of Mount Bianco, there was a kingdom, very remote and hidden deep within a circle of jagged stone and sharp cliffs. It was quiet there, and the people were left to themselves. Because the journey there was both difficult and dangerous, there were never any visitors.

"There in the kingdom, life was peaceful, and the people were happy. They were ruled by a benevolent king and queen, who had only one son—the little prince. The little prince was beloved by all who saw him. He was kind and generous."

"And handsome," he interjected.

"No," she replied, "not handsome."

His eyes flew open. "He wasn't handsome?"

"He was not. But his dearest friend was. They had grown up together as boys, and the little prince thought of the boy as a brother. He knew he could always rely on him for wise counsel. He was so beloved that when he grew up to be a man, he was knighted by the king and queen."

Rocco narrowed his eyes. "What is the name of this knight?"

Nico had to bite her lip to keep from laughing. "Dario."

Rocco made a face. "Okay, so he was a pretty knight."

"Indeed."

He sighed and closed his eyes.

"As I said, Knight Dario was very handsome. All the ladies of the court pined for him, longing for him to cast even one glance their way. He was known far and wide as the handsomest, prettiest knight who had ever lived."

Rocco's eyes flew open. "Is this going to be a story about the pretty knight or the little prince?"

Nico folded her arms and waited. Finally, he huffed and shut his eyes.

"But an astute eye might get tired of looking at handsome Knight Dario because his face was always the same, unlike the little prince's, which was always changing. One could never grow tired of looking at his face. Though not pretty like Knight Dario's, it was far more interesting."

She looked down to see him with one eye open, grinning. He quickly shut it when she caught him.

"All the women of the court fawned over the little prince. They were eager to bathe him and feed him when he was a baby; they combed his hair and dressed him. Even when he grew up to be a young man, that never changed."

"Even as a man?" Rocco said, grabbing a pillow. "This story is getting interesting."

Nico chuckled.

"They never tired in their efforts to make the little prince happy. They cooked him whatever he fancied, always trying to make the baby, the boy, and finally the young man happy. For they had never seen a boy more wonderful than he. Even though the king was generally known to be wonderful himself, they thought his son, the little prince, had surpassed him."

"It's good to be the prince," Rocco said.

"Indeed. Everyone who looked upon him thought he had sprung from the mountain itself. For in his face and body and character he carried the mountain with him.

"He had a face that looked as though it had been carved from stone. His cheekbones formed a bold precipice on which to hang his flesh. The descent from there to the hard rock that was his jaw was a perilous one. There was nothing subtle about him except for his eyes."

Nico's eyes drifted from the window down to Rocco's face.

Her breath shuddered in her rib cage as she saw him looking up at her. But he quickly shut his eyes when her gaze met his.

She waited a moment before she continued.

"While his face and body told the story of the mountain, his eyes told another story, a secret he kept hidden: his desire to see what lay beyond it. It would have pained the king and queen as well as the people of the kingdom to know this, so he kept it to himself. And because it was a secret"—Nico cast a sidelong glance at Rocco—"whenever he spoke of it, it was always in a whisper and only to himself.

"No one had ever ventured outside the kingdom. Why would they? They had everything they'd ever need and want. They were ruled by a magnanimous king and queen, and when they were gone, they knew the little prince would be as generous and kind to them as his father and mother had been.

"But the little prince had this restless desire. It was a mystery to him where it had come from, and because no one ever spoke of such a thing, he thought this desire must be a sin. The desire made him anxious. It weighed upon him. It was as though he had shackles around his ankles, and with every passing day those shackles became heavier because with every passing hour another massive link had been bound to the chain and thus to him—so that the chain of that desire became a heavy burden indeed.

"He discovered that the only way to release those shackles—even if only for a moment—was to race. And so he did. And no matter with whom he raced, he was always the fastest. Even pretty Knight Dario couldn't beat him. For Dario was too pretty for his own good. Many a lady would faint at the sight of him as he ran past them, and being the gallant knight he was, he could not help but stop to revive them. And since reviving them required a kiss, it was not unusual for the lady to require much kissing before she came to."

Rocco laughed.

"But after a while, the little prince began to slow down. He was still the fastest in all the land, but not as fast as he once was. They soon discovered it was because of his head, which had begun to grow in size and become quite heavy. At first, the queen thought it was because of his diet, then they thought perhaps it was the heat that was making his head swell."

Rocco's eyes popped open. "Is this going to have a happy ending?"

Nico hesitated. "I don't know."

He sat up. "Well it's a fairy tale, isn't it?"

"I hadn't really thought about it."

"You began with *Once upon a time*. That means it's a fairy tale. So, it has to have a happy ending."

"Is that some kind of law?"

"I think it is. In fact, I'm sure it is. I think I read it somewhere. I just can't remember where."

Nico sputtered as a laugh escaped her lips. But she quickly stopped when she saw the look on his face.

He looked almost serious.

"Not all fairy tales have happy endings," she said.

"Name one that doesn't."

Nico thought a moment. "Snow White."

"What do you mean? The prince revives Snow White with a kiss, and he takes her to the castle where they live happily ever after. The end."

"But that isn't the end. The queen is punished. They put shoes made of iron in the fire, and she's forced to wear them and dance until she drops dead. So, it's not a happy ending for the queen."

Just then the bells from the cathedral began to ring.

"It's midnight," he said.

"Time for you to go to sleep," she said, taking an intentionally light tone.

"What about the story? You didn't finish."

"I guess you'll just have to be left in suspense." She turned toward the door. "If you even remember it," she muttered, not intending for him to hear.

"I'll remember," he said. "By the way, I lied tonight when we were playing that drinking game."

"Good night," she said, hurrying out of the bedroom.

She'd lied too, but she wasn't about to admit it. Especially not to him.

Whatever he'd lied about, it wasn't what she'd lied about.

And then she recalled what Carolyn Wickham had said as she sat down.

Bottoms up, darling.

She'd said it with such confidence. Like she knew. The same way Celeste had known about Dario. But Rocco didn't drink.

She realized then that they had lied about the same thing—having a sexual dream about someone sitting at that table.

For Rocco, that someone was Carolyn Wickham. But for Nico, that someone had been him.

CHAPTER TWENTY-FOUR

ROCCO AND NICO

Rocco stood on the terrace, leaning against the balustrade and gazing up at the sooty ivory stone of the Berlusconi's villa, his eye drifting to the top floor and the covered corridor—the loggia adorned with purple bougainvillea.

He turned around and faced the lake, inhaling the heady, sultry scent of jasmine, wisteria, and freesia that ornamented the villa in the multi-tiered gardens below.

The sky had slipped from a violet twilight to a deep purple, and the lake's surface shimmered in the moonlight.

To the north lay the Tremezzina Bay, to the south the Isola Comacina. Farther in the distance were the verdant mountains, and farther still the snowy alpine peaks and Mount Bianco, where the story Nico had begun telling him took place.

He felt a hand on his back and turned around to see Dario.

"Well," Rocco said, "if it isn't Sir Lancelot. You know I'll have to leave in a bit for Carnival. My nieces are expecting me."

Dario nodded. "Too bad it turned out to be on the same night. You'll have to go back to the hotel and change."

"Why?"

Dario blinked. "You're not going to go like that."

"Why not?"

"Well, the laced-up tunic, suede vest, and boots might not be so bad. But that wig and moustache? If you were wearing a snug T-shirt and jeans, you'd look like a seventies porn star."

Rocco took a step back and pulled out his sword. "'Thinking of using Bonetti's Defense against me, are you?'"

Dario rolled his eyes. "I never know how to respond when you quote that stupid movie."

"Stupid?" Rocco took a couple more steps back and began swiping the sword through the air.

"You do realize you're taking on a knight." Dario tapped his own sword hanging from his hip.

"And you, sir, are taking on a Spanish fencer and henchman to the Sicilian criminal Vizzini. Prepare to die!" Rocco cried as he lunged forward.

Dario staggered back, his tongue lolling out of his mouth as he gripped the stone balustrade but then immediately righted himself. "I can't go down any farther. Celeste will be pissed if I do any damage to this costume."

Rocco laughed. "So, Lancelot is afraid of Guinevere."

"He is."

Both stood looking out at the placid, silent lake with the sounds of laughter, music, and tinkling ice in cocktail-filled glasses drifting out onto the terrace.

Finally, Dario spoke. "I've been meaning to talk to you about last night. You drank pretty heavily after . . ."

Rocco placed his hand on his cousin's shoulder. "I'm okay. We both know Carolyn was trying to rattle me. Don't worry. She didn't."

Dario nodded. "You know, I think she might be the one who's rattled. Her precious Anker might be atop the leaderboard now, but if you can keep performing like you did at Monza, I think you can take him—even win the whole thing. Monaco's next."

Rocco sighed. "Monaco."

"You know you can win it. You've done it before. Carolyn knows it too."

"Did you notice how rude she was to Nico?"

"Nico's probably used to it. She hasn't exactly been welcomed with open arms by everyone on the circuit."

Dario gave Rocco a significant look.

"Do you mean me?" Rocco asked. "That was in the beginning. I know I was an ass. Anyway, Nico paid her back. She poured some of her drink in Carolyn's purse when she wasn't looking."

Dario's eyes ballooned. "She didn't."

Rocco grinned. "She did."

Dario bent over and the two of them roared with laughter.

After the laughter subsided, Rocco exhaled. "She's an odd character, don't you think?"

"Nico? She's not bad. Celeste really likes her."

"Don't you?"

"Of course I do. I didn't say I didn't."

"Well, I didn't either."

"Okay, but you said she was *odd*."

"She is. But I meant that in a good way. She's . . . interesting. Different."

Dario peered at Rocco. "Last night—"

"What?"

"Things are going so well now."

"Yeah?"

"I just want to be sure last night didn't change things."

Rocco frowned. "Why would they?"

Dario shrugged.

"Nothing's changed," Rocco insisted. "Not for me."

Dario nodded. "Good. And not for her. I think. I hope."

"What are you getting at?" Rocco demanded.

"Just, you were pretty drunk, and you left together."

"We're staying in the same hotel, and I needed someone to help me home, drunk as I was."

Dario nodded. "Okay."

"We didn't sleep together if that's what you're wondering."

Dario sighed. "I figured as much."

Not that it's any of your business, Rocco thought, feeling annoyed by Dario's obvious relief.

"It's just those magazine photos and the one on social media and some of Celeste's comments. I mean, I can see what she's saying. It seems like there might be an attraction there."

"There's no attraction!"

Dario blinked. "Okay. Okay."

Why did I say it like that?

Rocco drew a deep breath. "Look, I told you what happened with that one on social media. It wasn't at all the way it looks. And as for that photoshoot. I would look at any woman like I looked at Nico in those photos if the woman looked like Nico did in that dress."

Dario sighed. "Yeah. Sure. Okay."

But in some of those photos, she was wearing her racing suit.

Dario seemed to have forgotten that fact, and Rocco wasn't about to remind him.

He looked down at his hands and thought of hers. How small and delicate they were.

Would it really be so bad if we did? Well, yes, if things didn't go well. I mean, we're teammates. But what if they did go well? Would it be so bad then?

Thinking about her hands made him wonder what it would be like to kiss her. Would her kisses be like her hands or more like her dark eyes and that hair? What would she be like in bed? When he thought of the things he'd discovered about her during that drinking game, he thought she must be wild in bed.

Rocco blinked when he saw Dario with an uneasy look, staring at him.

Laughing, he shoved him. "You've got nothing to worry about. I'm not stupid enough to start something with her. We're teammates. It would be a big mistake."

"Huge," Dario added.

"Besides, even if I tried, she wouldn't go for it. My nieces told her I called her a cockroach."

Dario burst out laughing. "What? When did—"

"Dario! Rocco!" Celeste cried, waving them over.

■ ■ ■

Nico entered the grand ballroom. The ivory and pale blue walls looked like works of art themselves. Every doorway and window was framed by swirling stucco delicate as lace and frescoes that looked as though they'd been carved from the walls rather than painted on them. A series of windows framed the lake, and in the center were French doors leading out onto a terrace.

She scanned the crowd of colorful characters—women dressed in flowing scarves, rich tapestries, and velvet. Nico eyed one dressed as Scheherazade, another Queen Anne Boleyn joined by a man dressed as King Henry VIII. There were men dressed in suits of armor, as pirates, and even a couple in suits looking very much like the characters from *Men in Black*. But no Guinevere and Lancelot. She didn't know what Rocco was dressed as. Perhaps she was looking at him right now and didn't know it.

Do I want to see him?

No. Not exactly.

That was in part true. And in part false.

She did want to see him—but so badly, it was unsettling. The result being that she wanted very much not to want to see him.

Adjusting her wig of dark rakish curls and making certain the moustache she was sporting was secure, she turned around. She spotted a hallway on her right, approached it, walked up a couple steps, and stopped almost immediately when she felt a hand on her shoulder.

"Seen the cockroach yet?" Dario said with a laugh.

Nico froze. He was standing directly behind her.

"By the way, don't go asking any questions about the stuff she revealed last night during that drinking game. Celeste told me to tell you that. Not that you would—but, don't. You said it yourself, she's a bit odd, and who knows what the rest of the story is."

He must think I'm Rocco.

She and Rocco must be wearing a similar costume—at least similar enough from the back. She was wearing padding in her shoulders, and her platform boots made her appear taller. She'd also walked up a couple steps to enter the hallway up ahead. Dario must not have noticed.

"Hey, look, I'm still a little worried. Not about you. But about her. I mean, what if Nico gets ideas—you know, the wrong ideas? That could make things awkward. Maybe even get in the way of your performance."

Nico stiffened. She wished she'd turned around immediately when he'd come up to her. Even if there would have been an embarrassing moment because of that cockroach comment, Nico could have explained that she knew about it and Rocco had apologized.

Too late now. There's no way I can turn around now.

"I'm just glad nothing happened last night," Dario went on. "Like you said, it would have been a real boneheaded move. I never even thought it until Celeste mentioned it. But you know Celeste gets these ideas into her head. She's closer to Nico, and I'm guessing she got the idea from her. Just know, the girl might have a crush on you; she probably does. Nothing serious, mind you. She'll get past it. As long as you don't encourage her. And definitely don't act on it.

"Now as for that blonde you were just introduced to, Tiffany Bright, you'd be a fool to let that one slip through your fingers. You're not the only one whose jaw dropped to the floor when she entered the room. She's one fine mermaid. And she's definitely interested. I would hit that if I were you. You have the perfect getaway to keep it from developing into anything serious. We leave for Monaco in a few days."

Nico could feel him turn as he removed his hand from her shoulder.

He's probably looking for that blonde.

"Dario!"

He patted her shoulder. "There's my dad. Better move quick if you want a chance with Tiffany. She's got a crowd of guys chatting her up now."

Nico waited and then glanced tentatively over her shoulder. Dario was nowhere in sight.

She needed to leave. Now.

You can't just disappear without saying anything.

I'll tell Celeste I don't feel well.

She would catch a taxi to the ferry and pray she hadn't missed the last one.

Nico looked anxiously around the room.

Where the hell is Celeste?

Maybe she was out on the terrace. She rushed across the room, weaving her way frantically through the crush of bodies until she reached the French doors. Once there, she opened them and stepped out.

The terrace was empty except for one lone figure who had his back to her, gazing out at the lake.

I'll text Celeste.

She'd have to. She had to get out of here now.

Suddenly the figure turned around, and she was faced with the mirror image of herself.

He took a couple of steps forward and brandished his sword. "'My name is Inigo Montoya. You killed my father. Prepare to die.'"

Her eyes ballooned. "Rocco?"

He stood up straight. His sword fell with his arm to his side as he cocked his head. "Nico?"

Fuck-a-dilly-dewdrop.

■ ■ ■

Rocco approached her, looking her up and down. "Are you supposed to be . . . Inigo Montoya?"

She lifted her chin. "As you can see."

She sounded, what? Annoyed? Perturbed?

Something.

"Why do you say it like that?"

"Like what?"

Rocco shrugged.

She did likewise, and he wondered if she was mimicking him.

"Maybe," she hissed, "because you asked like that."

"Like what?"

"Like you were shocked."

"Well, aren't you? I mean, what are the odds two people would be wearing the same costume? Especially when it's a character from a film that's what, something like thirty-six years old."

"It was a book first, and the book is something like fifty years old."

He lowered his brow. "I know that."

"You aren't just surprised that you found another person wearing the same costume, you're surprised that it's a woman."

"I didn't say that," he insisted.

Although, he had thought it.

"You didn't have to," she hissed.

He took a step toward her. Those dark eyes were perfect for Montoya. The kind of eyes he would imagine the character having.

"You're not exactly difficult to read," she spat.

"I'm not, am I? Okay, suppose you tell me what I'm doing outside here on the terrace?"

"Well that's obvious. You're talking to me, pretending that your surprise that I'm wearing the same costume has nothing to do with the fact that I'm a woman."

The corner of his lip quivered, and he quickly bit it to keep from grinning.

"All right, then, tell me what I was doing before you came out onto the terrace."

"I said you were easy to read. That doesn't mean knowing everything about you like some kind of mystic or fortune teller. But if I had to guess, I would say you were thinking about which of the women in that ballroom you planned to take back to your hotel room."

Now he did grin. She was wrong.

"If I had to guess," she said, "I would say you've chosen Tiffany Bright."

His brow wrinkled as he narrowed his eyes. Why had she chosen that particular woman? Had the thought crossed his mind when he'd been introduced to her? Yes. But it had left immediately after.

Nico looked smug. "I thought so."

What made her so certain? And so angry?

They'd done well in Monza. They were getting along fine. And now. This.

He plastered a smug smile of his own on his face. "Now that would be a good choice. She is very . . . very . . ."

"Very," Nico said.

Rocco grinned and growled, "Indeed."

"Humph. I told you, you're easy to read."

"Ah, but that wasn't what I was thinking about. Not that the thought hadn't occurred to me earlier in the evening."

"Well there you are."

"And what about you? There are some decent-looking guys in that room. Unless, of course, you prefer women. Please don't tell me we're going to need to brandish these swords for real and fight for the heart of one Tiffany Bright. Perhaps that's why you mentioned her. Are you, by chance, interested in her . . . for yourself?"

"No, you needn't worry. I'm not interested in anyone in that room, man or woman."

"Why not? Someone at home?"

"No."

"Well, then, why not? I mean, it's the perfect opportunity. You can have a pleasant evening, and then you have the perfect excuse not to complicate things. We'll be leaving for Monaco in a couple days."

"If I were looking for something like that, I would hardly call the evening I would be embarking on *pleasant*."

His breathing halted and then sputtered, sounding hoarse and ragged to his own ears just as a warmth that felt thick like honey began to spread between his legs.

Looking into her dark eyes, he had the sudden thought that she was telling the truth—that a night with her wouldn't be *pleasant* because that was much too tame a word.

She tossed her head. "But as I said, I'm not interested in anyone, so you don't need to worry about any competition from me."

"Why are you being so combative?"

She held out her arms. "I'm Inigo Montoya."

He laughed despite himself. But he quickly stopped. He wasn't about to let her off that easily.

"Costume aside. It's like you're looking for a fight."

"We've been fighting for years online. Nothing new. Nothing's changed."

But something was new. Something had changed.

He shook his head. "You know that's not true. Okay, it was true. But I haven't given you any reason today, yesterday, frankly since we were locked in that room in Barcelona, to be mad at me. At least I don't think so. But you're coming at me as though I have. You're making a point of being nasty and disagreeable."

"Nasty and disagreeable? That should hardly surprise you—cockroaches generally are."

Rocco frowned. "I told you I never called you that."

"Well, it's obvious you lied."

"I didn't lie."

"Should we ask Dario?"

"Dario?" And then it suddenly occurred to Rocco. "Did Dario just tell you that? Really? I can't believe he did that!"

"What? Tell me the truth?"

"No. I told him my nieces thought I'd called you a cockroach."

"Why would you tell him that? To have a good laugh at my expense?"

"No!" He hesitated. He didn't exactly want to tell her any of the rest of his conversation with Dario. "I only told him about that to explain to him that you would never—"

"Never what?"

"That there was no danger of—"

He huffed. *Just say it already.*

"I told him so that he would know you'd reject any move I made. If I did make a move. Which I have no intention of doing. So, you don't have to worry about it."

"What do you mean, 'make a move'?"

"You know what I mean. A move. Like the kind you think I want to make on Tiffany Bright."

"Why would you make a move on me?"

"I wouldn't."

"Well, then, why were you and Dario talking about it?"

"Because you took me home, and I was drunk. So, he was concerned. That's all."

"This wouldn't even be an issue if I were a man."

Rocco laughed. "No, it wouldn't. I'm not interested in men."

"It's not just that. I'm"—she placed one finger on her chin, tilted her head, and raised her eyes to the stars as though she were thinking hard—"odd." She turned back to him, snapping her fingers. "That's it! Odd!"

Without giving it much thought, he shrugged. "That's true. You are."

Her eyes sprung open wide. Maybe they'd grown even darker. Although he couldn't see how that was possible.

"I mean that in a good way."

"Odd? In a good way?" she sneered.

"Yes. As in. Unique. Different. Hell, you have a pet rat. Not to mention the fact you're one of only five women to have ever driven Formula 1. And in terms of the racing you're doing, actually more like one of three—you, Maria Teresa de Filippis, and Lella Lombardi. In fact, now that I think of it, you're probably really only comparable to Lella."

She didn't say anything and turned her gaze to the lake. But he could feel her anger coming down. It felt as though she'd lowered her sword.

Why had she used that word, *odd*? She must have overheard him talking with Dario.

He drew a quick but deep breath.

"Look, cut Dario some slack. I mean, it's not that difficult to understand why he might go there. Why he might have some concern. I mean, about me, making a move."

She turned her attention back to him. She was staring at him as though he were speaking a foreign language.

She couldn't be that clueless. Could she?

He sighed. "You possess certain characteristics that might, you know."

"That might what?"

"That might. Interest. A man. In that way."

"Oh really."

"I said might; I didn't say they did. And anyway, even if they did, I wouldn't—and you wouldn't. It would be stupid. To. Do. That."

"Right. Stupid. You're right, of course I would." She paused. "I mean, I wouldn't."

"You would or you wouldn't?" he heard himself asking as though it were someone else speaking.

Nico glared at him. "I suppose you're accustomed to women just falling at your feet. I hope you make certain to catch them before they fall completely."

He chuckled. "They do. And I do."

The French doors opened, and the sound of laughter floated out onto the terrace as a couple of people stepped out and walked over to the other side of the balcony.

He looked at his watch. "I have to get going," he muttered. "Carnival."

Should he? Probably not. But he found himself wanting to. "You want to come?"

She didn't respond.

He grinned. "Sofia and Beatrice will be there."

She smiled. "They will?"

He grabbed her hand, pulling her after him.

They ran down the winding staircase and stopped beside a speedboat tethered to the dock. He let go of her hand, undid the rope, and put his foot along the side of the boat to hold it.

"Hop on."

"I didn't say I'd go."

"You didn't?"

"No."

"Well you didn't say *no*."

"So?"

"Exactly."

"Exactly what? You aren't seriously saying my not saying *no* means I said *yes*."

"Look, I saw your face when I mentioned Sofia and Beatrice. You said *yes*."

"So, you're a mind reader now?"

He thought a moment. "Yeah, that's right. When it comes to you . . . I suppose I am."

She was gritting her teeth, which made it difficult to hear what she muttered. But he paid close attention. And he got it.

"Man, that little prince has nothing on you."

He narrowed his eyes, and she did likewise.

"Is this even your boat?" she demanded.

"No, I'm just going to borrow it."

"You mean steal it."

"No, I mean borrow. Now, come on already." He paused. "Or maybe you're only daring on the track when you're behind the wheel."

She scoffed. "You think using some kind of reverse psychology is going to get me onto that boat?"

"I don't really think I need to get you on this boat because I think both you and I know you want to get on this boat."

"Oh, we do, do we? Well in that case, why even bother with talking at all? Why not just channel your inner Neanderthal, haul me over your shoulder like a sack of potatoes, and throw me onto the boat?"

She crossed her arms and glared at him.

Was that an invitation? Or a challenge? Maybe both.

She doesn't think I'd dare.

Suddenly, he got the uncomfortable feeling she'd read his thoughts just now.

In one quick move, he picked her up, slung her over his shoulder, and jumped on board.

Once he set her down, he turned his back to her with the intention of sitting behind the wheel and taking off.

That was easy. Almost too easy.

She wasn't saying anything. Not a word.

Probably shouldn't have done that.

Shit. He'd have to apologize now.

He turned around, prepared to do just that. But before he could utter even one word, her knee made contact with his crotch, and he doubled over.

CHAPTER TWENTY-FIVE

NICO AND ROCCO

Is he okay?

She should not—would not—feel bad.

I do not. Feel bad.

She sighed.

She did feel bad.

He was still hunched over. "What'd you do that for?" he grunted.

"Do you really need to ask?"

"You could have used words."

"So could you!"

A burst of breath surged from behind his gritting teeth. "Fair enough. But I didn't hurt you."

"Sorry," she muttered.

She was about to add in a cheeky tone *Do you want me to kiss it and make it feel better?* But then realized where *it* was. She felt her cheeks burn.

"Are you okay?" he asked, peering up at her with a concerned look.

That made her wonder what her face looked like.

"I'm fine." *Deflect*, she told herself. "You?"

He drew another deep breath and stood up, wincing slightly. "I'm okay." He paused, giving her a pointed look, and added, "Now." He sighed. "Look, if you don't want to come, that's fine. You can go back up to the party. Hey, you might still have a shot at Tiffany Bright."

She laughed. She didn't want to. Well, okay, maybe she did.

"I'll go. But next time, ask." She walked past him and sat in the passenger seat. "So, whose boat is this?"

"Dario's parents'," he said as he sat behind the wheel, started the motor, and they took off. "They know I'm taking it. We'll dock across the lake, where I have a car waiting. It's faster than driving around the lake. Carnival's in a small village north of here."

Nico gazed out into the distance, trying to catch the horizon, but the lake was like black satin and the sky like black silk. She couldn't tell where the one ended and the other began.

"Are you cold?" he asked.

"No, I'm fine."

The costume—heavy boots, pants, and cloak—kept her warm enough. But her cheeks bristled from the cold bite of the wind. She kept pressing her moustache to make certain it was still there. Glancing over at Rocco, she noticed he didn't bother with his. And it stayed put.

The silence between them felt awkward. She wondered if it felt that way to him. But then, he had something to occupy him—driving the boat. And he was good at it. Hardly surprising. Was there anything he wasn't good at? She thought a moment. Yes. Apologizing. He wasn't very good at that. And drinking. That too. These thoughts made her feel better. The man was not perfect.

She sighed.

How could he sit there this long without uttering even a word?

She needed to fill this silence. And then it came to her.

"Why Inigo Montoya?" she asked.

He turned to gaze at her and blinked. He looked surprised. She was surprised too. The question felt as though it had come out of nowhere. But once she'd asked it, she realized, it hadn't. She wanted to hear his answer.

He turned his attention back to the lake so that all she could see was his profile.

"Because he's loyal, trustworthy."

Good answer.

She could feel her heart begin to throb more insistently. She felt as though it were trying to tell her something. She just wasn't sure what.

What if it were telling her to stop, she thought, at the very moment she heard the sound of her own voice.

"I suppose you think only animals can be that, and possibly men."

"Huh?"

"You said as much. You said 'Animals don't go around showing you one face and then turn around to show the world another. They don't make you think you can trust them, only for you to find out you can't.'"

He turned to look at her. "You remember that?"

Now it was her turn to gaze out at the lake. She shrugged. "I remember lots of things."

"Yeah, well, that's true. About animals."

She gave him a sidelong glance."And when I went on to ask you whether or not people do that, you said women do."

She tried to read his profile. It was all she had to go on. The only thing she could make out was that it looked as though his jawline had turned so hard, it looked like stone. It reminded her of the little prince in that fairy tale she had made up.

"Well," he finally said, "maybe not all women. I was thinking of one woman in particular."

Nico nodded. "I see."

She turned her attention back to the lake, figuring that was as far as he would go and thinking she was just going to have to put up with the silence until they reached land. She could see it up ahead, but she couldn't tell how long it would take them to get there.

And then she heard his voice.

"She's married. And was married when we were—I was going to say *together*, but that's not exactly right. But we had a relationship. I didn't know she was married when I first met her. But I didn't stop seeing her once I found out. Let's just say the way I found out wasn't ideal. Although I suppose there isn't an ideal way to discover a thing like that. Still, this way was really nasty. That's why I said what I said about women."

"Okay."

"Okay? That's it?"

"What do you want me to say? So, you had an affair with a married woman. Maybe it's not the best thing to do, but it happens. She's the one who made a promise to the man, you didn't."

"It isn't just that."

He turned and stared at her. She could see he was searching for something, but she couldn't tell what.

"What?" she asked.

"I'm just wondering whether or not I should say any more."

"You don't have to. But of course, you know that. Let's just drop it."

He's wondering whether or not he can trust me. That's what he's really wondering.

He turned back to gazing at the lake. She did the same.

"She's part of the F1 world," he said.

"Oh."

"It's because of her I got my start racing Formula 1. She made it happen. She's the reason I jumped from F3 to F1."

Nico frowned, puzzled. And then she recalled their discussion in Barcelona. When he told her that he didn't feel as though his promotion to F1 was entirely based on merit. That he had an advantage other drivers didn't.

"Wait a minute, you aren't thinking you only got the position racing Formula 1 because you're good in bed?"

Rocco shrugged with a sly smile. "Well…"

Nico laughed. "Nobody's that good in bed, including you."

That smile deepened and his eyes twinkled. "Well…"

Rolling her eyes, Nico groaned. "Are you forgetting that you'd won the F3championship trophy—three years in a row—before you moved up to F1?"

"You know that?"

"Of course I know that. Everyone knows that."

"Yeah, that's true. I'm not even sure why I'm telling you this. Especially now, given the way you and I are dressed. The whole thing is absurd. Maybe I told you because looking at you right now is like looking in a mirror."

She smiled. "So, you feel like you're talking to yourself."

They burst out laughing.

Once the laughter subsided and was replaced with silence, Nico thought about what he'd just told her.

It has to be Carolyn Wickham. When Rocco moved up to F1, he drove for Blue Jet Lightning. Carolyn's married to the owner. That last round of

Never Have I Ever. The dream? Her suddenly showing up, telling him to drink. Because she knew—he had—dreamed—of her.

But Nico understood why he didn't drink.

No one other than Charles and Templeton would ever know about the dreams she'd had.

She glanced over at him and felt a sudden warmth course through her veins when she saw him staring back at her. His was a strange look. One she couldn't read. It made her wonder about the way she was looking at him. Recalling what Dario had said, she had the thought that her poker face had failed her and she must be wearing her heart on her sleeve. Why else would Dario be worried? Clearly, Celeste was too.

Only it wasn't exactly her heart, and it wasn't exactly her sleeve.

She turned away and looked out at the lake wondering how cold the water was. She was seriously considering jumping overboard.

Stop thinking about that dream. Something obviously shows on your face when you do. That's why he's looking at you with that strange expression.

There were things she wanted to ask him. How long had he and Carolyn been together? Did he still have feelings for her? How had it ended? When had it ended? But then he hadn't even referred to her by name. He hadn't wanted to share that. None of it was her business.

"And," she heard him say, "because it's my favorite movie."

She turned to him. "What?"

"You asked why Inigo Montoya."

"Oh." She smiled. "Mine too."

Grinning, he gave her a sly look. "That and the fact that I naturally identify with the man. I mean, he's the greatest of his generation when it comes to fencing, and I—well, with respect to racing. You understand."

Laughing, Nico shook her head.

Okay, so he wasn't really so annoying, or an asshole, or a prick right now. But he was still arrogant.

■ ■ ■

They were approaching the small village nestled between the mountains.

After docking the boat and picking up the car, they'd been quiet the entire drive.

That gave Rocco time to think.

Why had he grabbed her like he had and brought her with him?

He didn't want her to think he was trying to get away from her. But it was more than that. He didn't want to leave things as they were.

And what about him telling her as much as he did? About Carolyn? Even though he hadn't mentioned Carolyn's name.

He must trust her.

He wanted not to trust her. But he did. He could feel it in his bones.

Rocco parked the car on the outskirts of the medieval village and shut off the engine.

"Don't forget your gloves," he said, handing them to her.

She shoved them in her pocket, and he did likewise with his own.

There was no one around.

"It's not what I expected," she said. "It's so quiet."

"Just wait."

Suddenly, something smacked against the window.

Nico jumped. "What's that?"

Rocco laughed.

It was a hook hanging on the end of a long fishing rod. On the other end of the rod was a man, and behind him, a crowd of people laughing.

"What is he doing?" she cried.

"It looks like he's trying to catch us, fish us out of the car, and reel us in."

"What do we do?"

She looked genuinely frightened. Rocco bit his lip to keep from laughing. There was something childlike about her. Something he'd first noticed when they were locked in that room in Barcelona.

He peered out the window. "He seems a decent fellow. I'd hate to kill him." Shrugging, he ran his fingers over his moustache. "But then, I'm Inigo Montoya."

Nico burst out laughing.

He jumped out of the car, brandishing his sword, and the man backed away.

At first the man and the crowd were stunned and remained silent.

Rocco opened the passenger door and held out his hand. "Come on!"

Nico got out.

“There’s a pair of ’em,” someone yelled.

“Throw ’em back,” cried someone else.

Everyone laughed. The man with the fishing rod came running after them.

Rocco grabbed Nico’s hand. “Don’t let go. It can get pretty crazy, and it’s easy to get lost.”

They took off and didn’t slow to a walk until they’d reached the middle of the village. He led her through a crowd of people until they came to some musicians playing a lively song while people wearing colorful costumes, hats, and black masks danced.

“The people dancing are the Mascher,” he said.

“I thought you said we have to watch out for them.”

Just then the music stopped, and one of them pointed at Nico and Rocco.

“We do,” he said as a group of them came running toward them.

“Come on,” he cried, and they took off.

They turned a corner, and another group of Mascher jumped out at them.

“This way,” he called as he pulled Nico after him.

They turned left and then right, running through a maze of streets until they came back to the village square, which was swarming with people. Rocco carved a path through the mass of bodies, heading for the center, looking to lose themselves in the crowd.

Suddenly, his hand felt empty, and it dropped to his side. He turned around.

“Nico!” he shouted. “Nico!”

He pushed his way back through the bodies, retracing his steps, his heart beating with such force that he felt as though it had leapt outside him and was propelling him forward rather than his feet.

“Nico!”

“Rocco!”

He stopped and looked around.

“Nico! Where are you?”

Suddenly, he saw her hand waving back and forth above the heads in the crowd.

“I’m coming,” he shouted, running toward it.

Finally, he saw her standing with a group of women wearing masks and done up like old hags.

"There's a pair of them!" one of them shouted.

"More to go around!"

Some of them made obscene gestures.

He gripped her hand, yelling, "Don't let go!"

"You don't let go!"

"I promise I won't! But you have to promise if I have to throw you over my shoulder like I did before, you won't kick me in the balls!"

She laughed, but it sounded forced to his ears.

"I won't!"

He wanted to look into her eyes. See what was wrong. He felt sure something was. But there wasn't time.

They ran through the cobblestone streets, weaving their way through the crowd until finally Rocco ducked into a quiet alleyway and pulled her in after him.

She looked down at their hands, and he released his hold.

"Did I hurt you?" he asked. "I didn't want to lose you again."

She had her back up against a building. She looked . . . scared.

"Are you okay?" he asked. "What happened?"

"I don't know. It was one of those Mascher, I think. Someone grabbed my other hand and . . . I tried to pull away, but then you were gone."

"I'm sorry if they frightened you. You don't have to worry. Nothing bad will happen. It's all a part of it. I told you it was crazy. But you're okay, aren't you?"

She nodded. "I was just surprised, that's all."

"It's my fault. I should have held on tighter. But your hands."

He picked one up and stared at it.

She flinched, but she didn't pull away.

He suddenly realized hers had not been the only hand held above the heads in the crowd. But he'd known instantly which one was hers.

"I should have held on tighter," he said, still gazing at her hand as if he were speaking to it. "But I'm afraid I might crush them. They're so small. And delicate." He looked up at her. "Did you know that?"

She smiled. "So I've heard."

He sighed—relieved. She was okay.

She glanced down at the hand he was still holding. He let go.

Staring back at him, she suddenly smiled. "You look ridiculous!"

He grinned. "Well, if I do, then you do."

They burst out laughing until they were nearly breathless.

But not quite.

He felt a sudden overwhelming urge to take what little breath she had left from her.

He wanted to kiss her.

He blinked. It was absurd. He was staring at the mirror image of himself. And what a mirror image. She had on that ridiculous wig and that outlandish moustache.

I don't care. I want to kiss her.

Real. Bad.

It's those eyes, he thought, staring into them.

Suddenly, he liked the idea that they were so dark he couldn't see what lay ahead.

He fisted his hands. There was that itchy feeling again—the one he'd only ever felt before a race.

Until.

He felt as though there were only one remedy.

Kiss her.

Now.

Her lips parted.

She's waiting for you to.

He leaned forward, but before his lips reached hers, he heard the voices of those two Tasmanian devils.

"Uncle Rocco!"

CHAPTER TWENTY-SIX

ROCCO AND NICO

ROUND 8: RACE 8: MONACO

Rocco sat in the car, waiting for them to signal him onto the grid. The forecast had said no rain, but Rocco had grown skeptical when he watched a large swath of ominous gray clouds drifting this way. They grew darker the closer they got, and sure enough, there was a sudden downpour. So the race had been delayed. They were going to have to start on wet tires, and the teams had quickly gone to work changing them.

He'd been worried about what it would be like in the paddock with Nico after Carnival. But she acted as though nothing had happened. In fact, she'd done so immediately after his nieces had shown up. She was so convincing, he'd begun to wonder if anything actually had happened. Maybe he'd imagined it—all of it.

Had she known what he was about to do in that alleyway? Did she want him to? He thought she did. But she was difficult to read.

Sofia and Beatrice had gotten a big kick out of seeing Nico dressed as Inigo Montoya. Afterward, they'd told him they invited her to come with him during the upcoming three-week break in the racing schedule. He was going to visit his family in the small Italian village where he'd grown up. But she'd told them she couldn't. She'd made other plans.

He felt a hand on his shoulder. "Second row," Dario said. "Good position."

But not as good as first, Rocco thought.

The two drivers from Blue Jet Lightning were on the first row; he and Clarke were on the second—Clarke at #3 and Rocco at #4. Nico was starting from the fourth row at #7. It was her best starting position yet.

Qualifying was everything in Monaco. It was virtually impossible and a death wish to pass on the tight and twisting narrow circuit that took you through the streets of the principality. Passing a car was usually a guaranteed crash. That's if you could even manage to find enough space to attempt it.

Where you started the race was nine times out of ten where you finished. Rocco wasn't in a position to see the podium, let alone win the race.

The rain made it even more difficult.

But Rocco saw the rain as an advantage, one he intended to exploit. Never did a driver's ability behind the wheel matter more than at Monaco—and in the rain, that truth seemed absolute.

He'd raced here before in the rain and won. Anker and Clarke hadn't.

■ ■ ■

Nico gripped the wheel as she sat watching the rain. It was coming down harder now. What had begun as singular drops now looked more like a sheet of water splashed against a gray wall. The streets would be slick, the visibility—poor.

She'd never driven an F1 car in the rain.

At least things seemed okay between her and Rocco. She told herself that was a good thing even though she felt a pang in her heart when she did.

You couldn't have been thinking there was something there.

And yet she had thought there was a moment. Before his nieces showed up.

A moment? What moment? That he might kiss you? Dressed up as you were? Wearing that wig? That moustache?

Now she could see how absurd that was.

Besides, there was Mickey.

Was it him who pulled me away from Rocco at Carnival?

The person was wearing a black mask like the Mascher and had whispered something to her, but it was too noisy for her to make out the words. She was grateful some drunken men had stumbled into them and broken his hold on her so she could get away.

She drew a deep breath and exhaled so forcefully, her breath echoed and bounced off the shell of her helmet.

Was it possible Mickey would try to get at her by targeting someone else?

He would only do that if he thought she really cared about the person.

Nico sighed.

Where was the woman who'd been in command at Drink and Dive? She'd left her behind because she wanted to leave that entire life behind. But now she might have to rally her back.

That woman cared for no one. She was distant, cool, untouchable. There was no way anyone could or would think that woman cared for Rocco Vittori. Not Mickey. Not even Dario and Celeste.

She drew another deep breath.

Focus. Focus.

Any minute now she'd be pulling out onto the grid. This would be her first F1 race in the rain. And in Monaco of all places! The circuit was difficult enough as is. Still, she'd put in her best qualifying performance yet.

Rocco had to be disappointed starting from the second row and in fourth position. It was difficult to see how he could win this one. He might still have a chance at coming in third and mounting the podium. But the odds were against it. Still, if they could work together as a team it might happen.

She could do that. And she felt confident he could too.

■ ■ ■

Rocco was driving through the tunnel. Anker and Mendelsohn had made contact with each other again. They were pressing each other too hard, and neither one would make way for the other. They were acting like they were the only two in the race. Rocco knew what was driving them—the desire to come in first. They were just in front of Clarke, who was right ahead of him. No position change since the start of the race.

Rocco: Those two are driving like a couple of maniacs!
Race Engineer: Just focus on your own driving, Rocco. How's the grip?
Rocco: Holding steady. Has the rain let up at all?
Race Engineer: A little. You're right on pace with Clarke. Stay close, but not too close.
Rocco: Copy.

He was nearing the end of the tunnel, approaching the fastest stretch of the track just before he'd need to break for the chicane—that serpentine curve in the road meant to reduce speed and slow down drivers. This was his best and possibly only shot at passing.

Just up ahead Rocco could see Mendelsohn attempt to overtake Anker and Anker squeeze him out, but Mendelsohn was too close and the two Blue Jet Lightning cars hit—this time with enough impact to throw the pair out wide and allow both Clarke and Rocco to shoot ahead.

Race Engineer: Well done, Rocco! You're on pace with Clarke.
Rocco: Copy. Where's Nico?

■ ■ ■

Race Engineer: Excellent, Nico. You're at P5.
Nico: Copy. Is that . . . Anker? And Mendelsohn?
Race Engineer: It is. They went for too much just before the chicane.

Nico felt her heart racing as a huge grin engulfed her face.

Nico: What position is Rocco at?
Race Engineer: He's at P2, but he's on pace with Clarke. How're the tires?
Nico: Good. Holding steady. Car feels strong. What was the pace on that last lap?
Race Engineer: Fastest yet. Two seconds faster than Anker and Mendelsohn up ahead.

Nico: What about the turn up ahead?
Race Engineer: No moves. Not now, Nico. Not with the two of them lined up like they are. You don't have room.

■ ■ ■

Rocco: Damn, they're right on my tail.
Race Engineer: Yeah, they've picked up the pace. Can you hold on? The checkered flag is just up ahead.
Rocco: Yeah. I can hold on.
I better fucking hold on.

■ ■ ■

Race Engineer: Nico, just hold steady. They've boxed you out.

Mendelsohn was in front of her, Anker ahead of him.

There was nowhere for her to go.

But while Anker was keeping close to the inside, Mendelsohn was riding the right rear tire of Anker's car. Nico knew what he was thinking. Up ahead was a turn, and about midway through the turn, the road widened.

He's positioning himself to pass Anker there.

I can't pass them. But I can make them think I'm going to try.

The more she could draw Anker to the inside, the more Mendelsohn will see the widest part of that turn as his shot.

She veered ever so slightly left. As expected, both Anker and Mendelsohn did as well, blocking her way. Nico inched back to the right, and they followed suit. She did it again, and so did they. But on the third attempt, when they were coming to that widening of the road on the turn, after inching to the inside almost immediately after she jerked right, Anker did likewise and ran into Mendelsohn, who was attempting to pass on the outside. That not only gave Nico room to pass on the inside but given they were all so close and bottled up, the impact between the two Blue Jet Lightning cars startled Clarke. He lost momentum, allowing Rocco to shoot past him.

The checkered flag was just up ahead.

Rocco crossed the finish line first. Clarke regained control and came in second. And Nico . . .

She could hardly believe it.

Did that just happen? Did she really come in third?

She could hear the cheers in the paddock on the radio. She placed her hand over her heart where she kept the drawing of her grandfather.

I did it, Grandpa. I'm going to be up on that podium.

■ ■ ■

Rocco watched Nico mount the podium as the crowd cheered. Clarke followed. He was next.

He was happy. But it felt different than the times he'd mounted the podium in the past. Different than what he'd expected. It was as though the joy had an anchor attached to it.

They handed him a bottle of champagne. Soon he was drenched as Nico and Clarke sprayed him and the crowd. He joined in.

He looked over at her. She was smiling back at him, her dark eyes shining. And then he saw it—a flash of light, as though she'd opened a window—but just for him. And suddenly, that anchor had sprung wings.

After he and Clarke had given each other a bro-hug and she and Clarke had hugged, they stood, staring at each other.

This is ridiculous, Rocco thought.

He stepped over and pulled her in for a hug. As he began to release her, he leaned in, thinking he would kiss her on the cheek and then staring at her lips, suddenly changed his mind. But she looked surprised and had already turned her head partway so that his lips landed clumsily, half on the edge of her lips and half outside them.

They quickly pulled apart.

Rocco was grateful for one thing. It had happened so quickly, given all the excitement and commotion, no one seemed to have noticed.

Afterward, there were dozens of press interviews.

When they were finished, they headed back to the Maverick complex. It was just the two of them. And neither of them had said a word. Should he say something?

That kiss.

They were both acting as though nothing had happened. But something had happened, even if that kiss sucked.

It irked him. A part of him wanted to right that wrong. Now. But then someone might come around that corner up ahead. And just as he had the thought, someone did.

Carolyn.

She smiled. "Congratulations! I'm not sure which is more of a surprise—you, Nico, on the podium, or you, Rocco, darling, not only back on it but in first. A pleasant surprise, of course. But a surprise nonetheless. I thought it might never happen again, dear," she said, placing her hand on Rocco's cheek.

"Surprise? Really?" Nico sneered. "I find *that* surprising."

Up until then, Rocco had avoided looking over at Nico. But now he turned. He only caught her profile, but by the look of that lifted chin and determined jaw, he would bet anything those dark eyes were blazing.

"Do you?" Carolyn said, more statement than question.

"Well, yes. Rocco has, what, three championship trophies? Not only that, but he's the only driver on the circuit who's shown that he can master Monaco in the rain. I mean, he's done it before—*five* times."

"Right," Carolyn hissed, her words spitting from behind clenched teeth. "Well. I'm sure I'll be seeing both of you tonight at the party."

Before Rocco could stop her, Carolyn leaned in and planted an intimate kiss on his mouth. He was just grateful he'd had the foresight to keep his mouth shut and so had she.

She turned to Nico. "You see, dear. That's how it's done. Just a little pointer in case you ever make it back up on the podium and try your hand at it again."

"Hmm. Looked tepid to me. I was thinking something more like this."

Suddenly, Rocco felt her hand around his neck. She pulled him down until his lips met hers, her lips slightly parted so that her breath, hot and sweet, entered him, and like a bolt of lightning, shot straight through his veins. She opened wider, and her tongue, slow and sultry, shattered that bolt into shards of electricity that sparked throughout every square inch of him and then suddenly lit a fire while that scent of hers, thick and viscous, landed heavy in his groin. He wrapped his arms around her, pulling her in closer, squeezing tighter and tighter until he could feel her heartbeat against his own and her breath falter in his mouth.

"I can't," he heard her whisper, their lips still locked.

He felt her hand on his chest.

"I can't," she whispered again, "breathe."

He finally released her. She looked stunned and then blinked.

Carolyn was gone.

"Well, we showed her," Nico said before turning on her heels and walking away.

CHAPTER TWENTY-SEVEN

NICO AND ROCCO

What do you think?" Nico asked Charles as she stood before him in a dusky violet-gray one-shoulder floor-length gown.

Charles didn't say anything. Not exactly the reaction she'd been hoping for.

"What's wrong with it?"

"Nothing's wrong with it. Turn around."

Nico did. The singular strip that hung over her shoulder crossed her back and attached to an O-ring set very low, leaving almost her entire back bare.

"Wow," Charles exclaimed. "It's very, very . . ."

Nico faced him. "Very what?"

"Very cherchez la femme la shark a la Drink and Dive."

Nico frowned. "What do you mean by that?"

"Don't get me wrong, you look gorgeous. It's just, I haven't seen you done up like this since—well, you know—only without the wig."

Nico began looking around the room, making a pretense of searching for her purse. "Well, why not? This is big. I want to celebrate. Why shouldn't I do myself up special for a special evening?"

"You can stop pretending to look for your purse to avoid looking me in the eye. It's right there on the bed—right in front of you—you're staring right at it."

"I'm not trying to avoid looking at you."

"Okay, then look at me."

Nico drew a deep breath and faced Charles, lifting her chin. "Satisfied?"

"No," Charles said, "because you're not being honest with me. But I guess I can hardly expect you to be when you're not being honest with yourself. The way you're acting right now, Nico, I swear the only thing stopping you from donning that platinum wig is the fact that you didn't pack it."

"What are you talking about? I'm not planning on sharking someone at poker or pool. Why would I? Even in the past, when I still did that, I never did it to anyone even remotely connected to the racing world."

"Other than that night at Drink and Dive."

Nico sighed as she plunked down on the bed.

"Okay, that's true. But I didn't know Rocco back then. Remember the things he was saying on social media? The annoying, arrogant, asshole, prick? I wouldn't do it now. For what possible reason? I don't want to go back to doing that. I'm not that woman. I'm the woman who just made it to her first podium in Formula 1. So, why would I— That makes no sense."

Charles sat down beside her. "It makes perfect sense. You've developed feelings for the man. Come on, admit it. That kiss wasn't just to irk Carolyn Wickham."

Nico remained silent. She'd intended to be that woman outside Drink and Dive when she'd kissed him. But as his lips met hers, she realized something was different. It was her kissing him—not that platinum blonde. And toward the end there, it had begun to feel like she was losing control and it was him kissing her.

What must he be thinking? He must have been stunned. For her just to grab him and kiss him like that?

It didn't mean anything. It couldn't mean anything. She had to make certain he knew she understood that.

It. Didn't. Mean. Anything.

"You care about him, Nico. And that scares you to death. You want to destroy any chance of anything starting between the two of you."

Nico shook her head. "Not true!"

"It is true."

"Okay, maybe, just maybe I'm attracted to the man, but so what?"

"It's more than that. You're forgetting I know you. You're also forgetting I saw you up on that podium. One might almost think you were happier for him than you were for yourself."

"What?! That's ridiculous!"

"I said *almost*."

Feeling agitated, Nico stood up and began to pace. "Look, suppose it's true, what you're saying, and mind you, I'm not saying it is. But if it were and I have developed feelings for him, then it's better I put a stop to it right now. He doesn't have those kinds of feelings for me. And if he did, that would only make things worse. We're finally doing well as a team. That's why Dario said those things he did at the masquerade party when he thought I was Rocco. He knows anything more than friendly teammates off the track would screw us on it. Even Celeste is worried about it. You can't be team members and, whatever you would call it, at the same time."

"A couple? Boyfriend and girlfriend? Lovers? In love? Those are some of the things you might call it. And who says?"

"What about just friends? Women and men can be friends. Look at us."

"That's different. And you know it. Why ask you to join him in that village for Carnival? He wanted you with him."

"So, what? I want you and Templeton with me."

"Yeah, but you don't want to kiss us. Not like that."

"No, I don't. You're right. And let's remember it's me that wanted to kiss him in that alleyway. Not the other way around."

"Uh-uh. He wanted to kiss you. I can tell by the way you described that scene. I can see it. He would have if his nieces hadn't showed up."

Nico sighed, rolling her eyes.

"Poor man. He must have it bad. He didn't even care that you had a moustache!"

"You're reading into this. Also, are you forgetting what I told you happened in that village? It might have been Mickey who pulled me away." Nico held up her palm like a traffic cop when Charles opened his mouth. "And before you say something to the effect that I give the man too much power. That's exactly what I plan on *not* doing. Don't you get it? If he's around and he sees that I have feelings for Rocco, he might try to get at me through him."

"How?"

"I don't know how. And I don't want to find out how."

Charles narrowed his eyes. Nico did likewise.

"And what about him inviting you to come to the town he grew up in and stay with his family? A man doesn't do that if he doesn't have feelings for a woman."

"He didn't invite me. His nieces did. And I've already told them I have plans."

"What plans?"

"Hanging out with you and Templeton. We'll go out, eat junk food, coffee ice cream, and chocolate. Invent new cocktails and watch movies. It'll be fun."

"He's made no mention of your joining him for a visit?"

"No. Just because his nieces want me to visit doesn't mean he does."

"He hasn't mentioned it because he thinks you have plans."

"He can't know that. We haven't talked about what we're doing over the break."

"His nieces told him."

"You don't know that." Nico stood up. "Are we going or what?"

Charles groaned. "Okay."

They walked silently down the hallway and into the elevator.

Charles looked her up and down as they descended. "You really are in grifter mode."

Exasperated, Nico huffed. "Just because I'm made up like I would be if I were going to con someone doesn't mean that's what I intend on doing."

Charles sighed as the elevator doors opened. "Guess there's no need to when you've already conned yourself."

■ ■ ■

Rocco leaned against a marble column in the Salle Empire. Three arched windows opened out onto a large terrace that overlooked Casino Square and a portion of the circuit they'd raced earlier today.

He watched, waiting for the moment he would find her alone.

She stood with a group of people, her hair swept up into a bun on top of her head. The dress hugged every turn her body took. He blinked when she turned and he saw her from behind—naked, exposed. His eyes drifted from her shoulders to the arch of her back, sliding down that olive flesh to her ass. He swallowed, pulling his collar away from his throat.

He wasn't even certain what he would say to her, but he knew whatever it was, he wouldn't say it with anyone else around. He bit his lower lip. He could still taste her, and her scent still lingered. It couldn't be on his clothes, given he'd changed, not even on his skin, given he'd showered. It must be lingering in his memory, but it was so powerful, it invaded more than his mind, it invaded his body. So that even when he wasn't thinking of it, it was here; he couldn't shake it.

He hadn't wanted to let go of her. He wouldn't have if she hadn't pushed him away. Did he linger in her the way she did in him? How could he not? After a kiss like that.

He turned when he felt a hand on his shoulder.

Carolyn.

"I really did mean it, you know."

He frowned. "Mean what?"

"Congratulations. It took me back, seeing you command those streets in the rain. Like it was years ago."

Nodding, he swallowed, attempting a smile.

"I feel as though I should apologize for that little scene afterward. But it's not easy to see that kind of public display with someone you once—you still—care about. And, in my defense, I thought, seeing how awkward it was up on that podium, I guess I thought, you weren't really—well, you know. But I suppose I was wrong."

"We aren't together. Like that."

"Really? When she kissed you like she did . . ."

"She was just trying to show you up, that's all."

"Well, that she did. On the track as well as off it."

Rocco chuckled, smiling at her, and in that moment recapturing some memory of what he'd liked about Carolyn, recalling why he'd fallen for the woman.

"Is that what she's doing now?" Carolyn asked, gazing at something over Rocco's shoulder.

Rocco turned to see Leo Clarke with Nico.

They looked good together. Even he had to admit it. Clarke's elegant features complemented Nico's dramatic ones. She touched his arm as she laughed at something he'd said. Why had she never done that with him?

His eyes shifted to Clarke. The man's eyes glinted—he was looking at her like he—

Is he interested in her?

He leaned in and whispered something in her ear.

She better not blush. Don't. Blush.

He waited. And watched. And then sighed.

She didn't.

She did, however, lean in and whisper something back.

Her eyes were sparkling, but he didn't see that window of light, did he? No, he didn't see it. He was 100 percent certain. His heart thudded in his chest as though it no longer knew how to beat in a steady rhythm.

Maybe 85 percent certain.

"Rocco?"

"Huh?" he turned, surprised to see Carolyn there and then immediately realized she'd been there all along.

"I wanted to talk to you about the possibility of coming back to Blue Jet."

■ ■ ■

"Congratulations!" Ceci said, giving Nico a hug.

She turned to Clarke. "You too, Sir Clarke Kent. Oh, look at that. Your tie is crooked."

It wasn't. But it was once Ceci got her hands on it.

Nico eyed the man with curiosity. Clarke, who just a moment before had exuded that effortless calm he was known for, now seemed shy, almost awkward.

"There now," Ceci purred, having finished fussing with his tie. "So how goes it, Sir Clarke, in your search for that damsel?"

His chin dropped to his chest as he shook his head, but Nico could see he was grinning. After a moment, he lifted his gaze and pinned those warm brown eyes on Ceci.

"Not so well. It's tough these days for a knight—with or without the shining armor."

"Is it now?"

"You haven't been able to find even one?" Nico asked.

"Oh, I've found more than one. There are plenty of damsels to go around."

"Ah, I see." Ceci held up her finger. "But finding one in distress, that's the difficulty."

"No, plenty of those to go around too."

Nico laughed.

Ceci frowned and then snapped her fingers. "Ah, I think I understand. There's an overabundance of stock. The difficulty lies in making a choice."

He shook his head. "No, that's not it."

"Clarke!" someone shouted. "Over here! There's someone I want you to meet!"

Relief flooded his face. "Excuse me, ladies," he muttered with a slight bow.

Once he'd left them, Ceci shook her head. "Hard to believe that guy can be such a brute on the racetrack. Once he's off it, I can't decide whether he's traveled forward in time, having come to us from the early nineteenth century, you know the Regency period, or journeyed back in time, having come from the future. I sometimes wonder if he's really a super sophisticated robot made of carbon fiber and bioplastics rather than flesh and blood."

"I don't know, Ceci. He seemed very much flesh and blood when you had your hands on him."

"Really?!"

"Have you ever seen carbon fiber and bioplastics blush?"

Ceci burst out laughing. "It's fun having you on the circuit." She glanced around. "Now, where's your teammate? I should congratulate him too. Ah, there he is. Guess I'll wait. It looks like I might be interrupting something."

Nico turned to see Rocco talking with Carolyn Wickham. She wondered if Ceci saw what she saw. A handsome couple engaged in an intimate conversation.

Ceci sighed. "It must be difficult to have been a driver, to know this business better than a lot of men, and to be relegated to the passenger seat by your husband just because he's the one with the money."

"Carolyn was a driver?"

"F3 some years back. When you think about what you have to put up with, what I had to put up with, just imagine what she had to put up with."

■ ■ ■

Rocco watched Carolyn walk away.

Race for Blue Jet Lightning?

Suddenly, Dario and Celeste were by his side.

"I didn't know Ian Anker could dance," said Celeste. "He's not half bad."

Rocco glanced over at the dance floor.

There was Nico.

Dancing with Anker.

Celeste was right. He wasn't half bad. In fact, he was actually good, Rocco thought, as he stood with his hands clenched watching the man sweep Nico across the floor.

Why did she have to wear a backless dress?

He stared at Anker's hand on her back.

It better not drift south.

Maybe he should butt in. People did that. Guys did that.

But just then the dance ended.

Good, he thought. Until he watched them walk away. Arm in arm.

He hurried after them. From the lobby, they entered the casino and, once there, sat down at a poker table.

Rocco stood some distance away, watching her. She seemed different. Not the girl who had dressed as Inigo Montoya and run through those cobblestone streets with him. Not the girl who drank GoGo squeeZ. Not the one he'd seen up on the podium.

There was a kind of artifice about her now.

He was debating whether to pull up a chair and sit between them when he felt a tap on his shoulder.

He turned around to see Charles.

"I wish I'd had the opportunity to meet Beatrice and Sofia at the race. Nico's told me a lot about them."

Rocco smiled. "The two Tasmanian devils, you mean."

Charles laughed. "They sound like great fun. I'm sure it'll be nice to have a break with them. Your sister told me about your hometown. It sounds lovely."

Rocco nodded before glancing back at the table. Nico laughed at something Anker said.

Anker was as groomed as he'd ever be. His tattoos were covered up by his tux, and his usually spiky and restless blond hair had been sleeked back. Hard to tell what gleamed brighter: that hair or those crystal and cobalt-blue eyes.

Did he have to sit so close to her? And why did he keep whispering in her ear? What was he whispering? Why couldn't he say what he was saying out loud?

"It's nice to have family," Rocco heard Charles say. He listened but kept his eye on that table. "I only have my mother, but trust me, she's family enough. She's asked me to come and visit over the next couple of weeks, but the timing couldn't be worse. I feel bad leaving Nico alone, especially in of all places—Vegas."

Rocco turned to Charles. "What's that?"

"I said I feel bad leaving Nico alone in Vegas over the next few weeks."

"She'll be alone?" He glanced over at Nico before he turned back to Charles. "What about her family? Are they away? Traveling? She told me they did a lot of that when she was growing up."

"Did she?"

Rocco frowned, unsure how to interpret Charles's expression and his tone.

"Well," Charles said, "they're all gone now. Dead."

Dead?

Rocco blinked. "Oh." He paused. "So she'll really be all alone."

He glanced back at the poker table and bristled when he saw Anker place his hand close to hers. Another inch, and they'd be touching.

He clenched his jaw. "She seems. Different—tonight."

Charles sighed. "She does that sometimes, puts on a tough femme fatale persona to bully that fragile part of her into a corner and silence it altogether."

Rocco turned to him. "Fragile?"

"Yes. That," Charles said, pointing at Nico as she tilted her shoulder and slivered her eyes, "tells me she's feeling vulnerable."

"Why?"

"I think she's fallen for a man."

Rocco felt his heart thud heavy and fast in his chest. Did he mean she'd fallen for Ian Anker?

"That frightens her," Charles said. "I might understand why, if that were the man she'd fallen for."

"Do you mean Anker?"

Charles nodded. "It's not him. Though it doesn't really matter. She can't find it in herself to trust any man. More than that, she can't trust herself. Not when it comes to matters of the heart—love—I mean, romantic love. I suppose it's understandable—given her past. You should know that about her."

"Wait? What? Why should I know that?"

"Wow!" Charles exclaimed. "How much do you suppose is in that kitty?"

Rocco turned to see more people crowding round the table. Now there were only three of them left in the game.

"Maybe I should try to stop her," he said.

"She knows what she's doing."

"How can she? She can't understand what she's risking."

"Trust me. She can. And does. Question is—do you?" Charles waved at someone behind Rocco. "Oh, there's Mateo." He placed his hand on Rocco's arm. "She won't come unless she thinks you want her to. And you'll have to hit her over the head with a two-by-four to get that message through her thick skull. I hope to hell you're not the same and you get my meaning." He patted Rocco's arm before walking away.

When Rocco looked back at the table, Nico and Anker were the only two left in the game. He weaved his way through the crowd and positioned himself directly opposite her. But she had yet to look his way.

"It's your bet, Mr. Anker," the dealer said.

Anker held up his finger as his crystal and cobalt-blue eyes rested on Rocco. The corners of his mouth slithered up his cheeks. He put his arm on the back of Nico's chair as he turned to her. And this time, he didn't whisper.

"That doesn't really interest me," he said, indicating the large kitty on the table.

Nico turned.

She sees me now.

He stared back at those dark eyes. And then his eyes drifted to Anker. He fisted his hands, seeing that grin sliver up Anker's cheeks. He wanted to smack it off the prick's face.

Anker leaned in and whispered something in Nico's ear.

Rocco watched her face, looking for something in her eyes, anything that might signal some kind of reaction to whatever he was whispering. But he got nothing.

"All right," she said nonchalantly.

"So, we agree to the terms?"

"We do."

Rocco's heart jumped to his throat and began to pound so hard it hurt.

"In that case," Anker said, shoving the remainder of his chips forward. "I'm all in."

Nico did likewise. "So am I."

CHAPTER TWENTY-EIGHT

ROCCO AND NICO

Rocco watched Nico walk out of the casino with her winnings. He took off after her. She was headed for the elevators. Once there, he saw her press the button.

Don't arrive.

Not yet, he thought as he shouldered his way through a crowd of people.

He saw her step forward,

Not yet.

He raced and, once arriving at the elevators, shoved his hand in between the doors just before they shut. He exhaled as they sprung back open and he saw her standing there—alone.

He stepped in.

"What—" she started but quickly stopped when a man raced up and was about to enter.

Rocco held up his hand. "This one's broken."

The man smiled. "Oh. Thanks." And then just as the doors were closing, the man seemed to realize his mistake. "Wait, if it's broken, then how come you're—" The rest of what he said was lost as the doors shut and the elevator began to rise.

Rocco leaned against the back of the elevator without pressing the button for his floor—the fourth floor. He folded his arms and looked straight ahead, telling himself he would wait until they reached her floor before he would say anything. He was angry and needed to cool down.

Out of the corner of his eye, he saw her finger poised to press the fourth-floor button. He took her hand in his and pushed it down, and with his arm across her body, he gently pushed her back and away from the panel.

She looked down at his hand holding hers. He let go.

"What was on the table back there?" he asked, not doing anything to mask the anger in his voice.

She wouldn't look at him. "You saw what was on the table. Do you want to count it?"

"What did Anker whisper to you?"

"Oh, that," she huffed.

"Yes, that!"

"He suggested we throw something else into the wager."

"And you agreed."

She shrugged.

"What?" he demanded.

"It doesn't matter. I won."

"And what if you hadn't?"

"That wasn't going to happen."

"You don't know that."

She didn't respond. Maybe he'd been wrong. Maybe he'd been wrong about it all. That look in her eyes on the podium. That kiss.

He drew a deep breath before he spoke next. "Or maybe it didn't matter whether you won or lost."

Just then the elevator stopped on the third floor, and the doors opened. She stepped out but paused and turned around. "What do you mean?"

The doors were about to close, but he held them open. "Maybe it didn't matter because win or lose, you were okay with the consequences. Whatever it was, you were prepared to give it to him. Maybe even wanted to. Maybe even still want to. Is that why you left the casino? Are you planning to meet him?"

"No!"

"Well, I don't know what else I'm supposed to think, given you won't tell me."

"I don't give a damn what you think. What's it to you anyway? Why do you care?"

He removed his hand, crossed his arms, and stood staring hard at her. The doors began to close.

"It was something stupid," she cried.

His hand flew up, and the doors sprung open again.

"Careful," she said. "Is your hand okay?"

He stepped out but remained silent, waiting.

She sighed and looked at his feet as she spoke. "If I lost, I would join him during the break. He'd asked me before when we were dancing, and I said *no*."

"Then why would you agree to it?"

"I told you. I knew I had him beat. Otherwise, I never would have. I had—have—no intention of doing anything with him."

Rocco sighed and smiled. "That's good. Because you're coming with me."

■ ■ ■

Nico's heart began to pound. He was asking her.

Was he asking her?

No, he's not asking you! Annoying, arrogant, asshole, prick doesn't think he has to ask. And he certainly doesn't think I have anything better to do.

She cast aside the obvious—she didn't.

She also cast aside her desire—how very much she wanted to. For most people, that would have them going all in. But for her, it had the opposite effect. It had her entire body working hard not to want it. It filled her with dread at the disappointment she felt certain was waiting on the other end of that desire.

It's because of that kiss. None of this would be happening if you hadn't kissed him.

She steeled her jaw along with her will.

"Look, I know what this is about. That kiss. I shouldn't have done it. I'm sorry."

"I'm not."

She blinked and opened her mouth, but all she could manage was, "Oh."

He took a step toward her, and she stumbled until she met up with the wall behind her.

He leaned in, placed one hand on her throat and his lips on hers as he whispered, "Say yes, Nico."

He left his lips there, barely touching her own.

Why did bourbon have to smell so damn good on him?

"Say *yes*?" She swallowed. "Yes to what? You haven't asked me anything." She felt her cheeks burn, her heart pound.

"I haven't?"

"Uh-uh."

He pulled back. "Nico."

His voice had changed. He sounded serious.

"Will you, please, come with me?"

"And if I say no?" she heard herself saying.

She also heard a voice that sounded like Charles. *You idiot!*

"You won't say no," Rocco said, "because I know you want to come."

"Aha, here we are again. You can read my mind."

"Will you come? That's twice I've asked you now."

He leaned in closer, his breath hot, smelling like bourbon and caramel.

"Say. Yes. Nico."

Those words and his breath surged through her like brush fire.

Her lips moved—barely—but no sound came out.

"Say. Yes. Now." His voice part whisper, part groan.

He placed his hands on either side of her face, threading his fingers through her hair. His lips gently plucked hers, grazing her upper lip with his teeth. His breath was like a drug, and without thought, she opened her mouth wider, letting his wet tongue enter her.

Something's different.

She placed her hands on his chest. Told herself to push him away. But he pulled her to him roughly, holding her tight as though he wanted to crush her. Only it didn't hurt.

Not at all.

And then she suddenly realized.

He's kissing me. That's what's different.

His fingers slid back until she felt them graze that scar.

She stiffened and pulled back.

He stopped. "Are you okay?"

She couldn't—wouldn't—meet his gaze. She felt sick.

"I have to go now."

"You haven't answered me yet. Will you come? That's three times now."

"And if I say *maybe*?"

It was the only thing she could think of to get him to leave.

"I'll accept it. For now." He grazed the top of her forehead with his lips. "Good night, Nico." He turned and began walking back down the hallway. "I'll call you tomorrow morning. And if you don't pick up, I'll be at your door."

She entered the room to find Charles and told him what had happened.

"He's so confident I'm going to go with him. He acted as though I didn't have anything better to do."

Charles bit his lip. "Well . . ."

"That's beside the point. He doesn't know that."

"Well . . ."

Nico blinked, staring at Charles. "What's with that look?"

"He might have gotten that idea from me."

"What?"

"I told him you weren't doing anything."

"What about our plans?"

"What plans? I'm going to visit mother in Booger Hole."

Nico still didn't believe Charles's mother actually lived in a place called Booger Hole. But she couldn't go there now.

"Fine. But you still didn't have to tell him I had no plans."

"Why not? What is wrong with him knowing? I know it's not just his nieces who want you to come. Why are you resisting this? I know it's complicated because you two are teammates, but can't you figure that out? I mean, look at how well the two of you did in this race!"

"It isn't just that. He kissed me."

Charles's eager eyes lit up. "All the more reason not to resist. What was it like?"

Nico sat down on the edge of the bed.

Charles gasped. "Like that, was it?"

"It was . . . it was . . ."

"Say no more. Your face says it all. After a kiss like that, I don't know why we're talking about any of this. It's obvious you're going. That *maybe* meant *yes*."

Nico shook her head. "No, it doesn't. It can't. Remember Mickey? Don't you see? When he was kissing me and his hands grazed that scar, I went cold. That told me everything I need to know."

"What do you mean?"

"If Mickey sees me getting close to Rocco and his family, he might try to get at me through them. Find some way to hurt them."

"J'accuse!" Charles cried dramatically, pointing his finger at Nico. "I was right! You do care about him."

"If I do, then I'll say *no*. And that's what *maybe* means—*no*. I'm turning off my cell. I'm having the hotel hold any calls. And if he comes to the door, I'm not opening it."

Charles stood up and turned on his heels. "Fine," he spat.

Nico got up and grabbed his arm. "And you're not either, Charles. Promise me. Right. Now."

Charles sighed, holding up his right hand as though he were about to testify in court. "I promise I will not open that door if he's knocking on it."

Okay, then.

After that, Nico tried to sleep but she kept glancing at the clock, wondering whether or not he would come, knowing how she would feel if he didn't. And hating herself for it.

Finally, she must have drifted off because the next thing she knew, when she opened her eyes, she saw Charles standing at the door and peering through the peephole.

"Charles, what are you—"

Before Nico could finish, Charles opened the door, and Rocco, who'd been sitting propped up against it, fell into the room.

Nico threw off her covers and jumped out of bed. She marched over to Charles, glaring at him. "You promised you wouldn't open the door."

"I promised I wouldn't open the door if he knocked on it." Charles looked down at Rocco lying on his back, gazing up at them. "How long have you been sitting out there?"

That's when *maybe* became *yes*.

CHAPTER TWENTY-NINE

ROCCO AND NICO

Rocco downshifted the Aston Martin to slow down as they approached yet another small cobblestoned village. The snow-capped mountain peaks lay ahead in the distance, but they loomed larger now that they were closer. Soon they would look as though you could reach out and touch them.

He glanced over at Nico, who was gazing out the window at the passing landscape.

"Do you need to—want to stop?" he asked.

"No," she said, shaking her head. "I'm fine."

Was she? Fine? She'd been quiet the entire drive.

She looked fine, he thought, glancing over at her and shifting in his seat, feeling that telltale tug in his pants. This was bad. Real bad. It wasn't as though she was wearing anything sexy. She was wearing a baggy sweatshirt and sweatpants. Even so as he pulled on his jeans, which were becoming unbearably tight, he wished she were wearing something else.

Like what?

Maybe a tent.

"Do you mind if I open the window?" she asked, pulling at the bulky collar of her sweatshirt. "It's hot."

It is.

"No, that's fine." He inhaled and exhaled so heavily he spotted her looking over at him out of the corner of his eye.

Once they'd passed through the village, he shifted up to sixth gear.

What had he been thinking? Was this a mistake? How in hell was he going to sleep under the same roof knowing she was in the room next to his?

Of course, they'd be in separate bedrooms. They weren't a couple. As far as the world and his family were concerned, they were teammates. And only teammates.

He knew why he'd asked her. He wanted to be with her. But now he felt how badly he wanted to be with her *alone*. How was that possible with his family around? It wasn't. But he couldn't not visit his family. They were expecting him. Maybe he could cut short the stay with them and go somewhere else with Nico. Alone.

He opened his window even though the car was moving at top speed and the wind was equivalent to a snowball hitting his face.

That snowball might as well have been the cold, hard truth.

His desire for her wasn't the only reason he'd asked her. He didn't like hearing that she'd be alone. Didn't like? It was more than that. It hurt—physically hurt—when Charles had told him. Yes, he wanted to be alone with her. But if that's all he'd wanted, he could have found time during the break to do that without inviting her to come to his family home.

I must want her to know them. Want them to know her.

He groaned.

Damn it.

He silenced himself quickly, glancing over to see if she'd noticed.

It didn't seem as though she had. She was still gazing out that window. She didn't seem to mind that snowball in the face either.

She was so quiet.

What is she thinking?

The quiet had to have something to do with why she'd resisted saying *yes*. He knew she'd wanted to come, but something was holding her back. What? Was it because they were teammates? It wasn't as though he hadn't thought about that.

I'm still thinking about it.

What will this look like when racing starts up again?

But it was more than that with her. There was something else. He could tell.

That scar. Is it that scar?

When I touched it, she turned into a block of ice.

He could literally feel her slip away at that moment.

They were approaching the turnoff onto the small country road that led directly to the village. Before they got to it, he swerved right, pulling off to the side.

"What are you doing?" she asked as he parked the car.

They were surrounded by trees. The mountains loomed, looking much closer now, and a creek threaded its way through the greenery.

"We have to walk the rest of the way," he said before getting out of the car.

The walk will be good. For her. And for me.

If it didn't manage to get his crankshaft to lie down, at least it would make it less squirrelly.

"How far?" she asked once she was out of the car.

"About five miles or so," he said, opening the trunk.

"What?!"

"It's the only way to get there."

He was glad he had an empty backpack in the trunk. He grabbed some stuff from his suitcase and tossed the items in.

"Okay," he said, "now you."

She sighed, pulling some things out and putting them in the backpack.

She pulled out a large T-shirt and a pair of baggy sweats.

More sweats?

"What's that for?" he asked.

"Sleeping," she said, stuffing it in the backpack.

"Where's the thing you were wearing this morning?"

It was a pale lavender short kind of slip. And sheer. A fact she'd clearly forgotten when she'd jumped out of bed earlier that morning and stood beside Charles, gazing down at him as he lay on the floor of her hotel room.

"I didn't pack it."

"I did," he said rummaging through her things. He'd grabbed it and threw it in her suitcase, stuffing it under the other items when she wasn't looking. He pulled it out. "Here it is," he said, smiling.

Her eyes opened wide as she stared at it. Glaring at him, she snatched it and threw it back in her suitcase. "I don't need that."

He went behind her back, grabbed it, and shoved it in the backpack when she wasn't looking.

Once they had everything, he shut the trunk and slung the pack on his back, and they set off.

"There's no road you can drive on that takes you to the town?" she asked, hurrying after him.

"Just a walking path. It's really small, not even a village, really. More of a hamlet."

"So, when your parents want to leave, they have to walk this far to get to their car?"

He hesitated. "More or less."

■ ■ ■

Most of the time, they walked a clear trail. But sometimes it disappeared, and she stumbled over a root or rock. But that was her own fault. Instead of watching where she was going, she was staring at Rocco's ass and wondering if he had those dimples above it.

He stopped, glancing over his shoulder. "Tired?"

"No," she huffed.

"Why don't you finish the fairy tale you were telling me? It'll help pass the time."

Okay, she thought, gritting her teeth and wanting to smack that ass. Hard.

She thought a moment, recalling where she'd left off, and then chuckled.

"The hours passed," she began. "The days and nights and the seasons too. And the little prince's head kept growing. It was making it more and more difficult to move. Soon he was unable to run and race; even walking had become difficult."

Rocco stopped and turned around. "Really?"

Nico smiled. "Yes, really."

She flitted her hand like she was shooing away a fly, and he resumed walking.

"There were no laws in the kingdom. The people did as they pleased. Life was good, everyone—happy. As a result, no harm was ever committed, and they had no need for laws. But now the king and queen made a proclamation. If the little prince could not run or race, no one would run or race. From thenceforth, running and racing was forbidden."

Rocco stopped so suddenly, she ran into him.

"No racing?! Come on!"

Nico bit her lip to keep from laughing and shrugged. "That's what happened."

"What do you mean that's what happened? You're making the story up, so it doesn't have to happen."

"That's. What. Happened. Now do you want me to finish the story or not?"

"Is it going to have a happy ending?"

She chuckled.

"Go on," he said gruffly as he turned around and continued walking.

"The people in the kingdom went about their daily lives much as they had before, but something had changed. They felt less joy. What's more, the little prince could hardly be called *little* anymore. His head was becoming so enormous it was too big for the doorways, hallways, and passages of the castle. Everything had to be renovated and fitted to accommodate the little prince's head, which was extremely difficult, given his head continued to swell.

"This put the king and queen in a bad temper. The women of the court were unhappy as well. They used to love to do things for the little prince. But now, bathing and dressing him had become very difficult with his overgrown head. What's more, the little prince, who once had been so charming, had now become ill-tempered. It was unpleasant to be around him, unpleasant to even look at him with that swollen head."

Again, Nico nearly ran into Rocco when he stopped. He peered at her. His jaw was rigid, and he'd clenched his fists. She had to bite her lip to keep from laughing. He drew a deep breath and only turned around and resumed walking once he'd exhaled.

"One day," she went on, "there was a big commotion when a stranger arrived. No one had ever visited the remote kingdom, given it was so far away and difficult to get to.

"The little prince was curious. He ordered the stranger to come to the castle. But the stranger didn't come. So, he decided to venture outside the castle in search of the stranger.

"He had to walk because his head had made him too heavy for the horses. It took him awhile because it was difficult to balance his head on his neck. Often his head toppled to one side, and his body was left to follow so that rather than walking in a straight line, he was forced to take a zigzag path.

"When he finally arrived in the village, he asked a villager where he could find the stranger. 'There,' the villager said, pointing the stranger out to him. But the stranger ran past him so quickly, the little prince only caught sight of a blur.

"He was angry. 'Running! Racing!' he cried. 'Running and racing are forbidden! There's to be no running! No racing!'

"The little prince took off after the stranger, but his heavy head bobbled back and forth so violently that he hadn't gone even three steps before he tumbled, and it required twenty villagers to carry him back to the castle.

"Once again he ordered the stranger to come to the castle, but the stranger didn't come."

Rocco turned around. "Tell me now, is there going to be a happy ending or not?"

She smiled. "Yes, there will be a happy ending."

"Oh, okay."

"For some," she added.

He sighed.

They continued walking, and she resumed the story.

"The little prince was anxious to see the stranger and hear about how the stranger was able to make the long and treacherous voyage to their village. But every order he sent was refused by the stranger."

Nico stopped.

Up ahead was a pathway made of stones. Looking down to the right, she saw that the creek had widened to become a river, to the left was the edge of a mountain, and at the end of the pathway were buildings that looked as though they'd been carved out of the mountain itself.

She pointed. "Is that it?"

He nodded. As they drew near, she saw a parking lot with cars situated at the start of the pathway. Then she spied the road that led to it.

"Why couldn't we park here?" she asked.

"Only residents."

"You're not a resident?"

"Not anymore."

"Nico!"

She turned to see Sofia and Beatrice running toward them.

"We've been waiting for you," Beatrice sputtered, out of breath.

"How come you didn't park in the parking lot?" Sofia asked.

"You mean that one right there?" Nico asked, indicating the one in front of the stone path.

"Yeah," said Sofia.

Nico turned around and glared at Rocco, but just then a dog came running. The dog passed them and ran directly to him.

"That's Cat," said Sofia.

Rocco avoided looking at her, crouched down, and began petting the dog, who slathered his face with his tongue.

"Dog is in the house," said Beatrice.

"I'm supposing Dog is a cat?" Nico asked.

Beatrice nodded. "Uncle Rocco found them in a dumpster."

"So I heard."

A dog named Cat and a cat named Dog, she thought, eyeing him with curiosity.

The girls each took a hand and pulled Nico toward the stone pathway. Rocco and Cat followed. Up ahead, the stone buildings of the hamlet glowed golden in the sun.

"You're the first girl Uncle Rocco's brought here," said Sofia.

Beatrice nudged her. "He must really like you."

They giggled.

Nico was grateful Rocco was behind them and couldn't see her face.

"Uncle Rocco said you have a pet rat named Templeton," Beatrice said.

Nico nodded. "I do."

"Like in *Charlotte's Web*," Sofia said.

"That's right."

"How did you get him? Did you find him in a dumpster too?"

Nico hesitated, her heart beating fast. She knew he was listening.

Should she tell them about this Templeton, who she'd gotten from a pet store? Or should she tell them about the original Templeton, her first rat? If she told them about the Templeton now, she would be telling them the truth. But if she told them about the first Templeton, she would be telling them a deeper truth.

She would be telling *him* a deeper truth.

If she were ever going to tell him a deeper truth, now would be the time to do it. Sofia and Beatrice were here, and she wouldn't have to look him in the eye when she did.

She swallowed. "No, I didn't find him in a dumpster. I found him in the apartment I was living in. He was a baby. His mother got caught in a trap and died. So, I took care of him."

"That's sad about his mother," Sofia said.

"It is."

Beatrice smiled up at her. "So, you became his mother."

"I guess so. I wasn't supposed to have any pets. So, I kept him a secret. He would have been taken away from me otherwise."

Beatrice's smile disappeared. "You mean, your mamma and papà would have taken him from you?"

"No, not them."

Nico was grateful to the girls. This way was easier. Their questions were so sincere and direct.

"My mother died when I was very young. I never knew my father. I was raised by my grandfather."

Sofia frowned. "So, your nonno would have taken Templeton from you?"

Nico knew enough Italian to know 'nonno' meant grandfather.

"No, he had already died by then. But the people who took care of me after he died would have."

"I'm sorry," said Sofia.

"Me too," said Beatrice.

Nico sighed. "Me three."

Finally, after walking five minutes, they came to a stone arcade.

"This is the gateway to the hamlet," Rocco said, coming up behind them. "On the other side, there's another one."

As they walked under the covered passageway, Nico felt as though the village had gathered around them. The stone buildings that clung to the side of the mountain huddled together. In some cases, they were connected with brick vaults hovering over the cobblestone streets. Nico looked around and thought, *This is how I imagined that kingdom in the fairy tale.*

They passed over a bridge and under a series of vaulted arches and finally arrived at the second gateway. Just beyond it stood a beautiful stone house, sitting on the edge of a slope overlooking the river below.

A group of people spilled out the front door. His parents, sister, her husband, and one set of grandparents. She recognized them all. She'd met them briefly and seen them at a few races.

It was easy to see the family resemblance. The warm brown eyes, the bold bone structure, the dark brown locks, the expressive mouths.

The house was warm and inviting with wooden floors and a beamed ceiling. Nico was surprised such a cozy house could still be filled with so much light, and then she realized it came not just streaming through the windows but from the people who inhabited it, who were so welcoming.

Rocco's mother took Nico by the hand. "Let me show you where you'll be sleeping."

Nico's eyes gaped as she entered the room and looked at the walls. They were covered with posters of Formula 1 drivers, which was hardly surprising. What was surprising were the posters of Lella Lombardi and Maria Teresa de Filippis.

His mother smiled. "I guess I don't need to tell you, this is Rocco's room—well, was his room, growing up."

Rocco suddenly appeared in the doorway. "You want to go for a ride?"

Nico felt her cheeks heat up, casting a furtive glance at his mother.

"Come on," he said, grabbing her hand and taking her outside where a collection of motorcycles were waiting.

She felt foolish. Of course this was what he meant.

She blinked at the sight of one particularly sleek cycle. "Is that a—"

"Kawasaki Ninja H2R?" He grinned. "It is."

The motorcycle he'd said he'd loan her in a direct message way back when, during their social media feud.

"Humph."

He placed his hands on the red one beside it. "This one's for you."

She smiled. It was a Superleggera V4 Ducati.

He came up beside her, and in one long sweep his eyes cast a flurry of sparkles that flickered up and down her flesh as though he'd pointed a magic wand and showered her in a cloud of pixie dust—cast by lurid and depraved pixies.

She narrowed her eyes. "Why did you make me walk five miles when we could have parked, what—five minutes away?"

"Didn't you like it? It's beautiful country."

"It is, but you didn't answer my question."

He sighed. "It just felt a little tense in the car, and I figured it would help." Pausing, he peered at her. "It seems to have worked. Telling that fairy tale of the formerly charming prince who is now repulsive seems to have done the trick."

She bit her lip but didn't succeed in stifling her laugh.

He folded his arms. "Are you going to finish that story?"

She grinned. "Eventually."

"At least tell me this. Does the stranger ever go to the castle?"

"Yes, once the little prince asks the stranger nicely. You'll have to wait to hear the rest."

He groaned. "We need to suit you up. I think you're about my sister's size. You can wear one of hers."

"Are we going out alone?" she asked, annoyed with herself for her voice sounding so breathy when she'd intended it to sound matter-of-fact.

Before Rocco could respond, Nico got her answer. Rocco's father and grandfather came walking toward them, suited up and ready to ride.

"Come on, get on your gear," Rocco's grandfather shouted.

His father shook his head. "For a couple of racers, you two sure do move slow."

CHAPTER THIRTY

NICO

Breathing heavily, Nico skidded to a stop. The trees in front of her were so dense, she couldn't see a way through. She'd gone off the main road some way back. Should she turn around? Rocco had been somewhere behind her. And behind him were his father and grandfather.

She turned at the sound of an engine. The Ninja came speeding toward her and then suddenly stopped a few feet away, skidding and sending up a cloud of dust.

Rocco.

She stared at him. As near as she could tell, he stared back. But that tinted helmet visor covered his eyes.

The wind had been so loud when she was racing down the path and now, suddenly—silence. She glanced up at the trees. Surely there must be a bird perched on a branch somewhere. Some small animal scurrying among the fallen leaves or burrowing into the ground. Some sound of life.

Something.

Nothing.

No sound at all. Not when he placed his feet on the ground. Not when he swung one leg over, dismounting. Not even when not bothering to kick down the kickstand, he shoved the motorcycle aside.

She watched it hit the ground with a thud. Only there wasn't a thud.

That can't be right. Of course there was a thud. There had to have been a thud.

Why didn't I hear it? Why can't I hear anything?

Not even the sound of his footsteps as he approached, crushing leaves beneath his boots.

He pulled off his helmet and tossed it aside. Those dark locks tumbled around his face, shedding beads of sweat that shimmered like crystals as they fell to the earth.

Once he was beside her, he removed her helmet and tossed it aside as well. He grabbed her around the waist and lifted her off the motorcycle. But once her feet hit the ground, he let go, and she stumbled.

The earth didn't feel solid.

No, it's not the earth that's not solid. It's me.

With his eyes fixed on hers, he moved toward her, and she stumbled again, taking a step backward on shaky legs. She grabbed hold of his arms, gripping the stiff leather of his jacket.

He kept coming and a sudden surge of heat seared the entire terrain of her body as though he were fire itself—his eyes, his lips, his chest, his thighs. She felt the weight of him—all of him—bear down upon her.

She couldn't be sure if it was the heat but something broke the sound barrier. And she heard it. A rushing sound.

Where is it coming from?

Her heart was pounding as she looked left and right. Were they near a body of water?

No.

It's not coming from outside. It's coming from me.

It was her own blood coursing through her veins, her own breath blazing through her lungs. And it was all she could hear.

He loomed over her, blocking out sun and sky.

He was all she could see.

She had nowhere else to go.

Her back was up against a tree.

CHAPTER THIRTY-ONE

NICO

He inched forward, and placed his lips on hers.

It felt as though that Ducati was still humming between her thighs.

She could feel his hard chest, his torso, those thighs—even the damp of him that was wafting from his flesh beneath the racing suit.

His hot, urgent breath entered her, hers entered him, until she couldn't tell where hers ended and his began.

She gripped his head, pulling him in deeper. She made a move to turn and put his back up against the tree. But he stood fixed, just like the tree behind her as though he had roots planted deep into the earth too. He pulled away, grabbed her wrists, and pushed her hands down beside her, holding her palms against the rough tree bark.

She thought of that kiss outside Drink and Dive.

There was no question in his eyes like there had been that night. And she suddenly wondered what her eyes looked like to him. He looked as though he knew something, and she couldn't escape the uncomfortable feeling that he could read her thoughts, that he was doing so . . .

Right. Now.

The bark of the tree was rough. His hands held her wrists so firmly, she couldn't move them. *It should hurt*, she kept thinking, *but it doesn't.*

He let go and placed one finger on her lower lip.

That finger drifted, gliding down the base of her throat, stopping when it reached the zipper of the racing suit. He'd kept his eyes on hers until he reached that point. But now he stared at the spot where his finger had landed, and he followed that finger as the zipper slid south.

"This suit doesn't fit properly," he muttered in a voice that managed to hum between her legs as though he'd placed his mouth there.

"It's too small. Here," he said, cupping her breasts, brushing his thumb across her rigid nipples. "And"—he gripped her hips with such force she rocked forward—"here."

He grabbed the tab and pulled the zipper down to her navel as far as it would go.

She opened her mouth, but he swallowed her words, placing his mouth upon hers. This time, the kiss—deeper and more urgent. He held his hands on either side of her throat, and her body went liquid and limp. When he pulled away, there was a moment she thought she might crumple to the ground like tissue paper. Before she realized it, the racing suit lay in a pool around her ankles, and he had his hands on the button of her jeans.

She made a move to unzip his racing suit. But he stopped her.

She was puzzled. "Don't you?"

"Don't I what?"

"Don't you want—"

"What I want, Nico, is for you to stop moving your fucking hands and getting in my way. If you must do something to occupy them, here." He placed one hand on his erection. "That's nice," he said, still working on the button. "Why do they make these things so fucking difficult?"

Her hand slid up and down the length of him.

He glanced up, gazed into her eyes, and leaned his torso into hers.

Underneath the thick racing suit, which he was wearing over jeans, she could still feel him. And then she had a sudden thought as he struggled with that button.

"Wait! Your father and grandfather . . ."

His eyes opened wide in mock horror. "Nico?! How can you think of my papa and nonno when your hand is on my cock?"

She blushed. Her mouth opened to say something. But no words came. What could she say?

The button of her jeans sprung loose.

Her hands flew on top of his. "Where are they? Will they?"

He shoved her hands aside. "No, they won't."

He leaned into her. She felt him. All of him.

Down went the zipper.

A cool breeze lay a trail of goosebumps on her thighs as he slid the jeans down her legs until they circled her ankles along with the racing suit.

He unbuckled one boot, took it off, and tossed it aside, not bothering with the other one. He lifted her foot, and foot and ankle sprung loose from suit and jeans.

As he rose, she felt his hands glide up her body followed by his hot breath until he was gazing back at her, his hands resting on her hips.

Her breath caught as one of his thumbs slipped under the elastic of her panties. He kept his eyes fixed on hers as he brushed her hip with it—back and forth.

"Are—you—sure?" Her words were forced between gasps of her faltering breath.

"Yes, I'm sure," he said as that thumb continued to move methodically, matching the beating of her heart. "You don't have to worry, Nico. But if you want to leave, we'll leave." He paused. "Do you want to leave?" he asked, his voice deep like the low throttle of a powerful engine.

The thumb stopped and he slid that hand under her panties and between her thighs. One finger slid along the slick lips of her vagina.

He grinned. "I'll take that as a no."

His finger slipped inside her.

He placed the elbow of his other arm up against the tree and leaned into it, hanging his head. She shivered as strands of his hair and his hot breath grazed her shoulder.

"Fuck," he muttered.

He'd said it so quietly, she thought maybe he didn't want her to hear him. She wasn't even certain she had heard him. Maybe it was her who had muttered.

His breathing began to mirror hers—heavy and labored, coming and going in deeper waves as though there wasn't enough oxygen to satisfy his lungs. She felt there might not be enough to satisfy hers. She could hear it but feel it too as his chest moved against her own.

"Fu—uuu—ck," he groaned. This time, more a guttural sound than an actual articulated word.

Her breath stuttered as she swelled and throbbed beneath his finger sliding . . .

Back and forth.

In and out.

"You must really like having my Ducati between your thighs," he murmured in her ear, his head still hanging to the side so that she couldn't see his face. He plunged his finger inside. "Damn," he whispered hoarsely, "I bet you taste good, Nico."

She trembled as she felt herself clench his finger.

She reached for his shoulders to steady herself, but just as she did, he began to lower himself and his finger slipped out. Now that heavy wet between her thighs began to throb.

She was going to fall. "I'm going to—"

"No, you're not," he said. "I've got you."

"What, what are you doing?"

"Isn't it obvious?" he said as he slid her panties down her thighs and sprung one ankle free.

He didn't need to ask. She opened her legs, and he placed his mouth there.

He made a groaning, guttural sound. When he spoke, his words with his breath vibrated, hummed, and then sank deep inside her.

"Damn, Nico, you taste like butterscotch," he said as he ran his tongue up and down.

Those words vibrated and sparked every cell from the top of her head to the ends of her toes so that every inch of her was humming. Her insides clenched. Her legs quivered. Her entire body began to shake so violently, there was no way he could hold her now.

But he did.

And his words, with his breath, with his mouth, with his tongue—entered her.

"You've made a great first impression, Nico. If they show up now, just think how great the second one will be."

CHAPTER THIRTY-TWO

ROCCO AND NICO

Rocco was hungry. But not for the feast laid out before him on the table. He was starved for what sat opposite him.

Nico.

What he'd done earlier should have sated him. It didn't. In fact, it made him even more ravenous. His mind was racing, trying to come up with all the possible ways he might get her alone.

He stretched his long legs under the table and gripped both of her feet, sandwiching them between his own.

It caught her by surprise. He watched her lips part just before she swallowed what he felt certain she wanted to say, what he felt certain she would have said if it weren't for the fact that his family was sitting at the table.

She glared at him. But that only made him grin. She tried to free herself. But that only made him hold on tighter.

I'm not letting go of you.

A flicker of light flashed in her eyes but then quickly disappeared, and she turned her head. He watched a soft blush bloom across her cheekbone as though it had been put there by the stroke of a paintbrush, and he suddenly wondered if she could read his thoughts just by gazing into his eyes.

He let go. She still kept her eyes averted, but she left her feet where they were between his.

What drove him to throw her off-balance like this? Like he had when he'd lifted her off the motorcycle and backed her up against that tree.

He'd liked when she'd grabbed hold of his arms. Liked that it had felt desperate and immediate—her body's response to his own.

Is that what had driven him to let her go on thinking there was the most minute possibility that his papa and nonno might show up when he knew full well they wouldn't? They were already headed home when he'd gone off the main road in search of her.

That thrill. That she would still give herself to him so long as he wanted her to because she wanted to that badly—so badly she would risk being exposed, naked, vulnerable. For him.

That surge. That surge of power when she'd held on to him. She must have known she could. She must have known she could trust him.

That surge that coursed through his breath and blood.

Was it possible it was greater than any he'd felt behind the wheel on a racetrack? He didn't know. He only knew he'd never felt it before with a woman. And he wanted to feel it again.

■ ■ ■

Nico stared at the table—the big bowl of pasta, the basket of crusty bread, the colorful peppers, gleaming in olive oil, the decanter of red wine.

Focus on the table—the food, all of it, even the cutlery. Just don't look up.

Every time she did and saw Rocco gazing back at her, she felt as though she might need a defibrillator.

If only she could send her brain to Brainerd and soak it clean of any thought of Rocco Vittori, at least while she sat around the dinner table with his family. Then again, she couldn't be certain the rest of her would be clean.

She didn't feel clean.

She felt dirty.

Really dirty.

Filthy. Filthy. Filthy.

Dirty.

"Rocco Vittori," she heard his mother cry, "did you wash your hands?"

Nico looked up. He was grinning at her. She stared at his hands, thinking about where they had been. And the minute she had that thought, it was as though the thought had placed his hands there again. On her breasts, on her thighs, in between her thighs.

Yes, please, in between my thighs.

That grin made her want to mount him and kick him under the table at the same time. When they were preparing to head back home and he was putting on her helmet, he had confessed that his father and grandfather had met up with him on the main road and told him they'd head for home while he went looking for her. She'd figured as much. Rocco never would have done what he'd done otherwise. Still, there had been the tiniest bit of fear in her. And yet she couldn't stop him. That had never happened before. She'd never lost control like that. And she couldn't even say she'd given that control to him. She felt as though he'd had it from the start.

She flinched when Beatrice nudged her, handing her the basket of crusty bread.

She was grateful Sofia and Beatrice were sitting on either side of her because they kept demanding her attention. As long as she could focus on one of them, she felt as though she could manage to make it through dinner without self-combusting.

Hopefully without self-combusting.

Please don't self-combust.

Charles told her phosphorus and coal could self-combust. He'd read it somewhere. One of the elements that made up the human body was phosphorus. Then too there was carbon. And coal was mostly carbon.

If she did self-combust, would she disintegrate into ash? Or would she set fire to anything and anyone nearby, she wondered, eyeing Sofia and Beatrice warily.

"Did you enjoy the ride, Nico?" Rocco's father asked.

Her heart. That defibrillator.

"What?" she cried.

They were all staring at her.

Rocco grinned. "I think she did, Papa," he said, rubbing his foot up her leg under the table.

"Yes," she said, trying to kick his foot away. "It's such beautiful country here."

And there.

She swallowed.

Right. There. Across the table.

One annoying, arrogant, asshole—I bet even his asshole is beautiful.

"Have you ever had casonsei, Nico?" his mother asked.

She started, surprised to hear the sound of her name and having no idea how to respond because she had no idea what had been asked.

Yes and *no* covered a lot of territory. *Have you been having lecherous thoughts about my son? Yes. Did you know said lecherous thoughts are like a match that can set all this carbon and phosphorus sitting around this table ablaze? No.*

She stared at Rocco. His eyes flashing, an evil grin slithering up his cheeks as his foot, like that Chilean snake with the slow and fast twitching tongue, slithered up her leg.

Slow-twitch. Fast-twitch. Yes-twitch. No-twitch.

He licked his lips.

Yes.

"No," she suddenly heard herself say.

Rocco's mother smiled at her and held out a plate. "Ah, well you will love it."

Nico sighed, relieved.

Smiling, she took the plate. "It looks and smells wonderful."

"Casonsei is ravioli with a sauce of butter, sage, and bacon," his grandmother said.

His grandfather leaned forward, looking past Beatrice. "You'll never taste anything more delicious."

"I don't know," Rocco said, catching her eye. "I think I might have tasted something more delicious."

Her eyes ballooned as his foot slid up and down her leg.

She jumped.

"Are you all right, dear?" his mother asked.

"Yes." Nico swallowed. "I'm, I'm fine."

Fast-twitch. Slow-twitch. Yes-twitch. No-twitch.

"That's sacrilegious," his grandfather said. "You have not tasted anything better, Rocco."

She glanced at him and saw on his face that he was enjoying this way too much.

It's payback for that fairy tale.

She glared at him.

Wait until I get my hands on you.

Thinking about what she would do when she did got her thinking about what he had done. Up against that tree. And that got her thinking about the things he hadn't done. The things she wanted him to do.

She wondered if there was enough phosphorus and carbon sitting around this table to self-combust, if her filthy thoughts could create enough heat so that everyone around them would disintegrate when she threw him on the table and they did those things. He did those things. In the middle of the Casonsei, the green salad, and the vinaigrette, the roasted peppers, the crusty bread, and the olive oil. Oh, the olive oil. Lots of olive oil. On his chest. On his thighs. On his ass. In those dimples. Would she ever find out if he had those dimples?

Don't rush things, Dr. Wily said, poking her so hard, she physically flinched.

Until she realized it was Sofia, handing her some roasted peppers. And she thought, *You were about to blast this girl and all of them, these warm-hearted, joyful, wonderful, welcoming people to smithereens just so you could have sex, rolling around in the roasted peppers, crusty bread, and olive oil.*

If there is a hell, surely it was made for you. To burn for all of eternity.

The snake curled around her leg.

Fast-twitch. Slow-twitch. Yes-twitch. No-no-twitch.

She stared into those warm caramel eyes.

Burn for all of eternity.

It might. Be. Worth it.

"Nico has a pet rat named Templeton," cried Beatrice.

"She found him like Uncle Rocco found Cat and Dog," added Sofia. "Not in a dumpster though."

His mother smiled. "Really?"

"Yes," Nico said. "When I was a kid in the apartment we were living in. The mother got caught in a trap and died."

"I didn't know rats could live that long," said his grandmother.

Nico swallowed. "The one I have now isn't the same one I found as a kid."

"But it has the same name?" asked Sofia, gazing up at her.

"Yes, actually, I've had a few pet rats, and they've all been named Templeton."

All of them were looking at her, but it was his gaze that felt like hands on her body.

"I know," she said, looking down at her plate. "It's—it's strange."

"I don't think it's strange," his grandmother said.

"I don't either," agreed his grandfather.

His father nodded. "Me neither."

"It's like Templeton never leaves you," said his mother.

"That's it," said the grandfather.

That's exactly it.

When dinner was over, Nico made a move to help clear the table, but Rocco's grandfather put a hand on her arm and shook his head.

Rocco smiled as he collected a pile of plates before carrying them into the kitchen.

"Come on, Nico," Rocco's grandmother said, taking her arm and leading her outside. "We made the dinner, so the men clean up. When they make the dinner, we clean up."

They sat on the terrace under a blanket of stars, drinking limoncello while Sofia and Beatrice were treated to hot chocolate before they ran off to play with Cat and Dog.

"Rocco's a lucky man," Nico said.

She blinked, surprised she'd said it aloud. She'd meant only to think it. Looking around at their smiling faces, she added, "I mean, to have all of you."

She kept waiting for them to fill the empty silence with some sort of polite response like, *Aren't you sweet?* and then to ask, And what about your family, dear? But they just looked at her with kind expressions. And somehow, she felt as though that empty space they'd given her with their silence and those gentle faces were a gift, and she could do with it whatever she wanted. That's when she realized her heart wasn't beating frantically, her palms weren't sweating, and her shoulders weren't hunched near her earlobes.

She looked at Rocco's mother. "I never really knew my mother. She died when I was very young. I carry her photo with me."

"Do you have it with you now?" Beatrice cried, suddenly running up and seemingly appearing from out of nowhere.

Nico nodded.

"May I see it?" Rocco's mother asked.

Nico reached in her pocket and drew it out, handing it to her.

Sofia had joined her sister. The girls looked over their grandmother's shoulder.

"She's pretty," Sofia said.

"Really pretty," said Beatrice.

"She is," said their mother, Isabella, who'd walked over to see.

"She's beautiful," said Rocco's mother, handing the photo to Rocco's grandmother. "Like her daughter."

"And loved," said the grandmother, running her fingers over the cracks and folds in the photo. "Loved deeply, still to this day."

Nico felt her eyes sting and drew a deep breath to still any tears.

Rocco's mother sighed. "There are all kinds of families, aren't there? Some you're born with, and others come to you." She looked over at Nico. "Rocco has told us about your friend Charles. We've seen him at a couple of the races. Will you bring him with you the next time you visit?"

Nico was afraid if her mouth or head made any movement or her vocal cords any sound, that might make the tears her eyelids had managed to hold on to spill over. She offered a tentative smile and hoped it was enough to convey what she was really feeling, which was a warmth and gratitude that felt bigger than the night sky.

Reaching over, Rocco's mother squeezed Nico's hand.

"And Templeton!" cried Beatrice and Sofia. "Can Templeton come too?"

"Of course. Templeton is always welcome."

Nico sighed.

"It's so good to have you here," his mother said. "We can see how happy Rocco is."

"Stop already," Isabella cried. "You're making Nico uncomfortable."

Nico froze. She couldn't think how to respond.

"I don't mean to make you uncomfortable, dear. I'm not presuming anything. That's why I put you in separate rooms." She reached over and placed a hand on Nico's arm. "It's just I know my son. I know when he's happy. And I see the way he looks at you."

"Mamma, stop!"

"Okay, okay, but don't tell me you can't see the change in him."

The grandmother nodded. "It's true. Such a difference. That woman made the last few years absolutely hell for him."

Are they talking about Carolyn Wickham?

"She never forgave him for ending the relationship," said his mother.

His sister sighed. "She never forgave him for not loving her."

The grandmother looked at Nico. "We thought she might ruin his racing career altogether."

His mother shook her head. "She tried."

"Yes, she did," said his grandmother. "It's been hard for him to trust a woman since then."

That word *trust*. Why did it hurt so much? Why did it make her feel sick to her stomach?

Why are you asking why? You know why.

After that, the men came out, and talk about Carolyn stopped.

As the sun set over the Italian alps and the sky turned from dusky gray to violet, deep purple, and finally black, Nico talked and laughed. But most of the time she watched and listened. She could see how much they loved one another. Really loved one another. And she was content to just sit back and absorb the warm glow that was Rocco's family, all the while thinking how very lucky this man was.

She was still thinking it when she turned off the bedside lamp and lay gazing up at the ceiling, wondering how she was ever going to sleep.

She wanted him. Wanted him now. Next to her. Inside her.

Does counting sheep really work? Do people really do that?

She sighed.

Is it possible? Am I happy? I feel happy.

Dinner, as much as she'd enjoyed it, had been difficult. She had kept waiting for the questions—the inevitable questions. Preparing herself for how she would answer them. *And what about your family, Nico? Who took care of you after your grandfather died? Where are they now? What do they do?*

But the questions never came. Not even after dinner when they sat outside, listening to the river, looking up at the stars, and sipping limoncello.

That in and of itself would have been surprising enough. But what was even more surprising was her. Talking. Not about her entire past. But some of it. The best of it.

I think I am happy.

Soon after, her eyes grew sluggish, and she drifted off—no sheep required.

■ ■ ■

Rocco shut the door quietly behind him. He pulled down the covers and smiled, seeing that T-shirt, and then slipped into bed beside her. He placed his hand on her thigh and slid his fingers up her silky skin.

Her eyes flew open. "What—"

He slapped his hand over her mouth and straddled her.

Placing his mouth next to her ear, he whispered, "You have to be quiet. Really quiet."

He removed his hand.

"But—"

His hand flew over her mouth again.

He shook his head. "You're a naughty girl, Nico. Do you never do as you're told?"

Those black eyes flared back at him while his other hand crept up her thighs and slipped under her T-shirt.

"Remember," he whispered, "quiet."

His hand slid between her thighs, and one finger slipped easily between the wet lips of her vagina.

Damn, he thought, gazing down at her.

Tell me you were dreaming of me.

Slowly, he removed the hand that was over her mouth.

Her chest moved up and down as he watched her struggle for breath.

Her lips parted. She was about to say something. As his finger skated smoothly back and forth, he held a finger from his other hand to his lips.

"If you want me to be quiet," she managed in a harried whisper, "you have to stop doing that."

"I don't want to stop doing that." He grinned as his finger slipped inside her.

The south pole definitely didn't want to. And he made sure she knew it, pressing into her.

He slid his finger slowly out, watching her, and then dipped it back in the pool of hot liquid. She looked like she was about to scream, but she swallowed it.

He grinned. "Do you want me to stop?"

She blinked but said nothing.

"I didn't think so." He shut his eyes and hung his head as his breathing became more rapid and his heart began to beat so hard, it felt as though every cell in him was throbbing.

"Damn, Nico. Are you always like this?" He pushed his finger deeper inside her. "Or is it just me?"

Her lips parted. But all he heard was her breath coming and going in deeper and deeper waves.

He waited until he could feel her throbbing and clutching his finger before he took it out.

You're evil, she mouthed.

He grinned as he lifted her T-shirt and pinched her nipple. Lowering his head, he took one breast in his mouth, sucking, then nipping, and then biting down. Hard. She arched her back and made a fist with one of her hands, hitting his arm. But he didn't stop. He only chuckled as he took the other breast in his hand, tweaking the nipple—hard.

Finally, he lifted his head, gazing down at her and grinning. "See, now these are definitely more delicious than casonsei."

She hit him again.

He took the first one in his mouth.

"Even better than chocolate."

Her breathing grew ragged, her breasts rising to meet his mouth.

"I—can't," she whispered.

He brought his face to hers, looming over her, and then lowering himself so his lips brushed hers.

"Do you want me inside you?" he whispered.

She nodded.

"Then you can." He slid his pajama bottoms down his legs and kicked them loose.

"And you will."

Fixed on those dark eyes, he felt himself slip into that dark abyss as he entered her.

She opened her mouth, but he shook his head.

Not yet, he kept telling himself as he moved slowly in and out.

But she was so hot and so wet. And she was gripping him so tight. He clenched his teeth, willing himself not to come. Yet.

She ran her fingers down his back and then stopped just above his ass.

She smiled. "You have dimples," she whispered.

He pushed deeper. He wanted to be so deep inside her, she wouldn't have breath enough to whisper. So deep she wouldn't have breath enough to breathe.

She crooked her finger, and he pushed deeper still as he lowered himself.

She gasped. "That," she whispered.

He pushed deeper.

She dug her nails in his back. "Little prince."

And deeper.

He watched her throat and heard her barely choke out the words.

"Is. Not. Getting. A. Happy. Ending."

He grinned, clutching her head, moving faster and deeper. "He's already got it. It's just. About. Here."

And with one final thrust, every cell in him exploded just before he collapsed.

CHAPTER THIRTY-THREE

NICO AND ROCCO

Nico stood looking out the window of the private home Rocco had rented. Her gaze slipped from the olive trees and citrus groves dotting the sloping hills below. Beyond that was another small medieval village situated on a peninsula that was bathed by the Adriatic Sea on the east side and the Ionian Sea on the west.

The days with Rocco's family had been lovely. She'd never tired of them although she was glad to be alone with Rocco now. At his family's home, every night he'd come into her room, and they'd made love in a way Nico hadn't thought possible. Quiet and hushed yet at the same time urgent and passionate. During the day, there was nothing obvious to indicate they were lovers—no holding of hands, no kissing. But there was the way they looked at each other, the fire in their eyes and the desire in their voices when they spoke. Nico couldn't tell whether or not his family noticed. Although she frequently caught Sofia and Beatrice looking at her and then at him, smiling and giggling.

She was glad there was no public display. She didn't feel altogether comfortable making their relationship known to his family. At least not yet. But, she thought with a pang, perhaps not ever. She still didn't know what this would look like when the season started up again. And more importantly, she still didn't know what he was thinking. He must be as uncomfortable about it as she was—possibly even more. After all, he never made any overture that would have told his family . . . what?

She couldn't say they were in love. That couldn't be true. If it were, he wouldn't be able to stop himself from making it known. Isn't that what happened when people were in love? How could she know when she'd never experienced it herself?

Her phone rang. She jumped.

Ever since Monte Carlo, those mysterious calls from Italian phone numbers had stopped. She couldn't decide whether she should feel relieved or more concerned.

Even now, she couldn't decide when she saw that it was Charles. Her first impulse had been to heave a huge sigh of relief, but on the tail end of that sigh hung a vague fear that never seemed to leave her.

"Hello, Charlemagne."

She'd already told Charles what had happened between her and Rocco. Charles filled her in on the latest details surrounding his relationship with Mateo and then made Nico describe where they were staying when she refused to describe the characteristics of Rocco's penis.

"What about once racing starts up? How are you guys going to handle it?" Charles asked.

Nico swallowed the stone that lodged in her throat and sank to her stomach whenever she thought about going back to racing. It should be something she was looking forward to. It was. She wanted to race. But now her relationship with Rocco had complicated the matter.

"We haven't talked about it. I keep meaning to bring it up and then something gets in the way."

"His dick?"

Nico laughed. "No!"

"His ass?"

"Stop it!"

"And he hasn't brought it up?"

"Uh-uh. But he must be thinking about it too. We return to racing in a week. You're even thinking about it." Nico paused. "Charles, why are you thinking about it? Are you thinking it can't work once we're back to racing? That we'll have to end it? That we can't have both?"

"No! Absolutely not! What I am thinking and what you two have to decide is whether or not you make it public."

"Well, we can't keep it private forever."

If *we continue after the racing starts*, she thought. She couldn't bring herself to say that out loud. It was painful enough just to think it.

Perhaps Rocco was thinking this was a romantic fling that would stop once racing resumed. That must stop once it did. He'd probably had such flings before, lots of them.

"I wasn't suggesting you keep it private forever," Charles said. "You might want to keep it private at the beginning. Or maybe until the season ends. And then take it from there."

If there was anywhere to take it by then.

Charles was right, of course. How could they make it public? What would Casey say? The press? The other drivers? No, no, and no. It would be a mess.

But if they kept it private, didn't that suggest all this was too much trouble, too much drama? It was bound to interfere with the racing.

How could they have been so stupid? How could she have been so stupid? Not to have thought about any of this?

But she had thought about it. It was just that other things drowned out such thoughts. Things like Rocco and how she felt when she was near him. How she felt when he did things. The smell of him. Even the sound of his voice. And it had gotten worse. Far, far worse. Because it had gone far, far beyond that. Being around his family. And seeing that sweet, endearing part of him. That feeling of pure joy when she'd seen him on that podium. When she'd seen him win in Monaco.

She was falling for him.

No, it was worse than that.

She'd already fallen.

And what about New Year's Eve at Drink and Dive? She might have been able to live with not telling him had they just remained teammates. But now?

Just then she heard the door open.

"He's back. Call you later?"

"Sure," Charles said.

Rocco came in, carrying coffee and a paper sack. He set them down. "What are you doing out of bed?"

He didn't give her a chance to respond. He picked her up and carried her to the bed, kicking and screaming, threw her on it, and then threw himself on top of her.

Nico laughed. "I don't know why we came to this beautiful location, when all our time here has been spent in bed."

"Because I want to have you all to myself. I don't want to share you with anyone. And that includes my family. Actually, now that we're here, I've realized I don't want to share you with any of what's out there either." He paused. "Are you disappointed? Do you want to go out?"

She shook her head. "But what took you so long? You said you were just going to get coffee and croissants."

"You missed me? Can't have me out of sight for even an hour?"

"Has anyone ever told you you're cocky?"

"Once or twice."

"There's a reason the little prince's head grew to be so enormous."

"You still haven't finished that fairy tale."

"Would you like me to finish it now?"

"Later," he said, reaching for the bag.

"What's that?"

"Take that off."

She was wearing the pale lavender negligee. "Why?"

"You don't want to get jam on it, do you? It might not come out."

"What?" she shrieked and began scurrying like a crab to get away.

He grabbed her ankles, pulled her down, and straddled her. Then he took the thin, transparent material in his hands and ripped it open.

"Hey," she cried.

"I'll buy you a new one."

He grabbed the bag. "I had to go to six pastry shops before I found some bomboloni."

"Bomboloni?"

"Jelly doughnuts." He pulled one out, broke it in half, dug his finger in, and scooped out some raspberry jam. "I've been wanting to do this for a long time."

He held his finger over her breast, watching while the jam dripped in fat sticky globs on her nipple. She could feel it sliding down the swell of her breast. Then he placed his finger there, sweeping the jam in slow and deliberate circles around her nipple.

He stared at it and then lifted his eyes to meet her gaze.

She shivered. Her breathing, slow, steady, and deep at first, started to catch, becoming ragged as she felt a warm glow flood her body.

"You're making a mess," she murmured.

"I'll clean it up."

He lowered himself, his hot breath like steam as he took her in his mouth and his wet, plump tongue licked up every last drop.

"You definitely taste better than casonsei," he murmured.

■ ■ ■

Rocco stroked her dark hair, liking the way it fell across the pillow, reminding him of Botticelli's painting *The Birth of Venus*—except with raven tresses rather than golden ones.

They were lying in bed after making love, eating jelly doughnuts and drinking coffee.

Nico warned, "If you get any of that jam in my hair—"

He grinned. "You'll what?"

"I'll curse the little prince with an ending more miserable than Snow White's stepmother."

He laughed and pulled her into him. "No, you won't. And you know why?"

"Why?"

"Because you like the little prince. No matter how cocky he gets." He paused, pressing himself into her. "In fact, you like him especially when he's cocky."

He was hard. Again. Already.

She laughed and tried to push him away, but he held her close.

"The little prince isn't all bad, you know," he said.

"I know. He rescued Cat and Dog."

"That he did."

"But why name the dog *Cat* and the cat *Dog*?"

"I guess I don't like things always going one way, the same way, the expected way. Like a girl having a rat for a pet. That's not expected."

She smiled. "I guess not."

He propped himself up on one elbow. With his other hand, he ran his finger along her collarbone. "Nico, when we were locked in that room in Barcelona, while you were asleep, I grabbed your racing suit to cover your legs because it was getting cold, and a photo and a piece of paper dropped out." He paused. "I wasn't snooping. They just fell out and I picked them up. I put them back. But I did look at them before I did. I'm sorry."

■ ■ ■

Nico clutched his hand in hers and kissed it. "You don't have to be sorry."

She wondered what her face must have looked like to make him think he should be and felt a small pang.

"The photo is of my mother, and the drawing is of my grandfather."

"That's what I thought."

"It's the only photo I have of my mother. I don't have any of my grandfather. Well, one that was given to me after he died. But you can't see his face. So, I draw a sketch of him every day so I don't forget what he looked like."

Now he's going to ask you why you have only one photo of your mother and none of your grandfather.

She waited. But the questions didn't come.

He lowered his head and kissed her forehead. A tender kiss. "Your nonno was a lucky man. To be loved like that by you."

He swept his thumbs gently across her lashes and down the sides of her face, sweeping the tears away.

Should she tell him? If not all of it, some of it?

She thought back to those things she'd admitted during that Never Have I Ever game. Should she tell him the truth about her being handcuffed to a bedpost? Tell him that Uncle Jack and Aunt Milly had done it in those early days to make certain she wouldn't run away when they went out? Should she tell him Uncle Jack and Aunt Milly weren't really her uncle and aunt? They were just a couple of grifters who found it useful to have a little girl when trying to con people.

Should she tell him about the black eye and the scar? That Mickey, the man she'd run away with when she was sixteen, had given them to her. That when she'd refused to do something he'd asked her to do and he told her it was okay and kissed her, that as he'd kissed her, he'd sliced the back of her head with a knife.

She shivered.

"Are you cold?" he asked.

She shook her head.

He must be wondering about the scar.

She stiffened every time he touched it.

It was one thing to tell him about Uncle Jack and Aunt Milly. But Mickey? She was older then. She was that woman he met on New Year's Eve in Drink and Dive. How could she tell him that? If she did, he would never look at her the same way again. He would never say her grandfather was a lucky man to be loved by her. All this would be gone.

■ ■ ■

Rocco watched her swallow. He could see her throat was tight. It seemed difficult for her to tell him even this much about her past.

He wondered about that scar. Whenever he touched it, she became rigid. He tried not to because he could feel her body grow cold; but sometimes in the midst of his passion and their lovemaking, it happened by accident.

He wanted to tell her she didn't have to tell him about it, but if she wanted to, she could. He wanted her to know she could trust him. He had the feeling that trust didn't come easy for her. And he knew what that felt like.

In a week, they'd be back to racing. It was hard to believe, given neither one of them had talked about it. He suspected Nico might have told Charles about their relationship. But he'd told no one. Not even Dario.

He'd intended to tell his cousin and had phoned him when he'd gone out for coffee, but then decided against it, recalling the concern Dario had expressed about this very thing. He hadn't even told Dario that Nico had come with him to visit his family.

His family knew. They knew without him telling them a thing. He could see it on their faces. But of course, they would leave it to him to make the news public. Did he want to? Did she want to?

He hated to think about what the press would do with such information. How Casey and the team would react. The other drivers. Even Dario might make things difficult. And Carolyn?

He felt a sudden desire to tell Nico. To tell her everything. He drew a deep breath. Maybe she'd already figured it out from what he'd said. But he needed to say the words—aloud—to her.

"The married woman I had an affair with. Maybe you've already guessed. That was Carolyn Wickham."

"Oh."

"When I met her, it was the night after my third F3 championship trophy. After celebrating with the team, I went alone to a bar. I couldn't get the thrill that ran through me to stop or even slow down. It was as though my blood were made of high-octane fuel. And she was there. And sure, she was attractive, but it was talking about the race that really roused my interest. She'd seen the race and seemed to understand what I was feeling."

He paused.

"I already told you it was really bad the way I found out she was married. It was the day I signed on with Blue Jet Lightning. I was so thrilled. I was going to be a Formula 1 driver. I shook her husband's hand as he welcomed me to the team with her standing by his side, acting as though we'd never met. She hadn't even warned me ahead of time. I felt like such an ass.

"I could have stopped things then. I should have. But I didn't. At first, I thought it was just a wild coincidence. Later, I discovered it wasn't, and what's more she'd been the one to suggest bringing me on."

Nico placed her hand on his cheek. "You don't have to—"

"I know I don't. I want to."

She placed her head back on his chest, and he stroked her hair.

"I began to have doubts. There were other F2 drivers every bit as good as me, not to mention a couple drivers in F1 who were without contracts. That kind of thinking—let's just say it wasn't good for my confidence. It didn't seem to matter if I won or not.

"I know my family and Dario want to blame the last few years on her, and I'm not saying she hasn't done things to undermine me and make it difficult, but she didn't have any power over me that I didn't give her. I was the one who doubted myself. Those doubts—that's why I was so raw about those tweets of yours."

She hugged him. "I understand."

"And it doesn't change things for you? I mean, with me?"

She lifted her head and gazed up at him. "No. Why would it?"

He shrugged. "Maybe I'm not the man you thought I was. Maybe it changes the way you see me."

She shook her head. "No. You're still the same annoying, arrogant, asshole, prick."

He laughed. "What?"

"It's what Charles and I *used to* call you. Before I really knew you. Said with affection, of course."

He grinned. "Of course."

She placed her head back on his chest. He felt her tremble.

He kissed the top of her head and stroked her cheek with his thumb.

"And what if you learned things about me that surprised you?" she asked. "Would that change how you feel? About me?"

He tried to look at her, but she kept her head on his chest and wouldn't look up at him. Her voice sounded different. He thought about that photo, the drawing, Templeton, and the fact that he knew nothing about her life after her nonno died.

But none of that matters.

"You're forgetting," he said, hugging her tighter, wanting to reassure her, "I already learned plenty of things when we played that drinking game. That doesn't change anything. Nothing you tell me will."

She remained silent.

It's because we start racing in a week. She's wondering about it too. Later tonight or maybe tomorrow, I'll bring it up, and we'll figure it out.

He held her tight, placing his chin on top of her head.

"You still haven't finished the fairy tale," he murmured, feeling himself drowning in all this uncertainty, and feeling certain about only one thing—she must feel herself drowning too.

She looked up at him and smiled, and he felt a rush of relief as though they'd both made it back to terra firma.

"Ah, yes," she said, "the little prince. Where were we?"

"I'll tell you where we were," he grumbled. "The dude has a swollen, enormous, and repulsive head. He can't run, he can't even walk without toppling over, and no one wants to bathe or feed him anymore. As a matter fact, he's so repulsive, no one wants to even look at him, including this mysterious stranger who refuses to come to the castle."

She giggled. "Right. Well, every command given by the little prince was refused by the stranger. So, finally the little prince asked politely if the stranger would please come to the castle, and the stranger did.

"The little prince was surprised when he saw the stranger. He was expecting a big, strong man, perhaps someone who he might befriend and knight as he had Knight Dario. But the stranger was nothing but an ordinary girl."

Rocco sighed. "Should have seen it coming."

"The little prince wondered how this girl could have managed to make the treacherous and difficult voyage to his remote kingdom.

"So, he asked her. And her answer was simple.

"She told him it was because she wanted to. And if she wanted to do something, she did it.

"So, the little prince asked her if she wanted to bathe him. He told her all the women in the castle did so and considered it a great honor. But she told him no, she didn't want to, and she left.

"The next day, he asked her again to come to the castle. This time, he asked if she wanted to feed him. She gave him a funny look and shook her head. But she told him she was hungry and that she would eat lunch with him, but he would have to feed himself.

"The little prince didn't like this answer, but he thought she must want to spend time with him or she wouldn't have suggested having lunch. So, they sat down to a splendid table and ate."

"Did they have casonsei?" Rocco asked.

Nico tilted her head, looking up at him and smiling. "They did. And chocolate."

"And jelly doughnuts."

"And jelly doughnuts," she echoed.

"After lunch," Nico continued, "the little prince asked her if she would like to stay. 'And do what?' she asked. The little prince thought. She had told him she didn't want to bathe him and she didn't want to feed him.

"'You can dress me,' he said.

"'But you're already dressed,' she replied.

"'But I'll need to change into my pajamas before I go to sleep,' he said.

"'But it isn't even dark out yet,' she said.

"The little prince glanced out the window. It was true. He hadn't thought about that. 'Well, then you can leave now,' he said, 'and come back later when it's dark.'

"She shook her head. 'No, I don't want to,' she replied. 'You can dress yourself.'

"He sighed, but before she left, he asked if she would come again tomorrow, and she agreed.

"When she came the next day, he asked if she would read to him. She said he could read himself. But she would sit and read a book alongside him. So, they sat by the fire and each of them read a book.

"The next day, he asked if she would take him for a walk. He told her that he needed to be wheeled around in a special carriage, given his enormous head. She told him she didn't want to, and he would have to walk himself.

"She told him she thought he could manage it because it looked like his head had gotten smaller.

"'I'll walk alongside you, and we'll see,' she said.

"And much to the little prince's surprise, she was right. It was true. His head had gotten smaller, and he was able to walk.

"Other people noticed his head had gotten smaller too, and the women in the castle wanted once again to bathe him, to feed him, to do everything they could for him. But he told them he could do it himself. And he thought he preferred to do it himself.

"After that, every day he would walk with the girl. Even when she didn't come to the castle, he would go looking for her and walk beside her. And every day, his head continued to shrink."

"It's not going to go the other way, is it?"

Nico frowned. "What do you mean?"

"Shrink to an abnormally small size, like a speck of dust."

Nico laughed. "No. Just listen. We're almost at the end. One day, the girl told him she was tired of walking and she wanted to run. But the little prince insisted they walk. Secretly he was afraid, thinking maybe he couldn't run, remembering what had happened the last time he had tried. But the girl said she wanted to run, and that's what she was going to do.

"She waved to the little prince and took off. He watched her and thought, *I want to run too*. And so he did, and the two of them ran side by side.

"They ran and ran and ran until they were too tired to run anymore.

"After that, the king and queen told the little prince they would cancel the proclamation that running and racing were forbidden. They told him he could resume the races he so loved. But the little prince didn't want to.

"He went to the girl and told her he wanted to see where she came from. 'Will you take me there?' he asked.

"She smiled and said, 'Yes.'

"And so, he waved goodbye to the king and queen, Knight Dario, and the villagers and said one day he would return.

"They all wished him well, and he and the girl set out.

"And that was just the beginning of their adventure. After seeing where the girl came from, they journeyed to other places. And the little prince got to see all the places he'd only dreamed of before, and he was happy."

Rocco waited.

"That's it?"

"You didn't like it?"

"I did. But you know, it's a fairy tale, so . . ."

"So . . . ?"

Rocco sighed. "'And he lived . . .'"

"Oh, right. And *they* lived happily ever after."

His phone buzzed.

"It's probably my mamma," he said as he reached for it. "I think she figured out we were going somewhere together after we left, and she wants us to come by there again for a couple days before the season starts. She hinted as much before we left. I didn't commit to anything."

Nico smiled. "Let's go! I love your family."

Rocco felt a pinch of jealousy. He knew it was foolish. It was his family. And he loved his family. He just felt such a deep want in him, a want to have her all to himself. But he saw the way her face lit up at the mention of his family. She looked happy—really happy—which made him wonder. Had he ever seen her happy before? Like this happy? He couldn't deny her that.

I have my whole future to be with her.

He paused at that thought. Surprised by it.

My whole future?

He'd think about that later.

He kissed Nico. "Okay, I'll tell her we'll cut short our stay here and head back there. We can leave tomorrow."

He frowned as he stared at his phone.

"I was right. It's a text from my mamma. She says your uncle is there. He just showed up at my parents' house, looking for you."

Nico's brow wrinkled. Her eyes had a look. Was it fear?

"My uncle?"

"Yeah. Your uncle Mickey."

CHAPTER THIRTY-FOUR

ROCCO AND NICO

Rocco surveyed the man as they sat around the table eating dinner. He was nice enough, charming enough. He'd definitely charmed his mother and grandmother, Sofia and Beatrice too. He glanced over at his father and grandfather. The particular kind of charm he had wouldn't work the same way on his father and grandfather, although they seemed to like him as well.

He looked young for an uncle—that is, to be Nico's uncle. He had a pleasant, handsome face, light brown hair with hints of gold that fell in playful curls around his cheeks, and warm brown eyes with lashes that were almost too thick and long. Rocco tried to find a weak feature—chin, mouth, nose—but he couldn't find one. He was tall, about the same height as Rocco, and definitely fit. His manner was kind and open, he wasn't boorish, didn't talk about himself unless asked, and seemed sincerely happy not only to see Nico but also to meet all of them and to visit this part of Italy.

So why don't I like the man?

Maybe because he seems too affable.

Nico hadn't offered much information about him after that text. Her answers to Rocco's questions had all been vague, perhaps even evasive. What's more, he couldn't escape the feeling that his family welcomed seeing the man more than she did.

He looked over at Nico, who was sitting directly opposite him and next to her uncle.

He looked nothing like Nico. There was no family resemblance.

Rocco stretched out his leg, touching her foot with his. But rather than her looking up at him, her eyes shifted to her uncle before darting back to her plate, and she moved her foot away.

He watched the man place his arm around her. He stared at the man's hand on her shoulder and waited for him to remove it. And then he blinked as he watched the man's fingers. Was he stroking her shoulder? *That can't be right,* he thought, clenching his fists as his heart began to thud so heavy he felt it ringing in his ears.

Rocco felt an urge surging through his bloodstream to take that hand he had resting on her shoulder and wrench it behind the man's back.

Sofia nudged him, handing him a basket of crusty bread. He took it and placed a piece on his plate. When Rocco looked back across the table, he was relieved to see the man had removed his arm.

I guess he has to if he wants to eat.

Rocco reminded himself that this man was Nico's uncle. But that didn't stop the ringing in his ears.

Is he the reason she doesn't want to talk about her past? About her family?

He needed to get Nico alone. He needed to talk to her. *After dinner,* he thought, sighing as he heard his nonno tell yet another story about Rocco karting as a kid.

Now Uncle Mickey jumped in with one about Nico. He sounded proud, but Nico's head was cast down, her eyes on her plate.

■ ■ ■

Nico thought about that first dinner with his family at this very table. She hadn't been able to look Rocco in the eye then either. But how she'd felt then and how she felt now couldn't be more different.

"Competitive?!" Mickey roared. "I know you've seen Nico behind the wheel, but she's like that with everything. Crafty too. Oh, the stories I could tell you."

Nico's heart began to race. Stories? He was speaking to her, not them. He was letting her know. He had stories to tell. Plenty of them

What did he want? Money, to be sure, but what was his plan for getting it? Con or blackmail? The con, if it was big enough, would be more money, but in the long run, maybe blackmail was the smarter move.

She cast a sidelong glance at him as he went on. It was difficult to tell which gleamed brighter, his eyes or his teeth.

"As I always told her and taught her, the mental game is everything. Knowing when and how to make a move. Sizing up your opponent. Recognizing their weakness. My little girl here's a master at that. You set up your opponent to lose every bit as much as you set yourself up to win. What did I always tell you, topolina? Make every easy shot and make every shot easy."

Her heart did a swan dive. She even heard it land. *Splat.*

Swallow. Her mouth was so dry and her throat so tight, she couldn't.

He might not remember. Those exact words. Look up. And you'll know.

She did. She could never have imagined she could wish he would glare at her—the way he had in the beginning. But she did. Anything would have been better than the cold look she saw now.

Afterward, she would wonder how she managed to hold the fork in her hand, bring it to her mouth, chew, and swallow the food on her plate. She must have done these things because no one acted as though anything out of the ordinary had happened. No one else had felt that seismic shift of the tectonic plates and saw the earth open up, her feet balanced on the edge, toes hanging over. It wouldn't take much, and she would fall. Time enough would do it. And time was inevitable and relentless. It could not. Would not. Be stopped.

She watched Mickey follow the family out onto the porch and Rocco turn down the hallway that led to the bedrooms. She knew it wouldn't be long now.

She entered his old bedroom, the room she was sleeping in. Suddenly, a hand on her wrist swung her around, the door slammed shut, and she was face-to-face with Rocco.

He took a step toward her. She stumbled backward, and he grabbed her arms, pinning her against the wall.

"Now, I want you to do that to me."

Nico shook her head. "I don't— What do you mean? Do what?"

"Put my back up against the wall."

"What?"

"Just do it!"

"Why?"

"I'll do it then!"

He swung her and himself around, only stopping when it was his back that was flush with the wall. She stared down at his hands. It was the first time his touch hurt.

"Now bring your lips to rest lightly on mine and say my name."

She struggled to pull away but his hold was too strong. He pulled her to him. Her lips on his.

"Now say my name," he murmured.

Nico swallowed. Her throat was tight. "No," she croaked.

He shook her. "Do it! Damn it! Say. My. Name."

"Rocco," she whispered.

His hands softened, opening like the velvet petals of a flower. They no longer gripped her, but they still held her, and she made no attempt to free herself from them.

"Now kiss me," he whispered. "Kiss me like it's the last time your lips will touch mine. Kiss me like you want to burn that kiss in my memory, so that even if I wanted to forget, I couldn't. No matter how hard I tried."

The words were more than sound. She felt them on her flesh, on her lips. She felt them enter her, like it was him entering her.

Nico shook her head but suddenly stopped when she felt the tears welling up in her eyes. She did not want them to break free.

"Do it!"

"No, I won't. Rocco, let go of me."

He pulled her to him, parted her lips with his own.

His hot breath blazed through her like a brush fire, scorching every square inch of her flesh.

She told herself to pull away, push him away. But she held on, as though he were the only thing that would keep her from falling. She felt herself dissolving in his warm embrace. That liquification of anything that was solid in her. And she didn't care. She would gladly be a puddle at his feet, even if in the end he did nothing more than step in that puddle and walk away. If only he would not look at her with that cold stare.

"Now," he growled, his lips still on hers, "bite my lip."

"No."

"Do it!"

"I can't!"

"Okay, then just say the words."

"What?"

"You know."

"I don't."

"You do. Say it. Make every easy shot, Rocco, and make every shot easy."

CHAPTER THIRTY-FIVE

ROCCO AND NICO

He stared into those black eyes. How could he not have seen it? His gaze drifted down to that collarbone. He fisted his hands, resisting the urge to trace the length of it with his finger.

He remembered that cool, in control woman on New Year's Eve, and the way she'd played him.

That was Nico? This woman? They're one and the same?

He felt a familiar sick cold sweat, the same sick cold sweat he'd felt when he'd had to stand with a frozen smile on his face and shake Carolyn's hand as she stood next to her husband as though he were meeting her for the first time. And with the entire Blue Jet team and crew looking on.

"It was you!" he cried. "I can't believe I could be so stupid. I kept telling myself there was something. Something familiar. But I still don't understand. Okay. So, you made me look like an ass, even more of an ass, given I turned out to be your teammate. But why didn't you tell me? Especially since— Why would you be with me, like— Fuck! The things I told you."

"I—I—can— I can explain. I wanted to tell you. I just didn't know how."

He thought about that woman and how smooth she'd been. She was like some kind of professional you'd see in a movie. That made him think about how little he knew about the woman who stood before him now. She was so guarded, revealed so little about herself and her past. And then it hit him. That night.

"The drinking game," he said.

She frowned. "What?"

"When we played Never Have I Ever. All those things you admitted to doing."

"You admitted to the same things."

"That's different."

Her cheeks were flushed. "Why? Because you're a man and I'm a woman? That's it. Isn't it?" Her head dropped, and she gazed at his feet. "I knew what I was doing when I admitted to those things. I got my answer. You're thinking of those things, even now. You could never get past my past, the things I've done. What happened at Drink and Dive hardly matters."

"What do you mean, your past?"

She shrugged, but as she turned her head, he watched her hastily brush away tears from her cheek with the back of her hand. "The things I admitted I'd done during that drinking game and other things. What I did to you on New Year's Eve. Conning a man for money. It wasn't the first time I'd done that."

"You've done that before?"

She nodded.

Now that cold sweat burned hot.

That's why she was so good at it.

He turned away and began pacing. He still couldn't figure out what she was playing at. Why all the rest of it? What did she want from him?

Those stories about her mamma and nonno. They must be lies.

So, what about Mickey? Who was this guy?

He swung around, glaring at her. "And Mickey? Why did he suddenly show up now? You've never mentioned him. Why is he here? How did he know we'd be here?"

"I don't know how he found out. But he has ways. He's a con artist."

"Of course he is. And you let him put his grimy paws all over you."

She met his gaze. "What?"

"I saw the way he put his hands on you at the dinner table, the way he stroked you. Not exactly the kind of thing an uncle does with his niece. Is he really your uncle?"

She looked down and said nothing.

He grabbed her shoulders and shook her. "Answer me. Is he your uncle?"

She shook her head and uttered a "no" that was so quiet he almost wondered if he'd imagined it.

He let go. "I suppose that's something. It would be even worse if he were. I know exactly what he is to you."

"He's nothing to me now."

"Now? But he was once."

"Yes. But not anymore."

"I don't believe you."

She looked up at him. "It's true!"

"Keep your voice down," he hissed. "I don't want my family—" His eyes flew open so wide and so suddenly, his head began to pound.

My family. Why come here? She had to have told him. What are they planning?

The whole thing was bizarre. She was an F1 driver. Why would she involve herself in anything like this? But then he thought back to New Year's Eve. She saw her chance, and she jumped at it. She hated him that much. Even after everything that had happened.

"What is he out there doing with them now?"

"I don't know," she muttered. "But I wouldn't trust him. Your family shouldn't trust him. I didn't know he was here until your mother sent you that text. But I did worry he might come, that he might find me."

"And you left a trail of breadcrumbs to lead him right to my parents' house."

She lowered her head, and plump teardrops fell from her lashes. "I didn't mean to. I'm so sorry, Rocco."

"Spare me the tears. My family!"

"I'm sorry, Rocco. Really, I'm—"

She reached for him, but he pushed her away and turned his back to her.

It was bad enough they were teammates, but this? Why had she gone on to be with him like this? To come to his family home? To make his nieces fall in love with her? To make him fall— No! He would not even think it. Would not convince himself of something that could not be true.

It cannot be true.

What kind of woman . . . ?

You know what kind of woman. Carolyn is that kind of woman. But this one, standing before you now, is worse. Because being with Carolyn had never been like this.

When he next spoke, his words sounded stuttered and halting even to himself. It felt as though they were choking him.

"Inigo Montoya, the rat, your nonno, your mamma, the stupid fucking little prince—man, you really are good. I believed it. All of it. I'm just trying to figure out what you planned to do with it all."

"There was no plan," she sobbed. "None of it was part of a plan."

"I don't believe you. Why should I? All this time, making me believe you were someone else, making my family believe it."

"That woman on New Year's Eve, that's not me, that's part of the past. Okay, yes, my past, but it's not me. Not the real me. The time spent with you and your family—that's me—the real me."

He swung around.

"You stay away from my family. Do you hear me? I don't want you going anywhere near them. Ever. Again. When I think of how you used my nieces to get to me . . ."

Tears were streaming down her cheeks.

He swallowed. But he lifted his chin, fixing on what looked like a spider making its way across the wall.

"No," she said, sobbing. "I didn't. I would never. I love Sofia and Beatrice."

"I don't even want to hear their names coming out of your mouth. I can't believe I did this again. You're worse than Carolyn." He turned and marched up to her, holding his finger a mere inch from her nose. "If you think you're going to ruin this season for me—"

Nico shook her head. "No, I'm not, I wouldn't."

"You're damn right you're not. Here's what you're going to do. You're going to pack your suitcase, and you're going to leave. You're going to make up an excuse why you have to go. I'll have a talk with your *uncle* Mickey. God, what a fool I've been."

"No, Rocco. That's not— Will you at least let me explain? I'm not even expecting you to forgive me, but will you please just listen? For yourself as much as for me. You haven't been a fool. I—"

"Stop. I don't want to hear it."

He shoved her aside and began to open the door. "And when we're back to racing—stay out of my fucking way—both on the track and off it."

He slammed the door behind him.

■ ■ ■

Nico stood numb. It was as though she were in some parallel world where it appeared as though she were in the same space and time as Rocco, but in reality, she wasn't. She was so far away, she couldn't reach him. So far away, she would never be able to reach him. So far away, not because she had traveled to some other space and time, but because he had. He was beyond her now. No matter what she said, she'd lost him. He was gone.

Why hadn't she stuck to her plan in Monte Carlo? She was supposed to channel that woman he met at Drink and Dive. The woman who couldn't be touched. The woman who couldn't be moved. The woman who could never love or be loved.

Why hadn't she just let those elevator doors close and let Rocco think there was something between her and Anker? Why did she care what he thought of her? Why had she let him kiss her? Why had she come here?

She should have left the hotel room that night after he left. Then she wouldn't have been there when he came back the next morning. Then that *maybe* would have been a *no*, like it should have been.

She'd wanted to tell him; it was her who had been the fool, not him.

Somehow, she managed to move her limbs, and with trembling hands, wiped her tears and packed her suitcase.

She would fall apart later. She had a few days before the season began. She would go back to Vegas. Have a complete breakdown. And then Charles and Templeton would help her put herself back together again.

■ ■ ■

Rocco paced back and forth in the living room of the apartment he'd rented for this weekend's race—the first race after the three-week break.

Dario and Celeste sat on the sofa, looking stunned after what he'd told them.

Dario shook his head. "That was Nico? I can't believe it."

Rocco could. Now. He'd sensed something familiar about her from the beginning. From the very beginning. It was those eyes. Those pitch-black eyes. Thinking about those eyes gave him a moment's hesitation. Should he have given her a chance to explain? *No*, he thought. *Explain what?* She was a con artist, and that made her a liar. What else had she lied about?

He thought about Barcelona. Even that— He stopped pacing and swallowed. All of it. She could have lied about all of it. He had more reason to believe she had than she hadn't.

Dario came up behind him and placed a hand on his shoulder. "Are you going to be okay this weekend?"

"Of course I am," Rocco said, shrugging him off. "Why wouldn't I be?"

Maybe there was a silver lining here. Tomorrow he'd be hitting the track for the first practice session. So would Nico. He hadn't seen her since she'd left his parents' house. But if none of this had happened, how was it going to look between them on the track? They never did figure out how they were going to manage a relationship while racing.

And he knew why. Because it wasn't possible.

You already knew that, you idiot. And then you go and not only start up something but do it with another driver, a driver on your team—Nico Angelini of all people!

Rocco blinked when he suddenly realized Dario was staring at him.

"Is there something you're not telling us, Rocco?"

"Like what?"

Dario remained silent.

"Like maybe you fell for the girl?" Celeste ventured.

Rocco's eyes widened as he felt the pulse in his wrists throb and his palms sweat. "What?! Why do you say that?"

"Maybe because your face says it?"

"I haven't been sleeping well, that's all."

Celeste peered at him so intently it felt like she was trying to pierce his skull and read his thoughts. He turned away.

Celeste sighed. "Rocco, I'm so sorry. But . . ."

"But what?" Rocco snapped.

"Well, when she did that on New Year's Eve, she didn't know you."

"She knew damn well who I was. She called me by name."

"She knew who you were, but she didn't know *you*. Remember what it was like between you two? The stuff that you were saying on social media?"

"She was saying shit too!"

"Exactly. That's my point. I don't believe she went into that bar with a plan to con you. How could she? She didn't know you'd be there. But once she saw you, well, I guess, given some of the things that were said when you two were feuding, I can understand her wanting to—well, do what she did."

"You're not serious."

"Can you honestly tell me that you wouldn't have looked to do something similar given the chance—back then? If you could? Remember that tweet about the coffee? I mean, think about it, she didn't even know you'd be racing on the same team."

"Even if I would have, and I'm not saying I would, it's not the same. I haven't made a career out of lying and conning people. What about everything after that? Why not just tell me? Who knows what that *uncle* Mickey had planned. He sat down to dinner with my family, slept in their house. I heard him talking about some business with my parents and grandparents. Who knows what kind of con he was planning, how much money he might have stolen from them."

"Okay, but that doesn't mean she was intending to do whatever it was he had planned."

"You don't know that. How can you believe anything she says? How can you trust her? You can't. Period. She conned not only me but my family the minute she stepped foot in that house. Even before that with my nieces. It's bad enough not owning up to what she'd done were we just teammates, but . . ."

He couldn't finish that thought. He felt sick thinking of what he'd told her, what he'd done with her, and all the while her knowing he was clueless, making him look like a fool.

"Everything about her is suspect," he huffed. "That business about, her mamma dying, her nonno, Templeton. It's all bullshit."

Rocco slumped in a chair, holding his head in his hands. He rubbed his eyes to forestall any tears.

"Okay," Dario said, "I get it, about not trusting her. But we don't know for certain that everything she said was a lie. And who is Templeton?"

"A pet rat—supposedly."

"Really?"

"Really."

"Wow. I've never known anyone who has a pet rat."

"You still don't," Rocco spat. "You can bet she lied about that too."

"I don't know," Celeste said. "It's hard to see her making something like that up. It's too random. Why would she come up with a lie about a pet rat? I think it's true. And if it's true, then some of the other stuff she told you might be true too. Just because she didn't tell you she was that woman on New Year's Eve doesn't mean she lied about everything. Remember some of the things she admitted to when we played Never Have I Ever?"

Rocco lifted his head and pointed his finger. "There you go! Look at the things she admitted to doing. I should have known then."

"Known what?" asked Celeste. "You admitted to the same things."

"That's different."

"Why? Because you're a man?"

Rocco turned to Dario. "You want to jump in here? Anytime?"

Dario shrugged. "I don't know what to say. I understand the way you feel, Rocco. Definitely. But even you have to admit Celeste has a point."

Rocco glared at him.

Dario held up his hands. "Maybe you can't see it now. That's fair. But . . . with time . . . eventually, maybe . . . you'll be able to see it."

"God," Celeste said, "now I'm thinking about that black eye. That scumbag Mickey probably gave it to her."

Rocco put his head down again, thinking of that scar on the back of her head.

I will not feel bad for this woman. I'm the injured party here. I'm the one who's been wronged. She's conned everyone—including Dario and Celeste.

Celeste sighed. "Well, what did she say? I mean, did she say anything about why she did what she did?"

"No," Rocco huffed.

Celeste narrowed her eyes. "Did you give her a chance to explain?"

"Why? So, she could come up with more lies?"

"No, so she could explain. I'm not saying you should forgive her. I'm not saying you have to get back together with her or trust her. But don't you want to know? I mean, there has to be a story there."

"Oh, there's a story, all right. But that doesn't mean it's a true one. Trust me, she's good at telling stories."

That stupid fucking little prince. God you're an idiot, Rocco Vittori.

Celeste sighed. "I think she was torn. She must have feared if she told you, she would lose you. Which, given what happened, looks about right. It's sad."

"Excuse me! I'm the victim here."

Dario groaned. "This is all we need on the racetrack."

Rocco stood up and resumed pacing. "It'll just go back to the way it was in the beginning, before Monza."

Dario shook his head. "And that would be a good thing? Do you remember how well you were doing back then?"

"I'll be fine. I just mean she'll steer clear of me, and I'll steer clear of her."

"What about that Mickey?" Dario asked.

"You don't have to worry about him. I paid him off, put him on a flight, and told him if he ever came near Nico again, the next time he got on an airplane it would be in the cargo hold in a body bag."

"You did that for Nico?" Celeste asked.

Rocco blinked. "What's that?"

"Getting rid of Mickey. You did that for Nico?"

"What? No! I didn't do it for her. I did it for my family and myself."

"But you said Nico."

Did he?

"Well, yeah," he stammered, "her too. If he's hanging around her, that means he's hanging around me and my family. She is my teammate."

At least until the end of this season, Rocco thought, recalling what Carolyn had said to him about returning to Blue Jet Lightning.

Nodding, Celeste peered at him. “I see.”

“What?”

“What what?” Celeste said. “I just meant, I see your point.”

“Then why are you looking at me like that?” he demanded.

“Like what?”

“Like you know something I don’t.”

Celeste shrugged. “Am I?”

When Rocco turned his back, she mumbled, “Maybe because I do.”

“I heard that!” Rocco roared as he stomped into his bedroom and slammed the door behind him.

CHAPTER THIRTY-SIX

NICO

Am I really going to do this?

Nico's heart was pounding so heavy and with so much force, she felt as though at any moment it would suddenly explode from her chest and land splat on the floor.

Yes, you're going to do this. You have to. You have to at least try.

They'd done dismally since coming back. In some of the races, neither one of them had even finished because they'd both crashed.

She would say that they were back to where they were when they first began the season. But that wasn't true. They didn't glare at each other and fight. They didn't even look at each other. And they didn't talk at all. The atmosphere felt heavy as though an ominous dark cloud hovered over the entire team, threatening a storm that never came. Nico had decided that the only way to rid themselves of it was for the storm to break, even if she was the one who had to make it break.

Nico was worried they might not earn a single point in all the remaining races combined, not to mention Rocco blowing his shot at winning the trophy.

If they kept going the way they were, the outcome might be even worse for her. She might be let go. If that happened, she feared no one on the circuit would be willing to take a chance on her again. Her dream of being an F1 driver would be over.

She could not let that happen. Would not let that happen. She had to do everything and anything within her power to stop it from happening.

She glanced at the clock as she paced the length of the room and back, trying to walk off her nerves. It was Barcelona all over again. Only this time, there would be no Casey.

None of this should surprise you. You knew that kind of happiness couldn't last. He was going to find out eventually. You can't be with a person—really be with a person—and keep your entire past from them.

She could never be a part of his life, a part of his family. They could never accept her once they knew, just like he couldn't. And she didn't blame them. She didn't blame him.

You always knew it wasn't possible. It would never happen for you—a normal relationship, a normal life. Not for someone like you.

She jumped at the sound of his voice.

"Where's Casey?" he demanded.

Nico rushed to the door and slammed it shut.

"He's not coming."

"Bobby told me he wanted to talk to me—us."

She shook her head. "I just told Bobby to tell you that to get you up here. You're not leaving until you hear me out."

"I've already told you, I don't want to hear anything from you. What makes you think I'd believe anything you have to say?"

Her throat was so tight, she found it difficult to swallow. She had told herself she would look him in the eye and force him to do the same. But now, hearing his voice and seeing that cold look in his eye, she couldn't bring herself to. It was a good thing the floor was made of tile, simple white tile with no fancy designs. She could stare at it as she spoke without getting dizzy.

She cleared her throat. "It doesn't have anything to do with matters outside racing. I know that's over, and I've accepted it. But what I can't accept is you fucking up on the racetrack like you have been ever since we came back. You may not be able to trust me in your life off the track. Okay. I understand that. I can accept that. But what I can't accept is you doubting me as a driver and your teammate. I had to work just as hard as you to get here. In fact, I probably had to work harder."

"Spare me!"

That sparked anger in her, and she looked up.

"Are you really that dense? Did it escape your notice that I gave you an opening out there, blocking three cars so that you could pass through? You could have been up on that podium—should have been up there."

"I don't need *you* to win a race. So, don't do me any favors and get away from that door! Now!"

Looking at him, Nico thought that he might push her away, but she stood her ground.

"I'm not saying you need me to win a race. It should be obvious you don't, given you've done it before. And don't go thinking I was doing you any favors. I wasn't being selfless, just realistic. It's my rookie year. I don't have a shot at that championship. Not this year. But you do. So stop pouting and do something about it."

"I'm not pouting, and I am doing something about it."

"What you're doing is losing any shot at that championship. You've been doing it ever since we came back. And while you're at it, you've been undermining me as well. But then maybe that's the point."

"What does that mean?"

"Look, I'm not saying you should think of me. I wouldn't expect you to. But think about your family—your parents and grandparents, who've done everything they can to get you to where you are. Think about Sofia and Beatrice and how much they look up to their uncle Rocco. You shouldn't be trying to find ways to disappoint them. You may be an annoying, arrogant, asshole, prick. Hell, you've mastered the art. But you are an annoying, arrogant, asshole, prick who can drive better than anyone else out there!"

She opened the door and then paused as she was walking through it. Should she say it? Damn it, she would.

"You may feel like you can't trust me just like you can't trust Carolyn. But there's a difference between me and her. I want you to win. Not for you—you annoying, arrogant, asshole, prick—but for your family. You don't know how lucky you are. It's not all about you, Rocco. You wouldn't be here without them, and I've got news for you, the world and everything in it doesn't revolve around you. Your head is big enough. If it gets any bigger, you'll be like the little prince, and it won't fit in the damn car."

She heard something. Was he laughing?

"I can't believe you just said that."

She sighed, bit her lip. "I can't believe it either. I don't know where that came from."

Suddenly she was laughing too.

But once they'd stopped, she drew a deep breath. She felt as though she were going to cry. She felt how very badly she wanted to.

Exit stage right. Now.

She kept her head averted. She couldn't trust herself to look at him.

"Okay, well." She swallowed, doing her best to sound businesslike. "I think you get what I'm saying."

"Yes."

His voice wasn't cold. It wasn't harsh. It was . . . what?

Tender?

No. Not tender.

Do not go there.

She quickly left the room, running down the stairs and out of the paddock.

It had gone well. Better than she'd expected.

I wish I was stronger, she thought, keeping her head down and wiping her eyes. *I wish I had it in me to walk out of the room holding my head high instead of running like a scared rabbit.* What was she so afraid of?

You know.

She was afraid her face would betray her. That he was still written all over it. That if she'd stayed just a little bit longer, he'd see it—the way she felt about him, the way she still felt about him even knowing he no longer felt the same way about her.

She drew a deep breath.

She needed to think of him as a teammate and nothing more.

And she needed to do something else.

She'd do it when they raced at Imola in Emilia-Romagna. It was only a few hours away. That would be her last chance before the final race of the season. After that, she might not get another one.

CHAPTER THIRTY-SEVEN

NICO

Nico had rented a car and drove until she reached the small country road that led to the village. She pulled off to the side of the road and parked. From there, she walked the rest of the way—all five miles of it. It wasn't until she'd reached the stone path that she remembered there was a parking lot much closer.

She'd called ahead. They were expecting her.

Now as she entered the house and followed Rocco's mother into the living room where they were all sitting, she tried to recapture that feeling of warmth and light she'd felt when she'd come here before. But all she could feel was weight—like an anchor that had been strung around her heart, her gut, and her legs and then flung out to sink to the bottom of the sea. Even her breath felt as though it were attached to that anchor. She hoped she could manage to find the words and say them aloud.

If you don't face your past now, you'll never get beyond it.

She was relieved when Isabella assured her that Sofia and Beatrice were outside and were instructed to stay there. There were some things she couldn't say with them here. They were so young. How could they understand? But then, how could any of them understand?

"I'm sorry that I left the way I did and just disappeared. You deserve the truth, and I don't know what or how much Rocco has told you."

She looked searchingly at their faces.

"He didn't tell us anything, dear," his mother said. "But we knew something happened when you and your uncle Mickey left like you did."

She swallowed. "He's not my uncle."

And there it was, she thought as she looked around the room at their faces. That same warm, welcome, and safe space.

No look of surprise. No frowns. No gasps.

"You don't have to do this, Nico," Rocco's father said.

"Oh, but I do. People talk about welcoming people into their home, and it's just talk. But the way you welcomed me—I just need you to know that I know. And I didn't—I don't—take it lightly. It means"—she placed her hand on her heart—"it means everything to me. And in return, all I gave you was Mickey. It's because of me he was here. That never should have happened. Never would have happened if it wasn't for me. He's a con man, a horrible man. And he could have ruined you. Because of me. And I'm so sorry about that. I'm not asking for you to forgive me. I'm not here for that. I just need you to know the truth. I owe you that."

She wished she could get up and pace. Do something with her body. All the words felt so heavy. That's because behind them lay a flood of water. Maybe the anchor was a good thing. It kept everything in place, including her tears.

Please let me get through this without crying. I don't want to make them feel obligated to feel sorry for me.

"I don't know where to begin," she muttered.

"Well," said Rocco's mother, "they usually say it's best to begin at the beginning. But sometimes it's not easy to see where that beginning is."

"True," his grandmother said. "Why not begin with your mother, dear?"

Nico nodded. "Well, you already know my mother died when I was less than two years old, and I never knew my father. You know I was raised by my grandfather, that he was a mechanic. That my love for racing comes from him."

She drew a deep breath. *Here goes.*

"What you don't know is that when I was twelve and we were at the farmer's market, Grandpa collapsed. Some people tried to revive him. But when the ambulance came, they said he was dead. He'd had a heart attack.

"I was standing with people I knew, friends of my grandpa's. He knew just about everyone who lived in that small Midwestern town. I still don't know exactly how it happened. At some point, somebody's hand was in mine. I think I heard them telling someone they were family, but I'm not sure if that's something I just made up in my head."

Nico drew a deep breath. "They weren't family. I'm still not sure how they did it. I can't remember if they'd convinced everyone, and everyone just watched me walk off with them, or if they'd taken off with me when no one was looking. It's all a blur. Uncle Jack and Aunt Milly, that's what they wanted me to call them."

She felt, looking at their faces, that she might not be the only one finding it difficult to swallow.

"They didn't abuse me," Nico said, feeling the need to reassure them. "They weren't all bad. They gave me a kind of home, I guess. They fed me and bought me clothes. I think they loved me in their way. Milly wasn't able to have children, and I think she'd wanted to have a little girl. But they were grifters, con artists like Mickey."

She glanced around the room, but their faces revealed nothing. *No,* she thought, *that's not right. They do reveal something—one thing.*

They're listening.

"In the beginning, they were careful about having me in public. I think they were afraid I might say something, that they'd be found out. So, they handcuffed me to the bed to make sure I wouldn't run away. I thought about it. But then I had nowhere to run to. If they hadn't taken me, I suppose I would have been placed in foster care.

"Eventually, we came to an understanding. I wasn't going to run away, and I wasn't going to reveal their secret because their secret was now my own. It was useful having me around. People were much more willing to trust a couple with a young girl."

Nico looked down at her hands. Her palms were sweating. Her heart racing.

"Is that how you met Mickey?" Isabella asked. "Through Milly and Jack?"

She lifted her face and nodded.

"He taught me how to play poker and pool, how to read signals, people's faces, and their body language. He was kind to me. Or as kind as anyone had been since my grandfather died. I told him about my grandfather and the karting and how much I missed it.

"He convinced Jack and Milly to let me do it, telling them there were people with money in that world. If I turned out to be good at it, there could be money in it. At that point, I wasn't doing any serious racing, but I still loved it. I could feel my grandfather with me when I raced."

Nico smiled, forgetting for a moment what she was about to tell them. She quickly looked down.

"When I turned sixteen, Mickey took me away—" She paused, shaking her head. "No, that's not right. I ran away with Mickey. We went to Massachusetts, where the age of consent is sixteen. With the money I made at poker and pool and some of Mickey's money, I was able to keep racing. Mickey was willing to put some money into it as long as he thought there would be some kind of payoff down the road."

Nico cleared her throat.

"Would you like some water, dear?" Rocco's mother asked.

She shook her head. "Thank you. I'm okay." She drew a deep breath. "I was pretty much a passive observer when I was with Jack and Milly. But that wasn't the case with Mickey. I did some things I'm truly ashamed of. I was the girl on his arm when he conned people—another set of eyes and ears. I was there to be a distraction, charm people, mostly men." Her cheeks burned, and as much as she wanted to face the truth by facing them, she found herself looking down and staring at the wood floors. "And sometimes charming meant sex."

Her eyes bristled, and she willed the tears to wait.

She drew another deep breath and exhaled.

"When I was racing, I knew that was the only place I wanted to be. But Mickey kept pressing me about targeting people in the racing world. Even at the level I was doing, there were people with money.

"So, late one night, I left him. I took what money I could and tipped off the people Mickey was conning at the time."

She felt her shoulders lower. There it was. But there was more.

"I went back to the town where I'd grown up and found my grandfather's tombstone in the cemetery. I thought there would be weeds, but there weren't. People in that town knew him and loved him. Someone had even placed some flowers there. True, they were old and dried out.

But someone at some time had thought enough of Grandpa to bring him flowers. And when someone pulled the weeds, they didn't take them away and throw them out. I suppose to some people they would have been trash. But I don't know. Even dried and withered flowers can be nice, you know?"

One plump tear escaped her eye, followed by another and another.

Damn it.

She hastily lowered her head and brushed them aside and then saw a wrinkled and weathered hand holding out a handkerchief. She took it and looked up. It was Rocco's grandfather. She noisily blew her nose.

"While I was standing there, I heard someone call my name. 'Nico, is that you?' It was a man who'd been a friend of my grandfather's. He used to bring his car into my grandfather's shop. He said they'd worried and wondered what had happened to me. They'd even put out an Amber Alert, but of course I was never found. I told them about Aunt Milly and Uncle Jack but not the truth. I told him they were family and that I'd had a good upbringing. He wondered if I was still racing and took me out to the track just outside town, the one Grandpa used to take me to, and there were a couple cars they let me take around the track. It was wonderful to be behind the wheel without Mickey there. The man said if I was really serious, he knew a guy out in Nevada, just outside Vegas, who might be able to help. And I thought, *Vegas, of course.* I could make good money there, doing the only thing I knew how to do, the only thing I was good at other than racing—playing poker and pool.

"So, I went. Eventually, the man sponsored me. After a while, he put me in touch with other people, and I was able to gain more sponsors. My racing career took off from there.

"I never knew what had happened to Mickey, but I figured he'd probably left the country to escape the authorities. Eventually, he was able to track my whereabouts, and he sent me threatening letters for a couple years but then stopped.

"And then just as I was about to sign with Maverick Racing, I received a letter postmarked from Italy. I knew at some point he would find me."

She paused.

Now that night at Drink and Dive.

"On New Year's Eve, the night before I was set to sign the contract with Maverick, I went to a bar—"

She blinked as she saw Sofia and Beatrice tiptoe into the room, holding their fingers to their lips.

"Sofia and Beatrice!" Isabella cried. "What are you doing?"

Sofia tilted her head, raising one shoulder. "We wanted to see Nico."

Beatrice mimicked her sister, raising the other. "Most definitely."

"It's okay," Nico said. "I think it's okay if they hear the rest."

"All right," Isabella said.

Nico drew a deep breath. She was close now. Almost to the end of it. "I wore a short blonde wig. Like I used to when I"—she glanced at Sofia and Beatrice before looking away—"when I, well, you know. I don't know why I did that. I don't know if it was nerves over the fact that I was going to sign a contract to race Formula 1 or that letter arriving when it did, but I didn't plan on doing what I did. Not until I entered that bar and saw Rocco."

She told them about the pool game and the money. She left out what had happened outside the bar.

"I never spent any of the money. In fact, here it is," she said, pulling it from her purse and placing it on a coffee table. "I never dreamed Rocco would turn out to be my teammate. And I certainly never dreamed . . ." She swallowed. "Well, that just seemed like the stuff of fairy tales."

And it is, she thought.

What you were playing at with Rocco wasn't grounded in reality at all.

She sighed. "Well, Rocco figured it out. I know I should have told him. I just couldn't think how. It's good he knows. He should know. I only wish I had had enough courage to tell him myself. I'm just so sorry that Mickey entered your lives. It was because of me he did. And that's it."

Nico stood up immediately. She didn't want to make this more awkward than it already was. She didn't want to make them feel like they had to say something—anything. She took a step, intending to move quickly to the door but was stopped when Beatrice ran over and blocked her way. The girl stood there, gazing up at Nico.

"Did you really wear a blonde wig?" she asked.

Sofia rushed to her sister's side. "Was it short and really, really, really blonde?"

Frowning, Nico hesitated. "Yes."

They faced each other, clutching arms.

"Saturn Girl!" Sofia cried.

"Saturn Girl," Beatrice whispered.

Their eyes blew up wide.

"And we sent her flying over the balcony—" Sofia said.

Beatrice nodded. "And she landed—"

They turned and stared at Nico.

"On *your* balcony . . . Spooky!" they said in unison.

This last word was expressed in a hushed and reverent tone as though there were unseen forces at work in an unseen world, and they had to be careful not to disturb any of it.

Isabella grinned. "Saturn Girl has the greatest telepathic powers of any of the superheroes."

Oh, thought Nico, *she's a superhero.*

"Yeah." Beatrice nodded. "Telepathy."

The girls stared at each other. "Spooky," they said, once again, in unison.

"Saturn Girl beat Uncle Rocco at pool," cried Sofia.

The girls began to giggle.

After that, Rocco's grandfather grinned, nudging Rocco's father. They began to chuckle until all of them were laughing.

Nico stood frozen, unsure how to respond.

"Tell me something, Nico," said Rocco's grandfather. "Did you cheat when you played pool? Did you play by the rules?"

"Yes," Nico said, nodding. "I mean, I played by the rules. Whether I was playing poker or pool. I didn't cheat. But I did lead people to think I wasn't that good. Led them to believe they were going to win and coaxed them into betting large sums of money. That night, I purposely lost the games I played before the game with Rocco."

"Who suggested you play for money?"

"I did. But not at first. We were just playing a game, and then Rocco suggested we make it interesting."

She really had lost her edge. She could feel her cheeks burning. She knew full well what Rocco was planning on winning if she'd missed that final shot. If she'd known then what she knew now, she would have given it to him. Happily.

"And he threw that money on the table," Rocco's mother said, taking Nico's hand. "You were just a child, dear. You were taken advantage of every bit as much as the people conned by the man and woman you called Uncle Jack and Aunt Milly."

"More," said his father.

"That's right," said his grandfather.

"But afterward," Nico insisted, "with Mickey—"

His mother placed her hand on Nico's cheek, shaking her head. "No, dear. You were still very young with no one to look out for you."

"You may have done some things you're not proud of," his father said. "But that's true of all of us. You did what you did to survive."

"And as for what you did on your own," his grandfather said, "it's not the same at all. Not even if you did make like you weren't so good at the poker and the pool. You won that money fair and square. Nothing wrong in that."

His grandmother came up beside her, placing her hand on the other cheek. "That's right. If those men couldn't best you at either, then that's on them. And that includes my own grandson. It's also on them if they couldn't resist your charms. They knew what they were doing. Including Rocco."

That's when the tears tumbled from her lashes down her cheeks while each and every one of them hugged her. She cried until finally, there were no tears left.

"Please don't tell Rocco I came here," she pleaded. "That's not why I came. We're good as teammates now." She paused, seeing the doubtful looks on their faces. "Really. We're okay. We've come to an understanding. You've seen how well we've been doing. Rocco still has a chance to win that trophy. Please promise me you won't tell him any of this."

They hesitated, looking at one another.

"Please," Nico insisted.

They looked reluctant but they all promised.

Nico glanced apprehensively at Sofia and Beatrice. Isabella nudged them.

"We promise," they said in unison, holding up their hands as though they were testifying in court.

After Nico waved goodbye, she drew a deep breath, admiring the beauty of the small hamlet sitting at the foot of the mountain. As she walked along the cobblestone road, she realized something.

She felt lighter.

That anchor was gone.

She smiled at the few people she passed, and they smiled back.

Mickey was still out there. She might never be rid of him. But she'd deal with him if she had to. She wasn't sure exactly how. But she'd figure it out.

Charles was right. The man had no power over her anymore. Not if she didn't give it to him.

She lifted her chin proudly.

I've never been the kind of girl who would turn myself into sea-foam.

I'm going to be okay. Even without Rocco, I'm going to be okay.

She felt a pang thinking of Rocco. But for the first time since he'd learned the truth about her, she didn't want to put her life on rewind and erase what had happened between them. Even if it hurt now, she wouldn't wish what had happened with Rocco away. She didn't think it was possible for her to feel like she had about him. Like she still did.

Up ahead, she saw a couple young girls and wondered how old they were. They made her think of Sofia and Beatrice. She smiled, watching them laugh as they skipped arm in arm and disappeared around a corner.

When was the last time I skipped?

She'd have to go way back to sometime when her grandfather was still alive. And then she stopped.

Did she? Have to?

No. She didn't.

Today.

Today will be the last time I skipped.

And so, she did; she flew her arms out, flung her feet forward, and bounced down the cobblestone road and under the archway, waving goodbye to the hamlet.

CHAPTER THIRTY-EIGHT

ROCCO

Rocco glanced over at Nico as Casey talked about today's race—the final race of the season. The championship was on the line. Not the Constructors—Blue Jet Lightning already had that one in the bag—but the Drivers. Anker, Clarke, and Rocco were so close in points, any one of them could take it. It was all riding on today's race.

Rocco wouldn't be in this position if it weren't for Nico. If he'd kept going the way he was once they'd returned from the break, this season would have been his last. Not only would Maverick have let him go, he felt certain no other team would want to take him on.

And here he was, with a real shot to win the trophy, which he hadn't won in years.

The atmosphere had drastically improved off the track as well as on it after Nico had set him straight. They were friendly now. She was always there when the team celebrated a win. But there were no more intimate moments between them. Whenever they encountered each other, there were always other people around.

While the animosity was gone, it still was tense—at least for him. He didn't know how she felt or what she was thinking.

He tried to get a sense of that from Celeste, who talked to Nico from time to time. But he didn't learn much. According to Celeste, they never discussed him. He'd consistently asked Celeste if she was seeing anybody, but Celeste was no help there either. Rocco wondered sometimes about Leo Clarke because he often saw the two of them talking. Clarke was handsome and charming and all those things women liked. But to Rocco's eyes, it looked like nothing more than friendly talk between drivers. But did it look that way because that's what it was or because that's what he hoped it was?

Rocco wished he could have a do-over, do things differently. But how exactly? Maybe if he'd had some time before he had to face her once he learned the truth about that night, some time to get past that initial anger, and . . . okay, damn it—hurt. He'd avoided using that word, but Dario and Celeste had used it.

He hadn't talked about Nico to his family, not one of them. Even though it kept them in the dark and clueless as to what had happened, he preferred that to them knowing the truth. They'd liked Nico when they met her, really liked her. His nieces loved her. As angry as he was, as hurt as he was, he didn't feel right about undermining that. Maybe it had something to do with what Celeste had said. Nico didn't know him back then. And more importantly, he didn't know her.

He suspected his family figured it had something to do with Mickey. After all, Nico had left when Mickey had. And from then on, Rocco wouldn't talk about her.

Casey clapped his hands. "Okay, let's go out there and give it our best!"

Rocco followed Nico out of the room and tapped her shoulder. When she turned around, he tilted his head toward an empty hallway to their right.

He kept as much distance from her as possible in the narrow hallway. But the distance did nothing to temper the violent influence her dark eyes had on him; it didn't change the fact that her collarbone was a thing of beauty or that his fingers itched when he looked at it; it didn't even stop that scent from reaching him like the fingers of some primitive creature that would not be stopped by space, time, or any sort of resolve the brain might try to put upon the body.

A strand of her raven hair fell in front of her eyes, and the temptation to sweep it back was so powerful he might have done it had she not.

He cleared his throat. "I wanted to talk to you before the race. I just want you to know I don't expect you—I mean, yeah, we're a team and yes, I have a shot at the championship, but it's up to me to win it. If I do, great; and if I don't, well that's okay too. It's still been a great season. I wouldn't change anything. I mean, on the track."

"I understand."

What was he trying to say? *Just talk about the racing.*

"There's a saying—you're only as good as your last race. So, let's make it a good one."

Why did he say that?

You sound like a fucking used-car salesman.

Smiling, she nodded and made a move to leave.

"Wait!"

She turned.

He swallowed. "You know, I owe you a lot. The way things were going before you, well, set me straight. I wouldn't have a shot at this if it weren't for you. I just wanted to be sure you know that—you know that I know it."

She shook her head but wouldn't meet his gaze. "That might be overstating—"

"No!" he said firmly. So firmly, he could see he'd startled her. She stared at him.

"I'm not overstating things. I'm just saying that I get that that little prince needed that girl to come into his life and his village to set things right."

She laughed. "I can't believe you brought that up."

He chuckled and then suddenly stopped, biting his lip. "Stupid, huh? I don't know why, exactly. I guess it just sticks."

She shrugged. "Maybe that's why fairy tales last and we keep telling the same ones over and over again." Finally, she met his gaze. "As you said, they sort of—stick."

He stared into those dark eyes, searching for that window. "Maybe because we wish life could be like that."

"Maybe," she said in a quiet voice.

"Nico, I'm sorry I didn't give you a chance." He swallowed. "I mean, I should have let you ex—"

"Uncle Rocco!"

Nearly breathless, Sofia and Beatrice came running up.

"We have some—" Beatrice sputtered, still trying to catch her breath.

"Thing to tell you," Sofia added, trying to catch her breath as well. "We've been looking all over for you."

"Most definitely and to be sure," Beatrice said. "It's important."

The two girls looked over at Nico and quickly looked away.

"We need to talk to you. Now," said Sofia, casting another swift glance at Nico.

"Okay," Rocco said. "What is it?"

"We can't say," Beatrice said, rolling her eyes in dramatic fashion toward Nico. "It's private."

Rocco frowned, looking over at Nico, who was staring at the girls. He saw red flames ignite on her cheeks.

Suddenly, Isabella appeared. "There you two are. I told you not to bother your uncle Rocco before a race."

Shoulders slumped, drooping mouths, the girls both sighed and allowed themselves to be dragged away by their mother.

Suddenly, Beatrice broke free and ran back. "Don't worry, Saturn Girl," she whispered to Nico, but still loud enough so Rocco could hear. "We've got your back."

"Beatrice!" shouted Isabella.

After his niece was gone, Rocco stared at Nico, but she wouldn't meet his gaze.

"Did she just call you Saturn Girl?"

Nico waved her hand and gave a little laugh. "Private joke. Well, remember . . ."

"'Speed has never killed anyone. Suddenly becoming stationary . . . That's what gets you.'"

She blinked, looking surprised. "Right."

She made a move to give a bro-hug, but they both pulled back from the sudden spark.

"These suits," she said.

"Yeah, these suits."

CHAPTER THIRTY-NINE

ROCCO AND NICO

ROUND 24: RACE 24: AUSTIN, TEXAS

Race Engineer: We go as planned, Rocco. Three more laps.
Rocco: I haven't gained anything on him.
Silence.
Rocco: Did you hear me?
Race Engineer: I heard you. You haven't lost anything either. You're holding steady; you both set the same pace on that last lap.

Anker had started on pole and had shot out fast from the start. He'd held on to first from the beginning. Clarke had started in second, Rocco in third, and Nico in sixth. But a few laps back, Rocco had managed to slip past Clarke into second, and Nico had gone up two positions to fourth when the two cars up ahead of her made contact and spun out, hitting the embankment with enough force to bring them to a complete stop.

■ ■ ■

Nico: Am I on pace to catch Clarke?
Race Engineer: About a second behind on that last lap. Sets him a couple seconds ahead of you.
Nico: Do we have more power?
Race Engineer: Hold steady on this turn up ahead and then push on the straightaway.
Nico: Copy.

■ ■ ■

Rocco: It looks like Clarke's making a move.
Race Engineer: He's gained another second on you. But you can hold him off if you stay out of DRS range.
Rocco: Copy. How close am I to Anker?
Race Engineer: Almost within a second. It's close. But not yet.
Rocco: Copy.

Two laps to go, and he was in the same position. But Clarke was getting closer. If Clarke got within a second behind him, he could employ the DRS, and that would increase his speed enough to catch and pass Rocco.

Rocco: What's Clarke's position?
Race Engineer: Just a fraction over a second. Can you pick up the pace?

Just before Rocco took a turn, he spied Clarke lose control, slide to the outside of the track, and crash into the embankment.

He was beyond the turn now and couldn't see what happened behind him. Now he only needed to gain on Anker and he had this.

■ ■ ■

Shit, thought Nico as she and Clarke made contact. She skidded but was able to regain control and avoided going off the track completely.

Race Engineer: Good job, Nico. You're okay.

But she wasn't. Something was wrong.

Nico: I'm losing grip.
Race Engineer: Nico?
Nico: Shit!

■ ■ ■

Race Engineer: Push, Rocco. Push. You're within a second. Employ the DRS.

Rocco shot out ahead of Anker.

Rocco: Yes!
Race Engineer: Excellent, Rocco! You're setting a blistering pace. Checkered flag is just up ahead. Push! You've got this.

Rocco wasn't sure which was racing faster, the car or his heart. That flag and that trophy were just up ahead. And they were his.

Race Engineer: Shit.
Rocco: What?
Silence.
Rocco: What's going on?
Race Engineer: Nothing. Keep your pace, Rocco. Anker's just behind, but he won't catch you if you can just manage to keep this pace. Half a lap to go before you see that checkered flag.

Why wouldn't they tell him? Everything felt good. Nothing wrong with the car. So, what . . . ?

Nico. Was it Nico?

Rocco: Is it Nico?
Silence.
Rocco: So help me if you don't tell me, I'm going to ram this car so hard into the embankment, you'll have to scrap the whole fucking thing!
Silence.
Race Engineer: Nico's crashed.
Rocco: What?
Race Engineer: When she made contact with Clarke. Looks like there's an oil leak, and she lost control of the car.

After the race, Rocco would think how people had got it wrong when they said at moments of high stress that everything slowed down.

Not true.

Time stood still.

Suddenly becoming stationary . . . That's what gets you.

Race Engineer: Rocco what are you doing? Why are you slowing down? Fuck, Anker's right on your tail. Push! Damn it! Push!

The checkered flag was just up ahead. And suddenly it didn't matter. How could it if she wasn't there to be happy for him? It meant nothing if she wasn't there. Without that stranger, without that girl, the little prince would go nowhere because there would be nowhere to go.

Because of all the things he wanted . . . of all those things . . .

Race Engineer: Fuck! He's gaining. Anker's coming up from behind, Rocco!
Casey: Tell him she's okay! Nico's okay!
Race Engineer: Did you hear that, Rocco? She's okay!
Rocco: What? What's that?
Race Engineer: Nico's okay.
Rocco: You're not just telling me this.
Race Engineer: Get her on the radio, damn it! Can you get her on the radio? Can somebody please?!

Rocco saw a flash of color inch up on his right.

Nico: Rocco? Can you hear me?
Rocco: Nico? Are you okay?
Nico: Anker! He's right there! He's going to pass you! Put your fucking foot on that fucking accelerator, you annoying, arrogant, asshole, prick!

Rocco felt his heart leap as the car surged ahead. Anker was out in front now. Not by much. But it looked like Rocco would finish second.

A small voice that was almost too small and too far away was telling him second wasn't so bad.

But then he heard another voice. This voice was not small. And it wasn't far away. It was here. In the car with him. *No*, he thought. Not in the car. In him. It was under his skin and it was screaming at him.

Put your fucking foot on that fucking accelerator, you annoying, arrogant, asshole, prick!

So that's what he did.

Could he catch Anker? He didn't know. He just kept listening to that voice.

The checkered flag was just up ahead. He could see it. And before he realized it, as though it were someone else crossing the finish line, it suddenly hit him.

The race was over.

CHAPTER FORTY

ROCCO AND NICO

Rocco made his way through all the smiles, the slaps on the back, and the cheers. People were saying things to him. He could hear sound, but he couldn't make out any words.

Where is she?

Soon he would be up on that podium, celebrating not only his win in this race but for the entire season. Frantically, he scanned the crowd.

And then he saw the dark hair and that small hand reach up and sweep back a strand that had fallen in front of those dark eyes. His heart raced. His hands itched.

Nico.

"Nico!" he shouted.

She smiled and waved. "Congratulations!" she cried in order to be heard above the roar.

He pushed through the crowd and grabbed her arm. How in the hell was he going to find some place private? And then it hit him. He weaved into the complex, made a quick right, and ducked into a restroom with her.

"Just tell me one thing, Nico. You didn't make that move, collide with Clarke for me, right?"

She stared at him a moment and then burst out laughing.

"I didn't sacrifice myself for you," she said. "Clarke hit me. I didn't hit him."

He sighed. "Oh, okay, good. I mean it's not good you crashed. But—"

She shook her head. "I know what you mean. I'm not the Little Mermaid. I'm not turning myself into sea-foam."

He frowned. "Huh?"

She bit her lip. "Get over yourself."

He grinned. "I don't know if I can. I've got kind of a big head."

Nico lowered her eyes, but he caught the corner of her lip twitch.

"It's okay to smile, you know."

Nico lifted her chin. "I know."

"So, you didn't hurt anything?"

She shook her head. "Just my pride."

He placed his hand under her chin, feeling her soft skin beneath his calloused fingers.

She flinched, but she didn't pull away.

He lifted her face and peered into her eyes. "No, I don't think so."

"Uncle Rocco! Where are you?"

He groaned.

Those girls have the worst timing.

Nico opened the door.

"There you are," shouted Beatrice.

The girls stepped inside and looked around.

"What are you doing in the girls' restroom, Uncle Rocco?" Sofia asked.

He frowned. "The girls'—"

"Most definitely," said Beatrice.

He looked around. No urinals.

Sofia waved her hands. "Forget it."

Beatrice did likewise. "To be sure. We need to talk to you, and it's private."

Sofia held the door open, and Beatrice shoved Nico out.

■ ■ ■

Nico stood with Charles. She held Templeton in her hands and was petting him. Charles had driven to Texas so that Templeton could join them for the last race of the season.

"So, he's going back to Blue Jet Lightning."

Nico nodded. “That’s what everyone’s saying. You can hardly blame him. It’s like playing for the New York Yankees instead of the Bad News Bears.”

Charles sulked. “Yeah but the Bears are so sweet. You want to root for them.”

“Well, good, because I’m still here.”

“Right!”

“Nico!”

Nico turned around to see Celeste and Dario. She made a move to hug Celeste, but then realized she was holding Templeton and handed the rat to Charles.

After hugging them both, Dario pointed at the rat. “Is that Templeton?”

Nico nodded.

Celeste gave Dario a look. “I told you there was a Templeton.”

Dario shrugged. “Okay, you were right.” He paused. “You did really well, Nico. That was just some bad luck there toward the end.”

“Yeah. But I think it might have been partly my fault. I really wanted to pass Clarke to be up on that podium with Rocco. I think I went for too much. But I feel good about the season overall. I’m just happy I’ll be coming back next year.”

“And you won’t be a rookie,” Dario said.

“That’s right.”

“And you won’t have to worry about Mickey,” Celeste said.

Nico’s heart sank. “Oh.” She swallowed. “Rocco told you.”

They both nodded.

She sighed. “Well, I can’t say for certain. He might still show up. But if he does, I’ll deal with it. I’ll have to.”

“I don’t think so,” Celeste said. “I think he’s gone. For good.” She looked over her shoulder at Dario. “How did Rocco put it?”

Dario opened his mouth, but Celeste had turned back around and was already speaking.

“Quote: ‘I paid him off, put him on a flight, and told him if he ever came near Nico again, the next time he got on an airplane it would be in the cargo hold in a body bag.’”

Nico blinked. “He did that?”

Celeste nodded. "He did."

Dario placed his arm around Celeste. "They're about to have the podium celebration. I want to catch up with Rocco before he goes up there."

"We'll see you later?" Celeste asked as they walked away.

"Sure." Nico smiled.

Although she wasn't at all sure.

■ ■ ■

"This is wonderful, Rocco." Carolyn beamed. "Another trophy! And next year, with us—just think of what we can do. You, Anker, and Ceci! We'll be unstoppable!"

"Yeah, about that—"

Dario came up from behind and slapped Rocco on the back as they announced his name. "Hey, they're calling your name. Get up there. This is it. Go get her."

Rocco smiled and mounted the podium.

After the champagne celebration, he waited for the inevitable questions. And for once, he got exactly what he wanted from the press. He couldn't have scripted it any better.

"So, Rocco, rumor is you'll be leaving Maverick Racing and signing up with Blue Jet Lightning for next season? Can you confirm that?"

"I've been thinking about it. Blue Jet is so prestigious. They're the team a kid grows up dreaming about. Like a fairy-tale princess. Snow White, for instance."

■ ■ ■

What the—

"Uh, what was that?" she heard Charles say. "Did he just say *Snow White*?"

Nico looked around at the puzzled expressions of the faces in the crowd—the press, the fans, the teams.

"Snow White's like the perfect woman," Rocco said, "a true fairy-tale princess—sweet and kind, innocent and naive. Not at all like her stepmother, the queen, who's not sweet and kind, definitely neither innocent nor naive. Actually, crafty—even conniving. You can bet she's not going to wait around for a prince to come and save her. She goes after what she wants."

Nico looked around. She couldn't spot one mouth that wasn't gaping.

"This has got me thinking. Who would you rather have in your corner? Who's really going to have your back? Snow White or that queen?"

What is he doing?

"Do you know what happens to that stepmother, the queen? In the original version? They put a pair of iron shoes into hot coals and the queen is forced to wear them and dance until she falls down dead. For what? For turning into a haggard witch and offering Snow White an apple? It's a pretty clever way to teach your kid not to accept food from strangers. It's not her fault Snow White was too stupid to get it."

Charles whispered in Nico's ear. "Has he gone mad?"

Rocco grinned. "I think I prefer a different kind of fairy-tale princess; a princess more like Diana Prince, Marla Drake, or Harley Quinn."

"Or Jessica Jones," shouted a voice Nico recognized as Sofia's.

"Or Jessica Drew," she heard Beatrice shout.

"Or Saturn Girl," they shouted in unison.

"Aha!" Charles said.

Nico swung around. "Aha, what?"

"I know what he's doing." Templeton had popped his head out of Charles's pocket. He looked at Charles and then at Nico. His black eyes were bright, and he was bobbing his head up and down.

Charles smiled. "You know too, don't you, Temple?"

Nico wrinkled her brow. "You do?"

"You don't?"

Puzzled, her only response was to stare back at him.

"Nico, don't be Snow White. It's not a good look on you."

"Like a woman," Rocco went on, "carrying on the legacy of Formula 1 drivers like Lella Lombardi and Maria Teresa de Filippis. A woman who's got what it takes to get to Formula 1 and works her ass off to stay here. A woman who not only has to endure a lot to get to Formula 1 but has to endure even more once she's made it. The kind of woman who won't quit and inspires hope in others, like my nieces Sofia and Beatrice."

Nico felt her eyes mist. She sniffed.

"Here," Charles said, tapping her shoulder.

As she turned, he handed her a tissue. She could hear the reporter shout again.

"But wait, Rocco! You didn't answer my question. Is it true? Are you leaving Maverick for Blue Jet?"

When Nico turned back, he was no longer on the podium. He was gone.

She'd see him again next season. He'd be racing, and so would she. But they'd no longer be teammates. It would be different.

She sighed. She was happy for Rocco. Really, she was. But now it hurt too much to be here.

"Come on, Charles, let's go."

Charles gripped her arm. "Not just yet."

He was smiling at something over her shoulder. When Nico turned around, she saw Rocco standing there, smiling down at her.

"I'm not going anywhere, Nico. I like my team. Can you put up with a— What did you call me?"

Charles leaned over Nico's shoulder. "An annoying, arrogant, asshole, prick."

Rocco laughed. "All that?"

Charles smiled. "It's really quite impressive when you think about it."

Rocco nodded. "It is. So, can you put up with all that next year?"

Nico stared. She heard the word loud in her head—*yes, yes, yes!* But when her lips parted, no sound came out. Until she flinched from a shove in the small of her back.

Charles leaned in and hissed in her ear. "Nico Angelini, so help me, if you insist on leaving your brain in Brainerd, neither Templeton nor I will come to visit."

Right.

She smiled. "I think I can manage."

"And what about the year after that?" he asked.

She blinked. Did she hear him right?

"What?"

"What about the year after that? Can you put up with the annoying, arrogant, asshole then too?"

"Prick," Charles's voice came from behind her.

"What's that?" Rocco asked.

Nico cleared her throat. "It's annoying, arrogant, asshole, prick."

He chuckled. "Right. Well?"

She smiled. So hard her teeth hurt.

"Is that a yes?"

She blinked, suddenly realizing she hadn't said anything. "Yes, yes, yes."

"And the year after that?"

This must be what it feels like to be a bird and have wings.

Please, she pleaded with her eyes as she gazed up at him.

Not now. Don't play misty now.

And then she had a sudden thought that squelched any tears.

"What did Beatrice and Sofia tell you?"

He grinned, shaking his head. "I can't tell you. I promised I wouldn't."

"I don't believe it! They promised!"

"Yeah, but they'd crossed their fingers behind their backs. I didn't, so I'm obligated to keep my promise."

"Crossed their fingers behind their backs," Nico scoffed.

Charles tapped her on the shoulder. "That does negate a promise. It's something that's understood universally. It's like some kind of law of nature. In fact, I think I read that somewhere."

Nico shook her head and turned back to meet Rocco's gaze.

"I'm sorry I didn't give you a chance to explain, Nico. I should have. I was just so—"

"Angry. I understand."

"No. Not angry. Hurt. But I realized something. You holding yourself responsible for what others did when you were just a kid is as ludicrous as me thinking Carolyn is responsible for me being an F1 driver."

She smiled. He was right. It was.

"I wouldn't change a thing, Nico Angelini." He paused. "Well, no that's not entirely true. Maybe one thing."

She knitted her brow. "What?"

"I'd have made that last shot at Drink and Dive so fucking difficult, there would've been no way you could've made it. Then I'd have gotten what I really wanted."

Feeling her cheeks burn, she hung her head, smiling until she heard his next words.

"Because of all the things he wanted," Rocco said, "he wanted her most."

Nico looked up at him and frowned.

"The little prince," he said. "He never would have listened to her. He never would have cared what she thought of him, and his head never would have gone back to the way it should be so he could run and journey with her to all those places he wanted to go." Rocco took her hand in his. "It's because he loved her. But it's more than that. It's because of all the things he wanted, all the things he could ever want, he wanted her most."

And suddenly Nico felt as though they were in an insulated bubble and no one outside it could reach them.

No one except for Charles.

Of course.

Leave it to Charles to penetrate that bubble. One shove from behind, and *pop*—Nico burst out into the real world.

And, she thought, *the real world isn't really half bad.*

Now she couldn't stop the hot tears as they flooded down her cheeks.

"And she never would have gone to the castle day after day, refused to bathe and feed him, or push him around in a carriage."

He grinned. "Now that's real devotion."

She laughed and then grew silent. "Because of all the things she wanted, all the things she could ever want, she wanted him most."

"Hey," a voice from the crowd shouted, "is there something going on between you two off the track?"

"Yes!" Rocco yelled, not taking his eyes off hers.

"Prove it!" someone else cried.

"Prove it!" other voices in the crowd cried until the crowd began chanting.

"Prove it! Prove it! Prove it!"

He pulled her in so close, she felt his heart beating against her own.

As she lifted her face, he cupped her cheeks. And when he held her face in his hands and those hands reached around and grazed that scar, this time she didn't stiffen or flinch. She welcomed his hands.

They're exactly where they should be.

"Make an honest man of me, Nico."

She leaned in as he did. And as her lips brushed up against his, she whispered, "As you wish."

ACKNOWLEDGMENTS

I was told it takes a village. Turns out I was misinformed. This book took a Pantheon of talented, determined, creative, both inspired and inspiring, and sometimes stubborn people. That, and a lot of dog biscuits.

Thank you to the entire team at Podium for taking this and me on. Thank you for your generosity, incredible work ethic and impeccable attention to detail in every aspect of the production of this book.

Thank you in particular to Cass Dolan, for putting together a stellar editorial team, for being a wizard at conjuring up book titles—she came up with this one—and for having nerves of steel when it comes to my allergic reaction to deadlines.

Thank you in particular to Kate Runde, for being willing to take a chance, for her keen eye and judgment when it came to assembling a dream team capable of creating a memorable and standout book cover, and for being unflappable in the face of my inability at times to make a decision.

Thank you in particular to my agent, Elaine Spencer, who took me on when all common sense should have told her not to, who saw things others did not, who prompted, pushed and cajoled me to write an F1 Romance, and for that early morning email telling me, "THIS IS IT!"

And finally, thank you to the three women who probably know more about what it took then they care to or should.

To Bonni, who's faith and confidence in me never wavered even when most people would say it should have.

To Cybele, who was my North Star, the one I could always count on to be there, to be right and to guide my way.

To Theresa, who was there at the very beginning, who has been there all the way and all the while, and who will be there until the very end.

I can honestly say this book would not be here now for you to read without them. And without the ever patient and long suffering Mr. Darcy, who was willing to lie at my feet and be bribed with biscuits all that time I was glued to my computer.

ABOUT THE AUTHOR

A. G. Starling is a romance author and college professor who received her PhD in philosophy from Columbia University. She likes her martinis just as she likes her wit: extra dry. As for her heroes and heroines? She likes them to channel Mae West—when they're good, they're bad, and when they're bad, they're even better. Starling has lived in multiple cities, including New York, but currently resides in Monterey, California, with Mr. Darcy, who, in this life, has four legs and a tail.